# Christmas Dessert Murder

# JOANNE FLUKE

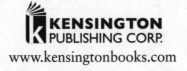

**KENSINGTON**
PUBLISHING CORP.

www.kensingtonbooks.com

KENSINGTON BOOKS are published by
Kensington Publishing Corp.
119 West 40th Street
New York, NY 10018

All Kensington titles, imprints, and distributed lines are available at special quantity discounts for bulk purchases for sales promotion, premiums, fund-raising, educational, or institutional use.

Special book excerpts or customized printings can also be created to fit specific needs. For details, write or phone the office of the Kensington Sales Manager: Kensington Publishing Corp., 119 West 40th Street, New York, NY 10018. Attn. Sales Department. Phone: 1-800-221-2647.

ISBN-13: 978-1-4967-3607-9 (ebook)

ISBN-13: 978-1-4967-3606-2

First Kensington Trade Paperback Printing: November 2021

10  9  8  7  6  5  4  3  2  1

Printed in the United States of America

Nov 2021

Books by Joanne Fluke

*Hannah Swensen Mysteries*

CHOCOLATE CHIP COOKIE MURDER
STRAWBERRY SHORTCAKE MURDER
BLUEBERRY MUFFIN MURDER
LEMON MERINGUE PIE MURDER
FUDGE CUPCAKE MURDER
SUGAR COOKIE MURDER
PEACH COBBLER MURDER
CHERRY CHEESECAKE MURDER
KEY LIME PIE MURDER
CANDY CANE MURDER
CARROT CAKE MURDER
CREAM PUFF MURDER
PLUM PUDDING MURDER
APPLE TURNOVER MURDER
DEVIL'S FOOD CAKE MURDER
GINGERBREAD COOKIE MURDER
CINNAMON ROLL MURDER
RED VELVET CUPCAKE MURDER
BLACKBERRY PIE MURDER
DOUBLE FUDGE BROWNIE MURDER
WEDDING CAKE MURDER
CHRISTMAS CARAMEL MURDER
BANANA CREAM PIE MURDER
RASPBERRY DANISH MURDER
CHRISTMAS CAKE MURDER
CHOCOLATE CREAM PIE MURDER
COCONUT LAYER CAKE MURDER
CHRISTMAS CUPCAKE MURDER
TRIPLE CHOCOLATE CHEESECAKE MURDER
CHRISTMAS SWEETS
JOANNE FLUKE'S LAKE EDEN COOKBOOK

*Suspense Novels*

VIDEO KILL
WINTER CHILL
DEAD GIVEAWAY
THE OTHER CHILD
COLD JUDGMENT
FATAL IDENTITY
FINAL APPEAL
VENGEANCE IS MINE
EYES
WICKED
DEADLY MEMORIES
THE STEPCHILD

Published by Kensington Publishing Corp.

# Contents

# CHRISTMAS
# CARAMEL
# MURDER

*This book is for lovely Frida Giselle*

# Acknowledgments

Big hugs to the kids and the grandkids.

Thank you to my friends and neighbors: Mel & Kurt, Lyn & Bill, Gina, Dee Appleton, Jay, Richard Jordan, Laura Levine, the real Nancy and Heiti, Dr. Bob & Sue, Dan, Mark & Mandy at Faux Library, Daryl and her staff at Groves Accountancy, Gene and Ron at SDSA, and everyone at Boston Private Bank.

Thanks to Brad, Stephanie, Eric, Amanda, Lorenzo, Nancey, Meg, Bruce, Alison, Cameron, Gabriel, Barbara, and everyone at the Hallmark Movies & Mysteries Channel who gave us the Murder She Baked Hannah Swensen movies. What fun to see Hannah on TV!

Thank you to my Minnesota friends: Lois & Neal, Bev & Jim, Lois & Jack, Val, Ruthann, Lowell, Dorothy & Sue, Mary & Jim, Pat and Gary at their Once Upon a Crime Bookstore, and Tim Hedges.

A grateful hug to my multi-talented friend and editor-in-chief, John Scognamiglio.

Thanks to all the wonderful folks at Kensington Publishing who keep Hannah sleuthing and baking up a storm.

Thanks to Meg Ruley and the staff at the Jane Rotrosen Agency for their constant support and their wise advice.

Thanks to Hiro Kimura, my wonderful cover artist for the incredibly delicious-looking caramels on this book cover.

My caramels don't come close to looking this delectable, but they *do* taste better!

Thank you to Lou Malcangi at Kensington Publishing, for designing all of Hannah's deliciously stunning covers.

Thanks to John at *Placed4Success.com* for Hannah's movie and TV placements, his presence on all of Hannah's social media, the countless hours he puts in on my behalf, and for always being there for me.

Thanks to Rudy for maintaining my website at **wwwJoanneFluke.com,** his talent behind the camera, and for giving support to Hannah's social media.

Big thanks to Kathy Allen for the final testing of every single one of Hannah's recipes.

Hugs to Judy Q. for helping with Hannah's e-mail at **Gr8Clues@JoanneFluke.com** and searching for answers to research questions.

Grateful hugs to my super friend, Trudi Nash, for going on book tours with me, for keeping me on an even keel, and for thinking of new and innovative recipe ideas for us to try.

Thanks to food stylist and media guide extraordinaire Lois Brown for her friendship and her talented assistance.

Hugs to the Double D's, Alicia, Fern, Leah, and everyone on Team Swensen who helps to keep Hannah's Facebook presence alive and well.

Thank you to Dr. Rahhal, Dr. and Cathy Line, Dr. Wallen. Dr. Koslowski, Drs. Ashley and Lee, and Dr.

Niemeyer *(who reminds me of Doc Knight)* for putting up with my pesky Hannah-book-related medical and dental questions. Norman and Doc Knight would be lost without you!

Grateful thanks to all of the Hannah fans who share their favorite family recipes with me, post on Facebook, watch the Hannah movies, and devour each and every book.
I hope you love reading *Christmas Caramel Murder* just as much as I loved writing it.

# Prologue

The dining room at the Lake Eden Inn was festive with corn shocks, hay bales, pumpkins, and giant beer steins made of papier-mâché. It was clear that the owners, Sally and Dick Laughlin, were getting ready for their Oktoberfest celebration over the weekend.

It was Thursday night, and Hannah Swensen smiled at Ross Barton as she finished the last delicious bite of her dinner. "That was wonderful. Thank you, Ross."

Sally, who was waiting on them personally, must have had a version of dessert radar because she approached just as soon as Hannah placed her flatware on the plate.

"I've got a new dessert for you to try," Sally announced, motioning to the nearest busboy to clear their plates. When there was room to display it, she placed a large silver dessert tray on the table.

"Something for Oktoberfest?" Hannah asked her.

"No, for Christmas. I decided to feature chocolate and caramel, the way you did in the children's gift bags last year. That's why I'm featuring chocolate flan with caramel whipped cream."

"I've never heard of caramel whipped cream before," Hannah told her.

"It's easy to make. I couldn't find a recipe, but I followed your advice. We were talking about recipes and you said, '*If you can't find a recipe, make one up.'* So that's exactly what I did."

"And it worked?"

"Not the first time, and not the second time, either. But I revised it again, and the third time was the charm. I tried it out on Dick first, and he said he loves it. The only problem is, Dick has a sweet tooth and he loves everything I bake. I'd really like to try it out on you if you'll promise to tell me exactly what you think."

"It looks wonderful!" Hannah said, watching as Sally cut two slices from the flan that was sitting in the center of the silver tray and placed them in crystal dessert dishes. She added several dollops of caramel whipped cream, and placed the dessert dishes in front of Hannah and Ross.

"Be honest," she warned them. "And be critical, too. Tell me if I need to add something to make it better."

Hannah and Ross picked up their dessert spoons and took bites almost simultaneously. Then both of them smiled.

"Delicious!" Hannah declared.

"Oh, yes!" Ross concurred, taking another bite. "The chocolate is really rich, and it's perfect with the caramel whipped cream."

"Thanks!" Sally said, looking relieved as she turned to Hannah. "I'm still trying to figure out how to decorate this flan to make it even more Christmassy."

"It looks great just the way it is," Hannah told her, "but it could be more festive for Christmas. I'll let you know if I think of anything. And I'll ask Lisa. She's my decorating expert."

"Just one more thing," Sally said, picking up the platter. "What do you think I should call it?"

"Call it exactly what it is," Hannah suggested. "Chocolate Flan with Caramel Whipped Cream. If you call it something else, your wait staff will have to answer questions about what it is."

Sally nodded. "That's a really good point. Thanks for the help and enjoy the rest of your dessert."

When Sally had left their table, Ross turned to Hannah. "I've never tasted Lisa's chocolate caramels. Are you making them for Christmas this year?"

"Only if you really want us to," Hannah said, frowning slightly. "I know it's silly to be superstitious, but . . . well . . . they were bad luck last year."

"What do you mean?"

"I mean, last Christmas was . . . pretty strange in the giant scheme of things. You weren't here, so you wouldn't know, but something bad happened with the caramels."

"Something bad?"

"Yes. I found some of them at a murder scene."

"Tell me all about it." Ross leaned forward and covered Hannah's hand with his.

"Well . . ." Hannah drew a deep breath. "This is going to take a while. It's a really long story."

Ross glanced at his watch. "That's okay. It's only six-thirty. What time does Sally close the dining room?"

"She's open until ten." Hannah was silent for a moment, and then she looked amused. "It could take almost that long to tell you. Are you sure you want to listen to a long story now?"

"I'm positive. You've got me curious, Cookie. Tell me."

"Okay." Hannah gave a mock sigh. "Just remember, you asked for it. But first, we'll need more coffee."

Hannah waited until one of the waitresses had brought a fresh carafe of coffee, and then she began her story.

"It was the first Monday in December, and Lisa and I were in the coffee shop at The Cookie Jar. It was early, an hour before we were due to open, and we were decorating for Christmas. We were almost finished when everything started to happen. . . ."

## Chocolate Flan with Caramel Whipped Cream

Preheat oven to 350 degrees F., rack in the middle position.

**For the Chocolate Flan:**

1 and ¾ cup whole milk
1 cup *(6-ounce by weight bag)* semi-sweet chocolate
  chips *(I used Ghirardelli)*
4 large eggs
1 can *(14 ounces)* sweetened condensed milk *(I used
  Eagle Brand)*
1 teaspoon vanilla extract
½ teaspoon salt

---

chocolate curls for a topping are optional *(Make
  them by scraping them from a dark chocolate bar
  with the blade of a sharp knife.)*

**For the Caramel Whipped Cream:**

1 cup whipping cream
5 Tablespoons caramel ice cream topping *(I used
  Smucker's)*

Select a round glass casserole that's approximately 10 inches in diameter.

Locate a baking pan with 4-inch or taller sides that is large enough to hold your glass casserole with at least an inch and a half of space on all sides.

Set the casserole you've chosen inside the baking pan. Eventually, this baking pan will hold hot water to "bathe" the outside of your flan casserole. This water bath, or *bain marie*, will keep your flan from baking too rapidly and becoming hard around the edges.

Spray the inside of the glass casserole with Pam or another nonstick cooking spray.

**Hannah's 1ˢᵗ Note: Don't use anything called "baking" spray on the inside of your casserole. It contains flour and you don't want flour on the outside of your flan.**

Put two potholders or oven mitts out on the counter where they will be handy.

Heat the cup and three-quarters of whole milk at MEDIUM heat on the stovetop in a medium-size saucepan until it almost comes to a boil. You'll be able to tell this is going to happen when bubbles start to form around the edges of the saucepan and steam begins to escape from the milk.

Pull the saucepan with the milk over to a cold stovetop burner and stir in the cup of semi-sweet chocolate chips.

Stir until the chips are melted and the mixture is a uniform color. If this doesn't happen, your milk was too cold. Put it back on the burner and stir constantly for another minute to make sure the chips are melted. Then pull it off the heat and turn off the stovetop burner.

In a large bowl on the counter, whisk the 4 large eggs until they're light-colored and fluffy.

**Hannah's 2nd Note: You can also do this in the bowl of an electric mixer.**

Add the can of sweetened condensed milk, the vanilla extract, and the salt to the bowl with the eggs.

Whisk the contents until they're well incorporated.

Carefully, feel the outside of the saucepan with the chocolate mixture. If it's not so hot that it will cook the eggs, slowly, add the chocolate mixture to the egg mixture. Whisk or beat until everything is well incorporated.

Pour the resulting mixture into your prepared casserole.

Set your casserole inside the larger baking pan.

Run water as hot as you can get from your tap, and fill a large measuring cup with a spout.

Pour hot water from the measuring cup inside the larger pan. Keep pouring until the water level reaches halfway up the sides of the casserole holding your flan.

Loosely cover your flan with foil and poke a few holes in the foil to let steam escape as it's baking.

Carry both pans to the oven and put them inside to bake.

Bake your flan at 350 degrees F. for 50 to 70 minutes, or until the blade of a table knife inserted one inch from the center of the flan comes out clean.

**Hannah's 3rd Note: If your knife has liquid residue sticking to it when you remove it, your flan is not fully baked. Give it another 5 minutes in the oven, wash and dry your table knife in the meantime, and test it again.**

When your table knife comes out clean, use oven potholders to take both pans out of the oven together and set them on a cold stovetop burner.

Use potholders or oven mitts to lift out the inner casserole with your flan and place it on a second cold burner or on a wire rack. Use potholders or oven mitts to dump out the water in the outer pan and set it aside to cool.

Set your timer for 20 minutes.

When your Chocolate Flan has cooled for 20 minutes, cover the top of the flan casserole with plastic wrap. Refrigerate your flan in the casserole for at least 4 hours, or until it's time to serve dessert. Overnight is fine too, if you want to make it the day before you plan to serve it.

To serve, run a table knife around the inside rim of your flan to loosen it slightly. Turn it out in a flat bowl or onto a plate with a deep lip. Then make the Caramel Whipped Cream.

In the bowl of an electric mixer, mix the cup of whipping cream and the 5 Tablespoons of caramel ice cream topping together.

Gradually, increase the speed of the mixer to MEDIUM-HIGH and beat until the resulting mixture will hold a soft peak. *(Test for soft peaks by shutting off the mixer and dipping the flat blade of a rubber spatula into the whipped cream and pulling it up quickly. If it forms a peak, but the tip droops slightly, you have achieved soft peaks.)*

"Frost" your flan with the Caramel Whipped Cream. People will ooh and ahh when you cut slices, place them in dessert dishes and serve it.

**Hannah's 4th Note: If you want to make your dessert really fancy, garnish the slices with chocolate curls and extra caramel whipped cream.**

Yield: This Chocolate Flan with Caramel Whipped Cream serves 6 to 8 people unless you invite Andrea's husband, Bill. Bill is absolutely crazy for this dessert. He boasted to me that he could eat a whole flan all by himself, and I believe him.

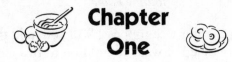

# Chapter One

"I'd better steady the ladder for you," Hannah warned as Lisa picked up the star ornament that fit on the very top of their Christmas tree and climbed up the first rung. "Are you sure you want to go do this? I really meant to get a new ladder after last year, but I forgot."

"That's understandable. The only time we use a ladder is at Christmas. But don't worry, Hannah. I can do it. I'm not afraid of heights, at least not usually."

"But you are right now?" Hannah asked, hearing the slight quaver in her young partner's voice.

"I'm a *little* nervous, that's all. It's just that the top of our tree seems like a long ways up."

"You're right, Lisa It *is* way up there. We got a sixteen-foot tree this year."

"I know, but it didn't seem this tall at the Christmas tree lot."

"That's probably because it was flanked by two blue spruces that were taller."

"How tall were those?"

"They were twenty-footers, and this one would have looked a lot shorter in comparison."

"I'm glad we didn't get a twenty-footer!" Lisa gave a little laugh. "I know it's impossible, but this tree looks like it's growing taller by the minute."

Lisa climbed up another rung. Then she reached down to

hand Hannah the star tree-topper. "Will you hold this until I get about halfway up? I want to hold on to this ladder with both hands."

"No problem. Just let me know when you want the tree-topper and I'll give it to you."

Hannah held the ornament with one hand while she steadied the ladder with the other. The ladder wobbled, and she wished she'd remembered to shop for a new one.

Lisa climbed up the fourth rung and looked at the top of the tree again. "Let's get a shorter tree next year."

"We will. I promise."

"And a new ladder."

"That, too. I'll call Cliff at the hardware store right after we're through decorating the tree."

"Sounds good." Lisa climbed up another rung, and then she stopped. "I'm almost up high enough. Hand me the tree-topper, Hannah. I'll bend down."

"And I'll stretch up." Hannah reached up with her right hand, but she kept her left hand firmly on the ladder. "Here you go, Lisa."

Lisa bent down even farther and grabbed the ornament. "Got it!" she said, straightening up again and reaching toward the top of the tree.

At that precise moment, the back door opened and a familiar voice shouted, "Girls! Come quick! It's an emergency!"

The ladder wobbled as Hannah reacted to the panic in her mother's voice. Lisa let out a little gasp of fright, but somehow she managed to attach the tree-topper and climb down two rungs before the ladder began to tip.

"I can't hold it!" Hannah exclaimed as the ladder tipped even further. "Jump, Lisa!"

Lisa didn't wait for a second invitation. She leaped down to the floor as the ladder collapsed with a clatter of old wood and stressed metal fasteners as it fell apart.

"Good heavens! What on earth happened?"

Hannah and Lisa turned to see Delores Swensen standing

in the doorway, staring at them in shock. "And where did you get that decrepit old ladder?"

"It was Dad's," Hannah said, resisting the urge to rail at her mother for startling them at such a critical point in their decorating endeavor. She took a deep breath to calm down, and then she asked, "What's the emergency, Mother?"

"Perhaps I shouldn't have used the word *emergency* to describe it," Delores replied, sounding slightly contrite. And then, in typical Delores fashion, she changed the subject. "How did you get Dad's ladder, Hannah?"

"I appropriated it from the basement of Dad's hardware store. I figured I might need a ladder so I brought it here when we sold the hardware store."

"You should have appropriated a new aluminum ladder, dear. This one was your Grandpa Swensen's ladder, and I tried for years to get your father to replace it. He finally got a new ladder for the house, but he must have kept this old one for sentimental reasons."

"I can understand that. That's why I wanted to keep it. But I should have propped it up in a corner and bought a new one for us to use. That's what I intended to do, but it slipped my mind."

"I'll remind you," Lisa said quickly. "Don't worry about that!"

"I won't forget again. This is the year we're getting a new one, and I'll order a metal ladder that won't rust. And I'll get one that has actual steps instead of rungs. I'll call to order it right after we hear about Mother's emergency."

"And after we have some coffee and cookies to calm down," Lisa added, turning to Delores. "Let's go to the kitchen. We just finished baking for the day and we made some of Andrea's Red Velvet Whippersnapper Cookies."

Delores smiled. "They sound good. . . . Of course everything you dear girls bake is good." She turned to Hannah. "What are you going to do with that rickety old ladder?"

"I don't know," Hannah admitted as she followed her

mother and Lisa into the kitchen. "I'll throw it out, I guess. It's too far gone for anyone to use."

"Don't do that!" Delores objected. "Are you getting your new ladder from Dad's old store?"

"Of course I am. It's the only hardware store in town, and I like Cliff Schumann and his dad."

"Then why don't you ask Cliff to deliver your new ladder and bring the old one to my house?"

"But it's in pieces! Really, Mother . . . I don't think anyone could fix it."

"I won't even try to have it fixed. I just want to keep it around for sentimental reasons."

Hannah stared at her mother in confusion. Delores wasn't usually this sentimental. But if Delores wanted the ladder, Hannah was perfectly willing to give it to her. "Okay. Whatever you want, Mother. I'll call Cliff right now."

"Thank you, dear." Delores took her usual stool at the stainless-steel workstation while Lisa poured coffee and filled a platter with Red Velvet Whippersnapper Cookies from one of the two baker's racks at the side of the kitchen.

Hannah headed for the wall phone in the kitchen, and less than a minute later, she'd ordered the new aluminum ladder for The Cookie Jar and given Cliff instructions to bag up the old wooden ladder and deliver it to her mother's house.

"Okay," she said, sitting down at the workstation and addressing her mother. "Now tell us about your emergency, or whatever it is."

"Just because it may have been downgraded a bit doesn't mean it's not important," Delores maintained.

"Agreed. Tell us, Mother."

Delores sighed. "All right. The emergency, or situation, or whatever it is, is Ricky-Ticky."

"Mayor Bascomb," Lisa said, knowing that Hannah's mother often used the nickname she'd given Mayor Bascomb when he was a small boy and she was his babysitter. "What else has he done?"

"What *else*?" Delores asked, and it was clear that she wasn't sure what Lisa meant.

"Yes, what *else* has he done? Whatever it is, it couldn't be worse than hiring Phyllis Bates and moving her here just because . . . well, you know why he did it. And then, when his wife, Stephanie, got wind of what was going on between the two of them, re-assigning Phyllis as Herb's assistant in the town marshal's office!"

Neither Hannah nor Delores knew quite what to say. They'd never seen Lisa quite so angry before. But there was no need to respond because Lisa didn't bother to wait for a reply.

"At least Stephanie Bascomb got her revenge! I saw that diamond ring she made the mayor buy for her and it's as big as a boulder!"

Hannah and Delores exchanged glances. Lisa sounded terribly bitter and they couldn't blame her for that. Lisa's husband, Herb Beeseman, had dated Phyllis Bates in high school and everyone had expected them to get married. But Phyllis's family had moved and Phyllis hadn't bothered to keep in touch with Herb or anyone else in Lake Eden. She hadn't been heard from in several years until Mayor Bascomb had somehow found her. And now she was back in Lake Eden, even more attractive than she'd been in high school.

"Don't keep me in suspense. Tell me what our esteemed mayor did this time," Lisa said, turning to face Delores. "Nothing you say about that man can possibly surprise me!"

"All right, but it's really bad." Delores took another sip of coffee and sat up a little straighter. "I'm warning you, Lisa. . . . This could be even worse than hiring Phyllis in the first place. I got the news this morning, straight from Rod at the *Lake Eden Journal*." She glanced at her watch. "The paper is coming out in an hour, and I wanted to give you advance warning."

"Advance warning of what?" Lisa asked, looking worried.

"Mayor Bascomb called Rod late last night and said he's

not holding the Mrs. Claus contest this year. Instead, he's using his executive authority to appoint someone to play Santa's wife."

Lisa began to look a little sick. "Don't tell me it's . . ." She stopped and swallowed hard.

"I'm afraid it is," Delores answered. "Ricky-Ticky has appointed Phyllis Bates as this year's Mrs. Claus!"

It was all Hannah could do to keep from speaking several words she would never utter around her young nieces. Everyone knew that Lisa had been hoping to be Mrs. Claus this year. Herb had played Santa for the past four years running, passing out gift bags with candy and cookies to the children in the audience right after the Lake Eden Players had performed their Christmas play. Lisa, as Herb's wife in real life, was the logical choice for Mrs. Claus. And everyone, Hannah included, had thought that this would be Lisa's year to have that honor. And now Mayor Bascomb had arbitrarily given the role to Herb's former girlfriend, Phyllis.

Delores reached out to pat Lisa's hand. "To tell the truth, I can't stand Phyllis either. She certainly could never be mistaken for a lady!"

Lisa responded with a shaky smile. "That's true," she said in a small voice.

Hannah wanted to say something supportive, but she wasn't sure what it should be. She didn't like Phyllis either. There had been several incidents in high school involving the bouncy blond cheerleader wearing too-tight sweaters and too-short skirts that had caused Hannah to harbor less than affectionate feelings for her. But telling Lisa about her own feelings wouldn't comfort her. Hannah's great-grandmother Elsa had always said that actions spoke louder than words, and Hannah reached over to give Lisa a hug.

"There's something else I have to tell you," Delores said. "We have to find another candy company. The one the town council used last year just went out of business. That means we can't sell candy during the intermissions. You have no idea how upset Tory is about that! This is her first play and she was hoping it would be a huge success."

"I can understand that," Hannah said. Victoria Bascomb, or Tory, as she preferred to be called, was the mayor's sister. A wealthy and successful actress who had recently retired from the stage, Tory Bascomb had moved to Lake Eden and taken over as the director of the Lake Eden Players.

"We won't have anything to sell at intermission," Delores continued, "not even popcorn now that we lost the popcorn machine."

"*Lost* it?" Hannah was puzzled. How could you lose a concession-stand size popcorn machine? It was huge!"

"Not *that* way! We didn't physically lose it. But we've always borrowed it from Jordan High, and theirs is broken. They're getting a new one, but it won't be here until after Christmas. The Lake Eden Players made a lot of money at the concession counter last year. And this year they won't make anything."

"Maybe we can do something about that," Lisa told Delores. "Hannah and I already agreed to make the candy and cookies for the gift bags that Santa will give to the children. There's no reason we can't just double that order."

"But you manned the concession stand last year," Delores pointed out. "Will you have time to do that again and make more candy and cookies, too?"

"We'll make time. It's important to support the Lake Eden Players, and I want to see the play anyway. My mother read *A Christmas Carol* to all of us every year, but I've never seen the play."

Hannah turned to look at Lisa in shock. Christmas was a very busy season for them. They'd been discussing it over their first cup of coffee this morning, attempting to come up with a schedule that would let them have a little more time off to enjoy the holidays with their friends and families. And now Lisa had volunteered both of them for more work! The play was being performed three times, and the concession stand would be open before the performance, and during the first and second intermissions. They'd have to be there early to set up, wait on customers as they filed in, handle the intermissions, and clean up after the performances.

Why had Lisa done this? For a brief moment Hannah was puzzled, but then she understood the reason why Lisa had taken on this extra work. Now that Phyllis Bates had been cast as this year's Mrs. Claus, Lisa wanted to be there to keep an eye on Herb. Herb and Phyllis would appear on stage together every night after the final curtain had fallen. They'd greet the children who were attending the performance, give them treat bags, and share a hug before they walked offstage. Lisa wanted to be right there to judge her husband's reaction to that very public hug. But Lisa had never been the jealous type of wife. Why was she so worried about Herb and Phyllis now? Hannah couldn't shake the feeling that there was something else wrong between Herb and Lisa, something that Lisa wasn't telling her.

"Just what we need!" Hannah muttered under her breath, but she managed to maintain her pleasant expression as she turned to her mother. "Do you know how much candy the Lake Eden Players sold at their performance last year?"

"I don't have a dollar amount, but I do know that all our local charities were extremely grateful for their donations."

"Could you get us a copy of last year's order from the candy company?" Lisa asked, clearly realizing why Hannah wanted that information. "We need to know the quantities to be certain that we make enough."

"Of course you need to know the quantity. I should have thought of that. I'll run over to Tory Bascomb's temporary office and ask her." Delores paused to take a bite of her cookie. "And by the way, dears . . . these cookies are fantastic. I love the fact that they have chocolate chips inside."

"I'll tell Andrea you said so," Hannah promised. "More coffee, Mother?"

"No, dear. I really must go." Delores got up from her stool. "I have a million things to do today. Have fun baking, dears. And be sure to save samples of any new cookies you try. I love to test new cookies for you."

Hannah waited until the back kitchen door had closed behind her mother, and then she turned to Lisa. "Okay, Lisa . . . give!"

"Give what?"

"There's more to this Herb and Phyllis thing than you're telling me."

"You're imagining things," Lisa said, but she looked down at the worktable, not meeting Hannah's eyes.

"I don't think so. And it'll probably help to talk about it. Tell me what's wrong, Lisa."

Lisa sat there in silence for a moment, and then she gave a deep sigh. "Herb's been working late every single night this month. I know he loves me and I know that I should trust him, but it's *every* night."

"When did this start?"

"A couple days after Mayor Bascomb transferred Phyllis to Herb's office."

It was Hannah's turn to sigh. "Did you drive past Herb's office to see if he was there?"

"Yes, after it happened five nights in a row. And Hannah . . . Herb wasn't there!"

"Maybe he was out on patrol?"

"No. His cruiser was in the lot, right where he always parks it. But his personal car was gone!"

That didn't sound good, and Hannah reached out to pat Lisa's shoulder. "Did you try to find him?"

"Yes. I drove past Dad's house because I thought he might have gone over there to help his mother with something. He wasn't there, and I didn't go in to ask if they'd seen him. I was too embarrassed. I didn't want them to think I was tracking him down!"

"Of course not. Did you try anywhere else?"

"Yes." Lisa gave a little nod. "I drove past every place I could think of, anywhere I thought he might go."

Hannah hated to ask the logical question, but there was no way she could leave that particular stone unturned. "Did you drive past Phyllis Bates's apartment?"

"Yes," Lisa admitted and she looked shamefaced. "I know that a wife should trust her husband, but when I couldn't find Herb anywhere else, I drove out to The Oaks. I didn't want to, but I just had to know!"

"Of course you did," Hannah reassured her partner, remembering the night she'd driven past the back of the Magnolia Blossom Bakery and spotted Mike's car there. "Was Herb there?"

"No. At least I don't *think* he was there. I didn't spot his car in the visitor parking section."

"How about Phyllis's car?"

"It was in her parking spot. I tried to convince myself that if Phyllis was home and Herb's car wasn't there, he couldn't be with Phyllis. But then I noticed that there were no lights on in her apartment."

"What time was that?"

"A quarter to ten."

"Maybe she was tired and she went to bed early," Hannah suggested, even though she doubted that Lisa would accept that explanation.

"On the *weekend*?" Lisa asked, sounding incredulous. "Phyllis is a party girl. Herb told me that, even back in high school, she'd stay up late and barely make it to school on time the next morning. Their first class was history, and Phyllis slept through it almost every day. Herb had to give her his notes or she would have flunked."

"Herb's right," Hannah conceded. "I sat right across from her and she fell asleep almost every morning. As a matter of fact, she asked me to poke her if she dropped her pen."

They sat in silence for a moment, and then Lisa gave a little shrug. "I can't help but wonder if Herb picked Phyllis up at her place and they went somewhere together. I shouldn't be thinking like that, but maybe Mayor Bascomb isn't the only married man Phyllis has set out to seduce."

## Red Velvet Whippersnapper Cookies

DO NOT preheat your oven quite yet—this cookie dough needs to chill before baking.

1 box *(approximately 18 ounces)* red velvet cake mix, the kind that makes a 9-inch by 13-inch cake *(I used Duncan Hines)*

1 large egg, beaten *(just whip it up in a glass with a fork)*

2 cups of Original Cool Whip, thawed *(measure this—a tub of Cool Whip contains a little over 3 cups and that's too much!)*

1 teaspoon vanilla extract

1 cup semi-sweet MINI chocolate chips *(I used Nestle)*

---

½ cup powdered *(confectioner's)* sugar *(you don't have to sift it unless it's got big lumps)*

small jar of red maraschino cherries, cut in half vertically and without stems

Pour HALF of the dry cake mix into a large bowl.

Use a smaller bowl to mix the two cups of Cool Whip with the beaten egg and the vanilla extract. Stir gently with a rubber spatula until everything is combined.

Add the Cool Whip mixture to the cake mix in the large bowl. STIR VERY CAREFULLY with a wooden spoon or a rubber spatula. Stir only until everything is combined. You don't want to stir all the air from the Cool Whip.

Sprinkle the rest of the cake mix on top and gently fold it in with the rubber spatula. Again, keep as much air in the batter as possible. Air is what will make your cookies soft and have that melt-in-your-mouth quality.

Sprinkle the cup of semi-sweet mini chips on top and gently fold the chips into the airy cookie mixture. Cover the bowl and chill this mixture for at least one hour in the refrigerator. It's a little too sticky to form into balls without chilling it first.

**Hannah's 1ˢᵗ Note: Andrea sometimes mixes whipper-snapper dough up before she goes to bed on Friday night and bakes her cookies with Tracey in the morning.**

When your cookie dough has chilled and you're ready to bake, preheat your oven to 350 degrees F., and make sure the rack is in the middle position. DO NOT take your chilled cookie dough out of the refrigerator until after your oven has reached the proper temperature.

While your oven is preheating, prepare your cookie sheets by spraying them with Pam or another nonstick baking spray, or lining them with parchment paper.

Place the confectioner's sugar in a small, shallow bowl. You will be dropping cookie dough into this bowl to form dough balls and coating them with the powdered sugar.

When your oven is ready, take your dough out of the refrigerator. Using a teaspoon from your silverware drawer, drop the dough by rounded teaspoonful into the bowl with the powdered sugar. Roll the dough around with your fingers to form powdered-sugar-coated cookie dough balls.

**Hannah's 2nd Note: This is easiest if you coat your fingers with powdered sugar first and then try to form the cookie dough into balls.**

Place the coated cookie dough balls on your prepared cookie sheets, no more than 12 cookies on a standard-size sheet.

If you haven't already done so, cut your maraschino cherries in half and place one half, rounded side up, on top of each cookie ball on your baking sheet.

**Hannah's 3rd Note: I've said this before, but it bears repeating. Work with only one cookie dough ball at a time. If you drop more than one in the bowl of powdered sugar, they'll stick together.**

**Andrea's Note: Make only as many cookie dough balls as you can bake at one time and then cover the dough and return it to the refrigerator. I have a double oven so I prepare 2 sheets of cookies at a time.**

Bake your Red Velvet Whippersnapper Cookies at 350 degrees F., for 10 to 12 minutes. Test for doneness by tapping them lightly with a finger to see if they're "set."

Let your cookies cool on the cookie sheet for 2 minutes, and then move them to a wire rack to cool completely. *(This is a lot easier if you line your cookie sheets with parchment paper—then you don't need to lift the cookies one by one. All you have to do is grab one end of the parchment paper and pull it, cookies and all, onto the wire rack.)*

Once the cookies are completely cool, store them between sheets of waxed paper in a cool, dry place. *(Your refrigerator is cool, but it's definitely not dry!)*

Yield: 3 to 4 dozen soft, chewy cookies with little nuggets of chocolate inside. Yield will depend on cookie size.

# Chapter
# Two

L isa wore a slight frown as she got out of Hannah's truck at Jordan High. It was clear that she didn't like what she felt compelled to do. "I feel like I'm spying on Herb by coming here," she confessed as their boots crunched through the freshly fallen snow as they walked toward the entrance of the school auditorium.

"Do you want to forget about it and go home?" Hannah asked her.

"No. I'd just sit there worrying about where Herb was and what he was doing. And thanks to your mother, we do have a perfect excuse for dropping in uninvited."

"That's right." Hannah pulled the heavy door open, and they stepped into the lobby of the auditorium. "We have to pick up the Christmas gift bags from Tory Bascomb. She told Mother she'd leave them on the table in the back of the theater."

Lisa still looked concerned. "Do you think Herb will think it's strange if we sit down in the back and watch the ending of the play?"

"Absolutely not. He'd be hurt if you told him you were here and you didn't stay to watch his Santa Claus appearance."

"Right," Lisa said, but she didn't sound convinced as she followed Hannah through the inner doors to the auditorium.

The Jordan High auditorium served dual purposes. It was a gymnasium for physical education classes and a basketball court during basketball season. When a theater setting was required, it was a simple matter to pull the velvet curtains partially closed and lower the wall-like curtains that were stored near the ceiling to form a stage at the front center of the court. The unused area at the sides and back served as a large backstage area where the actors could wait for their cues before they appeared onstage. The footlights were cleverly concealed below the floor at the very front, and the stagehands simply released the fasteners that held that section of flooring in place and engaged a lever so the lights swiveled up above the surface of the floor.

Since a rehearsal of the Christmas play was in progress, the basketball court that had been in use the previous night had been turned into a stage setting. The audience area was illuminated only by the lights from the stage, and Lisa and Hannah were quiet as they took seats in the back row to watch the end of the rehearsal.

On the brightly illuminated stage, the Cratchit family was seated around the table for their Christmas feast, and the actor playing Scrooge was with them. Now that Hannah's eyes had adjusted to the lighting, she glanced around the darkened audience area. Counting Lisa and Hannah, there were only six people watching the rehearsal. The director, Tory Bascomb, was seated in the exact center of the audience section, flanked by two non-performing members of the Lake Eden Players, Irma York and Bonnie Surma, who were acting as her assistants. Immediately in front of Tory was the costume designer, Trudi Schumann. Tory was making notes on a lighted clipboard, and Hannah assumed that she would go over her comments with the cast after rehearsal had concluded.

Bob Cratchit's wife entered, carrying a platter with what was supposed to be a roasted goose, but looked much more like a turkey to Hannah. Mrs. Cratchit set the platter down in the center of the table to a volley of cheers and applause from the diners. Hannah was so busy wondering where the Lake Eden Players' prop master had found a fake turkey that she almost missed the final line of the play. She returned her attention to the stage just in time to hear the boy Tory Bascomb had cast as Tiny Tim, the real son of the actor playing Bob Cratchit, deliver his famous, often-quoted line.

"God bless us, every one," the childish voice rang out loud and clear. There were several long moments of silence on-stage while everyone smiled at Tiny Tim, and then Tory Bascomb rose to her feet.

"Curtain!" she yelled. "It's not a tableau, for heaven's sake! Are you back there, Freddy? Or did you decide to take a coffee break?"

"I don't drink coffee, Miss Bascomb!" a male voice, somewhat muffled by the heavy curtains, responded. "Doc says it's not good for me because it makes me too nervous."

"All right then. Listen carefully, Freddy. I've told you this at least a dozen times and I'll skin you alive if you don't get it right on opening night! The instant Tiny Tim delivers his final line, I want you to count to five, and then ring down the curtain."

"I can't, Miss Bascomb."

"Why?"

"Because this curtain doesn't ring. Only bells ring. And this curtain doesn't go down, either. It only goes sideways."

The actor playing Bob Cratchit slapped his hand over his mouth and turned away from the audience. Hannah saw his shoulders shake, and she knew he was laughing. Freddy Sawyer had been born developmentally challenged, but he was a talented handyman and he was willing to work hard. And actually, Freddy did have a point. Tory Bascomb had told him to "ring down" the curtain, and she hadn't explained what that meant.

"Ring down the curtain is a theater phrase, Freddy." Tory did her best to modulate her voice, but she still sounded angry. "All it means is to close the curtains so the audience can't see the actors."

"And the actresses?"

"Yes, and the actresses, too."

"Oh. Okay. I can do that," Freddy said, sounding eager to please the famous actor-director. "I'm sorry I got it wrong, Miss Bascomb."

Irma York, who was acting as one of Tory's assistants, leaned over to whisper something in Tory's ear. Tory nodded, and cleared her throat.

"It's okay, Freddy. Irma's going to come backstage right before the play ends, and she'll tell you when to ring down . . . er . . . never mind. Bonnie will tell you when to close the curtains."

"Gee thanks, Miss Bascomb!" Freddy said, sounding greatly relieved. "I like Irma. She's a friend."

"All right. One more time, people. Let's take it from Mrs. Cratchit's entrance."

Irma climbed the four steps at the side of the auditorium that led up to the stage level and ducked behind the velvet curtains. The actors maintained the places, and the final moments of the play were repeated. Tiny Tim spoke his line, five seconds passed, and then the curtains closed.

"Perfect!" Tory called out. "Good job, Freddy! I'm going to let Irma stay back there and cue you for our Santa and Mrs. Claus appearance. Irma? Can you hear me?"

"Yes, Miss Bascomb."

"We'll open the curtains right after the actors clear and the stagehands dress the set for Santa. Cue Freddy when it's time, will you?"

"Yes, Miss Bascomb," Irma answered, sounding every bit as muffled as Freddy had earlier.

"Sound? Listen up. We'll need the sleigh bells. Make them soft at first and then gradually louder until they reach a peak."

"Got it, Miss Bascomb," someone said from backstage.

"Stagehands?" Tory raised her voice so that the crew could hear her backstage. "I'll need you to move the table to the back of the set just as soon as the actors clear. Then bring in the tree and light it. Set Santa's rocking chair next to the tree."

"Yes, Miss Bascomb," another male voice answered.

"Irma? Just as soon as the stagehands are clear, cue Herb and Phyllis to take their positions in the wings. Then cue Freddy to open the curtains to the dressed, but empty, set."

"Empty, Miss Bascomb?" Irma asked.

"Yes. And the moment the curtains are open fully, the sleigh bells will begin to ring to announce the arrival of Santa and Mrs. Claus. Does everyone have that progression?"

There were murmured assents from behind the curtains, and Tory continued her instructions. "When the sleigh bells reach a peak, Santa and Mrs. Claus will enter stage right. Santa will give us one *'Ho! Ho! Ho!'* and then go directly to his rocker. Once seated, Mrs. Claus will hand him his lap robe and retire to the table, where the Christmas gift bags will be arranged. Is everyone clear on that, so far?"

Again, there were assenting murmurs. Tory waited for a moment and then she called out, "Action!"

Once the curtains opened, Hannah turned to watch Lisa's face in the reflected light from the stage. She looked extremely nervous, and her hands were clasped so tightly in her lap that her knuckles were white.

"Relax. It'll be fine," Hannah whispered, even though she had no valid reason to think that it would be so. Then the sleigh bells began to ring, growing louder and louder, until Santa and Mrs. Claus walked out on the stage.

Hannah heard Lisa's sharp exhalation of breath, and she realized that she had also given a gasp of shock. When she turned to look, Lisa was staring at the stage with an expression of disbelief. Hannah couldn't blame her one bit. Phyllis was wearing a Mrs. Claus costume that was unlike anything Hannah had ever seen before in her life.

The red velvet bodice was so tight, Hannah wondered why she couldn't see the bulge of the fasteners on Phyllis's brassiere. Then she realized that perhaps Phyllis wasn't wearing a brassiere, and she was even more shocked than she'd been before. The red velvet skirt of the costume was short. Very short. And with the display of unadorned skin with no protection from the winter elements, Mrs. Claus would have been flash frozen like a Popsicle in no time flat.

Santa Claus was wearing heavy winter boots. The height came just under his knees, and the boots matched the ones that had been depicted on countless Christmas cards. Mrs. Claus, on the other hand, was wearing fire-engine-red patent-leather, knee-high boots that perfectly matched the color of her red velvet costume. The heels on the boots were pencil thin, and Phyllis looked erotically alluring. She was a modern, very sexy Mrs. Claus, and no one would ever mistake her for the overweight, jolly, grey-haired Mrs. Claus that smiled continually and baked cookies for Santa's elfin toymakers.

Hannah turned to look at Lisa, who appeared every bit as scandalized as Hannah was. Phyllis Bates wasn't playing Mrs. Claus. She was playing a *Playboy* bunny dressed up as a sexy, over-the-top Mrs. Claus.

Lisa gave an audible gasp as Mrs. Claus bent over to tuck in the lap robe around Santa's knees. Hannah felt like groaning, too. It wasn't her place to do it, but someone had better tell Phyllis never to bend over!

Trudi Schumann turned around to say something to Tory Bascomb. Tory nodded and rose to her feet.

"Mrs. Claus!" Tory called out.

Phyllis stopped arranging the lap robe and turned to face their director. "Yes?"

"Where did you get your costume? And don't try to tell me it was from our costume department, because I know we don't have anything like *that*!"

Phyllis tossed her head, which would normally cause her

blond hair to swing in a graceful arc. Now, however, the effect was lost due to the short, curly Mrs. Santa wig she was wearing. "The Mrs. Claus costume you have didn't fit me. I had to go to Minneapolis to get this one."

"Which doesn't fit you, either. It's much too short, much too brief, and much too tight."

"No, this one fits perfectly!" Phyllis argued.

Hannah held her breath. Tory Bascomb had a legendary temper, and Hannah expected it to manifest itself at any moment.

"You're right, Miss Bates. It certainly does fit. It's the perfect costume for a Christmas show in a strip club. But . . . my dear girl . . . *this* is not a strip club. This is general entertainment for men, women, and children of all ages. And there is no way that I will allow you on my stage in a lap dancer's costume!"

Tory turned to Trudi. "Is there any way you can alter our Mrs. Claus costume to fit Miss Bates so that she can return her lamentable and unfortunate choice?"

"Of course, Miss Bascomb. All I need are her measurements and I can have it ready by tomorrow." Even in the darkened theater, Hannah saw that Trudi's lips were twitching with laughter. "I can do it, no problem."

"Then get right on it after tonight's rehearsal. And thank you, Trudi. You've saved us from total disaster." Tory turned to face the stage again. "Now let us put this unfortunate incident behind us and rehearse the rest of the Santa appearance. Miss Bates?"

"Yes?"

Hannah's eyes widened. It was clear that Phyllis was not cowed by the famous director's tone.

"Please go to the table, pick up an imaginary Christmas gift bag, and carry it to Santa."

Hannah and Lisa watched as Phyllis walked to the table, pretended to pick up something from the surface, and returned to hand the nonexistent object to Herb.

"Very good. We'll have a silver tray for the bags the night of the performance. Our prop department tray will hold a dozen bags. All you'll have to do is pick up the tray, stand next to Santa, and hand the bags to him, one by one, after a child is seated on his lap." Tory stopped speaking to smile at Herb. "This year, Trudi has fashioned a new lap robe. Not only is it washable, she has wisely inserted a rubber sheet inside the lining. As our Santa knows quite well, some of the younger children in the audience become a bit too excited when they sit on Santa's lap. This new, improved lap robe should generate a goodly savings for the Lake Eden Players in dry-cleaning costs during the holiday season."

There was a burst of general laughter from backstage, and Hannah glanced at Lisa. Lisa was smiling, and she leaned over to whisper in Hannah's ear.

"They had to dry-clean Herb's costume three times last year. The rubber sheet was my idea."

Tory cleared her throat. "Are you ready, Miss Bates?"

"Ready for what?"

The question from Phyllis was casual, and Hannah realized that Phyllis was not at all intimidated, even after being dressed down in public by their famous director. Hannah glanced at Lisa, who was frowning slightly, and then she turned back to the stage just in time to watch Tory Bascomb give her next instruction for Herb and Phyllis.

"When the last child leaves, Santa will stand and toss his lap robe on the chair behind him. "Action, please, Mr. Beeseman."

Herb got to his feet and tossed the lap robe on the chair.

"Miss Bates? You will stand next to Santa. Santa will put his arms around you and give you a hug."

Hannah wasn't surprised by the instruction. In previous years, Santa had always hugged Mrs. Claus at the end of the show. She watched carefully as Herb put his arms around Phyllis and gave her a hug. Then she glanced at Lisa. Lisa did not look at all upset by the casual hug that Herb had given to Phyllis.

"Perfect," Tory said, cocking her head to the side. "But I think we'll try something new this year. Do you know how to deliver a stage kiss, Miss Bates?"

"I think so. That's a kiss that looks real, but isn't real. Is that right?"

"Basically, yes. This is what I want both of you to do. Mr. Beeseman will pull you into his arms. You, Miss Bates, will reach up to put your hands on his face. Then you will use your thumbs as a barrier and kiss your own thumbs right after Mr. Beeseman turns you to the side so that the audience cannot fully see what you are doing."

"I get it," Phyllis responded quickly.

"Are you sure? Stage-kissing often takes some practice." Phyllis shook her head. "No, it's okay. I got it."

"All right then. Let's try it. Mr. Beeseman? Please pull Miss Bates into your arms."

As Hannah watched, Herb pulled Phyllis into his arms, but he was careful to keep some space between them. It certainly didn't *look* as if Herb were interested in Phyllis, and that made Hannah doubt that Lisa truly had anything to worry about with her husband. Of course it was always possible that Herb had spotted Lisa in the audience and his apparent disinterest could have been for show. Hannah just wasn't sure.

"Proceed, Miss Bates," Tory directed.

Hannah glanced over at Lisa again. Her hands were clenched in her lap. It was clear that Lisa didn't trust Phyllis to follow the director's instructions.

"Action!" Tory called out, and Phyllis put her hands on Herb's face. Then, without waiting for him to turn, she began to kiss him.

Hannah gave a little gasp. This wasn't a stage kiss. This was real! And Phyllis was kissing Lisa's husband in a *very* passionate way. She reached out for Lisa, wanting to make sure that Lisa stayed in her seat and didn't make a scene right then and there, but her hand encountered empty air. Lisa wasn't there. Her seat was empty. Hannah swiveled around to locate Lisa and spotted her going out the door and into the lobby of the auditorium.

There was only one thing to do. Hannah got up quickly and hurried after Lisa, grabbing the box of Christmas gift bags from the table as she rushed past. The outside door was just closing, and Hannah raced after Lisa, almost slipping on the ice that had gathered on the sidewalk.

"Wait up, Lisa!" she called out, and Lisa stopped under the streetlight that illuminated the parking lot.

There were traces of tears on Lisa's face. Hannah could see them glittering in the light as she approached. Lisa hadn't been fooled for a moment by the stage kiss. And neither had anyone else.

"She kissed him! Like *that*! And she did it right in front of everyone!"

It was useless to deny the truth. Lisa was right. Phyllis had kissed Herb. "I know," Hannah said, reaching out to pat Lisa's shoulder. "But Lisa . . . Herb didn't kiss her. He was expecting a stage kiss. And he wasn't the one who kissed her. Phyllis kissed *him*. Just think about that for a moment. Herb was probably just as shocked as you were. He wasn't expecting it. And there really wasn't anything he could do about it."

"He could have moved. Or he could have pushed her away. He didn't do anything like that! He just stood there."

"Maybe he was too shocked to move or push her away."

"I really doubt that! They were an item in high school. And maybe, just maybe, Herb was enjoying it!"

Hannah remained silent. She knew that there was no way Lisa was going to accept any excuses for Herb right now. She was far too angry. The best thing Hannah could do to defuse the situation was to distract Lisa and give her something else to think about.

"Come on," she said, leading the way to her cookie truck. "Let's take these Christmas gift bags back to The Cookie Jar and see how many pieces of candy they'll hold. We need to figure out how much we need so that we can make out our work schedule. Christmas is a big busy season for us with all the family gatherings and parties."

"You're right," Lisa said, nodding quickly. "We had a lot more dessert-catering jobs than we expected last Christmas."

"That's right. We worked late every night the week before Christmas to fill all those orders."

"And we had to turn down a couple because we just didn't have the time," Lisa recalled. "I'm really sorry, Hannah."

"Sorry for what?" Hannah stopped in the act of buckling her seat belt to ask.

"I'm sorry I volunteered us for even more work by telling your mother we'd make the candy. I should have asked you first."

"Don't be silly. We're partners. I don't ask you every time I accept an order, do I?"

"Well, no. But . . ."

"Then you don't have to ask me," Hannah said before Lisa could go on. "I was just thinking I'd like to try something really different this Christmas."

"What did you have in mind?"

"Something with butterscotch. We've never done anything with butterscotch. I wonder if we could make butterscotch fudge with pretzels in it. Chocolate-covered pretzels are great. Do you think pretzels and butterscotch would go together?"

"I think so. Butterscotch is something almost everyone likes, and you need something salty with the sweetness. If the pretzels don't work, let's see what else we can come up with."

"Okay. We'll experiment."

"Good! I love it when we experiment." Lisa looked excited. "You never know what we're going to come up with, and sometimes it's wonderful!"

"And sometimes it's not," Hannah reminded her.

"I know, but usually something good comes out of it."

"Like, remind me never to try this again because it's yucky?"

Lisa laughed and Hannah breathed a sigh of relief. She'd managed to distract Lisa from her problems.

"Do you have time to do a little experimentation tonight?" Hannah asked her.

"I've got nothing but time. The only thing I have to do tonight is give the dogs their dinner, let them run around the backyard for a while, try my chocolate caramels one more time, and go to bed."

"How about Herb? Will he mind if you're late getting home?"

Lisa's expression changed to one mixed between sadness and irritation. "He hasn't been home before midnight for I can't remember how long, and there's no reason to think tonight will be any different."

Hannah was silent. She had no comment. She wished she hadn't asked the question. She wanted to comfort Lisa, to tell her that everything would be okay, but she wasn't sure that would be the case. Was it better to pretend that she wasn't as concerned as Lisa was? She knew that Herb loved Lisa. But sometimes a momentary passion superseded a steady and abiding love. It wasn't right, but it *did* happen and it would be fruitless to deny it. The better choice would be to pick up on something else Lisa had told her. And that was exactly what Hannah did.

"You made chocolate caramels?" Hannah asked, driving out of the snow-covered parking lot behind the school.

"Yes. I tried my great-aunt's recipe last night. It worked, but I want to try it one more time to make sure. Then I'll bring some for you to taste. I sent a dozen to work with Herb this morning, and he called me at The Cookie Jar to say he really liked them. He said he gave one to Phyllis and she wanted another, but he told her he was saving them for later." Lisa gave a little smile. "At least she didn't get *every-thing* she wanted from him!"

"Right." Hannah decided that the safest thing to do was to change the subject. "If your caramels work out tonight, we can make some for the Christmas gift bags. I don't know anybody who doesn't like caramels."

"Neither do I," Lisa concurred. "But I shouldn't have mentioned them, Hannah."

"Why not?"

Lisa gave a little laugh. "Because now I'm getting hungry. And I don't think there's much in the refrigerator at home ex-cept the bologna and cheese for Herb's favorite sandwiches in the morning."

"Now that you mention it, I'm getting hungry, too," Han-nah admitted. Then she thought back to her schedule for the day and gave a wry smile. "No wonder! I was so busy, I for-got to eat lunch."

"Me, too. We had a big lunch crowd today and I didn't even think of it. I guess I could have had a couple of cookies, but what I really wanted was meat."

"I know that feeling." Hannah drove down the alley and turned into the parking lot behind The Cookie Jar. "All I can think about is a double cheeseburger with crispy fries."

"And maybe a salad with bleu cheese dressing and some cheesy garlic bread?"

"Oh, yes!" Hannah's mouth began to salivate, and she swallowed. "I've got a proposition for you, Lisa."

"What's that?"

"Let's figure out how much candy the bags will hold and draw up a schedule of what to make when. And after we're through, we can go out to the Corner Tavern for salads, gar-lic bread, cheeseburgers, and fries."

"And maybe some of their Chocolate Coffee Cake for dessert?"

"Why not!"

Lisa began to smile from ear to ear. "That sounds really good to me, Hannah!"

As Hannah parked, Lisa grabbed the box with the Christmas gift bags for the children, and then she opened the passenger door.

"You're in a hurry?" Hannah asked.

"Yes! Come on, Hannah. I'm so hungry, my stomach is growling just thinking about the fries and onion rings at the Corner Tavern. And the sooner we get started, the sooner we can drive out there and eat!"

# Chapter
# Three

The bar at the Corner Tavern was crowded, but Hannah found a spot near one end. She ordered a soda water with a wedge of lime and sat there waiting for Lisa to arrive. Lisa had stopped at home to feed her dogs, Dillon and Sammy, and let them out to run in the backyard for a few minutes. Hannah had driven out ahead of her to wait for a table for the two of them in the dining room.

The scent of good beef was in the air, and Hannah smiled as she thought of a hot, fresh cheeseburger and crispy golden French fries. The Corner Tavern was a mecca for hamburger and steak lovers. As a nod to their patrons who were cutting down on red meat, they had a vegetarian entrée on their menu, and several fish dishes. The owner's wife, Nona Prentiss, had told Hannah that only two out of a hundred customers ordered a non-beef entrée, and Hannah believed it. As far as she was concerned, the Corner Tavern had the best beef of any restaurant in the area, perhaps even in the whole state of Minnesota. The reason most people went out there to eat was to get succulent beef, expertly cooked, and plenty of it.

"So, Hannah! How's it going?" a voice called out, and Hannah spotted Bonnie Surma sitting at the bar.

"Everything's fine, Bonnie," Hannah responded. Just then, the man next to Hannah got up to follow one of the waitresses to a table, and Bonnie moved over to sit down on the stool the man had just vacated.

"Can I buy the best baker in Lake Eden a drink?" Bonnie asked, smiling at Hannah.

"Thanks, but I'm just having soda water. Are you meeting someone, Bonnie?"

"Yes, Trudi Schumann. We're going to get a table in the back, as far away from the actors as we can get."

Hannah thought fast. There was only one group of actors in Lake Eden. "Are you talking about the Lake Eden Players?"

"Yes. And Tory Bascomb. She's got the big table in the middle of the room, and she's holding a meeting with the cast."

"And you're not invited?"

"I'm part of the technical crew on the Christmas play. I don't have to go to the actors' meetings, thank goodness. Tory's probably picking apart everyone's performances."

"You don't like Tory?"

Bonnie shrugged. "I like her well enough, but she's very exacting. We're not professionals, and our actors aren't really used to that. The only reason I'm here is that I'm waiting for Trudi. I told her I'd help her alter that Mrs. Santa Claus outfit for Phyllis Bates if she'd come out here for a cheeseburger and a pitcher of beer with me. I'm husband-less tonight. Gil's gone, and I hate to eat alone."

"Is Gil busy with school things?"

"He's in St. Cloud with the chess team. They drove up this afternoon and they're staying overnight. The boys have a competition tomorrow, and they won't be home until late tomorrow night."

Bonnie took a sip from her beer glass, and Hannah noticed that her hands were shaking. "Are you cold, Bonnie?"

"I'm freezing. I had to park all the way in the back, and the wind felt like needles of ice when I got out of the car." She glanced down at her beer glass. "I should have ordered a coffee drink. It's just that I know we'll have beer when Trudi gets here, and I didn't want to mix my drinks. They have Beck's on tap, and Trudi likes Beck's."

"Why don't you order a cup of coffee on the side? That way you can have your beer and warm up, too."

"Good idea." Bonnie crooked her finger at the bartender, and he came over. "Could I have coffee? I'm still really cold."

"No problem. It's on the house." The bartender poured a cup of coffee and set it in front of Bonnie. "Do you want some brandy in that?"

"No, thanks. I'm meeting someone in a while and we'll be drinking beer." Bonnie turned back to Hannah when the bartender had left. "Are you waiting for someone, Hannah?"

"Yes, Lisa. She had to go home and feed the dogs."

"I saw her in the audience at the rehearsal tonight." Bonnie cupped her hands around the coffee cup to warm them. "Was she terribly upset about that stage kiss that wasn't a stage kiss?"

"Let's just say that she wasn't exactly happy about it."

"I don't blame her for that. And she wasn't the only one who was upset! I saw Herb afterward, and he looked really embarrassed."

"Does Herb know that Lisa was in the audience?"

"I don't know. I didn't mention it, that's for sure. I figured the less said, the better."

"How about Herb? Is he here at Tory's meeting?"

"I don't know. He hasn't come in since I've been here, but I didn't come straight out. I stopped at the community center to drop off some books I collected for the library. And then I ran past the house to store some things that came for the school."

"Are you still filling in as the librarian when Marge can't make it?"

"Yes, I tried to get out of it this year, but they couldn't find anyone else. I'd like to back off a bit, but I guess I just can't say no, especially if something is school related. Gil doesn't like me to work, but he's okay if I do volunteer things. And I really do enjoy working with the students. And of course I love the Lake Eden Players. I've been working with them for years now."

Hannah was still thinking of that table in the center of the room and exactly who was attending Tory Bascomb's meeting. "Speaking of the Lake Eden Players, do you know if Phyllis Bates is here?"

"She hasn't come in since I've been here. If you want to pop in to look, I'll hold your stool for you."

"Thanks, Bonnie." Hannah got up from her stool and walked over to the entrance to the dining room. The Lake Eden Players weren't difficult to spot since Bonnie had told her that they had the big oval table in the center of the room. Hannah scanned all sides of the table. Herb wasn't there, and neither was Phyllis. She breathed a sigh of relief as she turned to walk back to the bar. If either Herb or Phyllis had been at the table, she would have called Lisa on her cell phone, made some excuse about how the Corner Tavern was too crowded to get a table, and suggested that they meet at Bertanelli's for a pizza instead. As it turned out, Hannah barely had time to finish her soda water before Lisa came in.

"It's a madhouse out there," Lisa said. "I'm just lucky I got here when I did." She noticed Bonnie on the stool next to Hannah and gave a little wave. "Hi, Bonnie."

"Hi, Lisa. What's wrong out there? Are people driving badly?" Bonnie asked, moving over one stool so that Lisa could sit next to Hannah.

Lisa shook her head. "No, it's not that. The drive out was fine, but everyone must have decided to come out here for a hamburger at the same time tonight. There were four cars behind me when I pulled into the parking lot, and I got the last empty spot."

Lisa slid onto the stool and ordered a hot lemonade. It had just arrived when the waitress tapped Hannah on the shoulder to say that their table was ready.

"Do you want to sit with us, Bonnie?" Hannah asked.

"Thanks for the offer, but Trudi should be here any minute now. I'll just stay here and wait for her. I don't want to go in the dining room quite yet. Tory is still holding court with the actors."

Lisa waited until they got to the doorway to the dining room, and then she leaned close to Hannah. "Is Herb here?"

"No."

"Good! At least I think it's good. How about Phyllis?"

"No." Hannah saw the expression on Lisa's face and hurried to reassure her. "But just because neither one of them is here doesn't mean that they're together."

"True. And I'm too hungry to worry about it right now." Lisa took a seat at the table the waitress had indicated and picked up the menu. "I don't really need this. I know exactly what I want. I've been thinking about it for almost an hour now."

Their waitress had carried in their drinks from the bar and she set them on cocktail napkins. "How do you like our new napkins?"

Hannah lifted her drink and saw that the napkin had a picture of a bear on it. "Is that Albert?" she asked, referring to the stuffed grizzly bear that guarded the entrance to the dining room.

"Yes, it's Albert. The boss hired a photographer to take the picture and had the napkins printed. Everybody loves Albert." The waitress pulled an order book from her apron pocket and turned to Lisa. "I can take your order right now, if you want."

"I want." Lisa gave a little laugh. "I'll have a double cheeseburger with a side order of onion rings and three pickles."

"Mustard or ketchup for your burger?"

"Both, please. And a bowl of bleu cheese dressing."

"You want a small green salad, too?" the waitress asked Lisa.

"No. I just like to dip my onion rings in the dressing." Lisa grinned at Hannah. "I got it from her. That's what Hannah does with her French fries."

"It sounds good. I'll have to try it sometime." The waitress turned to Hannah. "And what can I get for you?"

"Exactly the same thing, but I want French fries instead of onion rings. And just put a little extra dressing in that bowl for me."

The waitress laughed. "You can have your own bowl of dressing. It's not like I wash the dishes around here."

Hannah waited until their waitress had left, and then she leaned forward. "Well? Did you do it?"

"Do what?"

"You know what I mean."

Lisa nodded. "Yes. I didn't want to, but I couldn't help it."

"I figured you would. And we *are* talking about the same thing, aren't we?"

Lisa laughed. "I think so. You wanted to know if I drove past her apartment . . . right?"

"Right. Did you learn anything?"

"Only that her apartment was dark and her car was gone."

"How about Herb's office?"

"The lights were off, his cruiser was in the lot, and Herb's car wasn't there." Lisa reached for the small bowl of pickled vegetables that was sitting on their table. "I love these pickles."

"Me, too."

Hannah thought about the custom that the Corner Tavern had followed since their opening day. After the busboy cleared a table and reset it for the next diners, he dished up a small bowl of pickled vegetables and put it in the center of the table. It was a fresh bowl every time and, in the beginning, the original owner's wife, Nona's predecessor, had pickled all the vegetables herself.

"I love this pickled cauliflower," Lisa said, crunching down on the vegetarian treat.

"And I love these." Hannah reached for a green string bean

and bit off half. "Did you know that my great-grandmother used to call pickled vegetables *digestives?*"

"No. Are digestives something that helps you digest food?"

"Supposedly. Of course in the United Kingdom, they have digestive biscuits to take care of that. The first digestives were a sweet meal biscuit. They were meant to get the digestive juices flowing and make it easier for the body to process the rest of the meal."

"Believe me, my digestive juices are flowing!" Lisa smacked her lips. "These are really good. Can I have the last piece of cauliflower?"

"Knock yourself out. I'm enjoying the green beans and the button mushrooms."

For a few more moments the conversation consisted solely of crunching and chewing. Then Lisa looked down at the empty bowl. "Good heavens! We even ate the pickled carrots. And I don't like the pickled carrots!"

Their waitress overheard Lisa's comment and came over to take the empty bowl. "You two must really be hungry. I've been working here for over ten years and I've never seen an empty relish bowl. Nobody ever eats the carrots."

"Then why are they there?" Lisa asked her.

"Search me!"

"They're probably for color," Hannah offered an explanation. "Without them, the bowl would consist of green, white, and tan. That's not as eye-catching as a mixture with orange in it."

"You've got a point there," the waitress complimented Hannah. "Too bad they don't pickle those little red cherry tomatoes. They'd be really pretty."

Hannah thought about that for a moment. "You're right. And I wonder if you could pickle them. I think I'll give it a try."

"They'd be good in salads, too," the waitress said.

"And you could use them to decorate a bowl of coleslaw, or potato salad," Lisa suggested.

The waitress reached into her pocket and pulled out an electronic device. "Your food's up," she told them once she'd glanced at the display. "I'll go get it, and then you can eat something besides pickles."

"I'm positively stuffed!" Lisa remarked, as they got into their parkas and put on gloves and hats.

"Me, too. Maybe we shouldn't have had that Chocolate Coffee Cake for dessert."

"Or maybe we shouldn't have split that second order of French fries," Lisa added.

For once, the wind wasn't blowing as they went out the door, and the night was clear and icy cold. Both Hannah and Lisa shivered as they walked into the parking lot.

"Where did you park, Hannah?"

"I'm way in the back of the lot by the ditch."

"I'm back there, too. Let's walk over on the side, where there's fresh snow. It's not as slippery there."

The walking was easier once they'd moved to the side of the lot and they could avoid the deep ruts that the cars had made driving in and out. Hannah and Lisa had arrived at the back row when Hannah spotted something at the edge of the ditch.

"Wait up a second, Lisa," Hannah said. "Someone dropped something red in the snow and I want to see what it is."

"I see it. It looks like cloth."

"It's probably nothing but a mitten or a scarf, but whoever lost it might want it back."

"I can go with you."

"Better not. It's outside the plowed area and the snow's deep out there. It could go right over your ankle boots."

Hannah waded into the area that hadn't been plowed, heading straight toward the red object. As she got closer, she could see that Lisa had been right. It was something made of red cloth.

"It's a Santa hat!" Hannah called out to Lisa. "And there's something else here, too. Hold on and I'll see what it is."

As she waded even farther into the ditch, Hannah began to feel increasingly anxious. The anxious, uneasy feeling had nothing to do with the cold or the snow. There was something wrong, very wrong.

Hannah's first instinct was to turn around and retrace her steps up the side of the ditch and into the bright lights and safe haven of the parking lot. But she couldn't seem to turn around without knowing what had given her that anxious, uneasy feeling, and her need to know pulled her even deeper into the ditch.

The moon cast a cold, blue light over the surface of the snow. There were icicles with their sharp, lethal points hanging from the stark black branches of the trees. Hannah shuddered. She'd always felt menaced whenever she had to pass under icicles, but the trees with their glittering daggers dotted the sides of the ditch. There was no other path she could take to get to the second object she'd seen.

As she neared the bottom of the ditch, her heart was racing and Hannah was breathing in painful gasps. This wasn't from the exertion of wading through deep snow. It was fear of something she had yet to discover.

Her boot hit something beneath the snow, and Hannah barely managed to maintain her balance. She reached down to uncover the object that had tripped her, and her gloved fingers drew it out of the snow. She stood there staring for a moment, puzzled by the sight of one of the reusable lunch bags that Lisa had given to Herb for Christmas. Each lunch bag was a different color, and they all had Herb's name embroidered on the side in bold black letters.

There was something inside the bag, and Hannah made sure the contents didn't fall out as she flipped it over so that she could see the other side. A chill ran through her. The lunch bag was definitely Herb's. She could read his name quite clearly in the cold, blue moonlight. But why was Herb's lunch bag buried in the snow near the bottom of the ditch?

A possible explanation occurred to Hannah. Herb could have disliked the lunch that Lisa had packed for him and, quite literally, ditched it before he'd gone inside to eat lunch. This was possible, but very unlikely. Herb told everyone who would listen about the wonderful lunches his wife made for him and how much he enjoyed them. And even if he hadn't felt like eating this particular day's lunch and had thrown it out, Herb would have kept the lunch bag to take home to Lisa.

Her curiosity aroused, Hannah opened the lunch bag and peeked inside. There was no sandwich, or fruit, or cookies. The only thing left in the bag was homemade candy wrapped in waxed paper. Lisa's caramels. And Herb had told Lisa that he loved them. Why had he eaten part of his lunch and then thrown away his personalized lunch bag containing Lisa's caramels?

Hannah's mind was working on this new puzzle when she spotted something else only a few feet away. As she stared at the bulky, snow-covered mound, the anxious, uneasy feeling in her stomach began to intensify. She thrust the lunch bag in the pocket of her parka. She'd dispose of it later. There was no way she was going to let Lisa see what had happened to her caramels. Lisa would be devastated by the fact that Herb had lied to her by saying he liked her caramels and then throwing them away.

As Hannah stepped toward the mound in the snow, she had a very unwelcome thought. It was human-sized. "No!" she gasped as an awful suspicion took root in her mind. "It can't be!" she exclaimed, aloud.

"Hannah? Are you all right?" Lisa's voice floated down to her from above.

"I'm okay. I'm just . . ." Hannah thought fast. There was no way she was going to alarm Lisa before she found out what was in that mound of snow. "I'm just winded and I have to catch my breath. The snow is really deep down here."

Hannah was amazed at how strong and steady her voice was. Perhaps she should join the Lake Eden Players. It seemed as if she could act, since she felt just the opposite of strong and steady. "I'm just going to check out one more thing while I'm down here, and then I'll climb back up."

As she approached the hump of snow, Hannah realized that the anxious feeling in her stomach was what Mike had called her *slaydar*, her uncanny penchant for finding murder victims. *Please let it be wrong this time*, Hannah's mind begged, but that sick, sinking feeling grew with each step she took toward the snow-covered mound.

"Please not Herb!" she whispered as she brushed off a layer of snow with her gloves. She swept another layer to the side, and then another, until she had uncovered a cold, dead body that made her give an audible gasp of shock.

"What did you find, Hannah?" Lisa called out from the top of the ditch.

Hannah swallowed hard, and somehow she managed to form the words she needed to say. "Call Mike!"

"Mike? You mean . . . oh, no!"

"Yes!" Hannah answered, and then she swallowed again. "Tell him to get out here right away!"

"I will. Right now. Are you all right?"

"Yes. Hurry, Lisa. Tell him I'll stay where I am until he gets here."

Hannah listened as Lisa made the call. Her words were succinct and she sounded in control. Hannah was very grateful that Lisa had pulled herself together. The ditch was deep, and even though she had her cell phone with her, she might not have been able to get reception down there.

"He said to hang on, he'll be right there. Who . . ." Lisa stopped in mid-question and gave a little sob. "Who is it, Hannah?"

"Phyllis. Phyllis Bates."

"Is she . . . uh . . . is she . . . dead?"

Hannah glanced down at the cold, motionless body that had been very alive in a sexy Mrs. Santa costume not even two hours ago. Her eyes swept up to the damage that had been done to Phyllis's head, and she swallowed hard again. "Yes, Lisa. Phyllis is dead."

# Chapter Four

When Hannah unlocked the door to her condo, she stepped back three paces and braced herself. Then she leaned forward, pushed open the door, and waited for the feline missile that was about to launch itself in her direction. She waited... and waited... and then the orange-and-white missile hurtled into her arms.

"Moishe! Where were you?" Hannah asked, carrying her cat in to place him in his favorite spot on the top of the couch.

"Sorry," her sister Michelle said, rushing out of the guest bedroom. "I was just showing Moishe his new cat toy, and we didn't hear you unlock the door."

"Michelle!" Hannah greeted her youngest sister with a big hug. "How did you get here?"

Michelle laughed. "If you'd checked your text messages, you'd know. Mother picked me up at the bus station and dropped me off here two hours ago. I hope you don't mind that I used the key you gave me and came inside."

"Why should I mind? That's why I gave you that key in the first place." Hannah knew she probably looked a little crazy, but she couldn't seem to stop smiling. Seeing Michelle making herself at home in the condo was like basking in the sunshine. "I'm so glad you're here!"

"Uh-oh, this sounds like trouble!" Michelle said, hurrying

to the kitchen to take the glass of white wine she'd poured in preparation for Hannah's return from the top shelf in the refrigerator. "Sit down, kick off your boots, and tell me all about it."

Hannah peeled off her parka, kicked off her boots on the rug by the door, and took a seat on her old couch. "Just for starters, Phyllis Bates is dead."

"Mayor Bascomb's new squeeze?"

Hannah nodded. "That's right. I found her in the ditch behind the Corner Tavern parking lot."

"Murdered?"

"Oh, yes. As far as I know, people don't usually bash in their own heads as a preferred method of suicide."

It was clear that Michelle was attempting to control herself, but it didn't work. She laughed. "That's what I love about you, Hannah. You don't mince words."

"Well . . . perhaps that was a bit insensitive, but it's true."

"Yes, it's insensitive, but it was funny. And you found her?"

"Who else?" Hannah removed the plastic wrap from the top of the wineglass and took a sip. "I have slaydar, remember?"

"How could I forget? Mike says that all the time. Is he coming over tonight to take your statement?"

"That's what he said. Do I have any food in the house?"

"You do now. I brought some groceries with me on the bus, and I can make supper. The only thing I forgot was the Thousand Island dressing, but I guess I could get along without it."

"You don't have to get along without it."

Michelle smiled. "Great! Do you have some in the refrigerator?"

"No, but I have everything you need to make it. All it is is mayonnaise mixed with ketchup and sweet pickle relish."

"How much?"

"Just mix it to taste. It'll be exactly the same as the bottled dressing. What are you planning to make?"

"Grilled Ham and Double Cheese Sandwiches."

"That sounds like a really good sandwich!"

"It is. I made them for my housemates last night, and they said they loved them."

Hannah smiled. "I'm sure they did. You're a good cook, Michelle."

"Thanks. I'll make two for Mike and one for me. Do you want me to make one for you?"

"I'd love to try one, but I already ate a double cheese-burger, an order and a half of fries with bleu cheese dressing, and a slice of Chocolate Coffee Cake."

"Will you at least taste a corner of mine?"

"Of course I will. What kind of bread do you use?"

"Rye. There's a bakery near us, and they make really good breads."

"It sounds wonderful, and I almost wish I hadn't eaten. But I was *really* hungry."

"It only takes a few minutes to make them, so I won't start until Mike gets here. I'm experimenting with quick meals. One of my roommates is getting married right after graduation, and I want to give her a whole folder of easy, quick suppers. Her boyfriend's a teacher, and that's what she'll be when she graduates."

"That sounds like a great wedding gift, Michelle."

Michelle looked pleased. "I thought it would be better than monogrammed sheets or a set of fancy towels she'd only get out when company was coming."

After Michelle had gone into the kitchen, Hannah changed to her favorite wintertime at-home outfit which consisted of forest-green sweatpants, an oversized sweatshirt of the same color, and fur-lined slippers. Then she sat down on the couch again, picked up her wineglass, and took another sip. The Cookie Jar was doing good business, she'd finished her Christmas shopping early this year, and Michelle was in town. Life in Lake Eden was very good if you didn't consider the murder rate.

* * *

The knock on the door came twenty minutes later, and Michelle got up to answer it. "Good thing I decided to put together a double batch," she said as she saw that Lonnie was with Mike.

"A double batch of what?" Mike asked, sniffing the air as he walked into the living room. "Whatever it is, it smells great!"

"Michelle baked cookies earlier," Hannah told him, getting up to greet them, "and she's making Grilled Ham and Double Cheese Sandwiches." She turned to smile at Lonnie. "Hi, Lonnie. I guess you two guys are working late tonight."

"We're waiting for Doc to finish the autopsy," Mike explained. "And I have to complete your statement. After that, we're through."

"Except for being on call," Lonnie added. "We're on call twenty-four-seven during homicide investigations."

"Do you want to interview Hannah now?" Michelle asked Mike. "Or would you rather wait until after you eat?"

"Now. I've got most of what I need, and it shouldn't take more than ten minutes." Mike walked over to the couch, sat down, and patted the cushion next to him. "Come over here, Hannah. Lonnie can keep Michelle company in the kitchen."

Hannah took a seat on the cushion next to Mike. "What else do you need to know?"

"I need answers to a couple of questions that occurred to me after you'd left. Did you see the body from the top of the ditch?"

"No. The ditch is quite deep, and it was too dark to see much of anything. I just happened to notice something red in the snow, and I went to see what it was."

"Did you think it was blood?"

"No, not at all. Both Lisa and I could see that it was something made of cloth. I thought it was a mitten, or a glove, or maybe a scarf. And since it wasn't that far from the lip of the ditch, I told Lisa that I was going to climb down to get it."

"You told me that earlier, but you didn't tell me why."

For a moment, Hannah was puzzled. "Why what?"

"Why did you go down to get it?"

"Oh. Because somebody had obviously lost whatever it was and I thought they might have wanted it back."

Mike smiled at her. "That figures. You're just a helpful person by nature. Why didn't Lisa go with you?"

"She would have, but the snow was deep and she was wearing ankle boots. I had my regular boots on and they're knee-highs. It was a good thing, too. The snow was really deep down there."

"And the cloth you spotted was . . . ?"

"A Santa hat. I picked it up and I intended to climb right back up when I saw something else."

"The body?"

"Actually . . . no. I hadn't seen that yet. It was at the bottom of the ditch. I thought I'd spotted something else, but I couldn't find it again when I got down there. But I did find something else quite near the bottom."

"What was that?"

"I'll tell you, but it's something very . . ." Hannah paused, searching for the right word. "Let's just say that it was something very sensitive."

"Something sensitive in what way?"

"Well . . ." Hannah paused again and took a moment to formulate her answer. "Look, Mike . . . do you really have to put what I tell you in your report?"

"That depends on whether or not it has anything to do with the investigation."

"But if it's just personal and it doesn't have anything to do with the murder, then you don't have to put it in your report, do you?"

"I'll have to make up my own mind on that, Hannah. And I'll do that *after* you tell me what it was."

Hannah sighed deeply. She wished she'd never mentioned

that second object, but she had and now she was obligated to tell Mike.

"Hannah?"

"Yes. I know. I have to tell you. But first, I have to know if you really like Lisa."

Mike reared back in surprise. "Of course I like Lisa! She's like a younger sister to me."

"Okay. How about Herb? Do you like Herb?"

The puzzled expression on Mike's face didn't change with this new question. "Sure, I do. Herb's a regular guy. What's this all about, Hannah?"

"It's complicated." Hannah took a moment to phrase her answer. "Lisa's worried that Herb was getting a little too close and personal with Phyllis Bates, now that Mayor Bascomb reassigned her to Herb's office. Herb's been coming home really late almost every night, and Lisa knows he's not at work because she drove past his office and his car wasn't there."

"Okay. As far as I know, Herb's crazy about Lisa and I don't believe he'd get involved with another woman, but go on."

"Lisa made chocolate caramels last night and gave some to Herb in his lunch bag."

"That's nice, but what does that have to do with Phyllis Bates?"

"I'll tell you, but please be careful with this. If it gets out, it could cause a lot of trouble between Lisa and Herb."

"Okay. That's enough salad. Let's get to the main course. Spit it out, Hannah."

"The object I found was Herb's lunch bag. It was one of the reusable, personalized ones that Lisa gave him as a present. The lunch was gone, but the caramels were still there. I'm hoping that Herb was saving them for later, Phyllis grabbed Herb's lunch bag after he left the office, and Herb had nothing to do with the fact that she had it with her when she was killed."

"So you want me to sit on that piece of information until I find out if Herb has an alibi?"

Hannah nodded gratefully. "Yes, that's it exactly. Please, Mike . . . I just can't believe that Herb could kill anyone."

"Of course you can't, but both of us know that the most unlikely people can kill if they believe the circumstances warrant it."

"I know you're right, but I still can't believe it."

Mike reached out to slip an arm around Hannah's shoulders. "Okay. Just think about this for a minute. Say Herb *is* having a fling with Phyllis and Phyllis is threatening to tell Lisa about it unless he does something for her. And whatever that something is, Herb can't do it. He doesn't want to lose Lisa. He loves her. But Herb knows that Phyllis is the type of woman to make good on her threat and wreck his marriage. Herb's caught in a vise, and it's getting tighter with each passing day. He's desperate and he can see only one way out of it. He has to neutralize the threat."

Hannah shivered and Mike pulled her a bit closer. "By killing Phyllis before she can talk to Lisa?"

"Yes. You said that Lisa was with you when you found the body. Do you know where she was *before* she met you at the Corner Tavern?"

"Yes. You know that Herb's playing Santa and Mayor Bascomb appointed Phyllis as Mrs. Claus, don't you?" Mike nodded, and Hannah continued. "Lisa and I went to the rehearsal to pick up the Christmas gift bags we're filling with candy for the children. We sat down in the back of the auditorium and watched the last few minutes of the play. And then it was time for Herb and Phyllis to come onstage."

"Lisa wanted to watch Herb with Phyllis?"

Hannah nodded. "And that turned out to be a really bad idea. Tory Bascomb directed Phyllis to give Herb a stage kiss right before the final curtain, but Phyllis really kissed him. I mean, *really* kissed him. It was obvious to everyone who saw it that there was nothing staged about that kiss!"

"Go on."

"Lisa and I were sitting in the back, and we saw what everyone else saw. Naturally, Lisa was upset and she ran out of the auditorium. I caught her on the way to the parking lot, and since I didn't want her to go straight home when she was that upset, we went back to The Cookie Jar and we worked for a while. Then I suggested hamburgers at the Corner Tavern, and Lisa agreed. She said she had to go home to feed the dogs and let them out in the yard for a while before she could go out to eat, but she promised to meet me at the Corner Tavern just as soon as she could."

"Do you know what time you and Lisa left The Cookie Jar?"

"Yes. I looked at the clock before we went out the door. It was only a couple of minutes after nine."

"And what time did Lisa get to the Corner Tavern?"

"I don't remember. I went out there right away and sat at the bar for a while, waiting for a table in the dining room. I didn't look at my watch when Lisa got there, but Bonnie Surma was sitting next to me and she might remember."

"Okay. Give me your best estimate."

"Maybe ten o'clock or a little before that. I know we didn't leave the Corner Tavern until eleven. The receipt was time-stamped."

"Do you still have the receipt?"

"Yes. It's in my purse. I'll get it for you. But I don't understand why you need . . ." Hannah stopped in mid-sentence as the full implication of Mike's questioning hit her. "Do you think that Lisa killed Phyllis?"

"Anything's possible when jealousy is a motive. But no, I don't think that Lisa killed her. I just know that I have to clear her, especially because her car was parked in the back row of the parking lot and that's about where Phyllis would have tumbled down the ditch."

"The sandwiches are ready!" Michelle called out from the kitchen. "Are you ready to eat, Mike?"

"I'm ready," Mike said, giving Hannah a little hug before

he stood up to go to the table. "Don't worry, Hannah. I'll get to the bottom of this."

Hannah went to the table, tasted a corner of Michelle's sandwich, and pronounced it excellent. Then she sat there while the others ate and the conversation flowed around her. She made a comment once in a while, just so that no one would notice that she was preoccupied, and she gave a sigh of relief when the evening was over and Michelle went to bed.

Once the condo was silent, Hannah sat on the couch in the darkness with Moishe purring on her lap. She thought about everything that had happened during the day. Yes, even though it was unlikely, it was possible that Herb had killed Phyllis. And even though she felt like a traitor for admitting it, it was also possible that Lisa's temper had flared when she'd seen Phyllis in the parking lot, and she'd struck out with whatever hard object had been at hand.

Hannah shivered and bent over to hug Moishe. His purr was comforting, and she was glad he was keeping her company tonight. Phyllis had craved being the center of attention. She had gloried in causing trouble because it made her feel sexy and powerful. This time, Phyllis had caused trouble for two of Hannah's best friends, her partner, Lisa, and her former high school classmate, Herb. What Phyllis had done was far-reaching. It might have wrecked Lisa and Herb's marriage, and that made Hannah angry and sad at the same time. Perhaps it was a lucky thing that Phyllis wasn't here, sitting next to Hannah on the couch right now.

What Mike had said tonight was true. Anyone was capable of murder under the right circumstances. Even Hannah Swensen.

# Grilled Ham and Double Cheese Sandwiches

For each sandwich you will need:

2 slices of bread *(Michelle used seedless rye. You
could use any kind of bread you prefer.)*
softened butter to spread on the outside of the bread
and to put in the frying pan or grill if needed
Thousand Island dressing
1 slice of American cheese
1 fairly thick slice of fully cooked ham
1 slice of Swiss cheese
thin slices of sweet pickles, dill pickles, or sweet
onion *(optional)*

Butter two slices of bread. Place one slice, buttered side
down, on a piece of wax paper. Spread the bread with a
thin layer of Thousand Island dressing. This layer of dressing should not be too thick or your sandwich will get too
"gloppy" when you fry it. *(Feel free to add "gloppy" to
your list of cooking terms.)*

Place the slice of American cheese on top of the Thousand Island dressing you just spread.

Cut a slice of ham to fit the size of your bread and lay it
on top of the American cheese.

Place thin slices of pickle or sweet onion on top of the
ham if you decided to use them.

Place the slice of Swiss cheese on top.

Spread the top slice of bread with a thin layer of Thousand Island dressing.

Place the second slice of bread on top of the Swiss cheese, dressing side down.

Spread softened butter on top of your sandwich.

Make as many Grilled Ham and Double Cheese Sandwiches as you need for your guests.

Depending on how many sandwiches you made, put a helping or two of butter on your griddle or in your frying pan. Then preheat it at MEDIUM HIGH heat.

When the butter on the griddle or in the frying pan has melted and is preheated, fry your sandwiches, uncovered, until the bottom turns golden brown. *(You can test this by lifting it with a spatula and peeking at the bottom.)*

When one side is golden brown, flip the sandwich over, add more butter to the pan or griddle if needed, and fry the other side until it's golden brown.

Remove the sandwiches from the frying pan or griddle, cut them into pieces with a sharp knife, arrange the pieces on a plate, and serve immediately.

This sandwich goes well with piping-hot mugs of soup or a generous helping of coleslaw.

"**D**ad!"
Hannah sat bolt upright in bed and stared at the familiar shape that had materialized at the foot of her bed. "What are you doing here? You're . . . you're . . . I thought that you were . . ." Unable to say that awful, final word, she fell silent, merely staring at her father.

"Dead? I am, but they let me come here to be your Ghost of Christmas Past tonight."

"Then you're a . . . a ghost?"

"That's right. They're only going to let me maintain my human shape for a few more minutes. They wanted you to recognize me so that you wouldn't be frightened."

A million questions flew through Hannah's mind, and she turned to look at Moishe. He was staring at her with his one good eye and totally ignoring her father. Hannah turned back to look at her father again and found that he had been transformed into a white, amorphous shape that was hovering near the foot of her bed. "But, Dad . . . Moishe's not even looking at you. I thought cats could see ghosts."

"Some can, some can't," her father replied. "It's pretty obvious that you have a cat who can't."

Hannah smiled. Her dad had said, *a cat who can't*, rather than *a cat that can't*. It meant that her dad thought of Moishe as a person, just the way she did.

"I must be dreaming," Hannah said, considering the possibility.

"No, you're not dreaming. Throw something at me and see what happens."

"No, Dad! I don't want to hurt you!"

"You can't hurt me. I'm already dead. Pick up that pen you have on your night table and peg it straight at me. I taught you how to pitch, remember?"

"I remember," Hannah answered with a smile.

"Go ahead. Throw a strike. You used to be pretty good at that."

"No, I wasn't. You're just being nice."

"You caught me on that one, Honey-bear."

Hannah felt a rush of wonderful memories. Her dad had called her Honey-bear, the childhood nickname he'd used for her until Delores had informed him that Hannah was too old to have a nickname like that.

"Maybe you weren't the greatest pitcher in the world," her dad went on, "but you could hit a home run if you were mad enough at the opposing pitcher. Come on, Hannah. Do it. I don't have that much time here."

She'd always obeyed her father when he'd given her a direct order, and Hannah wasn't about to falter now. She picked up the pen, threw it directly at what she thought was the middle of the amorphous shape, and watched in astonishment as the pen passed directly through it and clattered to the floor near her closet.

"Do you believe me now?" he asked her.

Hannah nodded. And then she spoke aloud because she wasn't sure he'd noticed. "Yes, Dad. I believe you now."

"I love you, Hannah. I have to go soon, but they sent me here to give you a glimpse into your past. I hope it does the trick for you."

Hannah was about to ask which trick her father was talking about when his shape spread out flat, like a movie screen that was hanging on the wall. And as she watched, an image appeared.

There Hannah was in the bar of the Corner Tavern, sitting on a stool with her club soda in front of her. The man beside her got up to follow the waitress to his table, and that was when Bonnie came over to sit next to her.

The camera, or perhaps it was her eyes, traveled over to the stool that Bonnie had vacated. She was checking to make sure that Bonnie hadn't left anything behind. There was nothing on the bar in front of Bonnie's stool, and nothing on the floor except the sawdust the staff at the Corner Tavern spread out every morning after the floor was washed and swept. There were two footprints from Bonnie's shoes, but nothing else.

"Show's over," her father said as the screen coalesced into his amorphous shape again. "I love you, Honey-bear. If I'm lucky, they might let me come back again. You're scheduled for three ghosts just like the ones in the play. The difference is that we don't need makeup or costumes. We're really ghosts, and we don't rely on special effects and fake turkeys. Now go back to sleep like my good girl, and try to remember what I showed you when I visited you."

Hannah's eyelids felt suddenly heavy, almost as if they were weighted. She wanted to stay awake to see her dad leave, but it was impossible. She rolled over, reached out to pet Moishe's soft fur, and smiled as she slipped into a deep, restful sleep.

Hannah awakened to the scent of hot, strong coffee and something enticing that she couldn't identify. She sat up in bed, dislodging the cat who'd been sleeping on the pillow next to her head, and felt around under the bed for her slippers.

"Rowww!" Moishe complained as she thrust her feet into her slippers and got out of bed.

"I know. I don't really want to get up either, but something smells really good! Michelle must be making breakfast."

That comment elicited a purr from her feline friend. Moishe loved Michelle, especially after all the treats she'd brought with her. He'd even gotten some ham from last night's sandwiches, one of his favorite meats, and several fish-shaped, salmon-flavored treats that Michelle had given him before she'd gone to bed.

"Gingerbread!" Hannah exclaimed aloud as she thrust her arms into the sleeves of the gently worn chenille robe that she'd found at Helping Hands, the local thrift store. "At least I *think* it's gingerbread. It smells like gingerbread, and I can't think of what else it could be."

Moishe did not offer his opinion as he followed Hannah down the carpeted hallway, taking an occasional swipe at the hem of her robe.

When they reached the kitchen, Hannah took one step inside the doorway and into her brightly lit kitchen, sniffed the air again, and stared at her sister, who was standing at the stove. "Not gingerbread?" she asked.

"What?" Michelle looked puzzled.

"Not gingerbread. I thought you were baking gingerbread, but the oven's not on. What are you frying?"

Michelle looked pleased. "You're close, Hannah. I'm frying Gingerbread Pancakes. One of my housemates got the recipe from her grandmother. She said her grandmother used to make Gingerbread Pancakes every Christmas morning and that it was a family tradition. Since it's the Christmas season, I thought it was the perfect time for us to try them."

"They smell really good," Hannah complimented her sister. "What kind of syrup do you use on Gingerbread Pancakes?"

"I don't know, and my friend didn't know, either. She thought maybe her grandmother had served them with honey, but she couldn't really remember."

"We can experiment with syrups," Hannah suggested,

heading for the coffeepot to pour herself a cup. "It looks like you're making a lot of pancakes. Are you expecting anyone else for breakfast?"

"No, but my friend told me that her grandmother used to freeze her pancakes and then reheat them in the oven between sheets of foil. That sounded interesting and I thought I'd try it to see if it works."

"If it does, you could probably reheat them in the microwave, too. The only problem is that you can't use foil."

"You wouldn't have to use foil. You could reheat one pancake on a paper plate if you covered it with a paper towel. I've done that with frozen waffles before."

Hannah smiled at her sister. "You're right, and that would be an easy way to make breakfast on the run. You could thaw a pancake, butter it and sprinkle it with sugar, roll it up in a paper towel the way Great-grandmother Elsa used to do with *lefse*, and heat it in the microwave. Then you could eat it on your way to school, or the bus stop, or work."

"We'll try that to see if it works. But in the meantime, would you like a couple of Gingerbread Pancakes? This batch on the griddle is almost ready."

"Of course I would! You're the princess of breakfasts, Michelle."

"Thanks. I'll bring the pancakes to you when they're done, along with the honey, dark Karo syrup, butter and sugar, and molasses. We can try them out and see which topping is best."

In less than five minutes, Hannah had finished her second pancake. She was about to tell Michelle that she liked the molasses best when she thought of something she had to do. She got up to take a new spiral stenographer's pad from her kitchen drawer, grabbed the pen she'd found on the floor of her bedroom, and flipped to the first page.

"Is that your murder book?" Michelle asked.

"Yes." Hannah wrote the name *Phyllis Bates* on the first page. "Do you remember Phyllis Bates from school, Michelle?"

"Vaguely. She was the head cheerleader for the basketball team, wasn't she?"

"Yes."

"And for football, too?"

"That's right. And don't forget baseball."

"She was the blonde with a ponytail?"

"That's right. I know you were still in grade school, but do you remember your impression of her?"

"I *do* remember. Phyllis Bates was a bimbo."

"A *bimbo*?" Hannah repeated Michelle's words in the form of a question.

"Yes. And that was before I even knew what the word *bimbo* meant. Andrea called her that, so I did too. Andrea hated Phyllis Bates."

"How do you know that?"

"She told me so."

"But why?"

"Because Andrea knew I was too scared to tell anyone else."

"Not that. I mean . . . do you know why Andrea hated Phyllis?"

"Yes. It's because Andrea had a crush on Ryan Edwards, the football player that Phyllis was dating at the time."

"Good heavens! How old was Andrea then?"

Michelle shrugged. "Maybe seventh grade? I know Andrea was still in junior high because I had Mrs. Carlson in third grade, and she was Ryan's aunt. Andrea threatened to kill me if I ever mentioned anything about it in school. She would have, too. Andrea was scary when she was mad, and that would have made her really mad."

Hannah looked down at her steno pad. She supposed she should write down Andrea's name as a suspect, but all that was a long time ago and she was sure that Andrea hadn't harbored a grudge against Phyllis for over ten years.

"I *do* know somebody that hated Phyllis, though."

"Who?" Hannah was surprised. Michelle had been back

in Lake Eden less than twenty-four hours, and she'd already heard more gossip than Hannah had.

"Mayor Bascomb, that's who. Mother told me all about it. And the mayor's got a really good motive."

Hannah picked up her pen again. "Tell me."

"Okay. Mother took me to Beau Monde to buy me a new jacket before she dropped me off here. She said my old jacket was disreputable."

"That sounds like Mother."

"I know. The new one she bought me is a nice jacket, though. And she got me a new pair of jeans, too."

"That's nice. Now tell me how you know that Mayor Bascomb had a motive."

"I heard Mother and Claire talking about it while I was trying on jeans. The mayor dumped Phyllis when she asked him to set her up in her own furnished condo. And Phyllis got even with him by telling Stephanie Bascomb that she'd been having an affair with the mayor."

Hannah didn't hesitate. She wrote Mayor Bascomb's name on her list of suspects. "Did you hear any other gossip while you were there in the dressing room?"

"No, but I'm willing to bet that Claire knows more. And if she doesn't she can find out. She told Mother that Stephanie bought a whole new wardrobe from her. And Claire said that she had to alter everything before this afternoon because Stephanie was coming in to make sure everything fit."

The wheels in Hannah's mind were churning so fast, she could almost feel a breeze near the top of her head. It didn't take long for her to formulate a plan, and she began to smile.

"What?" Michelle asked, noticing the smile.

"I think we'll have to pay a visit to Beau Monde this afternoon. I'd like to try on a couple of outfits."

"You'd *like* to try on clothing? Come on, Hannah. Everybody knows that you hate to . . ." Michelle stopped and rolled her eyes. "Never mind. I get it. We're going to drop by a few minutes before Stephanie is due to come in?"

"That's the general idea. Let's drop by Claire's shop before The Cookie Jar opens. Claire probably knows what time Stephanie plans to come in."

"And if Claire doesn't know, maybe she can call to arrange a time," Michelle suggested.

"Exactly right." Hannah got up from the table, rinsed off her plate, and put it in the dishwasher. "Go get your jacket, Michelle."

"Okay. Are we going where I think we're going?"

"You'd better believe it! Claire's probably at the shop early, working on Stephanie's alterations."

"Do you want me to take Claire some pancakes for breakfast? I know she's got a microwave in her back room and I can reheat them for her."

"That's a great idea. And don't forget to bring some toppings, too. Claire's got a real sweet tooth."

# Gingerbread Pancakes

1 large egg
1 teaspoon vanilla extract
¼ cup molasses *(Michelle used Grandma's)*
1½ cups water
1 teaspoon ground ginger
1 teaspoon cinnamon
¼ teaspoon ground cardamom *(if you don't have it, just add a little more cinnamon)*
¼ teaspoon nutmeg *(freshly grated is best, of course)*
1 and ½ cups all-purpose flour *(pack it down in the cup when you measure it)*
¼ teaspoon baking soda
1 teaspoon baking powder
½ teaspoon salt

In a small bowl, whisk a large egg with the vanilla extract.

Add the quarter-cup of molasses and whisk that in.

Add the cup and a half of water and whisk that in.

**Hannah's 1st Note: You'll be adding the spices next, but Michelle says that's easier if you mix them together first. She uses a disposable paper bowl. Then you can add the spice mixture to your egg mixture all at once.**

Combine the ground ginger, cinnamon, cardamom, and nutmeg. Stir them around until they're mixed.

Add the spice mixture to your egg mixture and whisk everything together until they're thoroughly combined.

**Hannah's 2nd Note: Michelle says to remind you to rinse off your whisk and put it in the sink. If you let the egg dry on the whisk, it's really difficult to get clean.**

Get out your favorite stirring spoon. You'll be using it from here on out.

In a larger mixing bowl, combine the flour, baking soda, baking powder, and salt. Mix them until they're well incorporated.

Add the egg mixture to the flour mixture and stir until just incorporated. The batter may be a little lumpy. That's okay. You'll stir it again before you fry it.

**Hannah's 3rd Note: If you've made pancakes from scratch before, you know that they're tastier if you "season" them by covering the mixing bowl with plastic wrap and refrigerating the batter overnight. This is why I always mix my batter the night before.**

When you're ready to fry your pancakes, prepare your griddle or your frying pan by oiling it before you heat it, or using a mixture with equal parts of oil and butter.

Set your heat at MEDIUM-HIGH. You can test your frying surface to see when it's ready by putting a few drops of water on the surface. If the droplets of water skitter around and then evaporate, your pan is the right temperature to fry pancakes.

If you're using a griddle, you may want to pour on your pancakes rather than use a spoon. Simply transfer the batter to a pitcher and use that to pour. If you'd prefer to dip a large spoon or a small cup into the bowl and transfer the batter to the griddle or the frying pan that way, that's fine, too. (**Michelle used my** *quarter-cup plastic measure that has a little spout on the side. I measured this once, and when she empties the cup of batter in the frying pan, approximately 3 Tablespoons come out of the measuring cup.*)

Fry your pancakes until they're puffed and they look a bit dry around the edges. If you look closely, little bubbles will form at the edges. If you're not sure they're done, lift one edge with a spatula and take a peek. It will be golden brown on the bottom when it's ready to flip.

Turn your pancakes and wait for the other side to fry. Again, you can test your pancake by lifting it slightly with a spatula and peeking to see if it's golden brown.

If you don't have people sitting at your table waiting to eat breakfast, you can fry all your pancakes now and keep them warm until everyone comes to the table by separating them with layers of foil or paper towels, placing them in a 9-inch by 13-inch cake pan, covering the pan loosely with another piece of foil, and keeping them in a warm oven set at the lowest temperature.

Serve with plenty of soft butter and your choice of honey, dark Karo syrup, or molasses. These Gingerbread Pancakes are also good buttered, spread with jam, and topped with a dollop of sour cream.

# Chapter
# Six

"Keep your eye on the time," Hannah advised as she took another batch of cookies from the industrial oven at The Cookie Jar and placed the cookie sheets on shelves in the baker's rack. "We have to get to Claire's before Stephanie does, or our plan won't work."

"We've still got an hour," Michelle replied. "And I'm ready with a batch of Angel Jellies that we can bake first."

"Good, they're a favorite out front. Which flavor?"

"Raspberry. You had a whole big jar of seedless raspberry jam." Michelle stopped speaking and walked a bit closer to the swinging restaurant-type door that separated the kitchen from the coffee shop. "Lisa must be telling the story of the murder again. There's not a peep from any of the customers out there, and we've been packed ever since we opened this morning."

"I know. Everyone loves to hear Lisa tell stories. She keeps the customers mesmerized."

"And eating cookies," Michelle reminded her.

"That's right. It makes me feel a little strange to say it, but Lake Eden murders are good for our business."

Michelle raised up on tiptoe so she could see through the high window in the door. "She's got them all on the edges of their seats. Babs Dubinski is leaning forward so far, it's a wonder she doesn't tip over. And Grandma Knudson has her hand cupped around her ear so she doesn't miss a word. Lisa's a great storyteller, Hannah. She really ought to try out for the Lake Eden Players. I'll bet Tory Bascomb would love to have her."

"Agreed. Lisa could be the star of every show. She's a better actress than anyone else in town."

The phone on the kitchen wall rang, and Michelle hurried to answer it. They'd promised to answer the phone while Lisa was performing.

"The Cookie Jar," Michelle informed the caller. "This is Michelle speaking." She listened for a few moments, and then she said, "I'll tell her, Mother. Does Lisa know yet?" There was another moment of silence, and then Michelle laughed. "You might know that the Lake Eden Gossip Hotline would get it first. And he's on his way here now to tell her?" There was a pause, and then Michelle spoke again. "Okay, Mother. Thanks for telling us. We'll give Lisa a heads-up."

"What?" Hannah asked, the moment that Michelle had hung up the phone.

"That was Mother. Mayor Bascomb is on the way over here to tell Lisa that she's the new Mrs. Claus."

"How did Mother know that?"

"Luanne's mother was cleaning Mayor Bascomb's office this morning, and she heard him mention it on the phone to Rod McRae. She called Luanne from her cell phone to tell her, and Mother just happened to be at Granny's Attic when Luanne took the call. Mother asked Luanne what Mrs. Hanks wanted, and Luanne told her all about it. Mother figures she knew less than five minutes after Mayor Bascomb ended his call to Rod and hung up the phone."

"That's fast, even for the Lake Eden Gossip Hotline. The news on those jungle drums travels fast."

Michelle's eyebrows shot up. "Don't tell me you got up in the middle of the night to watch *Jungle Drums* on the old movie channel!"

Hannah sighed. "I did, but it didn't start out that way. I watched *Scrooge*, the nineteen fifty-one film with Alastair Sim. But I still wasn't sleepy so I stayed up to see what would come on next."

"And it was *Jungle Drums?*"

"Yes."

"And you actually watched it?"

"Yes, but I fell asleep about halfway through."

"That was probably a blessing. I can't believe you watched that long!"

"I didn't want to," Hannah admitted. "I really wanted to change the channel, but the remote was on the other side of the couch and I didn't want to disturb Moishe. He was sitting in my lap, purring so loudly that I could barely hear the dialogue."

"Moishe did you a favor. You should give him a shrimp. What woke you up in the first place?"

"Nothing *woke* me. I couldn't get to sleep in the first place. When I went to bed, I started thinking about Phyllis and who might have killed her. I was so busy going through lists of suspects in my head that I couldn't fall asleep."

"So you made yourself a cup of hot chocolate with miniature marshmallows, settled down on the couch with Moishe, and flicked on the television."

"That's right. I think you know me too well, Michelle."

"Maybe I do, but that doesn't mean I love you any less." Michelle smiled at Hannah. "I'll go out front and ask Lisa to come back here right after she does the crowd reaction. I think she's just about at that point in her story, but I'll check it out to make sure."

Both Hannah and Michelle moved closer to the door, where they could hear Lisa's voice.

*"She saw a mound at the bottom of the snow-covered ditch, a mound the same size as a body. She didn't want to think that way, but you know Hannah. Anyone else would have climbed back up to the top of the ditch just as fast as*

*they could and run back inside to get help. But not our Hannah. Do you think she hesitated?"*

"*No!*" the crowd in the coffee shop chorused.

"*Of course she didn't hesitate,*" a male voice called out and Hannah knew exactly who it was. "*Hannah's got slaydar!*"

"Mike?" Michelle asked.

"Who else?" Hannah confirmed it.

"I've heard Lisa tell this story twice, and she's winding down now," Michelle informed her. "I'll go out and give her the high sign."

"Do you think she'll know what you mean?"

"She'll know." Michelle sounded certain. "Lisa and I worked out a series of hand signals right after the last Lake Eden murder. If I stand at the back of the house and run my finger across my throat, it means I want her to end her story as soon as she can. And when I beckon to her and point toward the kitchen, she'll know that we want her to come back here right after she finishes."

Hannah glanced at the clock on the kitchen wall. "Okay. Go ahead. Marge, and Lisa's dad, should be here by now, and they can handle the coffee shop."

After Michelle had left, Hannah placed the trays of unbaked Angel Jellies inside the industrial oven. She had set the timer, poured herself a fresh cup of coffee, and taken a stool at the stainless-steel workstation when Michelle came back from the coffee shop.

"Lisa read my signal," she reported. "She should be here in a moment or two."

"Good. I don't want her to be caught unaware when Mayor Bascomb comes in."

"You don't think Lisa will turn down a chance to play Mrs. Claus, do you?"

"No. She really wanted to be Mrs. Claus. She mentioned it to me a couple of times. The only reason she might hesitate is if she thinks I can't handle the concession stand alone."

"You don't have to handle anything alone with me here,"

Michelle pointed out. "I'll help you, and Lisa can play Mrs. Claus. That should make Herb happy, too."

Hannah thought about the kiss she'd seen between Phyllis and Herb. "I hope so," she said.

"What's up?" Lisa breezed into the kitchen and took a stool at the workstation.

"Mother called," Hannah told her. "It seems Mayor Bascomb is on his way here to invite you to be this year's Mrs. Claus."

"Really?" Lisa looked both excited and pleased, but then her expression took on a worried look. "Do you think that would be right? I mean, after Phyllis and everything?"

"The show must go on," Michelle reminded her, "and there's nothing you can do about Phyllis. She's dead and she can't play Santa's wife."

"I know, but . . . do you think people will think less of me if I agree so fast? I'm just wondering if it's proper. She's been dead less than a day."

"They won't think less of you, Lisa," Hannah reassured her. "You know that the kids look forward to seeing Santa and Mrs. Claus every year. Their parents will be grateful that you agreed to step in and play the part."

"Well . . . there *is* that," Lisa conceded. "I'd hate to disappoint the children. But I'll have to get into my costume at intermission so I'm ready in time. Do you think you can handle the candy sales?"

"I'll help Hannah," Michelle spoke up. "I already told her that I would. This is important, Lisa. Santa and Mrs. Claus have appeared at the end of the Christmas play for as long as I can remember. I used to sit on Santa's lap when Santa was Earl Flensburg. And I loved it when Mrs. Claus handed me my gift bag of treats. Herb can't do it alone, and he needs you. You almost have to do it."

"Well, yes. You're right. I do." Lisa looked pleased at the prospect of playing Mrs. Claus.

"You're the natural choice," Hannah added. "Everyone

knows that you're Herb's wife. And now you also get to play his pretend wife on stage."

"Lisa?" Marge poked her head into the kitchen. "Mayor Bascomb is here, and he says he needs to talk to you."

"Of course. Please get him a cup of coffee and some cookies, Marge. And tell him I'll be right out." Lisa waited until Marge had left, and then she turned to Hannah. "I just thought of something. Is Mayor Bascomb one of your suspects?"

"Actually . . . yes. He certainly had a motive. Phyllis told his wife what was going on between them when he refused to set Phyllis up in a condo. And Stephanie made him pay for his mistake in designer clothes and expensive gems. I'd call that a motive, wouldn't you?"

Lisa nodded. "Yes, I would. So you think that the mayor might have killed Phyllis to get even?"

"There are worse motives," Hannah said. "Anger is a powerful emotion."

"So now all you have to do is find out if he had the opportunity . . . is that right?"

"That's right. If he has an alibi, he's in the clear. If he doesn't, he's still on my suspect list."

"And Herb's on there too, especially if he noticed me leaving the auditorium after that kiss Phyllis gave him. Is that right?"

Hannah felt like groaning, but she didn't. Lisa always went straight to the heart of the matter. "That's right. I'm sorry, Lisa. I don't really think that Herb did it, but . . ."

"But he had a motive. And we don't know if he had the opportunity because we don't know where he was until after midnight last night."

This time Hannah did groan. "I don't like it Lisa. But Herb's on my suspect list."

"And I'm there, too. I have to be. I have a perfect motive. After that kiss, I was so jealous, I couldn't see straight. I told you that I had to go home to feed the dogs, but you have no way of knowing if I actually did that, or not. Maybe I drove straight out to the Corner Tavern, spotted Phyllis getting out of her car, and killed her in a jealous fit of rage."

"But you *couldn't* have killed her. You were wearing ankle boots. I saw them. And you couldn't have climbed down into that ditch wearing ankle boots. You would have come in with soaked feet, and you didn't. I looked down at your boots when we were standing there in the parking lot. They're light-colored suede, and they weren't wet."

"Maybe I wasn't wearing ankle boots then. Maybe I had another pair of boots in the trunk and I used those. You don't know that I didn't. You didn't check, and neither did anyone else."

"Lisa!" Michelle sounded very upset. "Cut it out! You just gave yourself a motive and admitted that you had the opportunity!"

"I know that, but Hannah would have thought of that eventually, if it hasn't already occurred to her." Lisa turned back to Hannah. "I'm on your suspect list too, aren't I?"

Hannah visibly winced, but there was no reason to lie about it. "Yes, Lisa. You're on it. But I don't really think that you . . ."

"That doesn't matter," Lisa interrupted her. "You have to investigate me, too. That's one of the things I like best about you, Hannah. You're fair. I can tell you right now that I didn't do it, but that doesn't count for anything. Mike's going to zero in on me, too. He's a good cop, and he's bound to investigate me. I'm just hoping that you'll hurry and clear both Herb and me by catching the real killer. You'll do that, won't you?"

"I'll certainly do my best," Hannah promised.

"That's good enough for me. Now I'd better get out there and hear what Mayor Bascomb has to say to me. And I'd better help you either clear him or finger him."

Michelle and Hannah were silent for a moment after the swinging door had shut behind Lisa. Then Michelle shook her head. "*Finger him*? That dates back a couple of decades. Where did Lisa ever hear a phrase like that?"

"*Dragnet.* She told me that she watches reruns while she's waiting for Herb to come home. He's been working really late almost every night this month."

"Do you think he's really working?"

"I don't know, but I'm going to find out."

There was a knock on the back kitchen door, and Michelle turned to Hannah. "Mother?" she asked.

"No. Mother's knock is more impatient and she generally knocks in threes."

"Threes?"

"Yes. Knock-knock-knock. And then knock-knock-knock again. After that, she tries the door. And if it's unlocked, she comes in."

"How about Mike? He always checks in with you the day after a murder."

"It's not Mike. We heard him out front in the coffee shop."

"Unless he left and walked around to the back door."

"No." Hannah shook her head. "It's definitely not Mike. He always knocks like he's serving a search warrant. It's loud and demanding and staccato. I think it's probably Norman. He's got a firm knock, but it's not as commanding as Mike's and not as impatient as Mother's. Go let him in, will you please? I'll pour him a cup of coffee and get him settled at the workstation."

## Angel Jellies

Preheat oven to 275 degrees F., rack in the center position.

*(That's two hundred and seventy-five degrees F., not a misprint.)*

6 large eggs
¼ teaspoon cream of tartar
½ teaspoon vanilla extract
¼ teaspoon salt
1 cup white *(granulated)* sugar
2 Tablespoons *(⅛ cup)* all-purpose flour *(Pack it down when you measure it.)*
a little flour in a small bowl for later
a small jar of seedless raspberry jam *(or your favorite jam if you don't like raspberry)*

**Hannah's 1ˢᵗ Note: Make sure you use jam and not jelly in this recipe. I know the name is Angel Jellies, but that's because "Angel Jams" didn't sound as nice. I haven't tried jelly, but there's more liquid in jelly than in jam. Jam has pieces of fruit in it and although the liquid in jam will melt, those pieces of fruit won't melt. Jelly could melt and leak out of the bottoms of the cookies as they bake, making them soggy.**

Separate 6 large eggs and put the whites in one container and the yolks in another.

Cover the container with the yolks and put it in the refrigerator. You can use it to make yolk-rich scrambled eggs for breakfast in the morning, or a yolk-rich Chocolate Flan with Caramel Whipped Cream for dessert.

Set the whites on your kitchen counter until they've come up to room temperature. *(This will give them more volume when you whip them.)*

Prepare your cookie sheets by lining them with parchment paper *(this works best)* or brown parcel-wrapping paper if you don't have parchment. Spray the paper with Pam or another non-stick cooking spray and dust it lightly with flour.

**Hannah's 2ⁿᵈ Note: You can also use Pam Baking Spray or another brand of <u>baking spray</u> that has flour in it.**

**Hannah's 3ʳᵈ Note: These cookies are a lot easier to make if you use an electric mixer because you must beat the egg whites until they form soft peaks and, ultimately, stiff peaks. You can use a copper bowl and a whisk, but it will take some time and muscle.**

Beat the egg whites with the cream of tartar, vanilla, and salt until they are firm enough to hold a soft peak. Test this by shutting off the mixer and dotting the egg whites with the side of a clean rubber spatula. When you pull up the spatula, a soft peak should form.

Hannah's 4<sup>th</sup> Note: For those of you who haven't made meringues before, soft peaks slump a bit and bend over on themselves. That's what you want at this stage. A bit later on in the recipe, you'll want stiff peaks. Those stand straight up and do not slump or bend over.

With the mixer running on MEDIUM HIGH speed, sprinkle the egg white mixture with approximately one third of the sugar. Turn the mixer up to HIGH speed for ten seconds. Then turn the mixer down to MEDIUM HIGH speed again.

Sprinkle in half of the remaining sugar, turn the mixer up to HIGH speed for ten seconds, and then back down to MEDIUM HIGH speed.

Sprinkle in the remaining sugar and follow the same procedure, turning the mixer up to HIGH speed for ten seconds, or until stiff peaks form. Then turn OFF the mixer completely.

Sprinkle in the flour and mix it into the egg white mixture at LOW speed. You don't want to whip any air out of the meringue.

Take the bowl out of the mixer, give it a gentle stir with your rubber spatula, and place it next to your prepared cookie sheet.

Use a spoon to drop small mounds of dough on your cookie sheet, no more than 12 dough mounds to a standard-sized sheet.

*(If you make 4 rows with 3 dough mounds in each row, that should be perfect.)*

**Hannah's 5th Note:** The mound of dough should be no larger than a ping pong ball. (If you've never played table tennis, this is a little smaller than a golf ball. If you've never played golf, make the dough mounds the size of a large walnut in the shell. If you've never seen a large walnut in the shell, you'd better ask someone or you won't have a clue!)

Dip the pad of your impeccably clean finger in the flour. *(I use my pointer finger.)* Make an indentation in the center of your mounds of cookie dough, dipping your finger in the bowl of flour before indenting each mound. Make sure your indentations DO NOT go all the way to the bottom of the dough mounds. *(If the jam leaks out in the oven, it'll go all over and you certainly don't want that!)*

Use the tip of a small spoon to take a little jam from the jar and deposit it inside the indentation you made. Don't use too much jam. A little will do just fine.

Drop a little mound of cookie dough over the top of the jam to cover it completely. Then it will be a lovely surprise when everyone bites into your cookies.

Bake your Angel Jellies at 275 degrees F. for approximately 40 minutes or until the meringue part of the cookie is lightly golden and dry to the touch when you tap it lightly with your finger.

Take the Angel Jellies out of the oven. Cool the cookies on the paper-lined baking sheet by setting it on a cold stovetop burner or on a wire rack.

When your Angel Jellies are completely cool, peel them off the paper and store them in an airtight container in a cool, dry place. *(Unfortunately, your refrigerator is NOT a dry place. A cupboard shelf will do just fine as long as it's not near your stove.)*

Yield: 3 to 4 dozen crunchy, melt-in-your-mouth cookies with a delightful surprise in the center. Warning: Angel Jellies are like potato chips. You can't eat just one!

**Michelle's Note: My college housemates love these cookies. I've made them with strawberry jam, peach jam, apricot jam, pineapple jam, blueberry jam, and orange marmalade.**

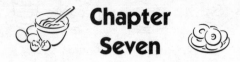

"Norman!" Hannah greeted him with a cup of coffee, a plate of cookies, and a smile. "How are you? I haven't seen you in a while."

Norman stood up as she placed the coffee and cookies in front of him and pulled her into his arms to give her a hug. "I know I haven't dropped in for a while. I've been busy at the house, directing workmen. And I've gone out to the mall every night for Christmas shopping. How about you?"

"Here," Hannah replied with a sigh. "Christmas and Valentine's Day are our busy times. And this year we're doing all the cookies and candy for the children's Christmas gift bags."

"Christmas is always a busy time. I hired Doc Bennett to take over for me until after the first of the year. He needs the work, and I need time off."

"Are you going away for the holidays?" Hannah asked him.

"Not a chance. I'm doing some construction at the house."

"What construction? I thought you loved the house the way we designed it."

"Oh, I do. But things have changed and I wanted to update. Do you know that you can buy a humungous LED big screen now?"

"I hadn't noticed. I'm perfectly happy with the television I have now."

"I'm not. You know those old movies you love, Hannah?"

Hannah began to smile. "You mean the old romantic comedies and the chick flicks?"

"Yes. And the old detective films. They're all remastered now. And I needed to enlarge the den so that I could get a hundred-and-twenty-inch screen on the wall without being crowded."

Hannah's mouth dropped open. "But . . . that's practically theater-sized!"

"That's right. And won't it be fun to watch our favorite classic films in a home theater with perfect surround sound and incredibly comfortable seating?"

"Maybe," Hannah said, but she couldn't hide her delighted expression. She loved to watch classic movies with Norman.

"Then you'll come out to watch films with me when my home theater is finished?"

Hannah's timing was perfect. She waited a beat before she answered. But when Norman started to look a little nervous, she relented. "Yes. You can bet I'll be there!"

"Wonderful!"

Norman looked very happy, and Hannah felt a little guilty about what she had planned to say next. But that didn't stop her. "You bet I'll come! But only if you've got a popcorn machine."

Norman's smile grew larger by the nanosecond. "I knew you'd say that!"

"I'm that predictable?"

"No, it's just that I know you so well. And because I know you that well, I've got one."

"You have a popcorn machine?"

"Yes. I bought one just so I could say I had it. Of course I don't know how to work it yet, but . . ."

"I'll figure it out," Hannah cut in. "When I was in high school, I made popcorn for every movie they ran in the auditorium. And when I got to college, I made popcorn in the big theater, the small theater, the concession stand for football, basketball, and baseball games, and any other special events where they thought they could make a profit selling it. There's not a popcorn machine on the face of this earth that I can't learn to operate."

"This one's digital."

"Ooooh! Fun! I've never seen a digital popcorn machine before. And that reminds me . . . is it portable?"

Norman looked slightly confused. "Actually . . . yes. It doesn't weigh that much. And it makes a ton of popcorn."

"You saved my life," Hannah told him.

"Okay." Norman's eyes narrowed. "How did I do that? Or will I be sorry I asked?"

"You may be sorry, especially when you have to lug that popcorn machine all the way over to Jordan High."

It took Norman a moment, but then he gave a nod. "I get it. Their popcorn machine is broken again, and you need one for the concession stand at the Christmas play. Am I on the right track?"

"Not only are you on the right track, you won the race! Will you lend it to me, Norman? It's just for three nights. Michelle and I are manning the concession stand at the play because Lisa's going to be Mrs. Claus. The Lake Eden Players usually borrow Jordan High's machine, but theirs is broken and the new one they ordered won't be here until after the holidays."

"You can borrow mine on one condition."

"What's the one condition?"

"It's simple. You have to teach me how to use it and let me make the popcorn for you. You and Michelle will be busy enough selling everything else. I want to help."

"Then you've got a job," Hannah said happily, reaching out to take his hand. "Thanks, Norman. You always come through for me in a pinch."

Norman gave her hand a gentle squeeze, and then he looked very serious. "Are you doing it again, Hannah?"

Hannah's first instinct was to ask him what he meant, but she already knew exactly what he was asking. "Yes," she admitted. "Lisa's a suspect and so is Herb. I have to clear them."

"By catching the real killer?"

"That's the plan. Lisa doesn't have an alibi for a critical period of time last night. She was with me until nine, and then she went home alone to feed Dillon and Sammy. She didn't join me again until around ten at the Corner Tavern."

"And Herb?"

"Herb told Lisa that he's been working late, but . . ." Hannah's voice trailed off. She really shouldn't be discussing Lisa's marital problems with Norman.

"But what?" Norman prompted.

Hannah sighed. "But Lisa has her doubts."

"Let me get this straight. You want me to find an alibi for both Lisa and Herb?"

"That's right. An alibi for one would be good. And an alibi for both would be even better."

"Okay. I'll keep my eyes and ears open. Do you know the time of death?"

"Not yet. Doc can't tell exactly, but he always puts a window of time in the autopsy report. My problem is, I don't have the autopsy report yet."

"It shouldn't be long now."

Hannah was puzzled. "What are you talking about?"

"I saw your mother on the highway when I drove to town. She was heading in the opposite direction, and unless she was going out to the mall three hours before it opens, she was heading out to the hospital."

"What time was that?"

"And hour or so ago. I stopped at Hal and Rose's for breakfast, dropped in at the office to go over the mail, and then I came over here."

"Perfect. Mother should be here any . . ." Hannah stopped

speaking as they heard a series of knocks at the door. "There she is now."

"Do you want me to get that?" Michelle asked from the other side of the kitchen.

"Yes, please," Hannah answered. "It's Mother."

"On my way, Hannah. I'll let her in, pour her some coffee, and then I'll put more cookies on the plate I was fixing for you and Norman. Mother loves these Angel Jellies, and they're cool enough to eat now."

A second or two later, Delores came in. She took a stool next to Norman at the workstation and plunked a manila envelope in front of Hannah.

"Is that what I think it is?" Hannah asked her.

"Yes, if you think it's the autopsy report." Delores tapped the envelope with one impeccably manicured nail, and smiled smugly. "I assumed that you'd need it?"

"You assumed right. Thank you, Mother. You're wonderful to do this for me."

"I like to help," Delores said modestly, but Hannah noticed that her smug smile was still in place. "And this time I took an extra precaution. I called Andrea last night and told her I was going to get it and she didn't have to sneak it out of Bill's briefcase and scan it before she put it back."

"Was Andrea grateful that you were getting it and she didn't have to?" Hannah asked the question, even though she thought she already knew the answer.

"Actually . . . no. I thought she'd be relieved. She takes an awful chance, you know. Bill would be so upset with her if he ever caught her. But she sounded almost . . ."

"Deprived?" Norman provided the word.

"Why, yes! That's right. And all I was trying to do was help."

"Of course you were," Hannah said quickly. "And I'm sure that Andrea realizes that. It's possible you just caught her at a bad time when you called."

Delores thought about that for a moment, and then she

gave a little nod. "You're right, dear. I *did* catch her at a bad time. Grandma McCann had taken Tracey and a friend ice skating at the school rink, and Andrea was trying to put Bethie to bed. I heard Bethie say that she wouldn't go to bed without *raffey* and Andrea had no idea what a *raffey* was."

"Does Bethie have a toy giraffe?"

Delores didn't say anything. She just stared at Hannah so intently that Hannah began to feel uncomfortable. "Don't look at me that way, Mother. It was just a guess."

"But you're right! Bethie has a stuffed giraffe and it's one of her favorite toys! You really should have children, Hannah. You have a natural flair for understanding them."

A host of replies occurred to Hannah including, *It takes two to have children, Mother!* and *I'll take that under consideration and let you know within a decade or so.* But she knew that anything she said would only make the situation more uncomfortable. And that was when Michelle arrived at the workstation with the platter of Angel Jellies and saved her the necessity of replying.

"Have a cookie, Mother," Michelle invited. "They're raspberry Angel Jellies."

"My favorite!" Delores declared, reaching for one.

"Norman?" Michelle offered the platter to him.

"Thanks, Michelle. I've never had these before."

"Hannah?" Michelle passed the platter to her. And then, in an undertone, she said, "I think you'd better put something in your mouth before you insert your foot."

Hannah had all she could do not to laugh. "Just set the platter in front of Mother, Michelle. She likes these cookies so much."

"Of course. I planned to do that." Michelle took the stool next to Hannah. "What are you giving Andrea and Bill for Christmas, Mother?"

"I don't know yet, dear."

"How about if we all go in on it together and give Andrea and Bill a few days in a nice hotel, just the two of them?"

"Why, that's a wonderful idea!" Delores agreed immediately. "But you girls don't have to contribute anything. I can afford to do it by myself and I'd like it to be *my* present to them. I wonder which hotel I should choose."

"Somewhere warm," Hannah suggested. "I think the cold is getting to Bill. When he came in the other morning, he was shivering."

"You're right, dear," Delores agreed. "This has been a particularly cold winter. I know that Bill has the week after Christmas off. Andrea mentioned it to me the other day. I could fly them down to Florida to a nice, relaxing resort. They could have a mini second honeymoon."

"That sounds nice," Norman said. "Mother and Earl went to Florida last March, and they loved it."

"Then that's what I'll do. I'll fly them down there the day after Christmas and they can come home the day after New Year's."

"You'd better act fast to get plane tickets," Michelle cautioned her. "Flights are hard to get over holidays."

"I know, dear. Don't worry. I'll rush right home and do it."

"Before you do that, it might be a good idea to check with Bill to make sure exactly which days he has off," Hannah reminded her. "I could be wrong, but I don't think Andrea would like to go on a mini second honeymoon all by herself."

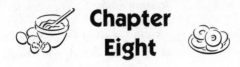

# Chapter Eight

"Here she comes!" Claire warned.

"Thanks," Hannah replied. She was sitting sideways on a settee in Claire's dressing room with her feet tucked up and her steno pad open to a fresh page in front of her.

"I'm ready," Michelle said from the opposite end of the settee. She'd assumed the same position and also held a notepad in one hand and a pen in the other.

"Come in, Mrs. Bascomb." Claire's voice carried easily to the dressing room. "I have everything all ready for you."

"Good. I don't have much time this afternoon. I'm meeting a friend for afternoon tea, and then Richard and I have a dinner party we must attend. Mayoral duties, you know."

Michelle rolled her eyes up toward the ceiling, and Hannah smiled at her youngest sister. Both of them knew that Stephanie had no plans for tea. If Stephanie was meeting a friend for tea, then *tea* was a euphemism for Stephanie's new favorite drink, a lemon drop vodka martini.

The doorknob on the dressing room rattled as Stephanie tried the door. But Claire had everything under control. "Please use the larger dressing room, Mrs. Bascomb. I've hung your lovely choices in there. The lighting's much better than it is in this one."

"Of course."

Michelle and Hannah heard the door to the adjacent

dressing room open and then close again, and Hannah put her finger to her lips. Michelle nodded, and both of them were completely silent as they waited for Claire to engage Stephanie in conversation. Claire knew exactly what they needed to know. They'd gone over it all this morning.

For long moments, there were no sounds except the rustling of cloth and the scratchy sound of zippers being closed. Then, at last, they heard the door to the adjacent dressing room open.

"Claire?" Stephanie Bascomb called out.

"Right here, Mrs. Bascomb," Claire answered. Her voice was a bit louder than Stephanie's, and Hannah realized that Claire must be standing just outside the dressing room where they were hidden.

"What do you think? Is it a bit tight over the hips?"

There was a pause, and Hannah assumed that Claire was assessing the fit.

"No, I think it's perfect," Claire gave her opinion. "Of course, if it makes you uncomfortable, I can always let it out a little over the hips, but I think it looks stunning on you just the way it is. It's too bad you didn't have this last night when you went out to dinner with the mayor."

"Oh, that's all right. We had to cancel anyway. Richard's meeting with the town council lasted until eight-thirty, and our reservations were for eight. We settled for going out for drinks and appetizers with Del Woodley. He's on the council, you know."

"I haven't seen Del in a while. He's well?"

"He seems to be, especially now that Benton has moved to Lake Eden permanently and taken over production at Del-Ray Manufacturing. Del was working too hard, and after Judith was gone, he had no social life at all."

"But now he does?"

"Oh, yes! Danielle has been very good for him."

This time Hannah did turn to look at Michelle, who appeared every bit as shocked as Hannah was.

"Danielle Watson?" Claire asked.

"Yes. Del called her right after the council meeting and invited her to join us for drinks last night."

"Danielle Watson is dating Del Woodley?"

"Heavens no! *Benton* is dating Danielle. And just between you and me, I think it could be serious. But Benton was still at the plant last night, and Danielle didn't want Del to feel that he was a third wheel. She's a very nice person, you know. She makes sure that Del is included in a lot of their social events. She even acts as a hostess for Del on the rare occasions when Del entertains."

Hannah jotted a note in her book to call Danielle Watson at her dance studio. If drinks with the mayor had lasted any longer than ten-thirty or eleven, Mayor Bascomb was in the clear.

"I'm sorry that you didn't get to go out to dinner, but that still sounds like a nice evening," Claire commented.

"Oh, it was. Richard came to the house to pick me up, and Del was already in the car. I joined them, and then we stopped to pick up Danielle at her dance studio. Richard was going to invite his sister, Tory, to join us but she was tied up with the people from the Christmas play."

"Has Del been dating Tory?" Claire asked, and Hannah felt like applauding. It was precisely the question she would have asked.

"Yes, a few times. They're both very well off, you know. I think both of them are comfortable with each other. Del knows that Tory isn't a gold-digger, and she knows that Del isn't after her money. It's difficult for people with money to find suitable companions, don't you think?"

"Well . . ."

"Of course you wouldn't really know about that," Stephanie cut off any answer that Claire might have given, thereby proving that she didn't give a fig about Claire's opinion on social matters.

"Was it a late evening?" Claire asked Stephanie.

"I didn't notice the time. Why do you ask? Do I look tired?"

"Not at all. You look fresh as a daisy and absolutely fabulous in that lovely outfit."

"Good. I'd better try on another one. We're wasting my time, chatting about inconsequential things."

"Of course," Claire responded quickly. "Try on the claret-colored pantsuit, Mrs. Bascomb. That color is so lovely on you."

"Yes. Isn't it."

It was a statement, not a question, and Hannah rolled her eyes ceiling-ward. Their mayor's wife was not shy and demure when compliments were offered.

"Come with me, Claire," Stephanie commanded. "I'll need help with those small buttons in the back."

The door to Stephanie's dressing room opened with a click. Hannah listened to the sound of two sets of footfalls entering the dressing room. She waited until the door clicked closed again, and then she turned to motion to Michelle. They had the information they needed, and they could sneak out while Stephanie Bascomb was trying on the pantsuit. And then they could dash back to The Cookie Jar to pick up some kind of sweet treat for Danielle, hurry down the street to her dance studio, and find out exactly what time drinks with the first family of Lake Eden had ended on the previous evening.

When they returned to The Cookie Jar, they found Lisa in the kitchen. "You look like you're in a hurry," she said as they rushed in the door.

"We are," Hannah told her. "Stephanie Bascomb just mentioned that she went out for drinks last night with the mayor. And Del Woodley. And Danielle joined them."

"Claire asked Stephanie what time that was," Michelle added, "but Stephanie didn't remember. My guess is that Stephanie had twee martoonis, or maybe more."

Hannah laughed. "You got that phrase from Dad, didn't you?"

"Yes. It used to crack me up when he said it. I always wanted to use it, but the time was never right . . . until now."

"So rather than go straight to the dance studio, you came back here to get something to take to Danielle," Lisa guessed. "Is that right?"

Michelle looked impressed. "That's very good, Lisa. You figured out Hannah's M.O."

"Of course I did. I've seen her do this before. Hannah always brings something tasty to exchange for information. It's the barter system. She makes people happy and content, and they tell her exactly what she needs to know. And they don't even know they're doing it."

Hannah began to frown slightly. "You're right, Lisa. But it doesn't sound very nice when you put it that way. And . . . actually . . . I've never really thought of it that way before." She stopped and considered it for a moment or two. "It *is* the barter system. Do you think that what I'm doing is wrong?"

"Not at all!" Lisa responded quickly. "You always bring something when you go somewhere. And there's nothing wrong with asking for information. After all, you're trying to catch a murderer."

"And she's trying to prove that the murderer's not you," Michelle added.

Lisa smiled. "There's that, too. I do have a vested interest. And it just so happens I've got the perfect treat for you to take to Danielle."

"What?" Hannah asked.

"You'll see." Lisa hurried to the walk-in cooler, disappeared inside, and returned with a tray of candy. "I happen to know that Danielle loves caramels. Try these and tell me what you think."

Hannah and Michelle each took a piece and bit into it. And then both of them smiled.

"Incredible!" Hannah pronounced.

"You said it!" Michelle took another bite. "These are worth a boatload of information."

"They're the chocolate caramels I told you about yesterday. Marge took over for me out front and I made a batch and stuck them in the cooler. And a couple of hours later, I came back here and wrapped them in wax paper. I hope Danielle likes them. And I hope she knows something about the murder. It's really unnerving to be a suspect."

"I've never been up here before," Michelle said, as Hannah pulled open the heavy door a few feet from the entrance to the Red Owl Grocery store.

"You'll love it. It was just an empty space until Danielle rented it, but it has big floor-to-ceiling windows in the front and Danielle's walled off part of the back for living quarters."

Hannah led the way up the long, carpeted staircase. As they climbed, she gestured toward the walls. "What do you think?"

"Very clever." Michelle obviously admired the sets of footsteps that diagrammed classic dances, each set depicted in a different color. "Listen, Hannah. I think I hear a waltz."

"You do. Danielle must have an adult class."

As they climbed, the music changed to a polka. "Music for a wedding reception?" Michelle guessed.

"It sounds like it. Danielle mentioned that wedding parties were a big part of her business."

"Because of the first bride and groom dance?"

"Yes, but there's a new trend around Lake Eden. After the bride and groom dance, the whole wedding party gets out there for the next dance. And then the bride's mother dances with the groom's father, and the groom's mother dances with the bride's father."

"That's a lot of dancing. Who started all that anyway?"

Hannah shrugged. "I don't know, but I wouldn't put it

past Danielle. She's always looking for ways to increase her business."

The music switched again and a slow dance began to play. It rolled out in a wave to greet them as Hannah opened the studio door. "Let's wait right here in the reception area until Danielle's class is over."

It turned out that they were in luck because right after the slow dance had ended, the music stopped and a few moments later, Danielle's customers began to emerge from the practice room and file out. After Hannah and Michelle had greeted the people they knew and exchanged pleasantries with the ones they didn't, Danielle came out and saw them sitting there.

"Hi, Hannah. Michelle. How are you?"

"We're fine," Hannah said, handing her the bag Lisa had filled for her. "We brought you something."

"Oooh!" Danielle began to smile as she peeked inside. "Candy! What kind is it?"

"Chocolate caramels that Lisa made."

"I love caramels." Danielle held out the bag. "Would you like one?" she offered.

"We already tested them down at The Cookie Jar," Michelle told her. "We wanted to make sure they were as good as they looked. Do you have a few minutes to talk, Danielle?"

"I have at least a half hour before my next class comes in. Come with me, and I'll put on the coffee." Danielle led them into the interior. They walked through the class area and into her living quarters. It was one large area, almost like an artist's loft, with a bedroom that was cordoned off with a curtain, a living room with a sofa and an easy chair, a tiny bathroom off to the side of the bedroom alcove, and a small, but workable kitchen.

"Sit down." Danielle gestured toward her kitchen table. "I'm sure you're here for a reason, and it's probably not for dance lessons."

"You're right," Hannah told her, noticing the coffee machine on Danielle's counter. "I thought you drank tea, Danielle."

"I do. Benton gave me this machine, and it makes both tea and coffee." She held up a small cup-like pod. "Would you like French roast, Italian roast, or espresso?"

"French roast," Hannah answered, choosing her favorite.

"The same for me," Michelle concurred.

"Just listen," Danielle said as she put a coffee pod into the machine and set an empty cup on the tray below. "It pokes holes in the pod and forces hot water through. And it takes less than a minute."

Hannah and Michelle watched as the machine worked. And less than a minute later, Hannah had her cup of coffee. Another thirty seconds or so, and Michelle had hers. And then Danielle made her cup of tea.

"You look too serious for a social visit," Danielle said as she sat down. "Is this about Phyllis Bates?"

"Yes," Hannah answered.

"And you're investigating?"

"That's right. I have to find the killer, Danielle. Lisa is a suspect and it's the only way I can clear her."

"She doesn't have an alibi?"

"No. We were together until nine at The Cookie Jar, but then she drove home to feed her dogs and let them run in the yard, and I went straight out to The Corner Tavern. She didn't meet me there until around ten."

Danielle looked concerned. "So there was an hour, from nine to ten, when Lisa was alone?"

"That's right."

"And the time of death was . . . ?"

"Between eight and ten," Michelle answered her. "Hannah and I looked at the autopsy report."

Danielle shivered slightly. "I get a sick feeling in my stomach every time I think of that."

Hannah wasn't sure whether Danielle was referring to the

autopsy, the fact that Phyllis was murdered, or if it had reminded Danielle of her own husband's violent death. Instead of asking a question that might be painful for Danielle, Hannah decided to change the subject, but Michelle spoke up before Hannah could open her mouth.

"Unfortunately, Lisa *does* have a motive," Michelle said.

"Because Herb dated Phyllis in high school, and now they're working together?" Danielle asked, looking a bit skeptical.

"That's part of it, but there's more," Hannah said. "Mayor Bascomb appointed Phyllis as this year's Mrs. Santa Claus."

Danielle nodded. "I know about that. The mother of one of my ballet students told me. And she said that Lisa was hoping to be Mrs. Claus."

"That's right," Hannah agreed. "Lisa and I went to the auditorium last night to pick up this year's Christmas gift bags. The Lake Eden Players were just rehearsing the end of *A Christmas Carol*, and we stayed because Lisa wanted to see how Herb and Phyllis would act when they played Mr. and Mrs. Claus."

"Herb with Phyllis," Danielle said with a nod. "That must have been hard for Lisa to take."

"Oh, it's not just that!" Hannah told her. "Usually Santa hugs Mrs. Claus when they've given out candy and cookies to the kids in the audience."

"Yes," Danielle said. "They always do that."

"Well, this year Tory Bascomb decided to do things differently. When she was through criticizing the Mrs. Santa costume that Phyllis was wearing . . ."

"Wait a minute," Danielle interrupted. "Isn't it the same costume that every Mrs. Claus wears?"

"It's supposed to be, but Phyllis claimed that the costume didn't fit and she rented her own costume from a place in the Cities. Tory said it looked like something a stripper would wear for a routine at Christmas."

Danielle gave a little laugh. "That figures. Was Tory right?"

"Oh, yes. The costume was very revealing."

"And that bothered Lisa?"

"That's only part of it. Tory directed Phyllis to give Herb a stage kiss right before they pulled the final curtain. But Phyllis didn't give him a *stage* kiss. It was a real kiss, and it was obvious that she was interested in Herb."

"Uh-oh," Danielle said. "That must have made Lisa very jealous."

"It did," Michelle told her. "And Herb's been out late almost every night this month. He says he's working late, but Lisa's not so sure that's the truth."

Danielle nodded. "I get it. Working late at the office, hmmm? Do you know that there used to be a bar in St. Cloud called The Office? That way, the guys who came there to drink could say that they were at the office and they wouldn't be lying."

"That's funny, but not really," Michelle said.

"I know." Danielle took a sip of her tea. "Poor Lisa! What can I do to help you, Hannah?"

"Give me a timeline for the drinks you had with the mayor and Stephanie last night."

"I can do that, but . . ." Danielle stopped speaking and her eyes narrowed. "I do understand. The mayor's a suspect because . . . well, you know why. And Stephanie's a suspect because she's always jealous of the women the mayor finds attractive."

"That's right," Hannah said.

"Let me think." Danielle shut her eyes for a moment or two, and then she opened them again. "The mayor and Stephanie picked me up at nine. And Del was already in their car. He told me he'd ridden over to their house to pick up Stephanie. I was watching out the window for them to pull up, and I looked at the clock in the reception area on the way out the door. And we got home at . . . oh, dear. I'm not sure that I even noticed what time. . . ." Danielle stopped speaking and began to smile. "Wait a minute. I can give you the exact time that I got back here."

As Hannah and Michelle watched, Danielle pulled out her cell phone and touched the screen. She touched it a second time and then she nodded. "Ten twenty-five," she told them. "I know because I sent a text to Benton to tell him that I was back so that he could come over when he finished work. The time's right here on the text."

"That clears the mayor," Hannah said.

Danielle looked slightly puzzled. "But it doesn't clear Stephanie?" she asked.

"No. I know that the mayor was in a city council meeting and he left with Del. That means he was with someone for the entire period between eight and ten. But Stephanie wasn't at the city council meeting. She was at home, alone. She had a whole hour, between eight and nine, to drive out to the Corner Tavern and kill Phyllis."

# Chocolate Caramels
## (Kathy & John's Yummy Nummy Caramels For Mummy)

To make this candy, you will need a candy thermometer. I use the kind with a glass tube and a sliding metal clamp that attaches to the side of a saucepan. And even though the recipe calls for a 3-quart saucepan, I always use my 4-quart saucepan. That way I don't have to worry about the candy boiling up over the sides.

½ cup finely chopped nuts *(I used walnuts)*
1 cup brown sugar *(pack it down in the cup when you measure it)*
½ teaspoon salt
1 cup dark Karo syrup
1 can *(14 ounces)* sweetened condensed milk *(NOT evaporated milk)*
2 ounces unsweeted baking chocolate *(I used Baker's)*
½ cup butter *(1 stick, 4 ounces, ¼ pound)*
1 teaspoon vanilla extract

Before you start, spray a 9-inch by 13-inch cake pan with Pam or another nonstick cooking spray.

Sprinkle the chopped nuts evenly across the bottom of the cake pan.

Place the cake pan on a folded kitchen towel on the kitchen counter.

Get out a 3-quart saucepan *(or a 4-quart saucepan)* and your candy thermometer. Place the thermometer inside the saucepan with the sliding clamp on the outside. Slide the thermometer through the clamp until it's approximately ½ inch from the bottom of the saucepan. *(If the bulb touches the bottom of the saucepan, your reading will be wildly off.)*

On a cold burner, combine the brown sugar, salt, dark Karo syrup, sweetened condensed milk, unsweetened chocolate, and butter.

Turn the burner on MEDIUM HIGH heat. STIR the candy mixture CONSTANTLY until it boils. *(This will take about 10 minutes, so pull up a stool and get comfortable while you stir.)*

Continue stirring until your candy thermometer reaches 250 degrees F. Continue to stir for one more minute and move the saucepan to a cold burner.

Add the vanilla extract to the candy mixture and stir it in. *(This could sputter a bit, so be careful.)*

Let the candy mixture sit on the cold burner for 5 minutes.

When 5 minutes have passed, pour the candy mixture evenly over the nuts in the cake pan. *(Use a heat-resistant spatula so that you can get every delicious drop.)*

Leave the cake pan on the counter for 20 additional minutes to cool. Then cover it with plastic wrap and put it in the refrigerator for at least 3 hours. *(Overnight is fine too.)*

When you're ready to serve your Chocolate Caramels, cut the caramels into squares with a buttered knife. Make sure you cut all the way to the bottom of the cake pan.

Pry out the caramels, one by one, and wrap each one in wax paper.

Yield: 3 dozen or so bonbon-size pieces of delicious candy, depending on the size of the pieces you cut. Store in a covered container.

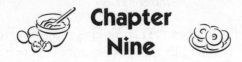

# Chapter Nine

"The kitchen smells wonderful!" Michelle said as Hannah pulled the last pan of Chocolate-Covered Mint Cookies from the oven.

"I know. I love to make these cookies. It always reminds me of Christmas. There's something about mint and candy canes that just goes with the whole season."

"And chocolate. Don't forget the chocolate."

"Chocolate's not seasonal. It's good any time of the year. Chocolate's like oxygen. It's elemental."

"You've got a point," Michelle said as she plucked a hot cookie from the baker's rack and juggled it from hand to hand. "Do you think these are too hot to eat?"

"Here." Hannah handed her sister a napkin. "You'd better let it cool a little or you might burn your mouth."

"I've got a better idea. I'll open the door, stand just inside, and stick out my hand with the cookie. It'll cool faster that way." Michelle opened the back kitchen door, extended her hand, and gasped as a shape materialized from the blowing snow and plucked the cookie from her hand.

"Thanks!" the shape said, stepping closer. "It's not every day that someone comes out to greet me with a hot cookie."

"Mike!" Michelle exclaimed as she recognized him. "You scared me half to death! Give me back that cookie. It's mine."

"Not anymore," Mike said, biting into the cookie as he

stepped into the kitchen. "This cookie's too young to be outside alone in weather like this. It's my duty to save it from the storm."

"You ate my cookie!" Michelle accused as Mike popped the rest of the cookie in his mouth.

"There's more where that came from," Hannah said with a laugh. "Sit down, Mike. I'll pour a cup of coffee for you."

Michelle walked over to the baker's rack and piled several more cookies on a napkin. "I'm not taking any more chances with these cookies. I'm going out front to eat them."

Hannah delivered Mike's coffee and dished up a plate of cookies for him. Then she sat down across from him at the workstation. "I figured you'd be here before closing," she said. "You always come around the day after a murder to find out if I've discovered anything."

"These are really good cookies, Hannah." Mike picked one up and took a bite. "Have you?"

Hannah knew exactly what he was asking, but she didn't get up to retrieve her murder book. "Not much."

"But you *are* investigating."

There were times when Hannah wished that Mike didn't know her quite as well as he did. "I'm asking questions if that's what you mean."

"You probably already know that I'll need to talk to Lisa."

"I know. And Lisa knows, too. She mentioned it to me this morning."

"Do you have her name on your suspect list?"

Hannah sighed deeply. "Yes," she admitted. "Lisa's name is there. But I intend to find an alibi for her."

"Any luck so far?"

"Not yet."

They sat there in silence for a moment, and then Hannah sighed again. "Is Herb one of your suspects?"

"Not anymore."

"Why isn't he?" Hannah was certain that she looked just as shocked as she felt.

"Herb has an alibi."

"Wonderful!" Hannah began to smile. "That's a big relief! Does Lisa know that Herb has an alibi?"

Mike shrugged. "I don't know, but I doubt it."

"Can I tell Lisa that you cleared Herb?"

"Sure, you can."

"Good! She'll be really happy to hear that Herb's got an alibi. What is it?"

"Sorry, Hannah. I can't tell you that."

Hannah began to frown. "Why not?"

"Because I promised Herb that I wouldn't tell anyone. And I don't break my promises."

Hannah's frown deepened. "Will Herb tell Lisa his alibi?"

"I'm sure he won't."

Hannah swallowed hard. "Please tell me that Herb's alibi doesn't involve a girlfriend."

"I can do that. Herb's alibi doesn't involve a girlfriend."

"Are you sure? I mean, he's been telling Lisa that he's working late and she's driven past city hall. Herb's not at his office and his car is gone. She's worried that he's spending time with another woman."

"He's not."

"Are you sure?"

"I'm positive." Mike reached out to take Hannah's hand. "Stop worrying, Hannah. And try to get Lisa to stop worrying. Herb isn't with another woman."

"Then where is he until after midnight almost every night?"

"That's privileged information between Herb and me. I can't tell you, Hannah. Now just let it go, okay?"

Hannah didn't like it one little bit, but she nodded. "Okay. I won't ask you any more questions about that. But now that Herb is cleared, who's left on your suspect list?"

Mike laughed. "I knew you'd get around to that, but I just

gave you a piece of information. It's your turn to cough up something for me. Who's on *your* suspect list?"

"Mayor Bascomb, but I cleared him."

Mike reached out to tip her chin up so that he could look into her eyes. "Do I detect a slightly disappointed look on your face?"

"Maybe. He *did* have a perfect motive."

"I know. And I cleared him, too. But I asked you who was *on* your list, not who you cleared."

Hannah sighed. She wished that Mike wasn't quite so logical. She had to give him something before he'd divulge any more information."

"Give it up, Hannah," Mike prompted her.

There was no choice. Hannah knew that she had to tell him. "All right. You win. It's Stephanie Bascomb."

"Stephanie?"

"Yes."

"But she got what she wanted from the mayor. I talked to Claire, and the clothes she bought cost a lot of money. And then I went out to the mall and talked to her jeweler. The mayor paid a small fortune for that ring. Stephanie got her usual revenge and then some."

"I know. I heard about the diamond. Lisa saw it and she said it was as big as a boulder."

"Well . . . Lisa's exaggerating a bit, but it *is* extremely large. But Stephanie already had her new clothes and her new diamond when the victim was murdered. What motive would Stephanie have for actually killing Phyllis?"

"I don't know. Maybe Stephanie thought that Phyllis would do it all over again. Or . . . maybe she wanted to get even with Phyllis for asking the mayor to set her up in an apartment."

"That's weak, Hannah."

"Okay, try this one on for size. Stephanie always supports the Lake Eden Players. She even introduces the actors when they take their curtain call. Maybe she didn't want Phyllis to be Mrs. Claus because she felt that Phyllis wasn't worthy of being included in a Lake Eden Players production."

"That's a little more plausible, but Stephanie has an alibi. She went out for drinks with the mayor after his council meeting."

"Yes, but he didn't pick her up until nine. She was alone before that. And Doc set the window for the time of death from *eight* to ten that night."

"How do you know that?"

"A little birdie told me."

Mike smiled. "A little birdie named Mother?"

"Whatever. I don't have to reveal my sources unless it interferes with your official investigation. We have a deal, don't we?"

"We do."

"If Phyllis was murdered at the beginning of the window of death period, Stephanie would have had time to kill her."

"You think that Stephanie had time to drive out to the Corner Tavern, bash in the victim's head, get rid of the murder weapon, drive back home, clean up, and be dressed and ready to go when the mayor picked her up at nine last night?"

"Yes. It would be tight, but if she was determined to get rid of Phyllis, she could do it. And there's even another possibility that would have saved Stephanie some time. She could have been in the school parking lot, waiting for Phyllis to come out of the auditorium. Rod published the rehearsal schedule in the *Lake Eden Journal*. Stephanie could have followed Phyllis out to the Corner Tavern and intercepted her before she could get inside. That would explain why Bonnie Surma didn't see Phyllis walk in. Stephanie killed Phyllis before she got anywhere near the entrance to the restaurant."

Mike thought about that for a few moments. "It's unlikely, but possible," he conceded. "You were there at the school, Hannah. Did you see Phyllis come out?"

"No. I told you this before. Lisa left before Tory Bascomb dismissed the cast and the crew. When we drove off, none of them had come out yet."

"Did you see Stephanie's car in the school parking lot?"

"No, but there were a lot of other cars and I wasn't looking for it."

"Fair enough. I'll have my team go through Stephanie's car to see if they can find anything."

"How are you going to do that? Are you going to tell Stephanie that she's a suspect?"

"There's no need for that. Don't worry, Hannah. I have a way to get her car so that my guys can go through it, and it won't arouse either Stephanie's or the mayor's suspicions."

"You're going to do something sneaky?"

"Some might call it that. Others would call it brilliant." Mike gave her the devilish grin that always made Hannah's knees turn weak. "What are you doing for dinner tonight?"

Hannah couldn't hide her look of surprise. "Are you inviting me out to dinner when you're in the middle of an investigation?"

"No. I'd like to ask you out to dinner, but I'm on call until this case is solved. I just want to know where you are at all times. I worry about you, Hannah."

"That's really . . ." Hannah paused, trying to come up with the perfect word. "That's really sweet."

"It's not sweet. It's necessary. You're really good at identifying the killer, but that usually gets you into trouble. I just want a little warning, okay? One of these times I might not be around to protect you. And I *do* want to protect you, Hannah. I care about you." Mike reached out for her hand and gave it a squeeze. "I don't want to see anything bad to happen to you."

Hannah's first instinct was to bristle. She wanted to recount the number of times she'd confronted a killer alone and taken the proper action to save herself. She wasn't some kind of delicate tropical flower that had to be kept in a hot-house and cosseted. But Mike did have a point. She'd gotten into trouble a couple of times and Mike had been there. He *had* saved her. There was no denying that. And she had no way of knowing the future. It was possible that a similar situation could happen again.

"Okay," Hannah told him, although it went totally against her fiercely independent nature. "I'll be glad to give you my schedule for the evening, if it'll make you feel any better."

Mike pulled out the small notebook that he always carried in the shirt pocket of his uniform, and unclipped his pen. "Okay," he said. "Shoot."

"Isn't that a rather dangerous thing for a cop to say?" Hannah asked him, unable to resist the joke.

"Not to you. I know you don't keep a gun in The Cookie Jar. Where will you be, Hannah?"

"I'll be right here until four-thirty. I'm going to let Lisa close up today. Michelle and I will head back to the condo to get something to eat and feed Moishe. And then we'll drive back to town to attend the last rehearsal of the play at the school auditorium."

"And after that?"

"Back to the condo until early tomorrow morning, when Michelle and I should get here about five. You're welcome to drop by then for coffee and cookies if you want to check up on me and get the schedule for my day."

"Thanks, Hannah. I appreciate that. And you won't go anywhere else?"

"I'm not planning on it."

Mike looked properly grateful for her cooperation, and Hannah couldn't help but wonder if they were on a new footing as she walked him to the door. When they got there, she opened it for Mike, but he didn't step out. Instead, he pulled her into his arms and gave her a hug. "If you deviate from the schedule you gave me for tonight, please text or call," Mike told her after ending the hug. "I don't want to remove another cold dead body from a snowbank."

# Chocolate-Covered Mint Cookies

Preheat oven to 350 degrees F., rack in the middle position.

1 cup salted butter, softened *(2 sticks, 8 ounces, ½ pound)*
1 small package *(makes 4 half-cups)* chocolate instant pudding mix *(NOT sugar-free)*
½ cup white *(granulated)* sugar
½ cup packed brown sugar
1 egg, beaten
1 teaspoon vanilla extract
1 teaspoon baking soda
¼ teaspoon salt
½ teaspoon ground cinnamon
1 and ½ cups all-purpose flour *(pack it down in the cup when you measure it)*
1 and ½ cups quick rolled oats *(not instant—the Quick 1-minute kind)*
1 cup chocolate-covered mints *(I used Junior Mints)*
1 cup semi-sweet chocolate chips *(a 6-ounce package—I used Nestle)*

In a medium bowl and using an electric mixer, on MEDIUM SPEED, beat the softened butter with the dry chocolate pudding mix. Beat until the mixture is light and fluffy.

Add the white sugar and the brown sugar. Continue to beat on **MEDIUM** speed until the contents are well-mixed.

Add the egg and the vanilla. Mix well.

Add the baking soda, salt, and cinnamon. Mix until they are well incorporated.

Add the flour in half-cup increments, mixing after each addition.

Add the rolled oats in half-cup increments, mixing after each addition.

Remove the bowl from the mixer and give it a final stir by hand. You will finish the rest of this recipe by hand.

Stir in the chocolate-covered mints by hand, being careful not to over-stir and crush them.

Add the semi-sweet chocolate chips and stir them in. Again, stir lightly so that you don't crush the mints.

Prepare your cookie sheets by lining them with parchment paper, or spraying lightly with Pam or another nonstick cooking spray.

Drop, by rounded teaspoons, no more than 12 cookies to a standard-sized sheet. You can also use a 2-teaspoon size scooper if you wish.

Bake the Chocolate-Covered Mint Cookies at 350 degrees F. for 10 to 12 minutes or until the edges are golden brown.

Cool the cookies for 2 minutes on the cookie sheet, and then remove them to a wire rack to complete cooling. *(If you've used parchment paper, you can simply leave the cookies on the paper and pull it over to the wire rack.)* Wait until the cookies are completely cool before you try to peel them off the parchment paper.

Yield: Makes approximately 5 dozen deliciously minty and chocolatey cookies.

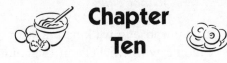

# Chapter Ten

"Thanks, Norman!" Hannah said, as Norman walked in the door of the Jordan High auditorium carrying a very large box. She knew exactly what was in the box because she'd called him earlier and asked him to bring his popcorn machine to the auditorium.

"No problem. I've got all the things you need to make a batch of popcorn in the car. I'll go get the other box."

Hannah quickly shrugged into her parka. "Hold on a second and I'll walk out with you."

"Okay, but I don't need help. Wouldn't you rather stay here, where it's warm?"

"No, I'd rather go with you. Come on, Norman. Let's get that second box so we can figure out how to use your popcorn machine before it's time for the first intermission."

"But there's no audience. It's just a rehearsal."

"I know, but the Lake Eden Players might like some popcorn to munch on between acts. And everyone on the makeup and technical crews would enjoy it."

"You're right, Hannah. Let's go."

Norman led the way outside and Hannah followed. The moment they got outside the door, Norman turned to her. "Okay, Hannah. Why did you need to talk to me alone?"

Hannah smiled. She should have known that Norman

would catch her true purpose in walking out with him. "Because Lisa was standing with Michelle at the counter and I wanted to ask you if you'd discovered anything that might help to clear her."

"Makes sense. And, as a matter of fact, I did discover a partial alibi for her."

"Oh, Norman! You're wonderful!" Hannah threw her arms around him and gave him a hug. It wasn't much of a hug because they were both wearing bulky, padded parkas and her arms barely reached around him. "Tell me what you discovered."

"I stopped by Mother and Earl's this afternoon. Earl was there, warming up after a whole morning of plowing out Lake Eden city streets, and Mother was making Janelle's Chicken Soup for him."

"I love that soup! I wish I'd gone with you."

"So do I. You know I love to spend time with you, Hannah. Anyway, I had a bowl of soup with them, and Earl and I got to talking. Earl said he was driving the snowplow last night."

"Last night," Hannah repeated, beginning to understand why Norman was telling her about Earl's snowplow schedule. "Where did Earl plow? And when?"

"That's what I love about you Hannah." Norman slipped his arm around her waist as they walked to his car. "You catch on right away."

"Maybe. What time?"

"He was going to plow Lisa's street at nine-thirty-five, but he noticed that Lisa's car was parked in front of the house. He knows that Lisa and Herb have a two-car garage and they always park there when they come home at night. Since Lisa's car was out on the street, Earl figured that she planned to go out again."

"That was smart of him," Hannah commented.

"I thought so, too. Earl told me that the plow he uses leaves a pretty high bank of snow and he didn't want to block Lisa in if she needed to get her car out again, so he passed by her street and started plowing a few streets over."

"Earl's a really nice guy," Hannah said, having trouble containing her excitement. "When did he come back with the plow?"

"He thinks it was about ten minutes later because he plowed the streets on either side of her."

"And when Earl got back there, Lisa's car was gone?"

"Yes. That helps, doesn't it, Hannah?"

"Yes! It proves that Lisa went home to feed the dogs. And it takes fifteen minutes to get from Lisa's house to the Corner Tavern."

"That means Lisa couldn't have gotten there until ten minutes before ten. And then there's only another ten minutes of her time that's unaccounted for?"

"That's right. It doesn't clear Lisa, but it makes her a much more unlikely suspect. Lisa met me inside at around ten. And that means she would have had only ten minutes to kill Phyllis, change to her ankle boots, and hurry into the restaurant to meet me." Hannah put her arms around Norman again and hugged him as tightly as she could. "Thank you so much! It helps a whole lot."

"Does it help enough to invite me to your place after the rehearsal is over?"

"Of course it does!" Hannah responded immediately. "You know you're always welcome."

"Good. I'll stop for pizza and meet you and Michelle at the condo. And now, we'd better get these supplies inside before the first act ends and we don't have time to figure out the machine and make the popcorn."

"That went well!" Hannah commented as she drove out of the school parking lot and headed for the highway."

"And everyone loved the popcorn," Michelle reported. "There were quite a few people who came straight from work and they were really hungry."

"I'm going to drive past The Cookie Jar to make sure our Christmas lights are on," Hannah told her. "I had to move the timer this morning, and I'm not sure I set the time correctly."

"Why did you have to move it?"

"Lisa told me that one of our customers almost tripped over the extension cord, so I decided to move the timer to a closer wall socket."

"That was probably smart."

"While I was at it, I put on a new timer, too. It's one that fits flat to the wall with the plug on the side." Hannah drove up to Main Street and turned at the corner. The lights were on, and she gave a satisfied smile as they went past. "I must have done it right. They're still on."

"And they look really good. I'm glad that all the businesses on Main Street leave their Christmas lights on at night."

"So am I. It really looks festive. Herb was smart convincing everyone that leaving on the Christmas lights was a deterrent to thieves."

"Speaking of Herb, did you manage to talk to Lisa?"

"Yes." Hannah turned onto the highway and drove toward her condo complex. "I think I convinced her that Herb isn't seeing another woman. I told her exactly what Mike told me, and that seemed to satisfy her. And she was very relieved that Herb had an alibi."

"Do you mind if I bake when we get to your place? It won't take long."

"I never mind when you bake. What are you making?"

"A Christmas Orange Raisin Cake."

"Is that a new recipe?"

"Not really. It's an adaptation of Grandma Elsa's Christmas Date Cake. I've been thinking about it all day, and I've got everything I need to make it."

There was very little traffic, and it didn't take long to drive to the condo complex, and Hannah parked in her designated spot in the underground garage. The two sisters walked up the outside staircase together, and Hannah gave a little wave as she spotted Moishe on the window ledge, waiting for them to get home. "I guess it's a little silly to wave to Moishe," she said with a laugh. "You're not going to believe this, but once he waved back at me."

"You're kidding, aren't you?" Michelle asked.

"No. When I climbed up the stairs and waved at him, he raised his right paw and put it up against the glass."

"Okay," Michelle said, but she didn't sound convinced. "Maybe he was after a bug or something."

"Maybe, but I prefer to believe that he was waving back at me." Hannah reached the landing first and waited for Michelle to climb the last few steps. "You, or me?" she asked.

"I'll do it." Michelle positioned herself for the furry orange and white ball that would jump through the air and land in her arms once the door was opened.

"Ready?" Hannah asked her.

"Ready."

Hannah unlocked the door and stood to the side. She reached out to open it, moved out of the way just in time, and watched as Moishe hurtled himself airborne and straight into Michelle's waiting arms.

"Oooofff!" Michelle said, and it was a cross between a laugh and a groan. "I always forget how heavy he is."

"Twenty-three pounds and counting," Hannah said as Michelle walked inside, placed Moishe on the back of the couch, and hurried into the kitchen to get the fish-shaped, salmon-flavored treats he loved.

"Here you go, Moishe," Michelle said, coming back with the cannister and placing three kitty treats in front of Moishe. "When Norman brings pizza and gives you sausage, you could gain another half-pound or so before the night is over."

## *Christmas Orange Raisin Cake*

Preheat oven to 325 degrees F., rack in the middle position

**Hannah's 1st Note: Michelle modified this recipe and Norman loves it. He wants me to make it for him every Christmas.**

**The Fruit:**

> 2 cups golden raisins *(you can also use regular raisins, but Norman prefers golden raisins)*
> 2 cups boiling water
> 2 teaspoons baking soda
> ½ cup triple sec or Grand Marnier *(substitute orange juice if you don't want to use alcohol)*
> ½ cup orange juice

*Mother, who's always frugal and absolutely doesn't have to be, says to tell you that triple sec is a lot cheaper than Grand Marnier.*

Place the raisins in a bowl. Pour the boiling water over the golden raisins, add the baking soda *(it foams up a bit)* and then add the liqueur and orange juice.

Set the raisins and liquid aside on the kitchen counter to cool.

While the raisins are cooling, place the following ingredients together in another large mixing bowl or in the bowl of an electric mixer:

**The Cake Batter:**

> 1 cup softened salted butter *(2 sticks, 8 ounces, ½ pound)*
> 2 cups white *(granulated)* sugar
> 4 large eggs
> ½ teaspoon salt
> 1 Tablespoon orange zest *(That's finely grated orange peel, but just the orange part, not the white under it.)*
> 3 cups all-purpose flour *(don't sift—pack it down in the cup when you measure it)*

Turn the mixer to MEDIUM speed and mix thoroughly, or beat thoroughly by hand.

Take a raisin out of your first bowl to see if it's plumped. If it's round and looks as if it's absorbed liquid, add the raisins AND the liquid to the mixing bowl.

Mix your cake batter thoroughly on MEDIUM speed or by hand until everything has been thoroughly incorporated.

Butter and flour a 9-inch by 13-inch rectangular cake pan. You can also spray the inside of the cake pan with Pam for baking *(the kind of Pam with flour in it)*.

Hannah's 2<sup>nd</sup> Note: This cake rises about an inch and a half, so make sure the sides of your cake pan are tall enough.

Pour the cake batter into the pan. Then sprinkle the following on the top, in this order, BEFORE baking:

**Cake Topping:**

12 ounces milk chocolate chips *(2 cups)*
1 cup white *(granulated)* sugar
1 cup chopped pecans *(you can use any nuts you like—Norman prefers walnuts—I prefer pecans)*

Bake your cake at 325 degrees F. for 80 minutes, or until you test it and it's done.

### Testing Your Cake for Doneness:

Use a long toothpick or a cake tester to tell if your cake is done. If you insert it one inch from the center of the cake, it should come out clean without batter sticking to it. If it doesn't, bake your cake in additional 5-minute increments until your tester comes out clean. Remove the cake from the oven.

Hannah's 3<sup>rd</sup> Note: If you happen to stick the toothpick in and hit a chocolate chip, it'll come out covered with melted chocolate—just wipe it off and stick it in again to test the actual cake batter.

Let the cake cool in the pan on a wire rack or a cold stove burner. It can be served slightly warm, at room temperature, or chilled.

Hannah's 4th Note: If you want to be fancy, cut this cake into pieces, put it on dessert plates, and top each piece with a dollop of sweetened whipped cream. Then garnish the whipped cream with chocolate shavings or chocolate curls scraped from a milk chocolate candy bar. Alternatively, if you don't want to use chocolate, you can top each slice with a dollop of sweetened whipped cream and put a red maraschino cherry on top.

# Chapter
# Eleven

Hannah wasn't sure what had awakened her. Perhaps it was the bluish-white light that had begun to glow at the foot of her bed, turning the dark night into something foreign, something unknown.

"Dad?" she asked, sitting up in bed.

"I'm here, Honey-bear. Or at least I'm almost here. Give me a minute to pull myself together, okay?"

Hannah wanted to laugh, but she was too amazed to do anything but stare. Her father *was* pulling himself together, right before her very eyes. The bluish-white cloud was forming itself into an oval. Once the oval was roughly her father's height, appendages began to grow, four of them in the proper places for arms and legs. The head was next, popping up from the top of the oval like a balloon on a string being jerked from above.

"Almost there," the head said in her father's voice. "They let me come to visit you again. I'm playing the Ghost of Christmas Present tonight. And all I have to do for the favor is to barbecue for the AITs next week."

"The AITs?"

"Angels in training. It hasn't been that long since they were human, and they still get hungry. We're having bratwurst and beans."

Hannah smiled. "That was your favorite meal to make for us when Mother was gone."

"That was because it was easy. Throw the sausage on the grill and heat a can of beans."

"But all of us loved it. We loved your chicken, beef, turkey noodle soup, too."

"Three cans of soup thrown in a pot and heated together. It was easy, too. It's not like I made the soup from scratch."

"But that's okay. It was good and we always had it with oyster crackers. All three of us loved the fact that you cared enough to cook for us."

"Of course I did. I still do. You never lose the love, Hannah. It survives forever."

Hannah blinked back the tears that had formed in her eyes. It was wonderful to know that her dad still loved her.

"Uh-oh. They just called me. It's time for your peek into the present, Hannah. Watch this."

As Hannah watched, the movie screen materialized and images appeared. It was morning in Lake Eden and she was walking down the street toward Florence's Red Owl Grocery. She didn't go inside the grocery store. She stopped by the door to Danielle's dance studio. There was a pretty wreath hanging on the inside of the glass door, and Hannah took a moment to admire it. Then she opened the door and began to climb the long, carpeted staircase.

The scene shifted to the reception area, and Hannah found herself sitting there, waiting for Danielle to finish with her class. Then Danielle came out and the scene shifted again to Danielle's tiny kitchen, the same kitchen Hannah and Michelle had visited less than twenty-four hours ago. This time, Michelle wasn't there. And then Hannah was leaving, going down the carpeted stairs. She stopped at the door to the street, pulled out her murder book and turned to the suspect page. She took a moment to jot down a name.

"That's all," her father said and Hannah squinted, trying

to read the name that was still faintly visible on the screen, but the screen went blank before she could decipher the letters. Her glimpse into the present was over.

"Remember, Hannah. You must remember this tomorrow. It's very important."

"Yes, Dad. I'll try to remember. Really, I will."

"I know. I love you, Honey-bear. I'm hoping they'll let me come back one final time to visit you. Until then . . ."

Hannah watched as her father's shape flickered and morphed into the bluish-white cloud again. The cloud moved, closer, closer, and then it surrounded her and she felt a kiss on her forehead. "Dad," she whispered, tears rolling down her cheeks. "Don't go, Dad! Please!"

"I must, Honey-bear. They're calling me. Just try to remember . . . remember . . . remember . . ."

"Remember," Hannah repeated, reaching out toward him and encountering nothing but empty air. And then her eyelids closed. And she slept a deep and dreamless sleep.

Someone with very rough lips was kissing her cheek. It was not completely unpleasant, but it was a bit disconcerting. Hannah opened her eyes to see Moishe staring down at her with his one good eye and purring.

"Good heavens!" she exclaimed, sitting up quickly. "What time is it?"

Of course Moishe did not answer, but one glance at her bedside alarm clock confirmed that she had, indeed, slept in. It was almost five in the morning and she normally got up at four-thirty. Hannah felt around for her slippers, located them under the side of the bed, and slipped them on her feet. Then she shrugged into her robe and sniffed the air.

"Coffee," she told Moishe with a smile. "And . . . something with raspberries?"

"Rrrroww!" Moishe concurred.

"Let's go see what it is." Hannah hurried down the carpeted hallway with Moishe trailing a bit behind her, swatting at the ties of her robe hanging down either side because she hadn't bothered to secure them around her waist.

"Great!" Michelle said as Hannah and Moishe entered the kitchen. "Now I won't have to wake you."

"Moishe took care of that. He licked my face to wake me up."

"That's probably because he was in a hurry for his breakfast. He knows I always give him something special when I stay with you."

Michelle scooped kitty crunchies into Moishe's bowl, followed by something from the frying pan.

"Shrimp?" Hannah guessed.

"No. I cut up a little piece of leftover chicken and warmed it on the stove."

"No wonder he's always so glad to see you!" Hannah exclaimed. And then she smiled. "Actually, both of us are. I smelled the coffee."

Michelle gestured toward Hannah's kitchen table and came over with the mug she'd just filled. "Here you go."

Hannah took a big sip and gave a grateful sigh. "Thanks. I really needed this. You made something else too, and it smells delicious. Does it have raspberries?"

"Yes. I baked Red Raspberry Muffins. I wanted something with fruit, and you had some frozen raspberries. The muffins should be cool enough if you want to try one now."

"Yes!" Hannah said emphatically. "You always make really good muffins, Michelle."

"Thanks. This one's an experiment. Let me know if you can think of any improvements."

Hannah accepted a muffin from Michelle, peeled off the double cupcake papers, and took a bite without even bothering to break it apart and butter it."

"Mmmmmmm!" she said, taking another bite just to be sure. "No improvements are necessary. These are perfect, just the way they are."

The two sisters ate in silence for several minutes, and then

Hannah got up to pour more coffee for both of them. When she came back, she was frowning slightly.

"What is it?' Michelle asked, noticing Hannah's frown.

"I'm not sure. There's something niggling at the back of my mind."

"Niggling." Michelle looked pensive. "You use that word all the time. Is that like jiggling and nudging at the same time?"

"That's exactly what it is! This time it's a feeling that I should go to see Danielle again. But I don't understand why. We found out everything we needed to know from her . . . didn't we?"

"I thought so, but I don't know for sure. Were you thinking that Danielle might know something more about Phyllis's murder?"

"Maybe. Were you in school when Boyd Watson was hired, Michelle?"

"Yes, except he wasn't the head coach. And I don't think he was married to Danielle yet. They were just dating, and she used to come to all of his games. I know she wasn't from Lake Eden because nobody at school knew her. And I think she was younger than Coach Watson was."

"And was that when Phyllis was a cheerleader?"

"I don't think so, but I'm not positive. Maybe you should ask Danielle."

"I think I will." Hannah was about to break her muffin apart and butter it when she felt a strange sensation. She dropped it back on her plate and put her hand to her cheek.

"Do you have a toothache?" Michelle asked her.

"No. No, I don't. Everything's fine, Michelle." Hannah was smiling as she picked up her muffin again and began to butter it. Michelle would probably have her locked up in a padded room if she admitted she believed that their dad had been with her for an instant, just long enough to give her a kiss on the cheek!

\* \* \*

At precisely nine o'clock, Hannah walked down Main Street with a bag of Red Raspberry Muffins in her hand, headed for Danielle's dance studio. She'd remembered even more about her strange dream, or whatever it was, and today was eerily similar to the one her father had shown on the movie screen. As Hannah neared the dance studio, she wondered what would happen if she walked on past the glass door. Would her father somehow push her back and guide her to where he wanted her to go?

Even though she was curious about what would happen, Hannah stopped at Danielle's door when she noticed the Christmas wreath that decorated the inside of the glass. It hadn't been there when she'd visited Danielle yesterday, but it was there now. And it was exactly the same as the wreath that her father had shown her.

Hannah felt an eerie sense of being directed as she climbed up the stairs, entered the reception area, and took a chair to wait for Danielle's class to end. She shivered slightly as she realized that everything was exactly the same as the scenes that her father had shown her. The implication was too much for her rational mind to handle, but she was here and she needed to talk to Danielle. Perhaps it was a coincidence. Perhaps it was due to her curious mind working overtime in her sleep. Or perhaps all this was something her mind refused to process. All she knew for certain was that she should forget about everything else and concentrate on how to get the answers she needed from Danielle.

# Red Raspberry Muffins

Preheat oven to 375 degrees F., rack
in the middle position.

**Muffin Batter:**

¾ cup *(1 and ½ sticks, 6 ounces)* salted butter
1 cup white *(granulated)* sugar
2 beaten eggs *(just whip them up in a glass with a fork)*
2 teaspoons baking powder
½ teaspoon cinnamon
½ teaspoon salt
2 and ¼ cups all-purpose flour *(pack it down in the cup when you measure it)*
½ cup whole milk
½ cup seedless raspberry jam
1 cup fresh OR frozen raspberries

**Crumb Topping:**

½ cup white *(granulated)* sugar
½ teaspoon cinnamon
⅓ cup all-purpose flour *(pack it down in the cup when you measure it)*
¼ cup *(½ stick, 2 ounces)* salted butter, softened

Grease the bottoms only of a 12-cup muffin pan *(or line the cups with double cupcake papers—that's what I do at The Cookie Jar)*

Melt the butter in a bowl or measuring cup in the microwave. *(This takes me about a minute in the microwave on HIGH.)*

Set the melted butter on the kitchen counter to cool.

Measure out the sugar in a large bowl.

Mix in the beaten eggs.

Add the baking powder, cinnamon, and salt. Mix thoroughly.

Cup your hands around the bowl containing the melted butter. If it's cool enough so it won't cook the eggs, stir it into your mixing bowl with the rest of the ingredients.

Add <u>half</u> of the flour to your bowl and mix it in.

Add the whole milk to your bowl and mix that in.

Add the <u>other half</u> of the flour to your bowl and mix until everything is incorporated.

Mix in the half cup of seedless raspberry jam.

If you're using a mixer, take the bowl out of the mixer, scrape down the sides of the bowl, and give the contents a stir with a spoon by hand.

Add the raspberries and mix them in by hand.

Fill the prepared muffin cups three-quarters full and set them aside. If you have muffin batter left over, grease the bottom of a small tea-bread loaf pan and fill it with your remaining batter.

Make the crumb topping by mixing the sugar, cinnamon, and flour in a small bowl with a fork. Add the softened butter and cut it in until it's crumbly. *(You can also do this in a food processor with chilled butter that you've cut into chunks. Use the steel blade in an on-and-off motion until the resulting mixture resembles coarse gravel.)*

Fill the remaining space in the muffin cups with the crumb topping. If you had batter left over and used the tea-bread pan, reserve some topping to sprinkle over that.

Bake the muffins in a 375 F. degree oven for 25 to 30 minutes. *(The tea-bread should bake from 5 to 10 minutes longer than the muffins, but test it with a cake tester or long toothpick when your muffins are done. Insert the tester in the center of the loaf. If your tester comes out clean, your tea-bread is done.)*

When your muffins are baked, take them out of the oven and set the muffin pan on a wire rack or a cold stovetop burner to cool for at least 30 minutes. *(The muffins need to cool in the pan for easy removal.)* Then just tip them out of the cups, or lift them out by the edges of the cupcake papers. Serve with salted butter for those who want it, and enjoy.

These muffins are wonderful when they're slightly warm, but the raspberry flavor will intensify if you store them in a covered container overnight.

Yield: 12 delicious muffins with a little batter left over for several more muffins or a small loaf of tea-bread.

# Chapter Twelve

"Do you have a couple of minutes to talk?" Hannah asked, handing the muffins to Danielle.

"Normally, no. I usually have a private class right after the one that just ended, but it's cancelled for today." Danielle looked down at the bag. "Whatever is in here smells divine! What did you bring, Hannah?"

"Red Raspberry Muffins. Michelle made them for breakfast this morning."

"I love raspberries! Let's go in the kitchen. I'll put on the coffee and then we can talk."

Several minutes later, Hannah was seated at Danielle's kitchen table, holding a cup of French roast coffee. "You make good coffee, Danielle."

"It's the coffeemaker and the pods, but thank you. I'm getting better in the kitchen, but I'm afraid I'll never be a really good cook. And I'd never be able to make anything as luscious as these muffins!"

"I'll tell Michelle that you like them."

"Good!" Danielle took another bite and smiled. "Heavenly! Now I'm almost glad that Bonnie cancelled her class this morning."

"Bonnie?"

"Bonnie Surma. She's taking private lessons from me to

learn some dance routines that she can use with the Jordan High cheerleaders."

Hannah knew that she must have looked completely puzzled, because Danielle went on to explain.

"Bonnie used to coach the cheerleaders ten years or so ago. That was about the time that you were in high school, wasn't it, Hannah?"

"Yes, it was. But I don't remember that."

"Were you a cheerleader?"

"Heavens, no! Andrea was the one who went to the tryouts, not me. I never was very athletic."

"Then that's probably why you didn't know that Bonnie was coaching the cheerleaders."

"I remember that Bonnie was always at the school for one thing or another. She did a lot of things there, but I never knew that she was involved with the cheerleaders."

"Well, she was. Boyd told me that she had classes for the cheerleaders in the gym after school on Mondays and Wednesdays. Bonnie was a head cheerleader in college and she taught the girls all the cheers she remembered. It was part of her volunteer work. She's always been very active with the school, and in the community, too."

"I know," Hannah said with a smile. "Bonnie belongs to as many clubs as my mother does. And that's a whole lot!"

"To tell the truth, I don't know how Bonnie does it. She never backs down when they ask her to do something, and she's on the board of almost every charity. She's very active with the children's home, and she even volunteers at the senior center."

Hannah's mind was spinning so fast at this new information, she wasn't quite sure what to ask next. But that didn't matter because Danielle began to elaborate.

"I think that's one of the reasons why Bonnie cancelled her class today. She must be very upset about what happened to Phyllis Bates. Phyllis was one of Bonnie's cheerleaders, and

Bonnie worked very hard to turn Phyllis's life around. Bonnie and Gil never had children and Phyllis was like a daughter to Bonnie. She took Phyllis shopping for the right kind of clothes, gave her advice on everything from schoolwork to dating, and picked her up for church every Sunday."

"Bonnie told you all that?"

"Yes. Bonnie's a fascinating woman, a real do-gooder, and I mean that in a positive way. She said that Phyllis was heading down the wrong path when she was in junior high, flirting with the older boys and wearing clothes that were too provocative. Bonnie just knew that Phyllis would get into trouble if she didn't change her ways, so she took Phyllis under her wing."

"By encouraging Phyllis to try out for the junior varsity cheerleading squad?" Hannah guessed.

"That's right. Bonnie said she did her best to teach Phyllis how to be a lady and maintain good grades and good moral values. And Bonnie was proud that her effort had worked. Phyllis gained self-confidence and began to date a really nice senior boy."

"Herb Beeseman," Hannah said.

"Yes. Bonnie said that Herb was a very good influence on Phyllis. Phyllis had never dated such a nice boy before. And then Phyllis's mother moved to Minneapolis, and Bonnie lost touch with Phyllis."

Hannah was beginning to see the whole picture. "And Bonnie didn't know what had happened to Phyllis until Mayor Bascomb hired her and Phyllis moved back here to Lake Eden?"

"Exactly. It just about killed Bonnie when she heard that Phyllis was involved with Mayor Bascomb. She didn't want to believe it at first. Phyllis was Bonnie's big success story, and she was doing everything that Bonnie had taught her not to do."

"Bonnie must have been terribly disappointed in Phyllis."

"Oh, she was. And Bonnie didn't know what she could do about it. She was desolate, Hannah, and horribly depressed. I've known Bonnie for quite a while now, and I've never seen her so upset."

Hannah felt a chill run through her. "Did Bonnie try to talk to Phyllis, to set her back on the right track again?"

"Bonnie was going to do exactly that, but before she had the chance, the mayor broke it off with Phyllis and reassigned her to Herb's office. Bonnie was sure that Herb would have a good influence on Phyllis, now that he was married and all, and everyone in town knew that he was in love with his wife."

Hannah asked the question again, just to be sure. "So Bonnie never talked to Phyllis about her . . . behavior with the mayor?"

"I don't think so. She would have told me if she had. And then the mayor appointed Phyllis as Mrs. Claus, and that changed everything for Bonnie. I talked to her on the phone right after I heard about it, and Bonnie said she thought that playing Mrs. Claus might be a turning point for Phyllis. She said she hoped that playing a sweet, kind woman on stage would have a real positive effect. Bonnie said that we learn by doing and she hoped that Phyllis would learn from the experience."

"I . . . see," Hannah said, scenes from the rehearsal she'd seen flashing through her mind. Phyllis's inappropriate costume, the way she'd kissed Herb, and the fact that Bonnie had been sitting next to Tory Bascomb and watching the whole thing.

"Poor Bonnie!" Danielle said with a sigh. "My heart goes out to her, especially now that she's so sick."

That got Hannah's attention. "Bonnie's sick?" she asked.

"Yes. That's why she cancelled her private lesson today. Bonnie caught a terrible cold and she's running a fever. She's blaming it all on the fact that she has holes in her boots and she got her feet wet in the snow. Bonnie's very frugal and she patched the holes with duct tape, but she admitted that it didn't work very well and she was avoiding deep snow."

"I'm sorry Bonnie's sick," Hannah said, hoping to keep the conversation going.

"So am I. Bonnie told me that it's just a cold, but I think it might be something more serious than that."

"Why do you think that?"

"Because doctors don't usually prescribe antibiotics for a common cold, and Bonnie told me that Doc Knight put her on antibiotics. My guess is that Bonnie got run down worrying about Phyllis and her immune system couldn't fight off the bug she got. Now she's not only sick, she's also grieving for Phyllis because she never got the opportunity to talk to her and try to help her."

*Or did she get that opportunity?* Hannah's mind asked the question, but this wasn't the time to say it out loud. She'd consider it later, after she was alone and could think clearly.

"Thanks for telling me, Danielle," Hannah said, getting to her feet. "I'll drop in on Bonnie later to bring her some soup or something. Do you know if she's home?"

"I don't know for sure, but I think she probably is. She sounded awful when she called me this morning, and I really doubt that she left the house. When you see her, please give her my best and tell her I said to get well in a hurry."

Hannah was thoughtful as she walked down the long staircase. Her mind was churning with unanswered questions. When she got down to the outside door, she stopped and drew her murder book out of her purse. She turned to the suspects page and was about to write down Bonnie Surma's name when she remembered that she had done the very same thing before.

"Not now," Hannah said out loud. She wouldn't think about her father, and the dreams she'd had, and anything else right now. She jotted down Bonnie's name, thrust her murder book back in her purse, and pulled open the outside door.

Hannah thought about Bonnie and Phyllis all the way back to The Cookie Jar. When she got there, she was glad to see that the kitchen was deserted and everyone was out in front, waiting on customers. She needed time to think. And she needed time to devise a way to get Bonnie to tell her what she knew.

Even though Hannah didn't think that Bonnie had murdered her former protégé, she couldn't dismiss that possibility. The Ghost of Christmas Present had shown her an image of what she'd written in her murder book. She had been unable to read it, but she was fast becoming convinced that it had been Bonnie's name.

Hannah thought back to her first visitation, the one from the Ghost of Christmas Past. Bonnie had been sitting on a stool at the bar in the Corner Tavern when Hannah had walked in. When the stool next to Hannah had become vacant, Bonnie had moved to join her and Hannah had looked over to make sure that Bonnie hadn't left any of her belongings behind.

"Shoes!" Hannah said aloud, remembering that Bonnie had been wearing bright red tennis shoes and gray and orange argyle socks. The socks were Gil's. Hannah was sure of it. Gil Surma had always been fond of argyle socks, and he wore them to school every day. Red shoes with a pair of her husband's gray and orange socks was an odd combination for Bonnie. She was someone who normally dressed conservatively. Bonnie's tennis shoes hadn't looked wet, and there had been no puddles of moisture in the sawdust on the floor. Had Bonnie worn her damaged boots inside the Corner Tavern and changed to her tennis shoes when she'd hung up her coat? And had the only dry socks in her car been a pair of Gil's?

Hannah jotted a note. Where were Bonnie's boots? Were

they still on the boot rack at the Corner Tavern? There was only one way to find out, and Hannah was just getting up from her stool at the workstation when Michelle came into the kitchen.

"Hi, Hannah. I didn't hear you come in. Did Danielle like the muffins?"

"She loved them. She was going to save one for Benton, but I'm not placing any bets that he'll actually get it."

Michelle laughed. "Did you find out what you needed to know?"

"I'm not sure. About the only thing I know for sure is that Bonnie Surma is sick. Danielle told me that. I thought it might be nice to take her something to cheer her up. What do we have that might be good for someone who's got a terrible cold?"

"Janelle's Chicken Soup," Michelle answered immediately. "I made a pot the last time I was here at The Cookie Jar, and I stuck some in the freezer. I'll get it out and thaw it for you."

"Perfect. Thanks, Michelle."

"Take some Butterscotch Crunch Fudge, too. Lisa and I made it while you were at Danielle's dance studio. It's in the cooler and it should be ready to cut by now. It's delicious, and Bonne's bound to like that. I'd give you one of the Cashew Candy Rolls we made for the opening night of the play, but they're not hard enough to cut yet."

"That's okay. I'm sure Bonnie will love the soup and the Butterscotch Crunch Candy."

"The recipe for the candy is on the counter. Take it with you if Bonnie wants to know the ingredients. I'll pack everything up for you right now."

"Okay. I'm running out to the Corner Tavern first to check something out. Do you want me to bring some food back for your lunch?"

"Thanks, but no. Lonnie's coming to pick me up and we're going down to Hal and Rose's Café for lunch. I was about to ask you if you wanted to come along."

"I haven't had one of Rose's roast beef sandwiches in ages. How long do you plan to be there?"

"An hour if that's okay with you. That's how long Lonnie has for lunch. And if Mike can get away to join us, it might be a little longer than that."

"An hour's fine with me, and so is longer. Take all the time you want, Michelle. It's not like I'm paying you for working here, or anything. I may drop by on my way back from Bonnie's house if you're still there. I'll give you a call on your cell when I leave Bonnie's."

"Okay, Hannah. Don't forget to stay in touch with Mike. I know he asked you to."

"I won't. And don't worry, Michelle. I'm just going out to the Corner Tavern and over to Bonnie's house. I'll be perfectly fine."

# Butterscotch Crunch Candy

You do NOT need a candy thermometer to make this candy.

half of a 15-ounce bag of salted stick pretzels *(the thin stick kind—I used Snyder's)*
14-ounce can of sweetened condensed milk *(I used Eagle Brand—do NOT use evaporated milk)*
¼ teaspoon salt
2 cups *(12 ounces)* butterscotch chips *(I use Nestle)*

**Hannah's 1ˢᵗ Note: you can make this candy in a heavy saucepan on the stove over MEDIUM heat or in a large, microwave-safe bowl in the microwave on HIGH. Either will work just fine.**

Put the pretzels into a bowl and break them into pieces. You don't have to be exact, but try to make sure each pretzel is broken into at least 4 pieces.

**Hannah's 2ⁿᵈ Note: When Lisa and I make this candy at The Cookie Jar, we put the pretzels in a large, sealable, plastic bag and crush them up with a rolling pin until there are no large pieces left.**

Prepare an 8-inch square brownie pan by lining it with a piece of heavy-duty foil that is large enough to stick up at least two inches above the sides of your pan. You will use these "ears" of foil to lift out your candy after it has cooled and hardened.

Spray the inside of the foil with Pam or another non-stick cooking spray.

Open the can of sweetened, condensed milk and pour it into another microwave-safe bowl.

Sprinkle the salt on top of the sweetened condensed milk.

Place the 2 cups of butterscotch chips on the top.

Stir everything up with a heat-resistant rubber spatula.

Set aside your spatula and microwave the contents of the bowl on HIGH for 2 minutes.

Let the bowl and its contents sit inside the microwave for 1 minute to cool.

Stir the contents of the bowl with your heat-resistant spatula to see if the chips are melted. If you can stir the mixture smooth, you're ready to complete your candy. If you can't stir the mixture smooth, microwave it on HIGH in 20-second increments followed by a 1-minute standing time until you can stir it smooth.

Quickly add your broken pieces of pretzels to the mixture in your bowl and stir them in.

Spread your Butterscotch Crunch Candy out in your prepared pan. Smooth it out on top with your heat-resistant spatula.

**Hannah's 3<sup>rd</sup> Note: This is going to look lumpy. That's because of the pretzels.**

Place the pan in the refrigerator, uncovered, for at least 2 hours.

Take the pan from the refrigerator, lift out the foil with the candy inside, and peel off the foil.

Cut your Butterscotch Crunch Candy into fudge-sized pieces.

Store the pieces in a covered container in the refrigerator.

Take the container out approximately 20 minutes before you want to serve your Butterscotch Crunch Candy.

Yield: 2 to 3 dozen pieces of delicious candy that both adults and children will love. The number of pieces depends, of course, on how large you cut them.

# Cashew Candy Rolls

**Hannah's 1ˢᵗ Note:** You do NOT need a candy thermometer to make this candy.

> 14-ounce can of sweetened condensed milk *(NOT evaporated milk)*
> 3 cups white baking chips *(18 ounces—see Hannah's 2ⁿᵈ Note)*
> 1 teaspoon salted butter
> 1 teaspoon vanilla extract
> ¼ teaspoon salt
> 1 and ½ cups roughly chopped salted cashews *(measure AFTER chopping)*

**Hannah's 2ⁿᵈ Note:** If you use Ghirardelli chips, that's one 11-ounce bag and a little <u>more</u> than half of another. If you use Nestle Chips, that's one 12-ounce bag and half of another.

If you haven't already done so, chop the salted cashews into pieces about the size of coarse gravel. Then measure out one and a half cups. *(Cashews are easy to chop if you have a food processor and use the steel blade in an on-and-off motion, but a knife and a chopping board will work just fine.)*

Measure out the 3 cups of white chips. *(See Hannah's 2ⁿᵈ Note.)*

Open the can of sweetened condensed milk and pour it into the bottom of a saucepan <u>or</u> a microwave-safe bowl that is large enough to also contain the white chips. Use a saucepan if you intend to melt this mixture on the stovetop. Use a microwave-safe bowl if you intend to melt the mixture in the microwave.

If you decided to use the stovetop, melt the mixture on LOW, stirring constantly, until the chips no longer maintain their shape.

If you decided to use the microwave, melt the mixture on HIGH. *(This will take approximately 80 seconds. Chips do retain their shape in the microwave, even after being melted, so let the bowl sit inside the microwave for approximately 1 minute before you try to stir the mixture smooth. If you cannot stir the mixture smooth, heat it on HIGH again in 20-second increments followed by a standing time of 1 minute, until the mixture can be stirred smooth.)*

When your mixture has melted smoothly, give it a final stir and then set it on top of a cold stovetop burner or on a thick towel on the kitchen counter to cool.

Let the mixture cool for 1 minute, and then mix in the butter, vanilla extract, and salt. *(Don't add the chopped cashews yet—they're for later when you make the candy rolls.)*

**Hannah's 3rd Note:** The week before the last Christmas, Lisa and I worked late making candy at The Cookie Jar. I was so tired that after I'd melted the chip mixture and let it cool on the counter for a minute, I dumped in the chopped cashews by mistake. I must have groaned out loud, because Lisa came over to look. She told me that was okay, got out a pan, lined it with foil, sprayed the foil with Pam, and put my mistake into the pan. It turned out to be all right after all. We kept it in the walk-in cooler overnight and the next morning we could cut it into pieces like fudge!

Put the saucepan or bowl in the refrigerator and chill the candy for 30 to 40 minutes.

Take the mixture out of the refrigerator and divide the candy in half. Place each half on a two-foot-long *(24 inches)* piece of wax paper.

Shape each half of the mixture into a roll with your fingers that's approximately a foot and a half long *(18 inches)* and about 1 and ½ inches thick.

Sprinkle the chopped cashews over the pieces of wax paper.

Roll the candy logs in the chopped cashews, coating them as evenly as you can. Press the cashews in slightly so that they'll stick to the outside of the rolls.

Wrap the finished logs in clean wax paper, twist the ends closed, and place them in the refrigerator for at least 2 hours to harden.

Hannah's 4<sup>th</sup> Note: You can store these candy rolls in the refrigerator for longer, if you don't want to serve them that day. Just take them out when you need them.

Cut your Cashew Candy Rolls into half-inch slices with a sharp knife. If the knife gets sticky, wash off the blade with cold running water, dry it off on a clean dishtowel, and resume cutting your candy.

Yield: Makes about 48 slices of delicious candy.

Hannah stood there in the cloakroom of the Corner Tavern, staring at the pair of light-brown boots at the end of the rack. They were Bonnie's boots. She recognized them. There were uneven patches of darker-colored brown on both of the boots from the sides of the soles all the way up to the ankles. There was no duct tape in sight, but it had probably lost its adhesive grip on the leather when the leather had gotten wet. But was the leather wet? Or was it simply discolored? Hannah had to know for certain.

She moved close enough to the boots to touch the area that looked wet. It was wet, very wet, so soaked that it had not yet dried out. The night that she'd seen Bonnie at the bar, the same night that Phyllis had been murdered, Bonnie had worn her soaked boots inside the Corner Tavern and then she'd changed to the only dry footwear she'd had in her car, her red tennis shoes and a pair of Gil's argyle socks. But the pair of wet boots didn't necessarily mean that Bonnie had anything to do with Phyllis's murder. Bonnie might have walked through some deep snow before she got to the Corner Tavern, realized that her boots were wet when she arrived, and carried her tennis shoes inside to put them on in the cloakroom.

A warning bell in Hannah's mind clanged insistently. Mike needed to know about Bonnie's boots. She really should take a photo and send it to Mike. She'd promised to keep him informed of anything she'd found that could relate to the murder. And even though she didn't believe that Bonnie had anything to do with it, she had an obligation to share this information with Mike.

Hannah pulled out her phone, took a photo of the boots, and tried to remember what her niece Tracey had taught her about attaching a photo to a text message. She titled the photo Bonnie's Boots and hit the proper series of buttons to send the photo to Mike.

"Yes!" Hannah said out loud when the attachment worked. And then she frowned. She'd sent the photo, but she hadn't typed a text message explaining anything about it. Hannah knew that she should send another text to explain, but it was getting late and she still had to stop to take the soup and candy to Bonnie before she would be free to join Michelle and Lonnie for lunch. She could always text Mike later.

For a long moment, Hannah debated whether she should take the boots with her and give them to Bonnie. But Bonnie had left them here and she probably didn't want them back. Bonnie's fix with duct tape had probably worked just fine on shoveled sidewalks and plowed streets, but it was quite obvious that deep snow had rendered the repair useless.

Had Bonnie killed Phyllis? She'd had the opportunity and her boots were wet, but that proved nothing conclusive. There could be a perfectly reasonable explanation for the wet boots. Bonnie was a pillar of the community, a deeply religious person who was active in her church, and a woman who worked tirelessly for the good of the Lake Eden community. Hannah was almost positive that there was a reasonable explanation for Bonnie's wet boots. She would ask when she took Bonnie the soup and the candy.

Hannah opened the front porch door and stepped inside. It was common practice for Lake Edenites to leave their front porches unlocked during the winter so that visitors could step in to get out of the wind or the snow. Hannah walked to the inside door and knocked, but there was no answer. She listened for a moment, but all she heard from inside was the sound of a television game show with buzzers and bells, and the excited voices of the contestants. If Bonnie had fallen asleep watching television, Hannah didn't want to wake her. Sick people needed their rest. But what if Bonnie hadn't fallen asleep? What if she'd taken a turn for the worse and she was too ill to get up to answer Hannah's knock at the door?

Tentatively, Hannah tried the doorknob. It turned and she pushed it open an inch or two. The enthusiastic utterances of the daytime game show host were louder, but she also heard a rhythmic creaking noise that she could not identify.

Hannah glanced at the coatrack as she hung up her winter things in the front hallway. Bonnie's coat was hanging there, along with a warm scarf, and a knit hat with earflaps and a tassel on the top. It was four degrees below zero today. Hannah had glanced at the indoor-outdoor thermometer that hung outside the kitchen window at The Cookie Jar before she'd left. That was much too cold to go anywhere without a coat, or a scarf, or a hat. Bonnie was home.

Uncertain but determined, Hannah opened the door all the way and stepped inside. She stood there for a moment, not sure what to do next, and then she hung her parka on the coatrack and headed toward the sound of the television set. She called out once, but Bonnie didn't answer. She'd leave the soup and the candy if she found Bonnie asleep, and call Gil at the school to tell him they were there.

The television was in the den. She remembered that from the last time she'd been invited to one of Bonnie's home meetings. Hannah hurried down the hallway, stepped into the den, and found Bonnie there. Bonnie was not asleep. She was sitting in a rocking chair with an afghan around her shoulders, and she was rocking back and forth.

It didn't take more than a moment to realize that the creaking noise had come from the rocking chair. Bonnie's eyes were closed, and Hannah approached quietly. "Bonnie?" she said softly. "It's Hannah. I brought you some soup because Danielle said you were sick."

Bonnie's eyes opened. They appeared huge and unfocused. "Hannah?" Bonnie asked.

"Yes. It's me, Bonnie. Would you like me to heat you some soup? Michelle made it."

Bonnie's expression changed to one of puzzlement. "Michelle?" she asked.

It was clear that Bonnie was not in control of her faculties, and Hannah proceeded carefully. "Michelle is my youngest sister. It's Hannah, Hannah Swensen. You recognize me, don't you, Bonnie?"

"Oh, Hannah. Of course I recognize you. But what are you doing here? It's a school day. Why aren't you in class?"

Something was wrong, very wrong, and Hannah knew it. Bonnie was either drugged or still half asleep because the normally cognizant woman that Hannah admired was slipping in and out of reality. Perhaps it would be best to stick with everyday questions at first.

"Are you hungry?" Hannah asked.

"I . . . I don't know. I could be, I think."

"All right then. I'll go heat the chicken soup that I brought." Hannah stopped and evaluated Bonnie's blank expression. "Is that all right, Bonnie?"

"Oh, yes. It's fine. Gil should be home and he'll be hungry. He always comes home for lunch on school days." Bonnie stopped and took a deep breath. "This is a school day, isn't it?"

"Yes, it is. I'll be right back, Bonnie."

"Oh, good. I like you, Hannah, but don't interfere. Never interfere in anything that doesn't concern you. My mother told me that, and it was some of the best advice I ever got. I just wish I'd followed it sooner."

Bonnie smiled once, and then her expression faded again

to a perfectly blank stare. It reminded Hannah of teddy bears in an arcade booth, waiting to go home with their lucky winners. "Are you sure you're okay alone?"

"I'm always alone. Everyone is. We're born alone and we die alone. It's a fact of life."

Hannah shivered. Bonnie's voice was devoid of inflection, almost like the recorded voice of the time of day on the telephone. "I suppose you're right, Bonnie," she said, attempting to smile as she went off to the kitchen to heat the soup.

It only took two minutes to heat the soup in the microwave. Hannah found a soup bowl in the cupboard and returned to the den. "Here you are, Bonnie," she said, placing the bowl and spoon on the table next to Bonnie. "This should make you feel better."

"Nothing will make me feel better until I go," Bonnie said, not even reaching out for the soup. "She was my daughter, you know."

Hannah's mind took a huge leap, and suddenly she thought she knew exactly what Bonnie meant. "Phyllis," she said, recalling Danielle's comment that Bonnie had regarded Phyllis as her daughter.

"Yes. She went bad, Hannah . . . horribly bad. She forgot my lessons, and she wouldn't listen when I tried to correct her. She said she wasn't in school, and she didn't have to listen to me. And then she pushed me away!"

Hannah felt a cold chill run through her as Bonnie's eyes began to glitter. Her mind was teeming with questions, but she didn't want to ask them for fear it would cut off the flow of Bonnie's words.

"I taught her what to do, how to act like a lady, but she reverted to type. She tempted men and used them for her own gain. Mayor Bascomb was weak. He couldn't help himself when she threw herself at him. And she was going to do it again. I saw that lunch bag, and I knew."

Bonnie rocked a little faster and the speed of her speech increased along with the creaking. "Herb would have fallen under her spell. I knew that and I had to stop her. Men are weak. Except for Gil. Gil tried to save me. And he did . . . for years and years. Gil is my savior. Gil is my rock. I put my trust in him and he will not fail me."

Hannah was silent. She wasn't sure what to say, but she knew she had to say something. She reached into her pocket, clicked the voice record button on her smartphone and said, "I found your boots, Bonnie. And now I know that you killed Phyllis."

Bonnie looked up at her again with those big, unfocused eyes. "But you see, I had to. She wouldn't listen to me when I tried to correct her, to set her on the right path again. She laughed at me. I kept trying. I reminded her of what it meant to be a lady and she told me to shut up, but I persevered. She could not get away from me, from the truth. She tried, but I followed her."

"Down into the ditch," Hannah said, knowing she was right.

"Yes. Yes, down in the ditch. And she slipped and fell."

The rocker slowed. And then it stopped. Bonnie's eyes attempted to focus on Hannah. "You won't tell Gil, will you? He sees the good in everyone. Do you have any idea how hard it is to live with someone who sees the good in everyone?"

Again, Hannah wasn't sure how to answer so she changed the subject, bringing it back to the murder. "I know why you killed Phyllis. But tell me how you did it. I want to understand."

"She did not suffer. I made sure of that. I found a branch. And I stood above her and I stamped her out. She was evil and it was my duty. You must stamp out evil wherever you find it. The angel helped me do it. The angel guided my arms. You know the angel, don't you, Hannah?"

Hannah took a wild leap into the morass of a twisted mind. "The angel of death?" she asked.

"Yes! I knew you'd understand. You're a good person,

Hannah, and I know that you'll be rewarded in the afterlife. The angel will help me with you, too. I'm sorry, Hannah, but I can't let you live. I can't let you tell Gil what I've done. He'd never understand!"

"Maybe he would," Hannah said quickly, hoping to keep Bonnie talking.

"I'd like to believe that, but I know it isn't so. You must go first and then me. We'll take the journey together, one right after the other."

Hannah thought fast. "I'll just heat some soup for Gil first. I'll do it right now and come back."

"No," Bonnie said, and her tone was as flat as the flagstone on the front of the fireplace in Bonnie's den. "You must stay right here so that I can release you from this earthly plane. Gil will be home soon, and the deed must be done before he comes home."

As Hannah watched in horror, Bonnie drew a gun from beneath her afghan and pointed it directly at Hannah. "It won't hurt, Hannah. I'd never hurt you. You're my friend, and we can be together in the hereafter."

Hannah knew she had to say something to stop Bonnie from using the gun. Her breakdown could be the result of guilt over the murder she'd committed, or she could be out of her mind from the fever that accompanied her cold. Hannah didn't really care what had caused Bonnie's mind to snap. She just knew that she had to get out of the den. And fast!

"Wait just a moment, Bonnie," Hannah said, as calmly as she could. "Give me a little time to heat more soup. It's comfort food, and Gil will need something to comfort himself when he sees both us here."

Bonnie's expression changed. She looked a bit thoughtful. "Do you really think so?"

"I do. It will be a shock, Bonnie. And everyone knows that you should give something warm, something comforting to people who are in shock."

"I've heard that. And you're right, Hannah." Bonnie nodded, but then her eyes narrowed. "But will you come back here so that I can release you?"

Hannah heard the sound of the front door opening, and she answered quickly so that it would mask the sound of the door. "Oh, yes. I'll be back. You're right, Bonnie. It'll only take a minute or two and then I'll be back with you."

And then Gil was standing in the doorway of the den, an expression of disbelief on his face as he stared at his wife with the gun in her hand. "Bonnie?" he said in the calm, friendly voice that Hannah assumed he used with his troubled students. "What are you doing, darling?"

"Don't you see?" Bonnie responded, turning toward him. "I have to release her, Gil. She knows I killed Phyllis. And then we can go, too. Together. Isn't that right, darling?"

"Yes, of course," Gil said. "Just let me think for a moment, dear." And then, when Bonnie's arm lowered slightly, Gil rushed toward her and grabbed the gun before Bonnie could raise it again. They tussled for a moment, as Hannah stood there, frozen. The struggle seemed to last forever, and Hannah's feet seemed glued to the spot. And then Gil forced Bonnie's arm up so that the barrel of the gun was pointing toward the ceiling.

"Run, Hannah!" he shouted at her. "Run for help!"

Gil's words served to release her and Hannah didn't waste any time. She ran out of the den and into the hallway, headlong toward the front door. She didn't stop to grab her coat, she just fled as fast as she could. She pulled the heavy inner door open, expecting to run to her truck, but she found herself engulfed in the arms of someone wearing a sheriff's department uniform. It was Mike and she'd never been so glad to see anyone in her whole life!

"Hannah!" Mike exclaimed. "Where's Bonnie?"

"The den!" Hannah managed to gasp out.

"Michelle's in the cruiser. Take her and get out of here. Now!"

"Bonnie's got a gun. Gil grabbed her arm, and . . ."

The sound of a gunshot drowned out any further explanation Hannah could give him. Mike drew his gun, motioned to Lonnie, who was standing behind him, and both men raced for the den.

Hannah knew she should go, but she couldn't, not without finding out what had happened. She drew a deep, shaking breath and turned around to follow Mike and Lonnie to the den. She arrived at the doorway just in time to see the gun on the floor next to the rocker, and Gil cradling his wife's body in his arms.

"I shot her," he said to Mike and Lonnie. "She was going to kill Hannah. You have to arrest me. I killed my darling wife."

# Chapter Fourteen

Hannah stared out of the passenger window at scenery she didn't see. The image of Gil holding Bonnie's body in his arms was too fresh in her mind.

"Are you all right, Hannah?" Michelle asked, as she pulled the cookie truck into Hannah's parking space at the condo.

"I don't know," Hannah answered truthfully. "It's like . . . too much for my mind to process. I can't take it all in. It's not right, Michelle. It never should have happened this way. Nothing's right!"

"Mike said that you were in shock and you have to rest. You haven't gotten a good night's sleep since this whole thing started. You're overloaded, overtired, and completely stressed. You need to stretch out on your bed and nap with Moishe until Mike gets here."

"But I should call . . ."

"No one," Michelle interrupted her. "You should call no one. You're in no shape to talk right now. You've always taken care of me, and now it's my turn to take care of you."

"I . . . I'm not sure . . ." Hannah's voice trailed off. Michelle was right. She was so terribly, terribly tired.

"Come on, Hannah," Michelle walked around the back of the cookie truck and pulled open Hannah's door. "Let's go upstairs and see Moishe. That'll make you feel better."

"Not if I have to catch him," Hannah said, eliciting a laugh from Michelle.

"I'll catch him," Michelle promised, leading the way up the covered outside staircase. "And I'll unlock the door, too. I want you to go in, walk straight to the bedroom, and take a nap. If you do, I guarantee you'll feel better by the time Mike comes to take your statement."

"Yes," Hannah said, and then she gave her sister a hug. "Thank you, Michelle."

She could see him at the foot of her bed. Hannah stared at him for a moment and then she sat up. "Dad?"

"Yes, Honey-bear. It's me. I'm back and I'm here to be the Ghost of Christmas Future."

"There is no future for Bonnie."

"I know. That's unfortunate. But there is a future for you, Hannah. It's a happy future, and I need to show it to you. And I need to show you something from Lisa's future, too. Don't tell her. It's going to be a Christmas surprise."

As Hannah watched, the movie screen materialized and images began to appear. The first image was of Lisa's house as a sporty red car drove up to park in the driveway. It was an older model but beautifully restored with fresh paint and new tires. As she watched, Herb placed a huge red and green bow on top of the car, and Hannah knew that it must be a Christmas present. Then Herb walked to the front door of the house and went inside.

A moment later, Lisa followed Herb outside. She saw the car and blinked and stared, as if she couldn't believe her eyes. And then, when Herb handed Lisa the keys, Lisa threw her arms around him and kissed him.

The scene changed. The whole family was sitting around a beautifully decorated Christmas tree in her mother's living room. They were exchanging presents on Christmas Day, and Delores handed Hannah a long, flat package in gold paper with little candy canes printed all over it. There was a tag on the front that read, *From Dad and Uncle Ed.* Hannah took off the ribbon and bow very carefully and handed them to her mother. Delores saved things like that. Then she took off the paper and stared down at the beautifully restored and refinished board inside. Someone had carved two names into the wood in childish block letters. One name was Ed and the other was Lars.

"Your uncle Ed was lucky," her father's voice said. "He only had to carve two letters. I had to carve four on the ladder we used to get up into our treehouse. I'm glad you kept our ladder, Honey-bear. And I'm glad your mother remembered what I told her about it."

Hannah's mouth dropped open. So *that* was why Delores had wanted the old ladder that had almost caused Lisa to tumble to the floor. She'd removed the board where Hannah's Uncle Ed and father had carved their names as boys and restored it as a plaque for Hannah.

The screen went dark and Hannah sighed. She was sorry the glimpse into the future was over. But her father was still here and she concentrated on the form at the foot of her bed. It was beginning to undulate and fade, and she knew that he was about to leave her.

"Dad!" she called out to him. "Will you come back, Dad?"

"I'm always here, Honey-bear. I always will be. And I promise that I'll always give you a kiss on Christmas morning, just the way I used to do when I woke you up to tell you that Santa had come."

Hannah opened her mouth to ask another question, but the amorphous form that had been her father changed into wisps of sparkling gold that floated up to the ceiling and then beyond.

"He's gone," she said to Moishe. "Dad's gone, but he promised he'd kiss me on Christmas morning."

Moishe began to purr and then he licked her hand. And Hannah gave him a scratch behind his ears, something he loved, and that made him purr even louder.

"Hannah?" a voice called her out of her half-awake state. "Mike's here. I'll give him some coffee and a couple of the Cherry Shortbread Bar Cookies I made. How do you feel?"

Michelle appeared in the doorway and Hannah smiled at her. "I feel good. You and Mike were right. Sleep was exactly what I needed."

# Cherry Shortbread Bar Cookies

Preheat oven to 350 degrees F., rack in the middle position

**The Crust and Topping Mixture:**

> 3 cups all-purpose flour *(pack it down in the cup when you measure it)*
> ¾ cup powdered *(confectioner's)* sugar *(don't sift unless it's got big lumps)*
> ½ teaspoon salt
> ½ teaspoon cinnamon
> ¼ teaspoon grated nutmeg *(freshly grated is best)*
> 1 and ½ cups slightly softened butter *(3 sticks, 12 ounces, ¾ pound)*

**The Filling:**

> 1 can *(21 ounces)* cherry pie filling *(I used Comstock)*

FIRST STEP: Use a fork to mix flour, powdered sugar, salt, cinnamon, and nutmeg together in a bowl.

Mix in the softened butter until the mixture forms little nuggets about the size of coarse gravel.

*(You can also do this in a food processor using cold butter cut into chunks, layered with the dry ingredients. Process with the steel blade in an on-and-off motion until it resembles coarse gravel.)*

Spray a 9-inch by 13-inch pan *(That's a standard-sized rectangular cake pan)* with Pam or another nonstick cooking spray.

Spread approximately HALF of the crust and topping mixture *(approx. 2 and ½ cups)* into the pan you prepared.

Bake at 350 degrees F. for 15 minutes. Remove the pan from the oven, but DON'T TURN OFF THE OVEN! You'll be using it again in just a few minutes and you won't have time to preheat it again.

Let the crust cool for 5 minutes.

SECOND STEP: Open the can of cherry pie filling and pour it out into a bowl. Use a knife to cut the cherries into smaller pieces.

Spread the cherry pie filling over the top of the crust you just baked.

Sprinkle the cherry pie filling with the other half of the crust and topping mixture.

Gently press the topping down with a wide, metal spatula.

Bake the bar cookies for another 30 to 35 minutes, or until the top is golden. Remove the pan from the oven, turn off the oven, and place the pan on a cold stovetop burner or a wire rack.

Cool the Cherry Shortbread Bar Cookies thoroughly.

When the pan is cool to the touch, cut the bar cookies into brownie-sized bars while they're right there in the pan.

If you want to be a little fancy, sprinkle your bar cookies with a little extra powdered sugar.

Cover the pan with foil and refrigerate your cut bar cookies until you're ready to serve them. Then use a small spatula to remove them and put them on a pretty platter.

You can also serve these bar cookies as a dessert if you cut them into larger pieces and warm them in dessert dishes in the microwave.

As a finishing touch, place a dollop of sweetened, whipped cream, OR a scoop of vanilla ice cream on top.

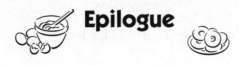

# Epilogue

"**H**annah?" Ross put down his empty coffee cup.
"Yes, Ross."

"I have a couple of questions for you."

"Okay." Hannah mentally prepared herself for some tough questions like *Do you really believe that you saw your father?* or *Don't you think that your subconscious was staging all these dreams because of the play the Lake Eden Players were doing, and your mind was working to form inferences from all the information you'd received during the day?* "What would you like to know?" she asked him.

"I know that Lisa has a red car. Did Herb restore it and give it to her last Christmas?"

"Yes, he did. He told us that he worked late every night out at Cyril Murphy's garage to get it ready by Christmas."

"And that's why Lisa thought he was going out on her?"

"Yes. And the reason Mike cleared Herb was because Cyril was helping Herb on the night that Phyllis was murdered. But Mike couldn't tell me that because Herb wanted it to be a secret so that Lisa would have a Christmas surprise."

Ross smiled. "Was she surprised?"

"And how!" Hannah used one of her favorite Minnesota expressions. "Lisa nearly had a cow when she saw that gorgeous car!"

"How about your present, the one your mother gave you?"

"It was a board from Dad's old ladder with Dad and Uncle Ed's names on it."

"And you pretended to be surprised?"

Hannah smiled. "I did."

"Is that the same plaque that you have hanging in your hallway?"

"It is. I love that plaque. There's no way you can know your parents as children, and sometimes it's nice to be reminded that they were really kids, just like you."

"A lot happened in Lake Eden last Christmas," Ross said, and he looked thoughtful. "Maybe you'd better not make those chocolate caramels again . . . just in case, I mean."

Hannah laughed. "We haven't made them since, but it's silly to think they're bad luck, isn't it?"

"Rationally, yes. Of course it is. And of course I want you to make them. I missed out last year. But you've got to promise me one thing."

"What's that?"

"You've got to promise that you won't find another body right before Christmas this year."

"But how can I promise something like that? Mike says I have slaydar. I don't go looking for murder victims, but I seem to find them more often than other people do."

"That's true." Ross gave a little sigh. "I know it's silly, Hannah. And I know it could happen whether you promise, or not. But . . . will you promise anyway?"

Hannah smiled at him. "If it'll make you feel better, I promise," she said.

# Christmas Caramel Murder Recipe Index

# CHRISTMAS
# CAKE
# MURDER

*This book is dedicated to my dear friend, Trudi Nash. Thank you so much for the Bundt cake concept! I had so much fun with it.*

# Acknowledgments

Big hugs to my family and my neighbors for their willingness to test recipes for me. TWO fresh-baked Raspberry Danish for everyone!

Thank you to Mel & Kurt, Lyn & Bill, Gina, Jessie & the boys, Dee Appleton, Jay, Richard Jordan, Laura Levine, the real Nancy and Heiti, Dan, Mark & Mandy at Faux Library, Daryl and her staff at Groves Accountancy, Gene and Ron at SDSA, and everyone at Homestreet Bank.

Grateful hugs to Richard Jordan for being a great cruise buddy and for helping me with book tours.

Hello to my Minnesota friends: Lois & Neal, Bev & Jim, Lois & Jack, Val, Ruthann, Lowell, Dorothy & Sister Sue, and Mary & Jim.

Kudos to my patient and brilliant editor, John Scognamiglio.

Thank you to all the wonderful folks at Kensington Publishing who keep Hannah sleuthing and baking up a storm.

Thanks to Meg Ruley and the staff at the Jane Rotrosen Agency for their constant support and their wise and knowledgeable advice.

Thanks to Hiro Kimura, my incredible cover artist, for his delicious cover art.

Thank you to talented Lou Malcangi at Kensington for designing Hannah's beautiful book covers.

Thanks to John at *Placed4Success.com* for Hannah's movie and TV placements, the cruise ship signings he organizes for me, his presence on Hannah's social media platform, the countless hours he spends helping me, and for always being there to help.

Thanks to Rudy for managing my website at **www.JoanneFluke.com** and for supporting Hannah's social media. And thanks to Annie for her help with social media and related projects.

Big hugs for Kathy Allen for the final testing of the recipes. And thanks to Kathy's friends and family for taste testing.

A big hug to JQ for helping Hannah and me for so many years.

Hugs to Beth for her wonderful embroidery work at Up In Stitches.

Thank you to food stylist, media guide, and friend, Lois Brown. I wouldn't dream of having a book launch party without you!

Hugs to the Double D's and everyone on Team Swensen who help to keep Hannah's Facebook presence alive and well.

Thank you to Dr. Rahhal, Dr. & Cathy Line, Dr. Josephson, Dr. Koslowski, and Drs. Ashley and Lee for answering my book-related medical and dental questions.

Grateful thanks to all of the Hannah fans who share their family recipes, post on my Facebook page, **Joanne Fluke Author**, and read Hannah mysteries.

Try one of the Ultimate Bundt Cakes. They're easy and yummy!

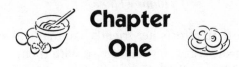

# Chapter One

## Hannah Comes Home From College

Hannah Swensen took her mother's potholders off the hook by the stove and removed a sheet of cookies from the oven. Since her mother only had a single oven, Hannah set the cookie sheet on a cold stovetop burner to let the cookies cool for a minute or two. Then she used a metal spatula to take them off the cookie sheet and move them to the wire rack she'd set on the counter.

The familiar scent of the cookies cooling brought tears to Hannah's eyes. These had been her father's favorite cookies. She brushed the tears that threatened to fall away with the back of her hand and sighed. Lars Swensen's funeral had taken place three weeks ago, and Hannah was worried about her mother. Delores was upstairs in the bedroom she'd shared with her husband and she was napping again. She'd taken a lengthy nap every day since the funeral and hadn't come downstairs until Hannah had called her for dinner. Even though Hannah had made some of her mother's favorite foods and Delores had complimented her on her wonderfully tasty meals, she hadn't eaten more than a few small bites. And when Hannah had dashed upstairs to straighten the bed after her mother's lengthy afternoon naps, she'd found her pillow wet with tears. Delores was crying in private, unable or unwilling to share her feelings with anyone.

She had cut off all efforts her friends had made to see her by claiming that she was too tired to visit with them.

Of course Hannah had discussed this worrisome situation with her sisters, and all three of them had attempted to pull their mother out of her self-imposed isolation. Hannah's youngest sister, Michelle, was still in high school, and she had tried to engage their mother's help in learning her lines for the lead she'd landed in the junior play. Michelle had even talked about cheerleading tryouts and how she hoped she'd get a spot on the cheerleading team, but Delores just didn't seem interested in her youngest daughter's high school life.

Andrea, Hannah's middle sister, was married to Bill Todd, a deputy sheriff with the Winnetka County Sheriff's Department. They had purchased a house only blocks from Delores, and Andrea was expecting her first baby. She had attempted to engage their mother's interest by inviting Delores to help her decorate the baby's room, an invitation that normally would have delighted their mother. But instead of jumping at the opportunity to help by doing something she loved, Delores had claimed that she was simply too exhausted to help Andrea.

All three Swensen sisters had tried every way that they could think of to get their mother into some activity that would get her involved in small-town life again, but everything they'd tried had failed.

Hannah looked down at the cookies she'd baked. They were almost cool enough to eat and for one brief moment, she considered taking some up to her mother for an afternoon treat. Then she'd discarded that notion, fearful that the sight of her father's favorite cookies might remind Delores of Lars.

Hannah gave a weary sigh as she realized that all three Swensen sisters were walking on eggshells around their mother, afraid that anything they tried might make things even worse. They knew that they had to do something to help their mother, but they were fresh out of ideas.

The doorbell rang, pulling Hannah away from the dilemma, and she hurried to answer the door. It was snowing again, a regular occurrence in Minnesota winters, and the temperature outside was well below zero. Hannah pulled the door open and began to smile when she saw Grandma Knudson, the unofficial leader of the Lake Eden Holy Cross Redeemer Lutheran Church. She was the current pastor's grandmother and everyone in Lake Eden called her "Grandma" as a term of affection and respect.

Standing next to Grandma Knudson was another one of her mother's friends, Annie Winters. Annie was the current head of the Lake Eden Children's Home, an orphanage situated just outside of town in a large, rambling brick mansion.

"Hello, Hannah. How are you?" Grandma Knudson greeted her.

"I'm okay," Hannah answered, giving her a smile before she turned to Annie. "Hi, Annie."

"Hello, Hannah. We came to call on your mother."

"Please come in," Hannah said, opening the door a little wider. Perhaps Grandma Knudson and Annie would know what to do to help Delores. Grandma Knudson always gave everyone wise advice, and Annie had her doctorate in psychology.

"Would you like tea?" Hannah asked them, leading the way to the living room.

"That would be lovely, Hannah," Annie answered. "Will your mother join us?"

Hannah shook her head. "I'm afraid not. Mother is napping upstairs."

"Again?" Grandma Knudson asked, looking more than a little distressed. "I've been here four times and it's the same story."

"Yes," Hannah admitted. "She's been taking long naps every afternoon."

Annie and Grandma Knudson exchanged glances and then

Annie spoke. "You look troubled, Hannah. Tell us why and perhaps we can help."

Hannah took a deep breath and blurted out her worries. "It's Mother. Andrea and Michelle and I have done everything we can think of to coax her out of her bedroom, but she still spends more time in there with the door closed than she does in the rest of the house. And when I go up to straighten the bed, her pillow is wet with tears. We're afraid that she's going to withdraw from life completely and we don't know what to do about it!"

Grandma Knudson gave a sad little smile. "It's a common reaction, Hannah," she said. "Some wives just don't want to go on with their lives when their husbands die." She turned to Annie. "Isn't that right, Annie?"

"Yes, and sometimes husbands feel the same way when their wives die," Annie added. "They think that getting involved in life again is a betrayal in some way."

"That's it exactly!" Hannah confirmed, feeling slightly relieved just telling them about it. "What can we do to convince Mother to start living her life again?"

"We have to come up with a project that only Delores can accomplish, a project that she can't refuse to accept," Grandma Knudson told her.

"That makes sense, but . . ." Hannah paused and wiped away a tear with the back of her hand. "Andrea and Michelle and I have tried everything we could think of, but . . . nothing has worked."

"Did you try things that your mother would enjoy doing?"

"Yes. Michelle was chosen for the lead in the junior play and she asked Mother to help her learn her lines. I know that, normally, Mother would have loved to do that, but she claimed that she was too tired to help Michelle."

"That's because she would have enjoyed helping Michelle," Annie explained. "And she didn't want to enjoy anything without your father. What did Andrea try?"

"Andrea asked her to help decorate the baby's room. And you know how Mother loves to decorate."

"Of course she does." Grandma Knudson gave a little smile. "And your mother claimed that she was too tired to help Andrea?"

"Yes, that's exactly what she said."

"And what did *you* do, Hannah?" Annie asked her.

"I made all of Mother's favorite meals for dinner, but she just pushed the food around on her plate and said she just wasn't hungry. And when I asked her if she'd go antiquing with me to find some unusual Christmas gifts, she told me that she wasn't interested in antiquing anymore."

"All right then," Annie said. "Grandma Knudson and I discussed the problem, Hannah, and we think we have a solution for you and your sisters."

"What is it?" Hannah leaned forward, eager to hear what two of the women she respected most in Lake Eden wanted them to try.

"We came up with a project that your mother won't really want to do, but one that she'll feel guilty about refusing," Annie explained. "Delores won't want to help us, but she's going to feel obligated."

Hannah thought about that for a moment and then she gave a little nod. "Yes, I can see how that could work. And you have a project like that?"

"Yes," Grandma Knudson said. "We think we have the perfect project. You know Dr. Kalick's niece, don't you?"

Hannah began to smile. "Of course I know Essie. She was married to Alton Granger, the owner of the Albion Hotel. I used to go to there for Essie's story-time on Saturday afternoons, and so did Andrea and Michelle. Essie's story-time was really popular in Lake Eden."

"So popular that they bussed in all the kids from the Children's Home," Annie added. "Everyone loved to hear Essie's stories, and it gave every mother in town a break for a couple of hours on Saturday afternoons."

"That's right." Hannah began to smile. "And I think I see exactly where you're going. Mother used to say that everyone owed Essie a debt of gratitude for telling those wonderful stories and entertaining all the children in Lake Eden. Mother used to drop us off there and go to yard sales and farm auctions."

"Perfect!" Grandma Knudson declared. "I think our idea is going to work, Hannah. We went to see Essie at the hospital last week."

"At the hospital?" Hannah felt a stab of fear. "Is Essie all right?"

"Not really," Annie responded. "We had a long talk with Doc Knight, and he says that Essie can't live alone in those two rooms at the hotel any longer. He said that she wasn't eating right and the flight of stairs to her rooms is simply too much for her to handle. She doesn't have running water, you know, and Essie has to go up and down the stairs to use the bathroom at the café."

"But the café closes at nine at night!"

"That's why Rose gave Essie a key. She can get in if she needs to."

"But you said that Essie can't handle the stairs any longer."

"That's right," Annie agreed. "She's fallen a few times, and the last fall was the worst. She was planning to go to your father's funeral, but she fell halfway down the stairs and broke her hip."

Hannah felt tears come to her eyes again. "That's awful! What can I do to help her?"

Grandma Knudson smiled. "That's exactly the reaction I hope your mother will have when we tell her about Essie. Doc Knight has her in the hospice ward at the hospital."

"You mean . . . Essie's dying?"

"No," Annie was quick to correct her. "Essie's not terminal, but she can't go back to living alone, especially with the stairs and the fact that she doesn't have electricity or running water. It's going to take her a couple of months to heal, and that's why he's keeping her in the hospice ward."

"I understand, but what, exactly, do you think Mother could do for Essie?"

"She can make Essie very happy," Grandma Knudson said. "You told me that Delores feels she owes Essie a debt of gratitude for inviting you girls to her story-time. That's why we think we know the perfect way for your mother to pay Essie back."

"How can she do that?"

"We'll tell both of you when your mother gets down here," Annie said. "Go get her, Hannah. Tell her she's got to come downstairs, that we need her help and we won't take no for an answer."

"I would . . . but . . ." Hannah stopped and gave a little sigh. "She'll just say she's too tired."

"Then we'll go up and get her," Grandma Knudson declared, springing up from her chair. "Go put on the tea, Hannah. Annie and I will have your mother down here in less than five minutes."

Hannah watched the two women climb the stairs to get her mother. If anyone could get Delores out of her bedroom, it would be Annie and Grandma Knudson. She watched them until they'd reached the top of the stairs and then she made a beeline for the kitchen to heat the water for tea.

# Chapter Two

Hannah was setting out the tea tray and a platter of cookies when she saw her mother coming down the stairs with Grandma Knudson and Annie. It had been five minutes since she'd heard them knocking on her mother's bedroom door and here was Delores, walking down the stairs with them.

Delores smiled when she saw the tea tray on the living room coffee table. "Oh, good!" she said to Hannah. "I'm so glad you made tea, dear. Do you happen to have any cookies that we can have with it?"

"I have Cocoa-Crunch Cookies," Hannah responded, lifting the napkin she'd placed over the platter of cookies.

"Perfect!" Delores turned to Grandma Knudson and Annie. "Lars used to say that they were like little bites of heaven. He loved those cookies and so do I."

Hannah began to smile. After three weeks of picking at whatever Hannah had made for her, Delores was finally enthusiastic about eating. This definitely reinforced her belief that Grandma Knudson and Annie were miracle workers.

Grandma Knudson picked up the cookie platter and passed it to Delores. "Have one, dear."

"Thank you," Delores said politely, selecting a cookie and taking a bite almost immediately. "These are wonderful cookies."

Hannah felt like turning cartwheels on the living room rug, and if she'd been more athletic, she might very well have been attempting it. "Thank you, Mother," she said as she filled the cups and passed the tea.

"As I mentioned upstairs, Annie was the one who found Essie," Grandma Knudson said, turned to Annie. "Tell Delores about it, Annie."

Annie drew a deep breath and Hannah could tell that the memory still upset her. "Essie and I had dinner every Sunday at the Children's Home. Essie always met me at the café and that night, she was late. I sat there for a while, waiting for her, but then I began to worry that she was sick, or she'd forgotten, or . . . worse."

"I had a key to the hotel." Annie stopped speaking and cleared her throat. "I used it and opened the door. And there was Essie at the foot of the stairs, just lying there and not moving."

"So Annie called the paramedics," Grandma Knudson reached out to pat Annie's hand and continued with the account. "They were there in less than fifteen minutes and they took Essie's vital signs, loaded her onto a stretcher, and took her to the hospital."

Annie nodded. "I followed them and when we got there, Doc Knight told me that Essie had broken her hip. He took her into surgery immediately and I waited until he came back to say that she was going to be all right."

"That must have been awful for you!" Delores said.

"It was . . . especially when she wasn't moving and I couldn't tell if she was breathing or not." Annie stopped again to take a sip of her tea. "I'm just so glad I was there that evening. I don't even want to think about what would have happened if it hadn't been our night to have dinner. Essie has been almost like a mother to us at the Children's Home. And she's like a grandmother to the children now."

"Annie grew up at the Children's Home," Grandma Knudson explained.

"Yes, and Essie was a volunteer. Then, after she married Alton and moved into the hotel, she started her Saturday story-time. She invited me and two of my best friends to come to the hotel after school every day. She always fixed us an after-school snack, and we sat at a booth in the Red Velvet Lounge." Annie stopped to smile at the memory. "You have no idea how special we felt, being in a grown-up place like that! Essie helped us with our homework and then Alton would give us a ride back to the Children's Home. It's a good place, Delores, and I'd like to think that, because of my back-ground, I was able to make it into an even better environ-ment for the children."

"You've done that, Annie. No question about it," Grand-ma Knudson said.

"Thank you. The point of all this is that I loved to take Essie out to the Home. Having her there was a chance for me to make sure she had a good breakfast, lunch, and dinner."

"That was kind of you, Annie," Delores responded.

"Perhaps, but it was also self-serving. Essie was wonderful with the children. They called her *Grandma* and they all looked forward to seeing her."

"It's so sad that Essie didn't have any children of her own," Delores said.

"That's not the saddest thing," Grandma Knudson told her. "Doc Knight says that Essie won't be able to go back to her home at the hotel again. I know that almost everybody in Lake Eden would be happy to help Essie out, but you do know how proud she is, don't you?"

Delores nodded. "Yes, she's never accepted help from any-one. Lars found out that there was no running water or elec-tricity in those two rooms she had on the second floor, so he found her a battery-operated electric blanket."

"How nice!" Annie commented.

"Yes, but Essie insisted on paying him for it. He tried to give it to her, but she wouldn't have it. He ended up telling her that it was a sample from the company and all she had to do was pay for the shipping and keep a record of any problems she had with it."

"Oh, that was really clever!" Annie exclaimed.

"Thank you. It was my idea," Delores beamed, and Hannah realized that she hadn't seen her mother look happy in weeks. "Just a little thing like that made both of us feel good. It's so rewarding to help someone you like."

"Exactly!" Grandma Knudson agreed. "That's why we came here today, Delores."

"What can I do?"

"We went to see Essie this morning and we had a very sad conversation with her. She was talking about the past and we could hear the longing for those days in Essie's voice."

"What did she say?" Delores asked.

"She told us about the first Christmas Ball she attended at the opening of the Albion Hotel. That's where she met Alton, you know."

"Of course," Delores responded. "He built the hotel."

"Essie was so excited when she described the Christmas Ball," Annie continued. "And for the very first time since her accident, she actually looked happy."

Grandma Knudson nodded. "She said she wishes she could go back in time just to see the splendor of that first Christmas Ball and something she called the Christmas Cake Parade."

"Yes," Annie continued. "We talked about it on the way over here to see you. Both of us wished that we could recreate that Christmas Ball for Essie again, just the way it was back then. It would mean so much to her. Of course it would be a huge project. Grandma and I would help all we could, but it would take a real community leader to organize such a large event."

Hannah watched her mother closely. It was clear that Delores was intrigued by the idea. "So you came here to ask me to spearhead this event?"

"Yes," Grandma Knudson admitted. "You're the only one we know who could pull it off in time."

"What time limit would I have to accomplish such a massive project?" Delores stopped speaking and gave a little sigh. "And I'm not promising I'll do it, but I need to know the time constraints?"

"Two and a half weeks," Annie responded. "The first Christmas Ball, the one Essie remembers, was held two weeks before Christmas."

Delores hesitated for a moment or two and then she squared her shoulders. "If I take on this project for you, how many people would be willing to help me?"

"You'd have everybody in the congregation at Holy Redeemer," Grandma Knudson promised. "We have carpenters, masons, painters, plumbers, you name it."

"And if you need muscle to unload things and carry things, I know the teenage boys at the Home would be happy to help," Annie offered.

"Well?" Grandma Knudson asked, giving Delores the look Hannah had always thought was made of pure steel wool. It was slightly flexible, but only to a certain degree. It reminded Hannah of a bundle of sharp-edged steel filaments that could wear anything . . . or in this case, *anyone* . . . down in seconds flat.

It was so quiet in the living room that Hannah could hear the old-fashioned windup alarm clock in her bedroom ticking off the seconds. That was when she realized that she was holding her breath, waiting for her mother to answer.

"Yes," Delores said, at last. "But only if Hannah will help me."

"Me?" Hannah was completely perplexed by her mother's request. "But, Mother . . . you know that I'm not very good at decorating and things like that. What could I do?"

"You can do what you do best, dear," Delores told her. "You can bake the cakes for the Christmas Cake Parade. I remember my parents talking about how beautiful it was when they shut off the lights in the ballroom and carried in the Christmas cakes. Each one was decorated with candles, and some of the older people in Lake Eden still talk about how stunning it was to see all those cakes when they were carried in and placed on the buffet table."

Hannah began to smile. "Of course I'll help bake the cakes, Mother. How many were there?"

"I'm not sure. I was too young to go to the ball since champagne was served and I was underage. I'd be happy to help you with the cakes, dear, but you know that I don't bake."

"Everybody in Lake Eden knows that, Delores," Grandma Knudson said, smiling to show that she was teasing.

Delores gave her a long-suffering look, but then she laughed. "You and Annie wouldn't want any cake that I baked," she said. "But both of you know that Hannah is an excellent baker. Tell me about the Albion Hotel Ballroom. Is it in good enough shape?"

"I'm not sure," Annie admitted. "I've never been up to the second floor."

"Then the first thing we have to do is talk to Essie and ask her to describe exactly what she remembers about that Christmas Ball. Do you think she's willing to see us this afternoon?"

Annie and Grandma Knudson exchanged triumphant glances. "I think she'd be delighted to see us," Annie said.

"And especially to see you," Grandma Knudson added. "She asked about you this morning."

Delores looked pleased. "How sweet of her!" Then she turned to Hannah. "Could you pack up some of those cookies, Hannah? We could take them with us when we visit Essie. I'm sure she'd love to have some." Then she turned back to Grandma Knudson and Annie. "I'll meet you at the hospital in forty-five minutes. That'll give me time to take a quick shower and freshen up. And after we visit Essie, we should go over to the Albion Hotel and find out which type of elevator is there. I've heard that the Otis Elevator people will fix any of their elevators. And if I talk to them and tell them about Essie and her situation, perhaps I can convince them to fix it for no cost to us."

"But, Delores . . ." Grandma Knudson began to frown. "What about the electricity? Elevators run on electricity, don't they?"

"Don't worry about the electricity. I'll talk to Mayor Bascomb about it. Recreation of the Christmas Ball is a project that the whole community should get behind. If enough people agree to help us, we can figure out some way to hook up the electricity. After all, Essie has lived in Lake Eden for most of her life and she's always been involved in charitable work. Now it's time for the community to give back to her, and I intend to make certain that they do just that."

## COCOA-CRUNCH COOKIES

Preheat oven to 350 degrees F., rack in the middle position.

1 and ½ cups softened butter *(3 sticks, ¾ pound, 12 ounces)*
1 and ¼ cups white *(granulated)* sugar
2 large eggs
½ teaspoon salt
2 teaspoons vanilla extract
¼ cup unsweetened cocoa powder *(I used Hershey's)*
2 and ¼ cups all-purpose flour *(pack it down in the cup when you measure it)*
1 and ½ cups finely crushed plain regular potato chips *(measure AFTER crushing. I used Lay's, put them in a plastic zip-lock bag, and crushed them with my hands)*
1 cup semi-sweet chocolate chips *(I used Nestlé)*

---

⅓ cup white *(granulated)* sugar for dipping

**Hannah's 1ˢᵗ Note: Use regular potato chips, the thin, salty ones. Don't use baked chips, or rippled chips, or chips with the peels on, or kettle-fried, or flavored, or anything that's supposed to be better for you than those wonderfully greasy, salty, old-fashioned, crunchy potato chips.**

In a large mixing bowl, beat the butter, sugar, eggs, salt, and vanilla extract until the mixture is light and fluffy.

*(You can do this by hand, but it's a lot easier with an electric mixer.)*

Add the quarter-cup of unsweetened cocoa powder. Mix it in thoroughly.

Add the flour in half-cup increments, mixing well after each addition.

Add the crushed potato chips and mix well.

Take the bowl out of the mixer and add the semi-sweet chips by hand. Stir them in so that they are evenly distributed.

Form one-inch dough balls with your hands and place them on an UNGREASED cookie sheet, 12 to a standard-sized sheet. *(As an alternative, you can line your cookie sheets with parchment paper.)*

Place the sugar in a small bowl. Spray the flat bottom of a drinking glass with Pam or another nonstick cooking spray, dip it in the sugar, and use it to flatten each dough ball. *(Dip the glass in the sugar for each cookie ball.)*

Bake your cookies at 350 degrees F., for 10 to 12 minutes, or until the cookies are starting to turn golden at the edges. *(Mine took the full 12 minutes.)*

Let the Cocoa-Crunch Cookies cool on the cookie sheet for 2 minutes and then remove them to a wire rack to cool completely. *(If you used parchment paper, all you have to do is pull it over to the wire rack and let the cookies cool right on the paper.)*

Yield: Approximately 6 to 7 dozen crunchy, chocolate, shortbread-like cookies, depending on cookie size.

# Chapter Three

"Where's Mother's car?" Michelle asked as she came into the kitchen from the garage.

"Mother has it. She's at the hospital with Grandma Knudson and Annie Winters."

"At the *hospital*?" Michelle looked anxious. "Is Mother all right?"

"She's more than all right. Mother's back!" Hannah gave a happy smile. "Mother's meeting them there and they're going to see Essie."

"You mean . . . Mother actually left the house?"

"She certainly did. Right after her visit with Grandma Knudson and Annie, she took a quick shower, got dressed, and went off to the hospital to visit Essie to find out about the first Christmas Ball at the Albion Hotel. Grandma Knudson and Annie asked her to recreate the ball for Essie, and Mother agreed to take on the project."

"Wow!" Michelle looked thoroughly shocked and it took a moment for her to digest this startling news. When she did, a huge smile spread over her face. "I don't know what you did, but it worked!"

"It wasn't me. Grandma Knudson and Annie Winters deserve all the credit for that."

Michelle noticed the cookies on the cooling racks and

began to look puzzled again. "You baked Dad's favorite cookies?"

"Yes. And Mother grabbed a plateful to take to Essie in the hospital. She said they were going to have cookies and coffee while Essie told them all about the Christmas Ball."

"You said Essie was in the hospital. Is she sick?"

"Not exactly. She has a broken hip and there was no way she could go back to the hotel. Doc Knight put her in the hospice ward at the hospital."

"But Essie's not dying, is she?"

"No, it's just that she can't go back home yet and Doc decided to use the hospice ward as a temporary solution."

"Oh, good! When you said she was in the hospice ward, I was thinking the worst. Let me see if I've got all this straight. Mother took a shower, got dressed, and she drove to the hospital to visit Essie with Grandma Knudson and Annie."

"That's right and there's more. Essie's going to tell them about the night she met Alton Granger, and Mother's going to spearhead a community project to recreate that Christmas Ball for Essie."

Michelle blinked a couple of times and sat down in a kitchen chair. "Wow!" she said again. "A lot happened while I was at school today!"

"Yes, it did."

"And this means everything's getting back to normal again with Mother?"

"That's exactly what it means."

"Oh, good!" Michelle turned to look at the cookies again. "Can I have a cookie, Hannah?"

"Of course."

"And is it okay if I call Lisa and invite her over tonight? She said she'd help me learn my lines for the junior play."

"Go ahead. You can invite her to stay for dinner, too. Mother likes Lisa and it'll be good for her to have company. Andrea's going to be here, too. Mother called to invite her right before she left for the hospital. She told Andrea that she'd be happy to help decorate the baby's room if Andrea would help her decorate the hotel for the Christmas Ball."

"And Andrea said yes?"

"Of course she did. You know that Andrea loves to work on decorating projects with Mother."

Michelle's smile grew even wider. "This is wonderful, Hannah! It just gets better and better. I can hardly wait to tell Lisa that Mother's getting back to her old self!"

"When you do that, you'd better warn Lisa."

"Warn her about what?"

"About Mother. She's in a recruiting mood and she'll probably try to recruit both of you to help her with the ball."

Hannah was just taking the spiral-cut ham out of the oven when Michelle and Lisa came into the kitchen.

"I was hoping you'd bake a ham one of these nights," Michelle said. "Do you want me to set the table in the dining room?"

"That would good," Hannah told her. "I'm going to cover this ham. It'll stay warm until Mother gets home. Then all I'll have to do is heat the rolls and make the creamed spinach."

"I'll help you set the table, Michelle," Lisa offered. "Just tell me what you want me to do."

"How many people are we having for dinner?" Michelle asked Hannah.

"We have you, Lisa, Mother, Andrea, and me," Hannah told her. "I invited Grandma Knudson and Annie, but Annie had to hurry back to the Children's Home and Grandma Knudson said she had to go back to the parsonage to cook because Reverend Bob loves her meatloaf."

"How about Bill?" Michelle asked.

"He's on night shift out at the sheriff's station. Andrea said she'd take leftovers home for him to eat when he got off work tonight."

"So we'll be five at the table then?" Lisa asked.

"That's right." Hannah turned to Michelle. "Use the green tablecloth. Mother likes that one. And see if you can find something to use for a centerpiece. This is a mini-celebration, so use the good china and the crystal champagne flutes."

"We're having champagne?" Michelle asked.

"Two of us are, but set out champagne flutes for all of us. Andrea's bringing her favorite ginger ale and I have a bottle of sparkling apple juice for you two."

"You have some winter border flowers left along the front walkway," Lisa said. "Would you like us to make a little centerpiece with them?"

"That would be nice," Hannah told her. "I'm going to finish up here in the kitchen. Mother called a few minutes ago and said she'd be back here in about twenty minutes."

"The table looks lovely, girls!" Delores complimented Michelle and Lisa as they all entered the dining room. Then she turned to Hannah. "Do I smell ham, dear?"

"You do," Hannah told her, taking the foil off the meat platter and revealing its contents. "Sit down, everyone, and I'll fill our glasses. Then we can have a toast."

"You have Perrier Jouët!" Delores exclaimed, beginning to smile when she recognized the champagne bottle in the silver wine server. "What's the occasion, Hannah?"

"Our mother is back with us again and we're happy," Hannah spoke for all of them.

"I'm happy, too," Delores responded, and then she noticed that there were crystal champagne glasses at all five place settings. "Michelle and Lisa aren't having champagne, are they?"

"No, Mother," Andrea answered quickly. "Hannah has sparkling apple juice for them and I have my favorite ginger ale."

"Oh, good! More for me!" Delores said, and everyone at the table began to laugh. They were laughing partially in relief that Delores had finally returned to the person they knew and loved, and partially because the comment she'd made was funny.

That night, Hannah's sleep was untroubled by worries about Delores and she woke up the next morning feeling more refreshed and well-rested than she had since her dad had died. She took a quick shower, dressed as fast as she could, and hurried down to the kitchen for a quick cup of coffee before she started to make breakfast for all three of them.

Once they had eaten breakfast and Michelle had left for school, Delores turned to Hannah. "Would you help me do something today, dear? It's important."

"Of course I will," Hannah responded immediately. "What would you like me to do?"

"I want to go over to the hotel and see if there's anything in Essie's rooms that she might need. If we find anything, I'll take it to her when I visit her this afternoon."

"That's a good idea, Mother. There may be photos or personal items that she'd like to have with her at the hospital."

"That's what I thought, dear. It'll make her room at the hospital seem more like home, and perhaps she'll recuperate faster." Delores stopped speaking and smiled at Hannah. "I'm going to change to old clothing and you should do that, too. Remember, Essie's rooms don't have running water, and I'm sure it must have been difficult for her to keep them clean."

It didn't take long for Hannah to change to jeans and an old sweatshirt. When she came down the stairs, she found her mother waiting for her at the kitchen table. Delores was wearing an old sweater that had belonged to her husband and she had pulled her hair up in a cap that Hannah hadn't known her mother owned.

"Ready?" Delores asked.

"I'm ready," Hannah said. "Are you driving, or am I?"

"I'll drive," Delores replied, grabbing the car keys and

leading the way to the attached garage. "There's an old duffel bag of your father's in the trunk. Grab it when we get there, dear. It should hold anything we find that we think Essie might like to keep with her."

"I'll do that, Mother."

Delores started the car and drove several blocks in silence. "It's a good thing there's no one on the street this early," Delores said as she pulled the car into a spot near the entrance to the hotel. "I wouldn't want anyone I knew to see me dressed like this."

"It wouldn't matter," Hannah said, unable to keep from teasing her normally impeccably dressed mother. "I doubt that anyone would recognize you with that sweater and cap."

Delores laughed. "You're probably right, dear. Let's go!"

"If it's locked, I can run over to the café and see if Rose has a key," Hannah said as she retrieved her father's duffel bag from the trunk.

"It's all right, dear. I have a key. Essie gave it to me when I said I planned to go up to her rooms to bring her some of her things. She even told me that there were several things she wanted to have with her."

"Which things did she want?" Hannah asked, following her mother to the side door of the hotel.

"The dress she wore at the first Christmas Ball. She said it would make her feel happier just to see it hanging in her closet at the hospital. And there was a beaded handbag that she made a long time ago and she wanted that, too. She even described it to me. It's made of crystals in a flower design and it has a gold-colored chain."

"How big is it?" Hannah asked.

"Large enough to accommodate a handkerchief, a comb, and a lipstick. She said that the gold-colored chain fits over a lady's wrist so that she can carry it with her when she's asked to dance."

The door opened when Delores turned the key and Hannah and her mother stepped inside. The old Albion Hotel smelled of dust and decaying wood, and it made Hannah wonder if the steps to the second floor were safe.

"Don't worry about the stairs," Delores said, noticing her daughter's worried frown. "Essie said they're perfectly safe if you stay next to the bannister. The weak spots are in the center of the steps."

Mother and daughter stayed close to the bannister and climbed the steps to the second floor. At the top of the stairs on their right was a door with a flower painted on it.

"Essie painted that," Delores told Hannah. "She told me that it was her favorite flower."

"What is it?"

"A hibiscus. She said that she tried to grow them several times, but they didn't do well for her."

Delores used the key that Essie had given her to unlock the door. "Be careful, dear. There's no electricity, but Essie told me that there should be plenty of light coming in the windows in the daytime."

"What did she do for electricity at night?" Hannah asked.

"She went to bed early and if she had to get up, she had a flashlight by the side of the bed."

"Did anyone know that Essie was living like this?" Hannah asked.

"I don't think so. She wasn't the type to complain. I know that she didn't mention it to Rose."

"How do you know that?"

"I called her right after I took my shower this morning. Rose said that if she'd known, they would have curtained off a spot in the back so that Essie could have spent her nights at the café where there was food, and electricity, and heat. Poor Essie would have almost frozen to death without the little gas heater and the battery-operated electric blanket that Lars gave her."

"Why didn't Essie ask for help? There are so many people with spare bedrooms who would have offered one to her."

"She was too proud, dear. Essie never wanted to ask for help. Some people are like that. They just try to manage on their own until something happens and they just can't go on any longer."

Hannah blinked back tears as her mother opened Essie's door and led the way in. The two rooms that Essie had were cleaner than Hannah had expected, and they were bright and cheerful with colorful blankets folded neatly on the cushions of chairs and several plants on the windowsills.

"It's cold in here," Hannah commented. "I wonder how those plants survive."

Delores walked over to examine one of the plants. "They're artificial," she told Hannah. "Essie must have bought them to brighten up her rooms."

Hannah noticed the sad expression on her mother's face and decided to change the subject. "Let's get started," she suggested, opening the duffel bag and placing it on one of the chairs. "I'll take the bedroom and you can start searching for things in here."

The bedroom that Hannah had referred to wasn't really a bedroom at all. It was simply a doorway without a door that had been cut into the wall between two studs. Someone, probably Essie herself, had taped heavy cardboard strips to the sides of the doorway to keep out the draft, and she had painted the cardboard with hibiscus flowers. Essie had done everything she could to make this arrangement cheerful, but Hannah knew that the little bottled gas heater would not have been adequate to heat the space.

There was a bed with heavy quilts piled on top and a closet that had been part of the second hotel room. Hannah opened the door and saw that the closet was filled with clothes and storage boxes. She started with the clothes and almost immediately, she found a lovely, old-fashioned ball gown. "I found it!" she shouted out to Delores. "I think this is the ball gown that Essie wanted you to bring."

Hannah carried the ball gown to the room where her mother was working and spread it out on a chair. "This is the only formal dress, so it must be the right one."

Delores walked over to look at it and gave a little sigh. "Essie was heavier then, but if there aren't any other ball gowns, this must be it."

"Do you think it'll fit her?" Hannah asked.

"No, but we can always talk to Claire about taking in the seams. I'm sure she'll be happy to do that for Essie."

"That's a great idea!" Hannah reached out to give her mother a quick hug. "I'm going back to see if I can find the purse that Essie described to you."

After looking in at least a dozen boxes, Hannah was beginning to think that she'd never find Essie's beaded handbag. She'd found several photo albums that she wanted to show to her mother, but not the crystal purse with the flower design. The last box was small and fairly heavy. Those two facts gave Hannah hope that the purse might be tucked inside. She took a deep breath, lifted the lid, folded back the tissue paper, and began to smile when she uncovered a beaded handbag nestled inside.

"I found it!" she announced, rushing back into the room that her mother was searching. "This is the purse, isn't it, Mother?"

Delores hurried over to look. "Yes, I think it is. Did you find anything else?"

"A couple of photo albums. I'll bring them in here to see if you want to take them to Essie." Hannah rushed back into the bedroom and came back with the photo albums.

Delores paged through the albums and nodded. "I'm sure Essie would like to have these. There are some pictures of her telling stories to a big group of children. Those should bring back happy memories for her."

Hannah noticed a small stack of items that Delores had set aside on one of the chairs. "Are you taking those things to Essie?"

"Yes, I thought she might like that multicolored blanket to put at the foot of her bed. It should make her room seem brighter and less institutional. The three little frog statues would look cute on her windowsill, and I thought we could stop at CostMart to pick up some nice guest towels to put in her bathroom to brighten that up."

"That's a great idea," Hannah said.

"Can you think of anything else she might like?" Delores asked.

"A warm, fluffy robe?"

"We'll look for one. It's always nice to have something soft and fluffy. Take a look at those notebooks on the chair, Hannah. They're numbered and I opened the first one. I'm not sure exactly what to make of it. And be very careful when you turn the pages. They're very old. The ink is beginning to fade and the paper is fragile."

Hannah walked over, picked up the top notebook, and carefully turned to the first page. Delores was right. The paper was fragile and the ink was faded. Enough sun was coming through the window to read the spidery writing on the first page and when she'd done so, Hannah closed the notebook and carefully put it back on the stack.

"What do you think they are, dear?" Delores asked.

"I'm not sure. Do you know if Essie ever lived in New York?"

"I don't think she did. She said something about living in Chicago with her parents, but she didn't mention New York."

"Then these can't be diaries," Hannah decided. "I think I know what they are, though."

"What is that, dear?"

"I think Essie was writing a book."

Delores smiled. "You could very well be right, dear. For years, Essie told stories based on books. Those were children's books, but perhaps she wanted to try her hand at writing a work of serious fiction."

"Do you think we should take the notebooks to Essie?" Hannah asked.

"I'm not sure." Delores thought about it for a moment and then she shook her head. "Let's pack them up and take them to the house, Hannah. That way we can make sure that nothing happens to them. Then we can ask Essie about them and see if she wants us to bring them, especially since we're not really sure what they are."

"All right, Mother." Hannah began to pack the notebooks carefully in the duffel bag. "Do you mind if I read them?"

"I don't mind, but you have to promise to be very careful with them. They represent hours of Essie's creative work."

"Don't worry, Mother. I was working on my doctorate in English Literature and I've read old manuscripts before. As a matter of fact, I think I brought my reading gloves home with me. Leaving the notebooks here will do more damage to them than I will."

"All right, dear, but you have to promise me two things."

"What are they, Mother?"

"You have to bake another batch of cookies. Grandma Knudson, Annie, Essie, and I simply gobbled them up with our coffee yesterday, and Essie asked me if I could bring some more cookies today. Will you have time to bake when we get home, dear?"

"Of course I will," Hannah agreed quickly. "You said there were two things. What else do you want me to promise?"

"I want you to promise to read Essie's book to me when I get back from visiting Essie. You seemed just as fascinated as I was when I read the first page."

# Chapter Four

"**I**s everyone ready?" Hannah asked, picking up the first of Essie's notebooks.

"I am," Delores declared, propping her feet up on a footstool and relaxing in her favorite living room chair.

"I am, too," Lisa agreed, leaning forward on the couch.

"Go ahead, Hannah," Michelle urged, tucking a couch pillow behind her back.

Dinner had been fun and Andrea had apologized when she'd left at seven. She'd told them that she wished she could stay, but she had several things to do before Bill got home from work. Once she'd left, Delores, Lisa, Michelle, and Hannah had retired to the living room, where Hannah had stacked Essie's notebooks.

"Okay, if you're ready," Hannah said, pulling on her reading gloves and opening the notebook. And then she began to read.

She had just finished totaling a column of figures when the phone on her desk rang. She let it ring twice, as her cousin had instructed her to do, and then she answered.

"Cappella Enterprises. This is Sharon speaking. May I help you?"

"Rose!"

"Yes, Tony." She felt her heart begin to beat wildly in her

chest. It was her husband and he'd used his private name for her, the name no one else knew. "Is it time?" she asked him.

"Yes, I'll be there in less than five minutes."

Her hand was shaking slightly as she hung up the phone and she felt their baby give a protesting kick. Her doctor had told her that babies, even when they were still in the womb, could sense when their mother was upset.

"It's all right," she told the baby, getting up from her desk and walking across the small office. She opened the closet to retrieve her coat and purse, and drew a deep, steadying breath. They'd talked about this day, rehearsed what each of them would do, and she knew exactly what was expected of her as she reached up to get the empty box from the top shelf. "It's all right," she repeated, attempting to reassure the baby and herself at the same time. "Daddy's coming to help us."

She'd just finished going through her purse to make sure she had enough money when the door to the office burst open. Her husband rushed in, locking the door quickly behind him.

"Are you ready?" he asked in a slightly breathless voice. "They're on the way. You know what to do, don't you, honey?"

"Yes," she said, trying not to look as frightened as she felt as she opened the bottom drawer of her desk and took out a bulky duffel bag. She had hoped this day would never come, but she trusted Tony to know when danger was imminent and it was time to flee.

"Let me," he said, taking the two ledgers out of the drawer and quickly stuffing them into the box, quickly taping it shut. "Go out the window and use the fire escape. Climb down to the second-floor landing. I opened that window a crack on my way up here. Push up the window and climb back inside, but don't use the elevator. Just walk down the stairs to the ground floor, go out the side door, and don't stop until you get to the post office. You have to mail that package."

"I will. But . . . what are you going to do?" she asked, her voice shaking with fear.

"I'll be fine as long as you're safe. They don't suspect me. Just take this and go, honey. You've got to protect our baby!"

"Yes, I know," she agreed. And as she watched, he unzipped the duffel bag and tucked a pouch inside. "Go!" he ordered. "Go now, and don't look back! I'll join you later, just the way we planned."

He helped her climb out onto the fire escape, gave her a quick kiss, and shut the window again, clicking the latch. Then he sat down in her desk chair and she knew she had no choice but to follow the plan they'd made together.

Her heart pounding in her throat, she hurried down the metal steps of the fire escape, holding the duffel bag and counting the floors as she went. When she reached the second floor, she pushed up on the window that he'd unlocked for her. One quick glance and she stepped in, a bit unwieldly as the baby kicked again, objecting to her sudden, panicked movement. She shut and locked the window behind her and told herself that it was going to be all right, that he'd be joining her in no time at all.

Cautiously, she peeked around the corner. No one was in the hallway. Heart beating rapidly in her chest, she hurried toward the stairs. Her legs were shaking slightly as she climbed down to the first floor, walked through the deserted hallway to the side door of the building, and opened it. One quick glance told her that there was no one on the street, no one at all. Had Tony panicked needlessly? But he wouldn't have done that. He was too well trained. This was a real emergency and she had to trust him for their baby's sake.

A moment later, she was out on the sidewalk, heading for the corner. She rounded it and walked as rapidly as she could without attracting notice until she reached the post office. She was just entering the building when she heard several cars screech around the corner she had left only moments before.

Hands shaking slightly, she handed her package to the window clerk, verified that the postage she'd prepaid was correct, and stepped aside to watch her package disappear down the conveyer belt to the sorting facility.

A city bus was just pulling up as she exited the post office. She boarded it, sat in an inside seat as far away from the windows as she could get, and breathed a sigh of relief when the bus pulled out into traffic. It was only after she'd ridden for over twenty minutes that she realized the bus was headed for Brooklyn, a place she'd never been before.

"I'm on the edge of my chair!" Delores said breathlessly when Hannah stopped reading.

"Me too!" Michelle echoed her mother's sentiment. When Delores had told them about the notebooks and mentioned that Hannah was going to read them to her, of course Michelle and Lisa had begged to listen. Delores and Hannah had agreed.

"It's scary and exciting at the same time," Lisa offered her opinion. "Essie's really a good writer."

"How many notebooks are there, Hannah?" Delores asked.

"Nine, but I only got about a third of the way through this one. I can't read too much at a sitting because my eyes begin to hurt. The ink is fading badly on some pages, and to add to that problem, Essie used paper that absorbed the ink. Since she wrote on both sides of the pages, it's bleeding through in spots."

"It's too bad Essie didn't use a ball point pen when she wrote it," Lisa said. "The ink never fades with ballpoint pens."

"How do you know that?" Michelle asked her.

"I got some ink from my ballpoint pen on my yellow blouse. I tried everything I could think of to get it out."

"Did you find anything that worked?" Delores asked her.

"No, I had to hide the ink by wearing the blouse with a sweater. And when the blouse wore out, there was still an ink stain on the pocket."

"Would you like some coffee, Hannah?" Delores asked

her. "It's only seven-thirty and I think coffee would perk me up."

"Coffee would be good. I'll go make some. And is there any dessert left? That Apple Crisp that Michelle made was really good."

"There's almost half a pan left, Hannah," Michelle told her. "I stuck it in the refrigerator. You make the coffee and I'll warm the Apple Crisp a little."

"And I'll bring Hannah a cold cloth to put on her eyes," Lisa announced. "And then, just as soon as the Apple Crisp is warm, I'll top everybody's slice with a scoop of vanilla ice cream."

"How about you, dear?" Delores asked Hannah. "Would you like Apple Crisp with ice cream? Or do your eyes hurt too much for a second helping of dessert?"

Hannah gave a little laugh. "You should know me better than that, Mother. Nothing could ever affect my appetite for dessert, especially if it's as good as the Apple Crisp."

"The dessert buffet!" Delores exclaimed, startling all three of them.

"What dessert buffet?" Hannah asked her.

"The one Essie told us about today. She said that they had champagne and a wonderful dessert buffet at the first Christmas Ball, and she just wished that she could remember all the desserts that were there."

"I wonder if there's a photo," Hannah said, looking thoughtful. "How long ago do you think they held the Christmas Ball?"

"I'm not sure," answered. You'll have to ask one of the older people in town."

Somehow, Hannah managed to keep the smile off her face. She doubted that Delores was more than ten years younger than Essie, and perhaps not even that much.

"Why did you want to know the year, Hannah?" Delores asked.

"I was wondering if there might be photographs of the ball in the archives at the newspaper office. Rod has copies dating back a long time ago, when his father was the editor."

"That's a wonderful idea, dear!" Delores said, looking pleased. "I'm afraid I don't remember the ball at all because I was in grade school at the time. There could be photos, or a detailed article. It was a huge event in Lake Eden. And that does give me a marvelous idea, dear."

Delores stopped speaking and Hannah knew that she was waiting for a dose of breathless prompting to share her idea. "Please tell us your idea, Mother."

"Based on how much help Michelle and Lisa were to you when you prepared dinner..." Delores turned to them, "Would you girls like to go with me to visit Essie at the hospital?"

"I'll go," Lisa agreed quickly. "Mother's in the hospice ward and sometimes I visit her after school. One of my teachers has a friend in the hospital and she gives me a ride there."

"I'll go, too," Michelle offered. "I've gone with Lisa to visit her mother a couple of times and there was always someone there who offered us a ride back to town. There's no reason why we can't go out to visit Lisa's mother and then meet you at Essie's room."

"Good! I'd like you girls to take notes when Essie describes the Christmas Ball. Grandma Knudson and Annie will meet us there, too. And if you girls aren't too busy, I'm hoping that you'll help Hannah bake for the Christmas Buffet."

"When will that be?" Lisa asked.

"Two weeks before Christmas, before everyone gets caught up in their own round of holiday baking and parties and entertaining."

"I'll help Hannah," Michelle agreed quickly. "The junior play isn't until the middle of January and they always suspend rehearsals during the holidays."

"I'll help, too, if Hannah wants us," Lisa agreed. "I love to bake and it'll be fun."

Hannah, who had been surprised at the news that Delores expected her to bake enough cookies, pies, cakes, and other sweet treats to fill an entire dessert buffet, felt a wave of relief wash over her. "I'd love it if you two would help me," she said quickly. "The baking will go a lot faster that way." She turned to Delores. "Please tell me what you remember about the buffet."

"Of course I didn't see it myself, but I do know that Essie was very impressed with the buffet and all the decorations. She told Grandma Knudson, Annie, and I that the grand celebration at the end was simply amazing."

"Tell us about it," Michelle urged, and Hannah gave her an approving look. Michelle had anticipated the question that she would have asked.

"As I told you before, I wasn't actually there, but everyone in Lake Eden was talking about it the next day. Everyone there was very impressed with the Christmas Cake Parade."

"What's a Christmas cake parade?" Lisa asked her.

"They turned off the lights in the ballroom and the waiters walked in with cakes that the Albion kitchen staff had baked for the occasion. Essie said one was shaped like a large Christmas tree, others were in various Christmas shapes and colors, and one had circles of glazed fruit on the top in red and green."

Lisa looked puzzled. "Cherries are red, but which fruit is green?"

"I really don't know, dear. I wasn't there, remember?"

"It could have been slices of melon," Hannah suggested. "Honeydew melon is green. Or perhaps it was kiwi if people used it back then."

"Whatever." Delores dismissed the speculation and turned to Hannah. "I was hoping that you girls could do a Christmas Cake Parade for Essie. She would love it so!"

"There's no way we can bake all those cakes on the day of the Christmas Ball," Hannah told her, "unless . . ."

"Unless what?" Delores, Lisa, and Michelle asked, almost simultaneously.

"Unless Mother will buy a big chest freezer and hook it up in the garage. Then we can start baking the cakes, wrap them and freeze them, and frost them on the day of the ball."

"I'll be glad to buy a large chest freezer," Delores said quickly. "It's a double garage and there are several electrical outlets. Since I'm using only one space for my car, we could put the chest freezer on the other side of the garage."

"Then I think we have a plan that'll work," Hannah said with a smile. "Let's all go out to look at the garage right now. We can figure out where we should put the freezer."

"Could we delay that for a few minutes?" Delores asked.

"Of course," Hannah agreed quickly. "Why don't you want to do it right away?"

"Because I keep thinking about that Apple Crisp and how good it was. I ate so much at dinner, I didn't think I could eat any more today, but I was wrong and I'm actually hungry for a second helping."

# HONEY APPLE CRISP

Preheat oven to 350 degrees F., rack in the middle position.

Graham crackers to line the baking pan
8 to 9 cups thinly sliced apples (*I used a combination of Granny Smith and Gala, peeled, cored, and sliced as thin as a quarter.*)
1 Tablespoon lemon juice
½ cup white (*granulated*) sugar
½ teaspoon cinnamon
¼ teaspoon nutmeg
¼ teaspoon cardamom
1 cup honey (*I used orange honey, but clover is also good—spray inside of measuring cup with Pam or another nonstick cooking spray to keep the honey from sticking to the inside of the cup.*)
½ cup brown sugar (*Pack it down when you measure it.*)
1 cup all-purpose flour (*Pack it down when you measure it.*)
½ teaspoon salt
½ cup (*1 stick, 4 ounces, ¼ pound*) salted butter

Prepare a 9-inch by 13-inch baking pan by spraying the inside with Pam or another nonstick cooking spray, or buttering it. Line the bottom with graham crackers.

Spread the apple slices over the bottom of a baking dish.

Sprinkle the apples with the lemon juice.

Mix the white sugar with the cinnamon, nutmeg, and cardamom.

Sprinkle on the white granulated sugar mixture.

Drizzle the honey over the top of the apples as evenly as possible.

In a separate bowl, mix the brown sugar with the flour and the salt.

Melt the butter in a microwave-safe bowl or measuring cup for 30 seconds on HIGH. Leave it in the microwave for an additional minute and then check it to see if it's melted. If it's not, heat it on HIGH for increments of 20 seconds, followed by 20-second standing times until it is.

**Michelle's Note: You can also melt the butter over LOW heat on the stovetop if you prefer, but stir it constantly and be careful not to brown it.**

Let the butter cool on a cold burner or a towel on the counter for 5 minutes and then pour it over the brown sugar, flour, and salt mixture in your bowl.

Use your impeccably clean hands to mix everything together until the mixture resembles coarse gravel.

Sprinkle the mixture over the top of your pan as evenly as possible.

Bake your Honey Apple Crisp at 350 degrees F. for 50 minutes, or until the apples are tender. You can test for tenderness by sticking a fork into the center of the baking pan. If you encounter resistance from the apple slices, bake it for another 10 minutes and then test again. When your fork goes all the way to the bottom of the pan and the crust on top is a deep golden brown, your Honey Apple Crisp is done.

Honey Apple Crisp is wonderful served either warm or cold. Serve in dessert dishes.

If you'd like to dress up your Honey Apple Crisp a bit, top each dessert bowl with a scoop of vanilla ice cream or a generous dollop of sweetened whipped cream.

Yield: Serves at least 12 unless everyone at the table wants more.

# Chapter Five

Hannah opened the door to the small building that housed their local paper and was immediately grateful that the printing press wasn't running. At least she'd be able to talk to Rod today. When she'd mentioned how loud the old printing press was, he'd pointed to the ancient linotype machine against the back wall of the main room. He told her that the press was fairly quiet compared to the clatter of the linotype machine, and he knew because he'd worked here as a teenager. He'd said that it had been a true cacophony when both machines had been running at the same time.

She had asked Rod how the linotype machine worked and he'd told her that one of his earliest memories was watching his mother, sitting on the stool in front of the mammoth machine, her fingers flying over the keyboard to make the molten metal type. Each piece that came out of the machine was stamped with an uppercase or lowercase letter that dropped down to cool in the metal type case that would be locked in a frame that printed the newspaper. Rod had bragged that his mother could proofread the lines of type in the frame even though they were upside down and backward.

"Hi, Hannah," Rod said, coming into the main room. "What can I do for you today?"

"I'm helping Mother with some things and I have a couple of questions for you."

"All right," Rod said, pointing to the chair in front of his desk.

Hannah sat down and drew a deep breath. "First of all, did you know that Essie was in the hospice ward at the hospital?"

"Yes, Doc Knight told me. He said that Essie didn't have electricity or plumbing in those two rooms of hers at the hotel, and she'd fallen down the stairs trying to get to the café to use the bathroom there."

"Did he tell you that Essie wasn't terminal?"

"He did. Doc said he's keeping her on hospice because she broke her hip and there's no way she can manage on her own again until it heals."

"That's what Grandma Knudson and Annie Winters told us yesterday. They stopped by the house after they visited Essie in the hospital and Essie described the first Christmas Ball that was held at the Albion Hotel. She said that was truly wonderful, and it was the night she'd met her husband."

"It's all true," Rod said. "The Albion was beautiful when it was new, and the second floor ballroom was magnificent. I wish you could have seen it. It's really too bad the highway department decided to change their plans for the Interstate. It would have made all the difference in the world to Alton and Essie."

"What do you mean?" Hannah asked him.

"The Interstate was supposed to run right past Lake Eden where the old highway is now. That's the reason why Alton built the Albion Hotel here. Everyone back then thought that Lake Eden would grow by leaps and bounds, that new businesses and industries would be built here. They thought we would become a big city instead of a small town. And that meant we'd need a nice hotel."

Hannah had never heard this story before and she was intrigued. "But that didn't happen?"

"No. I remember my father saying that there must have been some crooked dealing going on to move the highway project to another town, but no one was ever able to prove it."

"Poor Alton!" Hannah said. "And poor Essie, too."

Rod nodded. "It was a bad stroke of luck for them. They managed to keep the hotel going for a while, but the odds were against them even though people in Lake Eden loved that hotel. They operated it at a reduced capacity for a decade or two, but it was a losing battle. Lake Eden simply didn't get enough visitors to stay there and keep it open."

"I don't remember Alton at all," Hannah told him.

"You wouldn't. He died when you were quite young. The hotel was still partially open then, and Essie and Alton did a lot of the work themselves. The Red Velvet Lounge was still making a profit on their lunches and the bar was a popular spot at night. Essie supervised the hotel staff, and Alton set up a dance floor in the lobby with live music. That and the appetizers Essie served at the bar pulled in some revenue. And even though they were working long days, Essie still held her Saturday story-time for the kids."

"I remember. I was one of those kids and so were Andrea and Michelle. But Essie didn't make a profit on her story-time, did she?"

"Not a cent. She just liked children and wanted to do something for them and their families. I wish we'd known what dire straits Essie was in, but I guess she was too proud to ask for help."

"That's what Mother said and both of you are probably right." Hannah stopped and took a deep breath. "But we're all going to help Essie now."

"Do you mean because your mother, Grandma Knudson, and Annie are on the case?"

"That's part of it. Separately, each one is a force. Together . . ." Hannah paused as she tried to come up with the perfect word.

"They're indomitable," Rod supplied it.

"Exactly. When Grandma Knudson and Annie visited Essie in the hospital, Essie said that her fondest wish was that she could see the hotel ballroom the way it was the night she met Alton at the first Christmas Ball."

Rod held up his hand to stop her. "Let me guess. Grandma Knudson and Annie talked your mother into helping to recreate the Christmas Ball for Essie."

"Yes, and Mother recruited all of us to help her. Michelle, Lisa, and I are in charge of the dessert buffet and she wants us to recreate it, just the way it was then. She also wants us to bake all the cakes for the Christmas Cake Parade. The only problem is, we're not sure what they looked like. Mother can't help us with that part of it because she was still in grade school and children weren't allowed to attend the Christmas Ball."

Rod did his best to stifle a laugh, but he couldn't quite manage it. "Delores told you that she was in grade school at the time?"

"Yes. And I know that you were in her class, so I'm assuming that you didn't go to the ball either."

"Well . . ." Rod paused and Hannah could tell he was debating the wisdom of contradicting Delores. He was silent for a moment and then he must have come to a decision, because he went on speaking. "I was in your mother's class. That much is true. And I wasn't allowed to go to the Christmas Ball. But both of us were in high school, not grade school."

"That's what I thought and thanks for telling me. I thought that the age Mother claimed to be wasn't her real age. I'm curious, though. If you were in high school, why weren't you allowed to go to the ball?"

"Because they were serving champagne and my mother

was a strict teetotaler. She didn't want me anywhere near what she called *Devil Juice*. My dad wouldn't have gone either, but he managed to convince her that someone had to cover the event for the newspaper."

Hannah felt her hopes begin to rise. "Did your father take photos of the ball for the paper?"

"He certainly did. They're in the archives in the back room. You're welcome to look if you promise not to tell your mother that I ratted her out to you."

Hannah and Rod exchanged grins. "I promise I'll never tell her," Hannah said.

"That's good enough for me. Have at it, Hannah. And come out here when you need a breath of fresh air. It's pretty dusty back there."

After three trips outside to breathe the fresh, cold air, Hannah found what she needed. The newspaper photos were old and brittle, but Rod had a copier in the main room and she took the newspaper to him.

"I found it and there's a photo of the dessert buffet. Can you copy it for me?"

"Of course." Rod drew the newspaper out of its folder and carried it to the copier. He spread it out carefully, copied the photos and article, returned the original paper to its folder, and handed the copies to Hannah.

"Remember your promise," he warned her.

"I won't forget. Both of us would be in for it if I tell Mother that I know she's being creative with her age."

"*Creative?*" Rod laughed. "That's a nice way of putting it. Do you want me to give you a ride back to your mother's house, Hannah? It's cold outside."

"Thanks, but I'll walk. It's only a couple of blocks. It's not as cold as it was yesterday, and I want to stop at the hardware store. I need a new reading lamp." Hannah took her parka off the rack by the front door and put it on. Then she wrapped her warm winter scarf around her neck, and pulled on her gloves. "Did you happen to block out the date on the paper, Rod?"

"Relax. There's no date on anything I copied, Hannah. I used the copier to enlarge the photo to the size my father would have printed them in his darkroom. That way, you can tell your mother that I found the actual photos and I copied them for you."

"That was brilliant!" Hannah complimented him.

"I have my moments. There's no way I wanted to get either of us in trouble with your mother!"

Hannah was smiling as she went out the door, and she was still smiling when she let herself into her mother's house with her new reading lamp and the precious copies in hand.

"I'm home!" she called out, but no one answered. Delores, Michelle, and Lisa must still be at the hospital with Essie. She glanced at the kitchen clock and realized that she had time to make her mother's favorite meatloaf for dinner. Baked potatoes with sour cream and chives would be nice too, and since she had time, she could even try to make the peach pie that her mother loved for dessert.

Even though she knew that she couldn't carry a tune, Hannah hummed a Christmas carol as she mixed up the meatloaf and prepared the potatoes for baking. Her mother's favorite pie, Anytime Peach Pie made with canned peaches, was next and Hannah sang as she rolled out the crust and filled it. She was on the fifth verse of a Christmas carol that no one who heard her would be able to recognize, when the front doorbell rang. She hurried to open it and was surprised to see Michelle and Lisa standing on the front porch. "Where's Mother?" Hannah asked them.

"She dropped us off here and told us that she was going to drive over to see Carrie Rhodes to ask her if she'll help with the Christmas Ball."

"That's good news," Hannah said, beginning to smile. Carrie and Delores had been friends for years and even though Carrie had called and dropped by, Delores had pleaded exhaustion and said she couldn't see Carrie. "Mother is definitely feeling better if she went to see Carrie."

"That's what I told Lisa," Michelle commented. "What smells so good, Hannah?"

"Meatloaf, baked potatoes, and the Anytime Peach Pie I just made. I managed to get everything in the oven at once."

"I just love peach pie!" Lisa said. "Where did you get peaches this time of year? I went to the Red Owl two days ago and Florence didn't have them."

"That's why I called it Anytime Peach Pie. It's made with canned peaches so you can bake it even when the stores don't have fresh, ripe peaches."

"What a great idea! We'll set the table in the dining room again if you want us to," Lisa offered as they hung their parkas in the closet.

"Hannah made one of Mother's favorite meals again," Michelle told Lisa. "Mother just loves Hannah's meatloaf and her peach pie."

The two girls got to work and in less than ten minutes, the table in the dining room was set. Hannah stood in the doorway and gave an approving nod. "The table looks wonderful. I've always loved that wine-colored tablecloth. And I see you have some flowers arranged as a centerpiece again."

"Lisa did that," Michelle told her. "She's going to teach me about flower arrangement."

"How did your learn?" Hannah asked Lisa.

"From my mom. She took one of those adult classes out at the community college before she got sick." Lisa turned to Michelle. "It's really fun to make something beautiful. You'll see."

"Let's all go in the living room," Hannah suggested. "I bought a new reading lamp today and I want to show it to you. I thought it might make it easier for me to read Essie's notebooks."

Michelle and Lisa followed Hannah into the living room.

When she took the new reading lamp out of its box, the two girls agreed that it was bound to be an improvement over the tabletop lamp that Hannah had been using. They helped to set it up, choosing the proper sized bulb, plugged it in, and then they turned it on.

"It's much better," Lisa decided, giving a little nod.

"I think so, too," Michelle agreed. "Do you have time to sit down, Hannah?"

Hannah glanced at her watch. "Yes, I have a few minutes."

Michelle and Lisa exchanged glances and then Michelle went on. "Good. There's something we want to talk to you about."

"What is it?" Hannah asked, perching on the arm of the sofa.

"If you don't mind telling us, we were wondering what your future plans were now that Mother's finally getting back to normal."

"Plans?"

"Yes, plans," Lisa said. "Michelle and I wanted to know if you were going back to college to get your doctorate."

"I'm not going back to college," Hannah told them, making up her mind on the spot. "I've been in college for almost six years and it's time for me to decide what I want to do with my life."

"But I thought you wanted to be a college professor," Michelle said. "Don't you need a doctorate for that?"

"You do, but I changed my mind about that."

"Do you want to be a high school teacher?" This time it was Lisa who asked the question.

"I don't think so. Actually, I'm not sure I want to teach at all."

Michelle looked worried. "What *do* you want to do?"

"I don't know yet. I'll just have to get a job and figure it out. All I know is that I want to go in a new direction."

"But . . . you don't want to stay here and live with Mother, do you?"

"No, Michelle. I want to get my own place and that means I need to find a job."

"What kind of job would you like to have?" Lisa asked her.

"I don't know. Almost six years of college ought to qualify me to do something."

"You could always get a job out at DelRay Manufacturing," Michelle suggested. "They're hiring out there. I saw something in the paper about an executive secretary position and Mother knows Del Woodley. I'm sure he could find something for you."

Hannah couldn't help feeling slightly depressed at the thought of holding down a secretarial job or something on the assembly line for the rest of her life.

"I think we're asking the wrong questions," Lisa said, noticing Hannah's lack of enthusiasm. "If you could have any career you wanted to have, what would it be? Tell us your dream job."

Hannah thought about that for a moment and then she decided. "I love to bake and I'd really like to have my own bakery and coffee shop. That sounds a little crazy because I've never had any culinary training, but that's my dream job."

"Excuse me, girls."

Hannah, Lisa, and Michelle turned to see Delores standing in the living room doorway. "I came in through the kitchen and the stove timer's ringing. Is there something in the oven that has to come out now?"

"My pie!" Hannah said.

"I'll get it," Lisa said, jumping up before Hannah could move and hurrying to the kitchen.

"It smells marvelous, dear," Delores told Hannah. "Is it my favorite Anytime Peach Pie?"

"Yes, it is."

"I'm back," Lisa announced, coming in from the kitchen.

"I put the pie on a rack on the back porch. I thought it would cool faster that way. Is that all right, Hannah?"

"That's just fine, Lisa. And you're right. It'll be cool by the time we're ready for dessert."

"I'm sorry, but I couldn't help overhearing part of your conversation," Delores told them, taking off her coat and folding it over her arm. "Are you sure you don't want to go back to college, Hannah?"

"I'm sure," Hannah told her, knowing that the last thing she wanted to do was return to college and meet the associate professor she'd loved, walking across the campus with his new wife. It was just too painful to contemplate, but that wasn't the only reason she didn't want to go back.

"Why is that, dear?" Delores asked her.

"Part of the reason is exactly what I told the girls. I'm beginning to regret my career choice. I'm just not sure that I want to teach at the college level."

"Then I think I might have a solution for you," Delores told her. "Just let me hang up my coat and freshen up a bit and then I'll tell you about it. Is that all right, Hannah?"

"Of course," Hannah replied, wondering what possible solution her mother could have.

"Do I smell meatloaf, Hannah?" Delores turned back at the doorway to ask.

"Yes, you were right on two counts, the peach pie and the meatloaf. Can you sniff out what I'll be serving with the meatloaf?"

"No, but I hope it's baked potatoes."

"Now you're three for three," Hannah said with a laugh. "And there's a salad chilling in the refrigerator."

"Perfect! You're a marvelous cook, Hannah, and I'm simply starved! How long will it be before dinner is ready?"

Hannah glanced at her watch again. "Less than thirty minutes, Mother. Do you think you can wait that long?"

"I'm not sure, but I'll have to, won't I?"

"Yes, for the main course and dessert, but I have some cheese and crackers. Why don't I pour you a glass of champagne and we'll sit in here and munch until our dinner is ready?"

"Lovely! I'll join you here in a few minutes. Let's have a fire in the fireplace. That will be nice and cozy."

"I can start it," Lisa offered, glancing at the fireplace. "You have logs in the grate, but they won't last for long. If the wood is outside, I'll bring in more."

Delores laughed and Hannah and Michelle joined in. "Thank you for offering, Lisa, but we don't need more wood," Delores told her. "We have a gas fireplace."

"A gas fireplace?" Lisa looked surprised. "I've never seen one of those before."

"That's probably because most people in town have wood-burning fireplaces. Lars converted ours when we moved into this house. You girls show Lisa how it works and I'll be back as soon as I can. Then I'll tell you my solution to Hannah's problem."

Hannah waited until Delores had left the room and then she motioned to Lisa. "Come with me and I'll show you how to turn on the fireplace."

Once Lisa had followed Hannah to the fireplace, Hannah pointed to a switch on the wall. "Do you see that switch?"

"I see it. It looks like a light switch."

"It's not, but it operates exactly the same way. Flick it up, Lisa. That turns on the fireplace."

"Okay." Lisa looked a bit nervous as she flicked up the switch. And then she jumped back as the gas whooshed out of the gas line that ran beneath the concrete logs and burst into flames.

"It's easy, isn't it?" Michelle asked Lisa as she came up to join them.

"I'll say! It sure beats putting on a coat and mittens and boots and going out in the backyard to get more wood from the woodpile." She turned to Hannah. "Do you push the switch down to turn it off?"

"Yes, but don't do it now. We'll let this room warm up a little while we arrange the cheese and crackers on a plate."

"Your fireplace is just amazing!" Lisa was clearly impressed as she followed Hannah to the kitchen. "If we had one at home, I'd never have to shovel the ashes into a pail when I cleaned under the grate. And we'd never have to worry that sparks would jump out onto the living room rug. And I'd never have to go outside with Dad to split wood. The only thing that's missing is the smell of wood burning and that doesn't bother me at all."

"Me neither," Michelle agreed. "And the way our fireplace flickers looks almost real."

"It warms up the room too, because the flames are controlled, but real," Hannah added.

"How much does it cost to convert a wood-burning fireplace to one like yours?" Lisa asked Hannah.

"I have no idea. Dad owned the hardware store so he got everything at a discount from his suppliers."

"That must have been nice."

"Oh, it was," Michelle said. "Mother always had all the large and small appliances she wanted. I'll never forget when we got our first food processor. Hannah used it to chop up hard-boiled eggs and she made me egg salad sandwiches for a solid week."

Lisa laughed. "I'll bet you got sick of egg salad sandwiches."

"Nope, I still love them just as much as I ever did."

As she opened the refrigerator and took out the cheese, Hannah made a mental note to make egg salad sandwiches for Michelle. "Here's the cheese," she said, putting it on the kitchen table. "I'll get knives and cutting boards for both of you and then I'll look in the pantry to see what kinds of crackers we have on hand."

With all three of them working, the cheese and cracker platter was ready in a very short time. Michelle carried it to the living room and set it on the coffee table, Lisa laid out small paper plates and napkins, and Hannah opened her mother's favorite champagne. They had just taken seats when Delores came down the stairs and entered the living room.

"Oh, my!" Delores exclaimed when she saw the platter. "I didn't realize I had that many different kinds of cheese."

"You didn't," Hannah told her. "I stopped at the Red Owl on the way home and Florence picked out some of her favorites. The brie is closest to you. Florence told me that it was a triple cream. Over here," Hannah pointed to one of the cheeses, "we have a blue cheese. For sliced cheese we have white cheddar, Swiss, mild cheddar, Monterey Jack, and Havarti."

"We put the Ritz Crackers closest to you, Mother." Michelle began to describe the crackers. "Next is a stone-ground wheat cracker, and there's also a row of Carr's water biscuits."

"Wonderful," Delores said with a smile.

"The napkins are paper towels from the roll in the kitchen that I folded in quarters," Lisa told Delores. "And that's because I couldn't find any cocktail napkins."

Delores laughed. "And that's just fine, Lisa. They'll work just as well." She turned to Hannah. "Am I right in thinking that you and I have flutes of Perrier Jouët and the girls have sparkling apple juice?"

"You're right. Help yourself, Mother. The meatloaf is cooling in the kitchen and so are the baked potatoes. And I brought the pie in and placed it on a cold stovetop burner. We can eat our dinner in about twenty minutes."

"That's just perfect, dear." Delores picked up a Ritz Cracker, used the knife next to the brie, and cut a wedge to put on top of her cracker. "While I was upstairs, I called Andrea and asked her to meet me at the hotel tomorrow morning. We're going to make notes on what we should do to decorate the ballroom once the repairs are done. She sounded very excited about the Christmas Ball and promised to help any way she can."

"Good!" Hannah said with a smile. "Andrea's very talented when it comes to things like flower arrangements and table decorations."

"Exactly. And she was very grateful when I told her that since she'd opted not to go to college, there was money in her college fund to pay off the loan that they'd taken out for the down payment on the house."

"That was very generous of you, Mother," Michelle said.

"Thank you. And that brings me to you, Michelle," Delores continued. "You may not know this, but your father made some very wise investments before we were married. He had a good job and he still lived at home so he didn't have many expenses. He bought stock with the remainder of his paycheck and he invested heavily in a small company called Minnesota Mining and Manufacturing. Of course that small company turned into a huge corporation and by the time we got married, he'd already made enough profit on the stock to buy the hardware store. Your father was a very intelligent man."

"I know he was," Hannah said, and Michelle gave a nod of agreement.

"When we found out that I was pregnant with Hannah, we decided to start a college fund for her. We did this for each of you." Delores paused long enough to fix herself another cracker, this time with white cheddar cheese, and went on with her explanation after she'd eaten it. "Everything turned out very well for almost all of your father's investments. He only lost on one and he sold that before there was any real damage. He could have been a marvelous stockbroker or investment counselor, but he was more interested in running the hardware store."

"I never realized that Dad was that successful," Michelle said.

"Neither did I," Delores admitted with a little laugh.

"Your father did all of the banking, paid the bills, and took care of everything for us. He told me not to worry about money because that was his job, so I never gave it another thought. I had no idea that he'd established investment accounts for all three of you girls. It was only after he . . . he died that I realized that your college funds had grown enough for each of you to get your doctorate."

"You mean . . . I could go for my doctorate if I wanted to?" Michelle asked her.

"Yes, your father figured that it would take five years of college to earn a master's degree and another two years to earn a doctorate. He kept up with tuition prices at major universities and living expenses on and off campus. He wanted to make sure that his daughters could realize their dreams, and he wanted to give all three of you a good start in life. He put it all in a letter he wrote and left with Howie Levine for me." Delores turned to Hannah. "I'm sorry I never mentioned this to you, Hannah. I was just too depressed to talk about it before."

"I understand, Mother," Hannah said, and then she reached out to give her mother a hug. And her mother, who'd grown up in an undemonstrative family, surprised Hannah by hugging her back.

"And that brings me to you, Hannah," Delores told her. "You have two years of expenses left in your college fund. If you really don't want to go back to college for your doctorate, I think I have a plan for you."

"What is it, Mother?"

"Use the money to rent the bakery on Main Street. It's only been vacant for a few months and before she left, Veronica told me that all the major appliances are in excellent shape. Alex listed it for sale with Al Percy, but Veronica said that if it didn't sell within four months, they were going to rent it out with an option to buy. I'll give Al a call to make sure, but since that was over five months ago, it must be for rent by now. I think you should rent it, Hannah."

Hannah just blinked. She was too shocked to say a word. But suddenly the world was a much friendlier place than it had been only moments before.

"That's exciting, Mother," Michelle said. "Are you going to go down there and take a look at the bakery?"

"That's my plan, Michelle. I'll make an appointment with Al for tomorrow morning and Hannah and I will go down there. If everything is still functional and Hannah wants to rent it, I'll make a deal with Al for the rent." Delores turned to Hannah. "If it's in good shape, you can do all the baking down there for the Christmas Ball. And if the bakery doesn't have a freezer, I'll change the delivery address for the one I ordered on the phone yesterday. How does that sound, Hannah?"

Hannah, who'd always felt a bit resentful of the way that Delores had wanted to control her life, was so glad that her mother was back to normal again, she found that she didn't mind in the slightest.

"Of course it's your decision, Hannah," Delores said. "If you don't want me to do that, just say so and I won't."

Hannah began to smile. Delores had always simply done things and this was the first time Hannah could remember that she'd actually asked for anyone else's opinion.

"Hannah?" Delores prompted.

"It sounds like a dream come true, Mother," she said. "Thank you so much for thinking of it."

"Good." Delores glanced at her watch. "Only fifteen minutes to go until it's time for the meatloaf and baked potatoes. Have some more cheese, girls. And then we'll go in the dining room and eat my very favorite meal."

# Chapter Six

"That was superb, dear," Delores complimented Hannah. "Perhaps I should offer to send you to culinary school so that we could open a restaurant."

Hannah shook her head. "No thanks, Mother. I like to cook, but I *love* to bake. And there's no way I'd open a restaurant here in town."

"Why?" Delores asked her.

"I wouldn't like to compete with Hal and Rose at the café. If I open a bakery, I wouldn't be competing because I wouldn't be offering breakfast, lunch, or dinner."

It was clear by her expression that Delores was puzzled. "But I thought you wanted to open a coffee shop with your bakery."

"I do, but all I'm going to sell is baked goods."

"Rose has doughnuts, sweet rolls, and pies at the café," Michelle pointed out.

"That's true, but it's not the bulk of her business. Rose doesn't bake the doughnuts and sweet rolls."

"How about pies?"

"If I have them, it won't be often. And I'll check with Rose before I even consider it. I'm going to call my bakery The Cookie Jar. I'll have big jars filled with cookies on display and people can buy them to have with their coffee."

"That sounds good, dear," Delores said. "Rose shouldn't

have a problem with a coffee shop like the one you just described. Let's clear the table and put away the leftovers. And then we can have dessert."

"That sounds good to me," Hannah said. "I'll put on the coffee while the girls do that."

"Perfect," Delores agreed. "I'm really looking forward to that pie. And when we're done cleaning up, we'll go in the living room and listen to you read more of Essie's notebooks."

Once the bus arrived in Brooklyn, she peered out the window and wondered where to go. The driver had been stopping to let people off and she waited until she saw a small café in the middle of a block before she got up from her seat and stood in the front, indicating that it was her stop.

The driver nodded to acknowledge her, and pulled over at the bus stop on the corner. She got off and walked quickly to the café she'd seen from the bus window.

The café was small and very clean inside. Customers were sitting at the counter and there was a table open near the back of the room. She headed straight for the table, pulled out the chair, and sat down.

There was only one waitress working, an older woman with frizzy hair who seemed to know the customers at the counter. She took a moment to deliver two plates, one with an omelet and the other with a hamburger, and then the waitress, who was wearing a name tag, hurried over to the table. "What can I get for you, honey?" she asked.

"Coffee and a hamburger, please," she responded, glad that she'd cashed her last paycheck and had the money to pay for her meal.

"You haven't been in here before, have you?"

"No, we just moved here and we got a notice that our building is being tented tonight. I was wondering if you knew of a nice hotel where we could stay for a couple of nights."

"There's the Garden Spot, but I wouldn't go there. It's pretty run-down and from what my regulars tell me, it's not very clean. If I were you, I'd stay at the Dubuque. It's not fancy, but it's nice and clean, and they'll treat you right."

"Where is the Dubuque?" she asked.

"Two blocks back that way," the waitress pointed. "You can't miss it. It's just past the drugstore. I'd go there right after you finish eating, though. It's the nicest hotel around here and they fill up fast."

She glanced at the waitress's name tag again. "Thanks, Fern. I really appreciate the advice."

Less than an hour later, she was sitting on the edge of the bed in a third-floor room at the Dubuque Hotel. Fern had been right. It was clean and the man at the desk had been friendly when she'd checked in and paid for two nights in cash. She'd given him the same story she'd given Fern, that their apartment building was being tented for the night and they had to stay somewhere else. He'd asked her why she'd paid for two nights when their building was only being tented for one night. She'd quickly concocted an explanation and told him that since she was pregnant, her husband hadn't wanted to take any chances on anything that might hurt their baby.

"Smart man," the desk clerk had told her. "I'd make the same decision if I got married and my wife got pregnant."

She sighed as she opened the bag of items she'd purchased on her way to the hotel. She had a bottle of peroxide and blond hair dye, an oversize raincoat that she hoped would hide her pregnancy, and some snacks she'd picked up at the front drugstore counter. All this would fit in the duffel bag now that the bulky package had been mailed.

It was lonely in a hotel room all by herself and she wished that her husband was with her. Even though they'd discussed it, she still hadn't decided exactly where she should go. Sharon knew that she couldn't go to any of Tony's relatives in California. They'd talked about that and decided it would be the first place anyone would look for her. She would buy a ticket to

California, just to throw everyone off the track, but she'd get off the train somewhere in the Midwest.

"But how will you find me if you don't know where I am?" she'd asked Tony.

"Don't worry, honey. I promise that I'll find you," he'd told her. "I want you to get off the train somewhere in Minnesota."

"Why Minnesota?" she'd asked him.

"Because I've never been there. You haven't either, have you?"

"No, never."

"Then they'll never expect you to go there, especially in the winter. I've heard about Minnesota winters."

"What did you hear about them?" she'd asked.

"It's really cold in Minnesota and sometimes they have blizzards with lots of snow."

"It doesn't sound very nice," she'd commented.

"You'll be all right. I'll make sure you have everything you need. And I'll look for you there and find you."

A tear ran down her cheek and she brushed it away. She had to be strong for their baby. Tony would find her. He'd promised. She had to believe that her husband was all right and they didn't suspect anyone except her.

An hour after she'd transformed her appearance and her hair had dried, she finally gathered enough courage to look in the mirror. What she saw gave her hope that the plan she'd discussed with her husband would actually work. She'd cut her long dark hair short and since it was naturally curly, it had curled up in ringlets. The peroxide and blond hair dye had done its work, but the final result didn't look as ridiculous as she'd feared. No one she knew would recognize her now.

She pulled out the oversized raincoat she'd found in the thrift shop she'd passed, zipped out the lining, and tried it on. It covered her pregnancy fairly well. Anyone who saw her would simply assume that she was overweight. Even though it was cold in New York this time of year, she'd wear the raincoat without the liner when she bought the train ticket to California. The station would be warm and the train would be warm, too.

She stuffed the liner into the duffel bag and hoped that the conductor and the other passengers would assume that it was her carry-on luggage.

The hamburger she'd had at the café for lunch had been inexpensive and good. She considered going back there for dinner, but perhaps that wasn't a good idea. It would be best to eat the snacks she'd purchased and not take chances. She'd followed her husband's advice and been very aware of her surroundings. She'd watched and she knew that no one else had gotten off the bus when she had and no one had followed her to the café. She was safe, at least for now.

When she went to bed, her dreams were filled with fearful conjecture. The gunshots she'd heard as she'd rested on the bench at the bus stop in front of the post office still terrified her. She tried to convince herself that a car had backfired and they hadn't been gunshots at all, but she didn't believe that. They were gunshots. She was sure of it. What if one of those shots had killed her husband? And if he'd somehow escaped, what if he couldn't find her in the Minnesota winter? Neither one of them had ever been there, but she knew it was a fairly large state. How would he know where to look for her?

Another frightening problem was the money. She had some left from her paycheck and he'd tucked some money in the duffel bag, but it would run out eventually. Then what would happen to her? And even more frightening, what would happen to their baby?!

At last the long night was over and she could see the dim light of the dawning day outside her window. She was tired and depressed after her long night of frightening dreams, but she knew that she had to get up and devise a plan. She had to figure out the safest way to get to Minnesota. She couldn't stay here. It was too close to danger.

"I promise I'll keep you safe," she whispered to her unborn baby. "You don't have to worry. I'll find the best way to take care of you."

She took a quick bath in the spotless tub and used the clean bath towel that was hanging on the rack. Then she dressed in the same clothing she'd worn the previous day, picked up the duffel bag, and went out the door. She climbed down the steps to the first floor and glanced at the desk. The friendly clerk who had been there the previous day had been replaced by an older man with a mustache and glasses.

Breathing a sigh of relief, she walked past the desk and out the front door. She was on a mission to find out the location of the train station and learn how to get there. It would have been a simple matter to walk to the café and ask Fern, but that was simply too risky. She'd find another café, in a direction she hadn't gone the previous day, and ask someone there.

Four blocks later, she found a larger café, one with booths and customers sitting at a long counter. She went in the door and took a vacant stool at the counter next to a woman dressed in a business suit, who was just finishing her breakfast. The wall clock over the counter indicated that it was ten minutes before nine in the morning and she knew that if luck was with her, the woman would be hurrying off to her job soon.

"Excuse me," she said to the woman. "I'm new to the area and I have to get to the train station. Do you happen to know where it is?"

"Yes, I do. Are you traveling somewhere?" the woman asked, gesturing toward the duffel bag.

"No." She thought fast and came up with a plausible reason for carrying the duffel bag. "This bag belongs to my husband, but I always take it with me when I go out to shop. That way, I can put several other bags inside and I only have to carry one. I thought I'd just drop by the train station to pick up a schedule so we could go into the city this weekend."

"That duffel bag is a great idea!" the woman declared, giving her an approving look. "I think I'll start doing that, too. We don't have a car and it would be a lot easier than juggling bags of groceries on my walk home. And to answer your question about the train station, all you have to do to get there is turn right when you go out the door, go left at the second corner, walk three more blocks and you're there. There's no way you can miss it. It takes up the whole block across the street and it's a big commuter station so trains are coming in and going out all day."

"Thank you so much," she said, picking up a menu and studying it. It was a menu that covered the whole day and she read through the choices for breakfast, lunch, and dinner. She decided she'd have the cheapest thing on the menu, scrambled eggs and toast, for breakfast.

"Can I take your order?" the waitress asked, noticing her and bustling over, her order pad in her hand.

"Yes, thank you. I'll have scrambled eggs and toast, please."

The waitress nodded. "Do you want coffee with that?"

"Yes, please."

The waitress turned to the lady in the business suit. "Do you want a warm-up on your coffee?"

"I'd love it, but I have to get to work. My supervisor gets crabby if I'm half a minute late." The lady opened her purse, put some money down on the counter, and got up from her stool.

She watched as the lady picked up her bill, hurried to the cash register near the door, and paid for her breakfast. The obvious conclusion was that the money left on the counter was a tip. She noticed the amount of the tip and decided that she'd tip the same amount when she left. That way the waitress would have no reason to remember her.

Hannah stopped reading and frowned. "Essie's story is in the third person, but it's still very realistic. It's almost as if it happened to someone she knew."

"Maybe it happened to Essie, herself." Michelle looked excited at the prospect.

"It didn't happen to Essie," Delores said.

"How do you know?" Lisa asked.

"I talked to Essie while I was waiting for you girls to arrive and I told her that we'd found her notebooks. I apologized for starting to read the first one, and I said that if it was something personal, we'd stop reading immediately and bring them all to her in the hospital."

"What did she say?" Hannah asked.

"She said that they weren't personal at all, that she'd toyed with the idea of writing a novel and someone had told her to write about something she knew. She'd already written the first part about the girl in New York so she decided to have her go to Minnesota because she lived in Minnesota and knew what it was like. Essie said she even set part of the book in a fictional small town and based that town on Lake Eden."

"We're going to hear about Lake Eden in Essie's book?" Michelle asked.

"That's what Essie told me."

"I can hardly wait!" Lisa exclaimed. "This is really exciting. I've never read a book that was set in Lake Eden before."

"A fictional Lake Eden," Delores reminded her. "It may not be the same as our Lake Eden today."

"Did Essie ever type up her manuscript and send her novel to a publisher?" Hannah asked Delores.

"No, Essie said she got stuck partway through when she couldn't decide what she should write next. That's why she quit writing in the notebooks."

"So she just gave up?" Michelle asked, looking disappointed.

"That's what she said. Do you want to stop reading since Essie's story isn't finished?"

"No!" Hannah was the first to give her opinion. "I want to read everything that Essie wrote."

"Me too," Lisa agreed.

Michelle gave a nod. "I'd like to go on, too."

"Then it's settled because so would I," Delores told them. "How about another piece of peach pie, girls? I'll put on more coffee, Michelle can get out the clean dessert plates and forks, Hannah can divide the rest of the pie, and Lisa can put a scoop of vanilla ice cream on top of each piece."

# ANYTIME PEACH PIE

Preheat oven to 425 (four-hundred twenty-five) degrees F., rack in the middle position.

2 nine-inch frozen pie crusts *(or use your favorite pie crust recipe for a 2-crust pie)*
2 cans *(29 ounces net weight each)* sliced peaches
1 teaspoon lemon juice
½ cup white *(granulated)* sugar
3 Tablespoons all-purpose flour
¼ teaspoon ground cinnamon
2 Tablespoons *(¼ stick, ⅛ cup)* cold, salted butter

**Hannah's 1ˢᵗ Note: If you're using frozen pie crusts, leave one in the disposable pan to thaw on the counter and tip the other one upside down over a lightly floured surface, either wax paper or a bread board. Lift up one side of the disposable pan and try gently to pry it out all in one piece. If you can't do that, just leave it upside down on the wax paper or breadboard to thaw. You will use the upside-down crust later as the top crust of your pie.**

Open the cans of sliced peaches and drain them in a strainer. Pat them dry with a paper towel and place them in a large mixing bowl.

Sprinkle the sliced peaches with the lemon juice.

Wash your hands and toss the peach slices with the lemon juice using your impeccably clean hands.

Mix the granulated sugar, all-purpose flour, and ground cinnamon together in a small bowl. *(Use a fork from your silverware drawer to do this.)*

Sprinkle the sugar, flour, and cinnamon mixture over the top of the sliced peaches.

Again, use your impeccably clean hands to mix the dry mixture with the sliced peaches.

Place the pastry-lined bottom crust on a drip pan, either a foil-lined cookie sheet with sides or a disposable drip pan that's large enough to contain any liquid that might spill out of your pie when it bakes.

Place the sliced peaches in your pastry-lined pie pan.

If you used frozen pie crusts, check the second crust to see if it has thawed. If the disposable pie pan is still sitting on top of the crust, gently lift it to see if the crust has come loose and fallen down to the floured surface. If it hasn't, very carefully pry it loose, dust the top of the crust with a little more flour, and use a rolling pin to repair any tears and flatten it out into a smooth, round shape.

Cut the cold, salted butter into 5 to 8 slices and arrange the slices on top of the sliced peaches as evenly as you can.

Spread the top pie crust over the top of the pie, and tuck it under the bottom crust. If your top crust is not large enough to tuck under the bottom crust, spread it out until it covers the bottom crust and use the tines of a fork from your silverware drawer to press the top crust into the bottom crust, sealing it into place. Cut off any excess crust with a sharp knife or a kitchen scissors.

Use a sharp knife to cut slits in the top crust to vent the steam that will escape as you bake your pie.

Tear off narrow strips of aluminum foil to cover the edges of your crust to keep it from browning too much when it bakes.

Bake your peach pie at 425 degrees F. for 20 minutes and then remove the foil strips from the crust.

Bake for an additional 15 to 25 minutes or until the juice from the peaches begins to bubble up through the slits you cut in the top crust and the crust is a rich golden brown.

To serve, cut in wedges and top with sweetened whipped cream or vanilla ice cream.

Yield: 6 to 8 pieces depending on individual appetites.

**Hannah's 2nd Note: If you invite Mother to your house for dessert, you'd better bake two Anytime Peach Pies!**

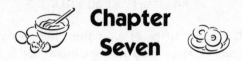

# Chapter
# Seven

When Hannah woke up early the next morning, she realized that she was smiling. Her dream had been filled with visions of people sitting at tables in her coffee shop and bakery, munching on her cookies and drinking coffee. It had been a lovely dream and she fervently hoped that her dream would turn out to be prophetic. Today was a big day. They had an appointment with Al Percy at Lake Eden Realty to look at the bakery rental.

It didn't take long for Hannah to shower and dress, and she was downstairs in the kitchen, pouring her first cup of coffee, at a quarter to seven in the morning. She'd just taken her first sip of the bracing brew when her mother appeared in the doorway.

"Oh, good! You're up early and you made coffee!" Delores said, taking a cup from the cabinet and pouring coffee for herself. "Good morning, dear," she said as she pulled out a kitchen chair and sat down. "Today's a big day for us. I'm really excited about this."

"I know, and so am I."

"Well, we'll find out everything we need to know at nine when Al takes us over to the bakery. It's a good location, dear. Veronica and Alex did very well there."

"All the town kids from Jordan High used to go in there

after school," Hannah told her. "I know because I used to stand in line to buy loaves of their cinnamon raisin bread for Dad."

"Remember how he used to want it slathered with butter and toasted?" Delores asked her.

"I remember. He said that the more butter the better and he used to have it for breakfast every morning."

Delores laughed. "And dip it in his egg yolks. Sometimes he'd drip yolk on one of his nice clean shirts."

"And you'd make him take it off and eat the rest of his breakfast without it. Then you'd rinse out the egg yolk and run upstairs to get another clean shirt for him to wear to work." Hannah drained her coffee cup and got up from her chair to get more. She didn't really want more coffee yet, but she didn't want her mother to notice the tears that had been gathering in her eyes.

"More coffee, Mother?" she asked, bringing the carafe to the table.

"Yes, please." Delores held out her cup so that Hannah could fill it. "This is going to be fun, isn't it, dear?"

"Yes," Hannah answered quickly. "Do you think we should take along a tape measure and a notebook?"

"That's a good idea. You'd better do the measuring, dear. Your father used to tease me by saying that if I measured a board three times, I'd get three different measurements."

Hannah remembered. She'd gone down into the basement of the hardware store with her father once and he'd shown her the three-tiered shelf that Delores had attempted to build for her houseplants. It leaned to one side like the Tower of Pisa, and any plants that her mother had placed on the top would have slid off on the floor.

"Dad told me about that," Hannah said, not mentioning that she'd seen the actual proof of her mother's measuring skills. "Don't worry, Mother. I'll measure and you can take notes."

* * *

"Hello, Delores, Hannah," Al Percy greeted them as they stepped into the real estate office. "Are you ready to take a look at the bakery?"

"We're ready," Delores told him. "I imagine it's pretty cold over there."

"Not really. They turned the thermostat down to a maintenance level, but they didn't shut off the gas or the electricity. The renter will have to take over the utilities, but that's a simple matter of switching it over when the rental agreement is signed."

"Then we can test the appliances to see if they still work?" Hannah asked him.

"Of course. They knew that no one who was going to buy a bakery would make an offer without checking out the appliances. And the same goes for a rental." Al got up from his desk chair, slipped into his parka, and clamped his winter hat on his head. "Come with me, ladies. I'll show you around the place and you can see if it's what you want."

There were snowbanks on either side of Main Street where the snowplow had driven through. The front blade had shoveled hard-packed snow to the side as it plowed, and the banks on either side were over two feet high. Hannah hopped over the one in front of the realty office, ran across the street to the other side, and hopped over the one in front of the bakery.

There was a large plate-glass window at the front of the building and Hannah peered in. There wasn't much to see except two bare walls and a third lined with display cases. There was a door at the back and Hannah had been in the bakery enough times to know that it led to the kitchen in the back of the building.

It took longer for Delores and Al to cross the street because they were walking down the shoveled sidewalk to cross at the corner. Hannah spent that time imagining what she would do with the front room if the bakery were hers. She knew it would be the coffee shop and she decided that she would need a counter on one wall with seating in front of it for her customers and a long shelf on the wall with a mirror behind it to showcase the large glass cookie jars she would use to display her daily cookie offerings. She wouldn't need all of the display cases, and she made a mental note to ask if there was a place she could store them. If she had those in storage, there would be room for more tables and chairs in her coffee shop.

"Are you planning what you want to do with the front room?" Delores asked her.

Hannah turned around to see that her mother had arrived with Al Percy. "Yes, that's exactly what I was doing," she admitted. "I don't remember ever seeing the kitchen and I can hardly wait to see the rest of the space."

"That's easy," Al said, stepping up to unlock the door. He pushed it open, flicked on the lights, and said, "Just follow me and I'll show you around."

As Hannah walked through the main room, she realized that it was bigger than she'd initially thought. She might keep one of the display cases, but she could move it to the space between the window and the front door. Then she could put shelves on the side that were deep enough to contain take-out bakery boxes and containers for coffee. The cash register, which the owners had left, could sit on top of the display case with a stool behind it.

Al led the way to the door that led to the kitchen. Hannah hadn't really noticed its construction when she'd been in the bakery as a customer, but it was a swinging door and there was a diamond-shaped pane of glass at slightly above shoulder level so the person who was leaving the kitchen could see if anyone in the coffee shop was coming in. Al held the door open and Hannah walked through with Delores.

"Oh, my!" Delores exclaimed, walking over to the huge oven. "You could roast a whole side of beef in here."

"Not really," Al told her, opening the door so that she could see the shelves inside. "It's a gas oven, Delores, and the shelves revolve inside so that the cookies, or pies, or loaves of bread get the same exposure to heat from the top and the bottom."

"That's very clever," Delores commented, and then she turned and pointed. "What's the door over there, Al?"

"The pantry. Come with me and I'll show you."

Hannah and Delores followed Al to the huge walk-in pantry. The walls were lined with shelves and there was plenty of room for large bags of flour and sugar.

"Very impressive," Delores said. "How about a bathroom? I assume there's one off the kitchen?"

"Right here." Al opened another door and led them into a small bathroom with a shower cubicle. "There are two more in the main room, just down the hallway that runs along the inside wall. Alex and Veronica put that in when they started serving coffee and pastries." Al pulled out a drawer under the long countertop that was built against one wall. "Veronica saved all the instruction manuals for the appliances and they're in a folder in this drawer. She also wrote out a list of repairmen and their phone numbers in case the person who rented the bakery needed it."

"She was very organized," Hannah commented, itching to get her hands on the manual describing how to operate the oven.

"Come this way and I'll show you the walk-in cooler," Al told them, leading the way to a large steel door. He opened it and flicked on the lights. "Veronica and Alex didn't leave this on, but I tried it just last week and it cools down fast."

Hannah pictured the shelves filled with dairy products and bowls of cookie dough waiting to be baked. Essentially, the walk-in cooler was a giant refrigerator and she was eager to start mixing up cookie dough to see how long it would take to chill.

"I can hardly wait to try out that oven," Hannah confessed when they emerged from the cooler. "It'll bake dozens of cookies at once, and it's a real time saver."

Delores smiled at her. "You'll need dozens of cookies when

you open your coffee shop. You and the girls can use the oven right now to get ready for Essie's Christmas Ball."

"I heard about that," Al told her. "And if you hadn't called me, Delores, I would have called you. Is there anything that I can do to help with that?"

"I'm sure there is, and thank you for the offer. Let me think about what needs to be done, and . . ." Delores stopped speaking and began to smile. "Yes! You can help me with something that's critically important to the project!"

"What is it?"

"You have someone who inspects houses before you list them, don't you, Al?"

"Of course. I don't want to list anything that needs a lot of repair unless I advertise it as a fixer-upper. I wouldn't be in business for long if I did that."

"That's what Andrea told me. She said the house they bought was inspected by a very nice man and he was someone you'd used for years."

"That's right. He's not only nice, he's reliable. He comes when I call him, and he's never failed to catch a serious flaw."

"Then I need your expertise and your inspector's expertise to go over part of the old Albion Hotel with me. We're going to try to restore the ballroom to its former grandeur and it's on the second floor. I'm going to try to get the old elevator in working order, but it's quite small and I know some people will choose to use the staircase. That's where you and your inspector come in. I need to know exactly what's wrong with the staircase so that we can fix it."

"Of course you do, and I'll be happy to help you with that."

"Do you think you can talk your inspector into assessing the hotel for a modest fee?"

Al laughed. "I think I can do better than that, Delores. I'm almost sure that I can talk him into doing it for free. Once he hears about Essie, he'll want to help us."

"Wonderful! We'll take it."

Al looked slightly puzzled. "You'll take my inspector's help?"

"That, too," Delores said with a laugh, "but I was really talking about the bakery rental." She turned to Hannah. "You want it, don't you, dear?"

"Yes, but how much is it?"

"You let me worry about that. Is there anything you want to ask Al before I make a firm commitment?"

"There probably is, but I can't think of anything right now."

"All right then. As your father used to say, *It's in the bag.* I wonder where that old saying came from."

"That depends on who you ask," Hannah told her. "The version I like is that shortly after the turn of the last century, the New York Giants baseball team was on a winning streak and someone carried the ball bag back to the locker room before the game was over because everyone on the team believed that they'd win the game."

"That's interesting," Al said. "My father used that phrase, too." He turned to Delores. "I'll get the paperwork in order for Hannah's rental. Could you two stop by tomorrow morning around ten to finalize everything?"

"Of course," Delores replied for both of them.

"Here, Hannah." Al held out the key to the bakery. "You'll probably want to do some planning later today and there's no reason why you can't have the key now."

"Thank you," Hannah said. She felt like jumping up and down in excitement, but she settled for giving him a huge smile.

Hannah followed her mother out of the bakery and after they'd thanked Al and said their goodbyes, they got back into the car.

"Let's stop at the Red Owl on the way back to the house," Delores suggested. "I want to put you to work baking desserts for Essie's Christmas Ball and that means you have to buy ingredients. I'll talk to Florence and open an account for you. And while we're there, we can pick up something for dinner tonight. And perhaps you can bake one of those desserts from those photos that Rod found for you."

"I'll be happy to do that," Hannah told her. "Since the highlight of the first Christmas Ball was the cake parade, I thought I'd bake a cake."

"That would be nice. And if there's any left, we can send a piece home with Lisa and I'll take a slice to Essie tomorrow. What kind of cake are you thinking of baking, dear?"

"I'm not sure yet, Mother."

"Whatever you choose, I know it'll be wonderful. Essie has quite a sweet tooth and she loved the last treat you baked for her. I checked with Doc Knight before I left the hospital yesterday and he said that Essie has no restrictions on her diet. He also told me that she needs to gain weight, so anything you bake will be perfect for her."

Delores pulled into a parking spot in front of the Red Owl Grocery store and they both got out of the car. When they stepped inside, Delores went off to find Florence and Hannah went to the rack to get a shopping cart and select the ingredients for dinner. For dessert, she'd bake a lemon cake. A neighbor she'd had in college had given her a slice of the lemon cake she'd baked and it had been so good, Hannah had immediately asked her for the recipe. She hadn't had time to bake it then, but she still remembered all the ingredients. If Delores liked it, perhaps it could be part of the cake parade at Essie's Christmas Ball.

Luckily, Florence carried all the ingredients that Hannah needed. She'd frost the cake with her favorite Cool Whip frosting and it would be ready when Delores, Michelle, and Lisa came back from visiting Essie at the hospital. Since Hannah liked to give credit where credit was due, she'd use Kim's name for the cake and she'd call it Ultimate Lemon Bundt Cake.

Hannah glanced at her watch. It was only ten-thirty and she'd be home by eleven. That was plenty of time to make something in the slow cooker for dinner. If Florence had a nice boneless pork roast, she could cook it with mushrooms and the strips of tri-colored bell peppers she'd seen in the frozen vegetable section. If her creation turned out well, she'd call it Melt-in-Your-Mouth Pork Roast. She'd serve it with her favorite potatoes mashed with butter and cream cheese, and they could have the mushroom gravy with peppers that would cook in the bottom of the slow cooker. She'd need to serve another vegetable for a well-balanced meal, but that was easy. She'd pick up a package of frozen green beans, cook them at the last minute on the stovetop, and toss them with butter and bits of bacon.

Once Hannah had planned their evening meal, she gathered the rest of the ingredients she'd need and arrived in the checkout line only seconds before her mother did.

"Do you have everything you need for tonight's dinner?" Delores asked her.

"Yes, I do. You still have that slow cooker I gave you for Christmas two years ago, don't you?"

Delores nodded, but Hannah noticed that she looked slightly embarrassed. "It still works, doesn't it?" she asked.

"I . . . assume it does," Delores replied, and then she sighed. "I hate to admit it, Hannah, but I never got around to taking it out of the box. I really was going to try to learn to use it, but you know that I'm not a very good cook."

"That's okay, Mother. If you can still find it, I'll use it to make our dinner tonight. Then you can decide if you like it or not."

"Of course I can find the slow cooker." Delores looked slightly affronted. "It's sitting on the top shelf of the pantry. I really should have taken it out of the box, at least, but . . ." Delores stopped speaking and sighed again. "I didn't mean to hurt your feelings by not using it, Hannah."

"That's all right. I'm just glad you still have it. And if you like tonight's dinner and want to learn how to make it, I'll be glad to teach you."

"You could try, but I really don't think it'll do any good."
Delores gave a little laugh. "And by the way, that was nicely
done, dear. You're very understanding, but I'm a terrible
cook. You were trying to save my pride, but I don't have any
pride when it comes to cooking. I know how hopeless I am."

"That doesn't matter, Mother. You have lots of other tal-
ents."

"I do?"

"Yes, you do. You're a genius at finding gorgeous antiques
and buying them for incredibly low prices."

Delores began to smile. "I *am* good at that, aren't I?"

"That and many other things. We'd be standing here for
the rest of the morning if I tried to list them all."

"I can name the most important talent I have," Delores
said with a smile.

"What's that, Mother?"

"I raised an extremely thoughtful and kindhearted daughter who wouldn't hurt her mother's feelings for the world.
And I believe that's my finest achievement to date."

# MELT-IN-YOUR-MOUTH PORK ROAST

Made in a 4 or 5 quart capacity slow cooker.

2 cans CONDENSED cream of mushroom soup *(I used Campbell's 10 and ¾-ounce cans)*
1 can CONDENSED cream of celery soup *(I used Campbell's 10 and ¾-ounce can)*
3 or 4 pound boneless lean pork loin roast *(rolled and tied with string is okay, but it won't look as pretty when you slice it)*
1 large yellow onion, chopped into small pieces
2 stalks celery, chopped into small pieces *(don't use the leaves)*
2 packages DRY pork gravy mix *(I used Schilling, the kind that you heat with one cup of water)*
1 package frozen 3-color pepper strips *(I used C&W 14-ounce bag)*
¼ teaspoon garlic powder
¼ teaspoon onion powder
salt *(for later when you adjust the seasonings)*
black pepper *(for later when you adjust the seasonings—freshly ground is best)*
hot sauce *(for later when you adjust the seasonings—I used Slap Ya Mama hot sauce)*

Spray the inside of the crock of your slow cooker with Pam or another nonstick cooking spray. *(This will make it easier to clean later and prevent sticking.)*

Open the three cans of soup and mix them together in a bowl.

Use approximately 1/3 of the soup mixture to spread out in the bottom of your slow cooker.

If your pork roast has a layer of fat on top, cut it off as best you can with a knife.

Spread out the chopped onion on the bottom of your slow cooker.

Spread out the chopped celery on top of the chopped onion. Lay the pork roast on top of the onion and celery bed.

Slather half of the soup that is left in your bowl on top of the pork roast.

Sprinkle 1 packet of DRY gravy mix on top of the condensed soup.

Sprinkle the frozen peppers over the dry gravy mix.

Add the onion powder and the garlic powder to the condensed soup that is left in your bowl and mix them in.

Slather the rest of the condensed soup over the frozen peppers.

Put the lid on your slow cooker and make sure it's plugged in.

Hannah's 1st Note: Don't laugh. When I was in college, I put a lovely meal in my slow cooker one morning and forgot to plug it in. I turned it on, but with no electricity it didn't heat. During the day I ran into several of my college friends and invited them to my apartment for dinner. When I got home from my last class, the slow cooker was stone cold and I had to call out for pizza.

Turn your slow cooker on HIGH and cook for 4 hours.

At the end of 4 hours, turn your slow cooker down to LOW and cook for an additional 3 hours.

Hannah's 2nd Note: Your meal will be ready to eat in approximately 7 hours, but you don't have to serve it immediately. It will hold in the slow cooker for an additional hour if necessary.

Twenty minutes before your guests arrive, take the pork roast out of the slow cooker and set it on a carving board. Cover it loosely with foil.

When you're ready to serve, slice your pork.

Taste a bit of the gravy that has formed in the bottom of the crock and adjust the seasonings. If the gravy has thickened nicely and you don't think you'll need the second package of DRY gravy mix, it's okay to add more salt if you think it's needed. If the gravy is thin and you plan to use that second gravy package, DO NOT add more salt. The gravy package is quite salty.

Feel free to add a bit of hot sauce and put the bottle on the table for any guests who want their meal spicier.

Use a slotted spoon to remove the peppers, onions, and celery and make a ring of the savory combination around the outside of a meat platter.

Arrange the pork slices in the center of the platter.

If the gravy in the bottom of the crock is too thin, add the second package of DRY gravy mix now. Turn the slow cooker up to HIGH and it will cook rapidly. *When the gravy is ready, place it in a gravy bowl. If it thickens too much, thin it with a little water.*

Serve with baked or mashed potatoes, a vegetable or a salad, and hot rolls with plenty of butter.

Yield: This meal will serve 6 to 8 people, depending on their appetites and how many sides you serve.

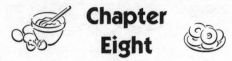

# Chapter Eight

"That was a wonderful meal, Hannah!" Delores complimented Hannah. "I love pork and your roast was so nice and tender."

"And the peppers added a lot," Lisa said.

"I loved the mushroom and pepper gravy," Michelle added her praise. "I had two helpings of mashed potatoes and gravy, and I never have more than one."

"Thanks," Hannah acknowledged the compliments. "We'll have leftover pork roast for sandwiches tomorrow." She turned to Lisa. "Does your dad like pork?"

"He always says he's a meat and potatoes man, and I know Mom used to fix pork a lot when I was growing up."

"Then I'll send a couple of slices home with you so you can make a sandwich for his lunch tomorrow."

"Come on, girls," Delores picked up her plate and stood up. "Let's clear the table and put away the leftovers."

"Do you want me to put on the coffee now so we can have dessert?" Hannah asked.

"No, dear. We can have it later. We'll take care of everything in the kitchen. All I want you to do is go into the living room, turn on the fireplace, and get ready to read more of Essie's exciting story."

\* \* \*

She opened her eyes early again, too nervous to sleep longer. Today would be a dangerous time and she prayed that she could get on the train without any of her bosses' men identifying her. She couldn't let any of her anxiety show. She had to be calm and collected, just another traveler who had somewhere to go and some time she had to arrive. She would take her cue from the other travelers, watching them carefully and mimicking their actions. She couldn't call attention to herself in any way and she had to act as if it were just another morning on the train, a day very much like the one the other commuters were having.

"Don't worry," she whispered to their unborn baby. "I know I can do it. I'll convince anyone who sees me that it's just another day for us, just another morning of commuting to work in the city. The only difference is that we won't be getting off the train in New York. The city's not safe for us. We'll be staying on with the other people who are traveling to places beyond that."

Once she'd bathed and dressed, she unzipped the duffel bag and gathered her belongings, preparing to pack them inside. That's when she noticed a packet that had slipped down to the bottom of the bag. Since she hadn't seen it before, her husband must have put it there when he'd tucked the money inside.

She drew out the packet and sat down on the edge of the bed to open it. The folded envelope was crisscrossed with layer after layer of tape. Since she didn't want to tear it, it took her several minutes to open it.

When she finally succeeded in removing the tape, she opened the packet and stared down at the contents in shock. There were a number of glittering stones inside, and they looked similar to the diamond in the engagement ring that her husband had given her. The only difference was that these gems were larger and more brilliant.

Were they real? She touched one, but it gave up no secrets. Since she was not an authority on precious gems, it would probably take a jeweler's expertise to answer that question.

One look at the packet told her that it was no longer usable. She had effectively destroyed it by pulling off the layers of tape. She had to think of a secure place to store the precious gems that her husband had given her. Her handbag would not be secure enough. There were purse snatchers on the streets, and some might be loitering in the train station, hoping to prey on hapless commuters. She needed a secure place where she could conceal her husband's gift.

She glanced down at her dress and an idea flashed through her mind. Her older relatives had once mentioned that immigrants who fled their home countries had concealed gems and other small valuables in their clothing by sewing them into the hems of dresses and the collars of blouses and shirts.

It only took a moment to find the small sewing kit she carried in her purse. It was a simple sewing kit consisting of two needles and three colors of thread in a small pouch. The sleeves of her dress had been turned up twice to make the cuffs and that would be a perfect place to hide this treasure.

She knew she couldn't simply sew the gems inside her hiding place. She had to wrap them in something so that their shape would not be noticeable. She tore off a piece of the original paper packet, folded the gems inside, and loosened several stitches on the underside of her cuff. The paper with the gems slipped in easily and she threaded a needle with dark blue thread, the same color as the material of her dress, and stitched the cuff shut again. She double-knotted the thread and since there was no scissors in her packet, she bit off the thread and tucked it back into the cuff.

"I did it," she said to their unborn baby. "Your father's treasure is safe with me."

Hannah paused to take a sip from the water glass that Michelle had placed on the table for her. Then she looked up again and realized that both Lisa and Michelle were leaning forward on the couch.

"Sewing the diamonds into her cuff was really smart," Michelle commented.

"I think so, too," Lisa said in agreement. "I just hope she remembers to take them out when she gets to a place where she can wash her dress."

Delores laughed. "I'm sure she'll remember, especially if she thinks they're real diamonds. I wonder if they are."

"I think they are," Michelle offered her opinion.

Lisa nodded. "Me too. It wouldn't be a good story if they were fakes."

"Do you want to read more, Hannah?" Delores asked.

"Yes, but I don't think we'll find out right away," Hannah replied, taking another sip of water and picking up the notebook again.

"Why do you think that?" Lisa asked her.

"Because there's a lot more of the story left and Essie's so good at building suspense in her story. If she told us they were fake in the next couple of paragraphs, we might stop reading."

Hannah's three listeners thought about that for a moment and then all three of them nodded.

"Please go on, dear," Delores told her. "We want to find out what happens when she gets to the train station."

It didn't take her long to finish packing her possessions in the duffel bag. She refolded the liner from her oversized raincoat and put that in the bottom. The coat she'd worn to work three mornings ago went in next and the new hairbrush, toothbrush, and toothpaste she'd purchased from the drugstore went on top. Before she zipped up the duffel bag, she briefly considered packing one of the towels from the bathroom, but it simply wasn't in her nature to take anything that didn't belong to her. She left the towel on the rack and closed the zipper on the duffel bag. There was nothing more to do. She was ready to go.

She wanted to move, to hurry, to leave, but it wasn't yet

time. There was no way she would arrive at the train station early and double the risk of being spotted. She sat down on the edge of the bed and attempted to relax until the alarm clock on the bedside table reached the time she'd planned to leave.

"It's time," she told their baby. "We're going to leave now." Then she got up to leave her room key on the dresser, picked up the duffel bag, and went out the door, shutting it behind her. She felt almost as if she were a bird leaving the nest. She had been safe here, but it wouldn't be safe to stay any longer. She had to get out and go far, far away where the danger was less and they would be safe.

She took the back stairs, as she had the day before, and she was relieved to see the older clerk with the mustache sitting at the front desk. He was engrossed in some kind of paperwork and didn't even look up as she passed his desk and went out the front door of the hotel.

The streets were filled with people this time of the morning. Some well-dressed employees were rushing to get to work in the surrounding office buildings, housewives who were up early were shopping in the markets that were open, workers who were employed in the factories bordering the train station were hurrying to punch timeclocks, and still others who had worked the night shift were heading back home to sleep. She let the tide of humanity carry her along with everyone else until she arrived at the train station.

The woman who'd told her how to get to this train station had been entirely correct. The train station was bustling with people going in and coming out. It was definitely a commuter hub and she moved to the right of the sidewalk to join the people who were entering the station so that the people who were going to work would have the other half of the walkway.

Once she got inside the station, she was surprised at how large it was with its cavernous ceilings and huge expanse of polished stone flooring that was peppered with benches for those who were waiting for trains. There were multiple windows with grates behind them for the ticket sellers, and some had signs identifying commuter windows. Other windows had no signs and she assumed that they were intended for passengers who were buying tickets for longer distances.

The line she chose had only seven people in front of her and she felt exposed to hundreds of eyes by standing at the rear. The feeling lasted only a moment or two because a man rushed up and got into line behind her.

"Out of state?" he asked her.

For a moment she was confused. Was he asking her if she was from out of state, or was asking her if this was the line to buy out-of-state tickets?

He repeated his question and she decided to take a chance on the latter choice. "I hope it's for out-of-state tickets," she told him. "There's no commuter sign above this window."

"Hold my place and I'll find out. I've never been in this station before."

She watched nervously as he left the line, but he was only going to a station guard in a uniform who was standing near a row of rental lockers. If he had been one of her bosses' men who'd recognized her and was going for help, he certainly wouldn't be talking to a station guard!

She observed the silent tableau since she was too far away to hear their conversation. After they'd spoken for a few moments, he nodded to the guard and hurried back to her.

"We're in luck," he told her. "It's actually the next line over, but the guard told me they sell out-of-state tickets here, too. Where are you going?"

"California," she replied quickly. "I'm going to visit my husband's aunt."

"It's Michigan for me," he said. "I just got a job in Detroit."

The man was pleasant and they passed the time in line by chatting about the weather in New York until she reached the window. Then she opened her handbag and drew out her wallet.

"One ticket to Los Angeles, please," she told the ticket agent.

"Coach or first class?" he asked her.

"Coach," she said. And when he told her the price, she removed the money from her purse and slid it under the grate. He pushed her ticket and her change out to her through the grate, she dropped the change in her purse and said, "Thank you."

The whole transaction had taken no more than thirty seconds, but she found that her hands were shaking as she left the window. She turned to give a little wave to the man behind her, and then she walked away toward the benches along the wall.

She looked around her and felt a bit relieved as she noticed that no one was watching her. She was just another passenger who'd bought a ticket.

She spotted a newspaper stand in the corner and crossed to it, choosing a popular New York paper from the rack and handing the clerk the correct change. Then she located her gate where people were already standing in line, tucked the newspaper under her arm, and joined them.

The loudspeaker burst into life with a completely unintelligible list of stops, but she didn't bother listening for her destination. The number of the gate was printed on her ticket and it also listed the time of departure. According to the huge clock on the wall above the gates, she had only ten minutes to wait before she could board her train.

The minutes passed slowly. She watched for anyone who appeared to be observing her and found, to her relief, that no one was. The train must have been on time, because the line began to move forward in exactly ten minutes. As she followed her fellow travelers out of the station and onto the platform that bordered the tracks, she told herself that her ordeal was nearly over and she was almost safe.

There were several trains waiting for their passengers to board, and the sound was deafening as one train pulled forward and accelerated away from the station. The engineer blew the whistle and she had to fight the urge to cover her ears. No one around her seemed to mind the noise of the revving engines, blaring whistles, and loud speakers cautioning passengers not to get too close to the edges of the platform. They must all be used to the cacophony of sound and she didn't want to be the only passenger to approach her train with her hands clamped over her ears.

It was windy on the platform and a sudden breeze blew her raincoat open as she was about to board. The porter motioned to another porter, who gestured for her to come with him.

"The platform slopes up near the front of the train and it's easier to board there," he told her. "I'm working this train and I'll help to get you on board."

"Thank you, but I'm back in coach," she told him. "The front cars are reserved for first class, aren't they?"

"Yes, but I'm going to take you through to the club car, where you can relax. We have nice chairs and sofas in there."

"But isn't the club car just for first class?"

"Yes, but I won't tell if you won't tell. Train travel's not easy in your condition. My kids are all grown now, but I still remember how miserable my wife was with our first when we went back on the train to visit her mother."

"I . . . I don't know how to thank you enough," she said, fumbling for words.

"No need. I'm in first class on this trip and I'll keep an eye out for you."

"She really lucked out with that porter!" Lisa said as Hannah stopped reading and closed Essie's notebook.

"You bet she did," Michelle echoed her sentiment.

"Is it time for dessert?" Delores asked, standing up from her favorite chair.

"It is." Hannah put the notebook back on the end table. "I'll take the cake out of the refrigerator and slice it."

"I'll get out the dessert plates and forks for you," Lisa offered.

"And I'll make the coffee," Delores promised.

"What shall I do?" Michelle asked. "There's nothing left for me to . . ." She stopped and smiled. "I know! I'll get out the coffee cups, sugar, creamer, and spoons."

"I don't know about you, but I can't wait to taste that cake," Hannah said. "I hope we're not disappointed. It's the first time I've baked it and I modified the recipe a little."

"We'll let you know, but I'm sure it'll be wonderful," Delores told her. "Everything you bake is fabulous, dear."

# ULTIMATE LEMON BUNDT CAKE

Preheat oven to 350 degrees F., rack in the middle position.

4 large eggs
½ cup vegetable oil
¼ cup water
¼ cup lemon juice
8-ounce *(by weight)* tub of sour cream *(I used Knudsen)*
box of Lemon Cake Mix, the kind that makes a 9-inch by 13-inch cake or a 2-layer cake *(I used Duncan Hines Lemon Supreme)*
5.1-ounce package of DRY instant lemon pudding and pie filling *(I used Jell-O)*
12-ounce *(by weight)* bag of white chocolate or vanilla baking chips *(11-ounce package will do, too—I used Nestlé)*

Prepare your cake pan. You'll need a Bundt pan that has been sprayed with Pam or another nonstick cooking spray and then floured. To flour a pan, put some flour in the bottom, hold it over your kitchen wastebasket, and tap the pan to move the flour all over the inside of the pan. Continue this until all the inside surfaces of the pan, including the sides of the crater in the center, have been covered with a light coating of flour.

Crack the eggs into the bowl of an electric mixer. Mix them up on LOW speed until they're a uniform color.

Pour in the half-cup of vegetable oil and mix it in with the eggs on LOW speed.

Add the quarter-cup of water and the quarter-cup of lemon juice. Mix them in at LOW speed.

Scoop out the container of sour cream and add the sour cream to your bowl. Mix that in on LOW speed.

When everything is well combined, open the box of dry cake mix and sprinkle it on top of the liquid ingredients in the bowl of the mixer. Mix that in on LOW speed.

Open the package of instant lemon pudding and pie filling and sprinkle in the contents. Mix it in on LOW speed.

Shut off the mixer, scrape down the sides of the bowl, remove it from the mixer, and set it on the counter.

If you have a food processor, put in the steel blade and pour in the white chocolate or vanilla baking chips. Process in an on-and-off motion to chop them in smaller pieces. *(You can also do this with a knife on a cutting board if you don't have a food processor.)*

Sprinkle the white chocolate or baking chips in your bowl and stir them in by hand with a rubber spatula.

Hannah's 1<sup>st</sup> Note: Florence, down at the Lake Eden Red Owl Grocery, carries mini semi-sweet chocolate chips, but she can't get any other flavor of chips in a mini version and she doesn't even think anyone makes them. The regular-size chips are larger and heavier than the mini version, and they will sink down to the bottom of your Bundt pan if you don't chop them into smaller pieces.

Use the rubber spatula to transfer the cake batter to the prepared Bundt pan.

Smooth the top of your cake with the spatula and put it into the center of your preheated oven.

Bake your Ultimate Lemon Bundt Cake at 350 degrees F. for 55 minutes.

Before you take your cake out of the oven, test it for doneness by inserting a cake tester, thin wooden skewer, or long toothpick. Insert it midway between the outside edges of the pan and the metal protrusion that makes the crater in the center of the pan. If the tester comes out clean, your cake is done. If there is still uncooked batter clinging to the tester, bake your cake longer until the tester comes out clean.

Hannah's 2<sup>nd</sup> Note: The Bundt pan was invented by a man from Minnesota so that it would be easier to cut uniform slices of cake. The crater in the center is there so that the cake will bake evenly all around.

Once your cake is done, take it out of the oven and set it on a cold stove burner or a wire rack. Let it cool in the pan for 20 minutes and then pull the sides of the cake away from the pan with the tips of your impeccably clean fingers. Don't forget to do the same for the sides of the crater in the middle.

Tip the Bundt pan upside down on a platter and drop it gently on a folded towel on the kitchen counter. Do this until the cake falls out of the pan and rests on the platter.

Cover your Ultimate Lemon Bundt Cake loosely with foil and refrigerate it for at least one hour. Overnight is even better.

Frost your cake with Cool Whip Lemon Frosting. *(Recipe and instructions follow.)*

Yield: At least 10 pieces of sweet and tangy lemon cake. Serve with tall glasses of ice-cold milk or cups of strong coffee.

# COOL WHIP LEMON FROSTING

This recipe is made in the microwave.

1 heaping cup *(6 to 7 ounces by weight)* of white
  chocolate or vanilla baking chips *(I used Nestlé)*
1 ripe lemon large enough to produce ½ teaspoon
  lemon zest *(just the yellow part of the peel, finely
  grated)* and ¼ cup lemon juice
8-ounce *(by weight)* tub of FROZEN Cool Whip
  *(Do not thaw! Leave in the freezer.)*

**Hannah's 1st Note: Make sure you use the original Cool
Whip, not the sugar free or the real whipped cream.**

Start by chopping your white chocolate or vanilla baking chips into smaller pieces or placing the chips in a food
processor with the steel blade and processing in an on-and-
off motion to chop the chips into smaller pieces.

If you haven't done so already, zest your lemon and
measure out ½ teaspoon of zest.

Juice your zested lemon and measure out ¼ cup *(4
Tablespoons)* of lemon juice.

Place the Cool Whip in a microwave-safe bowl.

Add the white chocolate or vanilla baking chips to the
bowl.

Sprinkle the lemon zest on top of the chips.

Drizzle the lemon juice on top of the zest.

Stir everything up with a heat-resistant rubber spatula.

Microwave the contents of the bowl on HIGH for 1 minute and then let it sit in the microwave for an additional minute.

Take the bowl out of the microwave. Stir to see if the chips are melted. If they're not, heat them in 30-second intervals with 30-second standing times on HIGH in the microwave until you succeed in melting the chips.

Once the chips are melted, let the bowl sit on the countertop or on a cold burner for 15 minutes to thicken the icing.

When the time is up, give the bowl a stir and remove your cake from the refrigerator. Frost your Ultimate Lemon Bundt Cake with the frosting and don't forget the sides of the crater in the middle. You don't need to frost all the way down to the bottom of the crater. That's almost impossible. Just frost an inch or so down the sides of the crater.

Return your cake to the refrigerator for at least 30 minutes before cutting it and serving it to your guests.

Hannah's 2nd Note: You can also use this icing on cookies. Simply frost and let your cookies sit on wax paper on the kitchen counter until the frosting has set and is dry to the touch.

Yield: This frosting will frost a batch of cookies, a 9-inch by 13-inch cake, a Bundt cake, or a round two-tier layer cake.

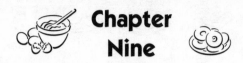

# Chapter
# Nine

For the second morning in a row, Hannah woke up energized and eager to start her day. She smiled as she got out of bed and pulled on her slippers and robe. She walked to the window, pushed aside the curtains, and looked out on a morning that matched her mood.

The sun was just rising over the steeple of Holy Cross Redeemer Lutheran Church and it bathed the streets of Lake Eden in a pale golden glow. The church sat on top of a hill and Hannah's new business rental, the eventual home of her bakery and coffee shop, was only a few blocks from her mother's house. Her new bakery was opposite the church, only one block down the hill, and centrally located on Main Street. She was looking forward to going there alone to test out the appliances and revel in the fact that her dream was about to become a reality.

Hannah hurried through her shower. She could hardly wait to dress, fix breakfast for Michelle and Delores, and then walk to her new place of business. She anticipated the thrill she'd feel at unlocking the door for the first time with the key Al Percy had given her. Once she stepped inside the main room, she would stand there for a moment, imagining the transformation that would take place. There would be more tables and chairs, and a fresh coat of paint in a color she hadn't yet chosen. Perhaps she'd leave that up to Andrea and Delores since they were more artistic than she was. The scene she imagined seemed so real, she could almost see herself standing behind the counter pouring hot, fresh coffee for her customers as they munched on the cookies she'd baked that morning.

This would be a daunting project to tackle alone, but she would have lots of help. Andrea had a real talent for interior design, Michelle had a gift for devising practical solutions to complex problems, and their mother could find amazing buys on all sorts of items that Hannah would need for her business. She would ask her whole family to help her spruce up the bakery and make it into a popular, friendly place.

Hannah stood there by the side of the bed, visualizing the interior of The Cookie Jar. Perhaps she should order aprons with the name of her business embroidered on the bib. The aprons should be forest green. She looked good in forest green. And the embroidery should be in bright red, her favorite color and one that, unfortunately, clashed with her curly red hair. There were other personalized items she needed, too. She'd have paper napkins, forest green and white striped, with the name of her business printed in red, bakery boxes designed and manufactured especially for The Cookie Jar, and signature coffee mugs with the name of her business printed on them in bright red. She should also have disposable to-go cups that identified her business for customers who stopped by for takeout coffee, and personalized paper bags, both in small size and medium for local business owners who dropped in to take their coffee and cookies to work with them. Then there were individual creamers, and sugars, and sugar substitutes, and . . .

Hannah gave a little laugh at the turn her thoughts were taking. She was being a prime example of the phrase her great-grandmother Elsa Swensen had used to refer to anyone who was getting ahead of himself. If Great-Grandma were here right now, she'd accuse Hannah of *putting the cart before the horse.* There was a lot of work to be done before she could even consider ordering personalized items for The Cookie Jar. Her immediate concern should be what to fix for breakfast this morning.

Now that she had stopped daydreaming in lieu of practical matters, Hannah hurried to finish dressing, visions of pancakes, French toast, and other breakfast dishes flitting through her mind. By the time she'd made her bed, walked down the stairs, and reached the kitchen, she knew exactly what to make for their first meal of the day. They would have Bacon and Sausage Breakfast Burritos.

The first thing Hannah did was put on the coffee. Cooking took concentration, and she needed the caffeine to wake her up completely. The moment the coffee began to fill the carafe under her mother's coffeemaker, Hannah jerked the carafe away and replaced it with a cup. When the cup was full, she removed it and replaced it with the carafe again. Then she sat down at her mother's kitchen table and took her first sip.

As she drank her coffee, Hannah thought of other mornings, the mornings she'd spent during her last few months in college. And even though she tried to push the memories out of her mind, she couldn't help thinking of the last time she'd cooked for the man she'd thought she was going to marry. She'd been so sure, so very sure that he loved her, too.

They'd talked about getting married in the summer, of buying a house near the campus so that Hannah could finish the last year of her doctorate. They'd planned how, when her thesis was accepted, she would apply for a faculty position and they'd be able to see each other every day on campus. She'd really thought that was what she wanted until the night all her dreams of happiness turned to ashes and she'd discovered what kind of man Assistant Professor Bradford Ramsey really was.

*Don't think about it!* Hannah's mind warned her. *Dwelling on shattered dreams is too painful and it doesn't do any good. Think about your new career in Lake Eden and how you'll never have to see Bradford again.* Hannah knew that was good advice, but it was difficult to erase all thoughts of the man she'd loved with all her heart.

"Get busy," she said aloud as she went to her mother's refrigerator to take out some of the ingredients she'd purchased at the Red Owl the previous morning. Soon sausage and bacon were sizzling in a frying pan on her mother's stovetop as Hannah gathered the other ingredients for her burritos.

Just to make sure that she hadn't chosen a salsa that was too spicy, Hannah opened the container and tasted it. It had a nice little bite, but not too much heat, and it was perfect for Michelle and Delores.

Once the bacon slices and sausage patties had cooked through and browned, Hannah removed them from the frying pan and placed them on a plate that she'd lined with several layers of paper towels. She would let the breakfast meat sit for a minute or so and then flip it over so that the paper towels could blot the fat on the other side. Once they had cooled enough to handle, she would crumble the meat and put it aside for her breakfast burritos.

There was some fat from the bacon and sausage left in the frying pan and Hannah poured it off into a container with a lid and stuck it in the bottom of the refrigerator. She would let it harden and then she'd take it to Grandma Knudson for her winter bird tree. Hannah had helped Grandma Knudson "decorate" her winter bird tree every year in grade school and when they were old enough to help, she'd taken Andrea and Michelle with her. They'd placed fat that they'd saved in little plastic cups that Grandma Knudson helped them hang from the branches. Winter birds needed fat, or what Grandma Knudson called suet, in their diets to survive the sub-zero temperatures that were common in Minnesota winters.

Once the children who'd helped with the bird tree were back inside the parsonage, they'd sipped hot chocolate and watched the birds fly back to the tree. Grandma Knudson had pointed out some particularly colorful winter birds, and

Hannah still remembered the names of some of them. There were red cardinals, black and white downy woodpeckers, purple finches, and white-breasted nuthatches. When visitors came to the parsonage in the winter and looked out the window in Grandma Knudson's sitting room, they saw the winter bird tree in all its glory, decorated like a Christmas tree with yellow, red, blue, and purple winter birds that were perched on bare black branches like Christmas ornaments, pecking at suet and black sunflower seeds that Grandma Knudson and the local children had hung there for them.

Hannah used another paper towel to wipe the grease from the frying pan, leaving just a bit for flavor. Then she added a bit of salted butter and prepared to scramble eggs. She broke the eggs into the frying pan, turned it on medium heat, and stirred them with a fork as they cooked. The tines of the fork kept the eggs from sticking together to form large pieces. Instead, the scrambled eggs were crumbly and that was exactly what Hannah needed for her Bacon and Sausage Breakfast Burritos.

When the bacon and sausage had cooled, Hannah crumbled the pieces into a bowl and went back to the refrigerator for the shredded Mexican cheese that Florence carried in her grocery store. The large flour tortillas were already out on the counter, and Hannah smiled as she began to prepare the burritos.

Ten minutes later, she was finished. She wrapped each burrito in plastic wrap and stuck them in the refrigerator. She would take off the plastic wrap and rewrap them in paper towels when she heated them in the microwave, but she planned to freeze any leftover burritos after their breakfast was over so that she could serve them for another breakfast.

As Hannah thought about freezing the burritos, she began to smile. The chest freezer her mother had ordered would be delivered today. She'd make a list of all the baked goods they planned to make for the Christmas Ball dessert buffet, and they'd bake those first and store them in the freezer. She wasn't sure how a cake frosted with Cool Whip frosting would fare in the freezer since the Cool Whip had already been frozen once, but the frosting was very easy to make. They'd freeze all the cakes they planned to eventually frost with the Cool Whip Frosting, thaw them the morning of the Christmas Ball, frost them, and store them in her walk-in cooler. There was plenty of room on the shelves to hold that many cakes until it was time to transport them to the kitchen at the Albion Hotel.

Hannah checked the coffeepot, realized that there was more than enough left for breakfast, and poured herself a second cup. As she sat down to drink it, she heard the master bedroom shower running and she knew that her mother would be downstairs in fifteen minutes or so. Michelle was up, too. She always blow-dried her hair and Hannah could hear the hair dryer running upstairs. It wouldn't be long before both of them came downstairs for breakfast.

Ten minutes later, Michelle entered the kitchen. She saw Hannah sitting at the kitchen table and smiled. "Good morning, Hannah," she greeted her older sister. "I bet I know where you're going today."

"And I bet you're right," Hannah responded.

Delores stepped into the kitchen a scant moment later. "I heard that," she said, and then she turned to Hannah. "Would it be too disappointing to delay your plans for an hour or so, Hannah?"

"Of course not, Mother," Hannah responded immediately. "Do you have something you'd like me to do for you?"

"Not for me, *with* me. I need to take my car out to Cyril's Garage and I'd like you to drive your father's car out there for me."

"That's not a problem, Mother. I'll be glad to do it."

"Is something wrong with your car?" Michelle asked Delores.

"Not a thing, dear. It's running perfectly and it's a year newer than your father's car."

"Then is there something wrong with Dad's car?" Hannah asked, drawing the obvious conclusion.

"No, it's running perfectly, too. I'm just following up on something that Grandma Knudson suggested to me yesterday when I told her about the bakery and your plans to start a business."

"What did she suggest?"

"She asked me if it made me sad to see your father's car sitting in the garage. I admitted it did, and she suggested that I sell it. That's why we're going out to Cyril's Garage. If you girls don't have any objections, I'm going to follow Grandma Knudson's advice."

Hannah thought about that for a few moments. "That makes sense," she said. "You shouldn't keep it if it makes you feel bad. I'll be happy to go out to Cyril's with you."

"I'd go, too, but I have to get to school," Michelle told her. "And I think it's a good idea to sell it."

"Good. Let's have breakfast, girls. It smells like bacon and sausage, but I don't see it anywhere. What are we having, Hannah?"

"Bacon and Sausage Breakfast Burritos. They're already assembled and they're in the refrigerator. All I have to do is heat them in the microwave."

"I'll get out the orange juice," Michelle said, hurrying to the refrigerator.

Delores went to the cupboard to get a coffee cup. "And I'll pour the coffee. Would you like a warm-up, Hannah?"

"Yes, please." Hannah got up and went to the refrigerator, got out three of the burritos she'd made, unwrapped them from the plastic wrap, and rewrapped them in paper towels so that she could heat them in the microwave.

A short time later, all three of them were sitting at the kitchen table, eating the burritos that Hannah had made.

"These are wonderful!" Delores told Hannah. "And they're so filling that I don't think I can eat more than . . ." She stopped talking and gave a little laugh. "Second thought, I may have two and skip lunch."

"Me too!" Michelle echoed her mother's sentiments. "You should serve these at The Cookie Jar, Hannah."

Hannah shook her head. "And compete with Rose's breakfast business?"

"No," Michelle answered quickly. "You're right, Hannah. I didn't think about Rose's breakfasts at the café. She makes some really good things."

Delores nodded as she wiped her mouth. "Yes, she does. Let's go there tomorrow morning for breakfast so that Hannah can get an early start at the bakery." She turned to Hannah. "You haven't been to the café for breakfast since you've been home from college, have you, dear?"

"No, I haven't."

"Then it's a date," Delores declared. "And tonight, we're all going out to the Corner Tavern for hamburgers. I want to give Hannah a break from cooking." She turned to Michelle. "Invite Lisa for me, will you, dear? I think she said her sister was cooking for Jack this week."

"But I'm perfectly willing to . . ." Hannah started to object, but Delores cut her off by holding up her hand for silence.

"No, dear. You're going to be busy all day today, learning how to use the appliances down at the bakery. And I haven't had a Corner Tavern Double-double hamburger for months." She pushed back her chair and got up from the table. "I'll pour more coffee for both of us, Hannah. Did you have many leftover breakfast burritos?"

"Yes, the batch made twenty-four and we only ate six. I thought I'd freeze the rest so that we could have them for snacks for another couple of breakfasts."

"What a wonderful idea! If you leave them in the refrigerator, I might be tempted to have another before I leave to see Essie at the hospital. As a matter of fact, I *know* that's what I'd do. And then I'd be too full to have a Double-double tonight, and that would be a true tragedy."

## BACON AND SAUSAGE
## BREAKFAST BURRITOS

No need to preheat the oven. These are made on the stovetop.

1 pound pork breakfast sausage *(either links or pat-ties)*
1 pound bacon *(regular and NOT thick sliced)*
½ cup thick, chunky salsa, drained *(measure AFTER draining)*
4-ounce can chopped green chilies, drained
Hot sauce, optional *(I used Slap Ya Mama brand hot sauce)*
2 cups shredded Mexican cheese *(I used Kraft)*
12 large eggs *(Yes, that's a whole dozen!)*
1 ounce *(2 Tablespoons)* salted butter
24 burrito-size flour tortillas
Salt *(as needed)*
Black pepper *(as needed)*

**Hannah's 1st Note:** Choose the spiciness of your salsa according to your family's preference.

**Hannah's 2nd Note:** If you can't find shredded Mexican cheese, you can use shredded Italian cheese or shredded cheddar.

If you bought breakfast sausage patties, cut them into 4 to 6 pieces and place them in the bottom of a large frying pan. If you used sausage links with casings, leave them whole. *(You will remove the casings after they are fried and have cooled.)*

Cut each bacon strip into 4 pieces and place them in the frying pan on top of the sausage.

Fry the sausage pieces and bacon pieces at MEDIUM-HIGH heat, stirring frequently, until the meats are brown and crisp, and can be crumbled when they are cool.

Take the frying pan off the heat, turn off the hot burner, and use a slotted spoon or slotted spatula to drain the meats onto a platter or a medium-size bowl lined with layers of paper towels.

Scrape the bottom of the frying pan to remove any bits of meat that may have stuck to the bottom and place it on a cold burner to wait for the eggs you will scramble.

Carefully *(the meats could still be hot)* pat the top of the meat with paper towels to blot the grease.

Wipe out the inside of the pan with paper towels. *(Be careful! The pan will be as hot as the meats were when you blotted them!)*

If you haven't done so already, drain the salsa in a strainer, pat it dry with a paper towel, and measure out ½ cup. Place the drained salsa in a small bowl on the counter.

Open the can of chopped green chilies and use the strainer again to drain them. Dry them with a paper towel and then add them to the salsa in the bowl. Stir the contents of the small bowl together.

Taste the salsa and green chili mixture. If it's not spicy enough for your family, add a few drops of hot sauce.

When the pieces of meat are cool enough to crumble, remove the paper towels from the platter or bowl and use your impeccably clean fingers to crumble the meat.

After your meats are crumbled, stir in the cheese.

Add the salsa and green chili mixture to the bowl with the meat and the cheese mixture.

Crack all twelve eggs into another bowl and use a whisk to beat them into a smooth mixture that is uniform in color. Let them sit on the counter while you prepare the frying pan.

Place one ounce of salted butter in the frying pan you used for the bacon and sausage. Set the frying pan on the burner again and turn it on MEDIUM heat to melt the butter.

Spread the melted butter around on the bottom of the pan with a spatula or a wooden spoon so that the entire bottom is coated with butter.

Give the eggs a final stir with the whisk and then pour them into the frying pan.

Scramble the eggs until they are thoroughly cooked.

Move the frying pan to a cold burner, shut off the stove, and stir the meat, cheese, salsa, and green chili mixture into the scrambled eggs.

Check for seasoning and add salt and pepper if needed.

Take the flour tortillas out of the package and wrap them in paper towels. Heat them in the microwave for 20 to 30 seconds, or until they are warm and you can bend them without breaking them.

Spread out a sheet of plastic wrap on your counter. It should be about 12 inches long when you tear it off the roll.

Center a tortilla on the sheet of plastic wrap.

Place ½ cup of your filling *(that's the egg, meat, cheese, salsa, and green chili mixture)* in the center of the tortilla.

Pull the bottom edge of your tortilla over the filling and up to meet the top edge. This will roll the filling into the proper place.

Fold one side of the tortilla over the filling. Then fold the other side of the tortilla over the filling. *(The sides will overlap a bit and that's the way it should be.)*

Starting from the bottom, roll the burrito up tightly, creating a roll that will not leak when you eat it.

Place another tortilla in the center of the sheet of plastic wrap and wrap it the same way, pulling the bottom sheet up to seal to the top, pulling the sides in to cover the burrito, and then rolling it up to the edge of the plastic wrap.

When you finish rolling all your Bacon and Sausage Breakfast Burritos, place them in a pan and refrigerate them until you're ready to heat them in the microwave.

**To serve:** Remove the plastic wrapper, rewrap in a paper towel, and heat in the microwave until they're heated through. Alternatively, you can heat a whole batch that has been refrigerated by removing the plastic wrap, rewrapping in foil, and placing them on a cookie sheet in a preheated 350 degree F. oven for 10 to 12 minutes.

**To freeze for later use:** Wrap your burritos in foil, place them in a closeable freezer bag, put them in the freezer, and take them out as you need them.

**Hannah's 3rd Note: Although you can thaw Bacon and Sausage Breakfast Burritos in the microwave once you've taken off the foil and rewrapped them in paper towels, I've found it works better if you thaw them on the kitchen counter or in the refrigerator before you rewrap them in paper towels and heat them for breakfast.**

Yield: 24 Bacon and Sausage Breakfast Burritos.

# Chapter Ten

A light snow was falling as Hannah followed her mother to Cyril Murphy's garage. It was located several miles out of town and it had grown both in size and reputation over the years. Now it served the whole Tri-County area, and Cyril had become a highly respected businessman with a reputation for honesty and competence.

Hannah was careful as she turned off the highway and onto the Winnetka County road that led to the garage. It wasn't as well-plowed as the highway, and there were a few small snowdrifts in fields and other areas that were not protected from the wind by trees. She passed farms she knew, red barns set back from the road with farmhouses placed in spots that the farmers and their wives considered close enough to the barn to get there in a blizzard, but more scenic.

She smiled as she spotted Winnie Henderson's farm. Very few people knew exactly how old Winnie was and if they did know, they didn't dare say. In that respect, Winnie was a bit like a countrified Delores. Winnie had been a rancher all her life, and her passion was raising and breeding horses. She'd been raised by her father and older brothers and she would tell anyone what she thought about a controversial subject with no punches pulled. Winnie was smart and tough, and she'd outlived multiple husbands. Even though Winnie's current one was a decade younger than she was, Hannah had no doubt that Winnie would outlive him, too.

Hannah waved as she recognized the driver of the Winnetka County snowplow that had pulled over to the side of the road to let her mother and her pass. It was Earl Flensburg, one of her father's friends. He'd looked slightly startled when he'd seen Hannah driving her father's car, but since her mother never drove it, he probably hadn't seen it on the road since Lars had died.

Cyril's Garage was only a mile down the road and Hannah pulled into the driveway behind her mother. Delores took a parking spot right next to the door, and Hannah took the spot on the other side. There weren't many cars in front of the building, but that was normal for a workday. Cyril opened at seven for people who had to drop off their cars for servicing or repair but still get to work on time.

Delores waited for Hannah to join her and then she opened the door. "Cyril knows we're coming," she said. "I called right before we left the house. How did the car run, dear?"

"Just fine. I'm no mechanic, but it seemed to be in perfect working order."

"That's all to the good, dear. That means we'll have a good trade-in value."

Hannah was a bit puzzled at that comment. "Trade-in? Are you planning to trade it in, Mother?"

"That's right, dear. We are."

"I don't understand. Are you planning to replace Dad's car with another car?"

"That's exactly what we're going to do."

"But I thought you *liked* your car."

"I *do* like my car. I'll probably keep it for years."

Hannah could feel her confusion grow. "But you just said that you were going to trade Dad's car in on another car. And then you said you were keeping your car. You don't need *two* cars, do you?"

"No, but *you* need a vehicle," Cyril said, coming up behind them. "Your mother told me all about your bakery and I'm going to be one of your first customers. I still remember the last batch of cookies you brought out here and I think I've got the perfect SUV for you."

Hannah just blinked for a second. She wasn't sure what to say.

Cyril laughed as he turned to Delores. "Now we've done it, Delores. We've rendered Hannah speechless."

"And that's no easy trick," Delores replied, and then she joined in the laughter.

Hannah just stared at the two of them as if they'd suddenly gone crazy. That made them laugh harder, and even though she tried to refrain, she was compelled to join in their laughter.

"You should have seen your face!" Cyril said between chuckles.

"Your startled expression was priceless," Delores managed to gasp out.

"A deer in the headlights," Cyril described it.

Gradually, they all stopped laughing and Delores turned to Hannah. "I'm sorry, dear. Perhaps I should have discussed this with you earlier."

This brought on another chuckle from Cyril. "Maybe it's a good thing you didn't do that, Delores. She just would have argued with you."

"I . . ." Hannah paused and gave a deep sigh. "You're probably right. But don't you want the money for Dad's car?"

"I don't need the money," Delores said. "But you *do* need a truck or a van to move all those cakes and the other baked goods to the hotel for the ball." She turned to Cyril. "You said you had something in mind when I talked to you this morning. What is it?"

"I've got a Chevy Suburban that came in last week. It's only two years old, but it needs a little body work."

"What kind of work?" Delores asked.

"We have to hammer out a few dents and the passenger-side door needed to be replaced, but we've already done that. And of course it'll need to be repainted. We don't do that here, but I know a good place and I can take care of it for you once Hannah picks out the color she wants. Everything that's left is cosmetic, Delores."

"Sometimes cosmetic work is more expensive than mechanical work," Delores commented. "How much do you estimate that the cosmetic work will cost? If it's too much, perhaps you could suggest something else."

Hannah turned to look her mother in admiration. She should have remembered the remarkably low prices Delores had paid for valuable antiques at auctions and estate sales. Her dad had often said that his wife was a horse trader from way back, and now Hannah knew exactly what he'd meant.

"It won't be that much, Delores. We got the door from a junkyard and hammering out the dents will only take fifteen minutes or so. My painting place gives me a discount and they do excellent work."

"Then it's not one of those cheap, overnight places in the Cities?" Delores asked him.

"No, the place we use takes their time and they do it right." Cyril turned to Hannah. "What color do you want for your Suburban, Hannah?"

Delores reached out to put her hand on Hannah's arm. "It's too early to ask that, Cyril. Hannah and I need to see the Suburban first and test-drive it. And then I need the price, minus the trade-in of course."

"Of course. Follow me, ladies. I'll take you to see the Suburban right now."

"Get the keys," Delores told him. "If we like the looks of it, we'll want to test-drive it."

"They're right here in my pocket." Cyril patted his uniform pocket. "I brought them with me when I saw you out here."

Hannah smiled, coming to the conclusion that she'd had

the privilege of watching not one, but *two* horse traders in action. And the show wasn't over yet. She found that she was looking forward to seeing the vehicle that Cyril had chosen for her. Her dad used to say that Cyril had a gift for choosing just the right car for the right person and she really hoped he'd been right.

Thirty minutes later, Hannah and Delores left Cyril's office. Hannah was now the proud owner of a Chevy Suburban that one of Cyril's mechanics would drive to the paint shop before noon. Cyril had demonstrated his uncanny gift once again when both Delores and Hannah had decided that the Suburban was exactly the right vehicle to be Hannah's cookie truck. Hannah had decided to have it painted candy apple red, and she planned to put signs on both sides advertising The Cookie Jar.

"I really don't know how to thank you enough, Mother," Hannah told her as Delores pulled onto the two-lane road that led to the highway.

"Just help me make the Christmas Ball a success, dear. That's all the thanks I need. And make a success of your business, too. Your sisters and I will help you in any way we can. Andrea and I will lend a hand decorating the place and if I need a little respite from decorating, I know Michelle will go hunting with me."

For a moment, Hannah wondered if the strain of the last few days of constant activity had been too much for her mother. Lars had gone deer hunting every year with a group of his friends, and although Delores enjoyed eating the venison he brought home, she had refused to even look at the photos he'd taken of his successes.

"You're going *hunting* with Michelle?" Hannah asked, almost afraid to hear the answer.

Delores laughed. "Not *that* kind of hunting, dear. Michelle and I are going to look for that counter you wanted in your coffee shop and the mirror that'll go behind it. There must be some small neighborhood bars that have gone out of business in the Tri-County area. You wouldn't mind a bar and bar stools, would you?"

"Not at all. And bars usually have mirrors, too."

"That's what Michelle said. And you'll be proud of me, Hannah."

"I already am. But why do you say that, Mother?"

"I didn't ask Michelle how she knew that bars had mirrors. I decided it was more important to ask her what she thought of finding small cafés that had gone out of business and seeing if there were tables and chairs in the building that we could buy. And then she mentioned lunch counters and how the little neighborhood drugstores often had soda and ice cream counters with stools attached."

"Those are great ideas, Mother."

"I know. Michelle is the practical one. I'll tell her that you appreciate her suggestions." Delores drove in silence for a few minutes and then she glanced at Hannah. "You're going to test all the appliances today, aren't you?"

"That's my plan, but I'll have to call the utility companies and put everything in my name first."

"Al told me that he was going to do that when I talked to him last night. The only thing you have to do is buy the ingredients you need from Florence and mix up a batch of cookies."

"The first batch I bake is for you, Mother. What kind do you want me to bake?"

"Surprise me, dear."

"But what if you don't like the kind I choose?"

"Impossible. I like everything you bake."

"Thanks," Hannah said with a smile. "Let's narrow it down a little."

"That's easy," Delores answered immediately. "I'd love to have something with cashews. I haven't had salted nuts since your father died. We'd buy the mixed nuts and he'd pick out all the walnuts while I ate all the cashews. Then we'd munch on the rest of them while we watched a movie on television. Did you know that if you mix a few chocolate chips in with the cashews and eat some with every bite, the taste is simply delicious?"

"I haven't tried it, but I will," Hannah promised. "And now I know which kind of cookie I'm going to bake for you."

"Tell me, dear."

"I'll bake Cashew Butter Blossom Cookies. It's a new recipe I want to try and it has cashews and chocolate."

"Wonderful!" Delores declared, a delighted smile spreading across her face. "How many cookies will a batch make?"

Hannah tried to come up with a number, but since she was baking this recipe for the first time, she decided not to commit to a number. "A lot, Mother."

"Will I have enough left over to send some to Lisa's father and take some to Essie?"

"I'll make sure that you do."

"Perfect," Delores said, pulling off the freeway and driving down an access road that Hannah didn't recognize. She pulled into a condo complex, identified herself to the guard at the gate, and he used a remote control to raise the wooden bar that blocked her entrance.

"Where are we going?" Hannah asked her.

"You'll see," Delores told her, traveling down a narrow, winding road that led to a parking lot. "We're here."

"We're where?" Hannah asked. "And why? Do you know someone who lives here?"

"As a matter of fact, I do. I know several people who live here."

"And you're going to visit one of them?"

"No, we're meeting Al Percy in one of the units." She shut off her car and opened the door. "Come on, Hannah. It took a little longer than I expected at Cyril's and I don't want to keep Al waiting. He has another appointment after ours."

There was nothing for Hannah to do except open her own door, get out of the car, and follow her mother as Delores led the way down a curved walkway. There were shrubs planted at the side of the walkway, and the buildings were nestled beneath tall pine trees. The buildings, which looked as if they housed four units each, were painted a shade of forest green that mirrored the color of the pine trees that surrounded them.

"Do you see those planters that separate the buildings?" Delores pointed to one planter.

"Yes."

"All they have in the winter is juniper and they're year-round, but the gardeners plant flowers between the shrubs every spring. You can't see them now because they're covered with snow, but there are stepping stones in a line across the center of the planter for people who want to take a shortcut to their unit. We could have parked anywhere, but I decided to take the walkway so that you could see how scenic this complex is."

Hannah's curious mind searched for answers as Delores pointed out the virtues of this particular condo complex. It was almost as if her mother was pretending to be a real estate agent who was taking a client on a guided tour. Hannah gave a little gasp as the most plausible explanation for her mother's behavior occurred to her. Delores had rented a condo for her before Hannah had even seen it!

# Chapter
# Eleven

"Just a minute, Mother," Hannah said, stopping short on the walkway.

Delores stopped and turned back to look at her. "What is it, dear? Am I walking too fast for you?"

"No." Hannah paused for a moment, searching for the right words. Her mother looked totally innocent. Did that mean that Hannah was wrong in her assumption? The last thing she wanted to do was accuse her mother of something she hadn't done.

"What is it, Hannah?" Delores asked, looking concerned.

Hannah wanted to know what was going on, and the only way to find out was to ask. She took a deep breath for courage and blurted out her question. "Did you rent a condo unit for me here?"

"Of course not!" Delores exclaimed, looking completely shocked. "I'd never rent an apartment without asking you! Living accommodations are personal, like . . ." Delores paused, attempting to find just the right analogy. "They're like purses," she declared. "Purses and perfume are personal. You shouldn't choose them for someone unless you know exactly what they want. I let you buy your own purses, dear." Delores glanced at Hannah's saddlebag-size purse. "Obviously, I do. And I try not to criticize your choices, although at times it's difficult."

"I imagine that's true," Hannah admitted.

"You have no idea how many times I've wanted to buy a smaller purse for you, something that's more stylish. But I knew that if I bought a smaller purse for you and gave it to you for one of your Christmas presents, you'd feel obliged to use it every time you thought you were going to see me. I'm right, aren't I, dear?"

"Yes."

"And you'd hate that, wouldn't you?"

Hannah laughed. Her mother had a valid point. "Yes, I'd hate that. If I had to switch to a smaller purse, I wouldn't have room for the things I want to carry with me."

"Exactly. And wouldn't you be disappointed if I bought an expensive bottle of perfume for you and it wasn't a scent you liked?"

"Yes," Hannah agreed.

"And wouldn't you resent it if I chose an apartment for you and you felt you had to pretend that you loved it to keep from hurting my feelings?"

"Yes, I would," Hannah answered honestly.

"Then I can assure you that I didn't put a deposit down on the place we're about to see. It's something Al told me about this morning, and both of us are seeing it for the first time." Delores stopped at the base of a covered staircase that led up to a second-floor bridge that connected two four-unit buildings. "Wave at Al, dear. He's standing outside the front door of the place I want you to see."

Hannah looked up and waved. Al waved back and motioned for them to climb the outside staircase. As she climbed, Hannah thought of how clever it was to have a roof on the outside staircase. The sides were open to let in the air and the light, but the roof protected the concrete steps from rain in the summer and snow in the winter.

"I like the covered staircase," Delores commented as they neared the top.

"So do I," Hannah agreed, following her mother. The stairs were wide enough to fit the largest and longest feet, and they were perfectly spaced for the easiest climb possible.

As they reached the top of the staircase and stepped out on the bridge that connected the buildings, Hannah stopped to admire the view. The highway was not visible, even from this vantage point, and that meant there would be no traffic noise. The towering pines promised privacy for the entire complex, and she could see a pool and Jacuzzi, next to a large building that she assumed was the clubhouse. It was centrally located and convenient to all of the residents.

"Hello, Al." Delores stepped forward to greet him. "You said that this place comes with some furniture?"

"That's right. The owners didn't want to take anything with them except a few small pieces and their personal items. They only lived here for six months before they had to leave, and they didn't have time to buy much furniture."

"Why did they move?" Hannah asked, hoping the reason wasn't that they'd found something wrong with the complex or the unit that Al was about to show them.

"He taught at the community college and he landed a much better position at the University of Georgia. Since most of her family live only forty minutes away from the campus, both of them wanted to move back there."

"But they liked it here in this complex?" Delores asked, and Hannah silently applauded her mother's probing question.

"They loved it. They said they were hoping to find a place this nice close to his campus. I talked to them a few minutes ago and they agreed to a rent-to-buy option."

"I don't know anything about that option," Hannah admitted.

"It was your sister's idea. She's very interested in real estate."

"Which sister?" Delores asked.

"Andrea. When they bought their house, she asked me some very good questions about real estate in Lake Eden. I think she'd make a great real estate agent, but please don't tell her I said that. She might just open her own office and put me out of business."

"I had no idea that Andrea was interested in real estate!" Delores said, looking very surprised. "She never mentioned it to me."

Hannah was just as surprised as her mother was. "I didn't know either. If Andrea had gone on to college, I assumed that she'd major in art or interior design."

"What does it take to get a real estate license in Minnesota?" Delores asked Al.

"My advice would be to take a pre-license course at the community college. It prepares students who want to take the exam."

"And if they pass the exam, they qualify as an agent?" Hannah asked him.

"It's not quite that easy. Once you pass the exam, you need to work as a licensed real estate salesperson and then you can go on for a broker's license. I have my broker's license, but it was easier to get one back then."

"And it's more difficult now?" Hannah asked.

"Yes, and it takes longer. Most really large real estate companies also run a real estate school. That's another source of revenue for them. And I was talking to an agent in Minneapolis the other day who said the broker's exam is a lot harder than it was when we took it."

"Food for thought," Delores said, and when Al opened the door to the condo unit, he motioned to Hannah. "Come on, Hannah. Let's all take a look."

Hannah followed her mother through the door. There was a carpeted landing just inside the door with three steps leading down to the main room. It was a combination living room and dining room with a dining room table sitting next to the large picture window. The living room was spacious with room for comfortable, overstuffed furniture.

"It's very nice," Hannah said.

"How about the dining room table and chairs?" Delores asked Al. "Did they leave those behind?"

Al nodded. "They come with the place."

"And the couch?" Hannah asked, motioning toward the long sofa that was placed with its back toward the dining area.

"The couch, too," Al confirmed.

"With the sofa placed like that, it separates the dining area from the living room," Delores pointed out. "I like it." She noticed the fireplace against another wall and turned to Al. "Is that a gas-burning fireplace?"

"Yes, with a gas log. And I know it works because I checked it out before they left."

Hannah noticed the balcony outside the sliding doors in the living room and looked out. Again, the view featured the tall pines with some of the other buildings nestled between them. "Where's the kitchen?" she asked Al.

"Right through there." Al pointed to a doorway close to the dining area. "The electricity is on. Take a look. Just wander through the place and look at everything. I'm going to step outside to make a phone call."

Hannah flicked on the lights and stepped into the kitchen. It was longer than it was wide, but there was plenty of space. There was a window over the sink to let in the light and it could be opened for fresh air.

She walked to the center of the kitchen and looked around. There was plenty of counter space with cupboards above it, and a nook where the residents had probably placed a kitchen table and chairs. There was even a wall phone that could be reached by someone at the table.

One glance at the appliances caused Hannah to wince. The owners had obviously purchased a used stove and refrigerator. The only new appliance was the dishwasher. At least she wouldn't have to replace that.

Hannah gave a little gasp as she realized that she was already thinking of renting this condo. So far, she liked everything about it, but she hadn't yet looked at the bedroom and bathroom.

"The first thing we'll have to do is replace the stove and refrigerator," Delores remarked, entering the kitchen behind Hannah.

"That's just what I was thinking," Hannah admitted, "but let's not rush things, Mother. We haven't looked at the bathroom and the bedroom yet."

"Make that plural, dear," Delores told her. "This unit has a master bedroom with an attached bathroom and a guest bedroom with a guest bathroom right across the hall."

Hannah began to frown. "That's more room than I need, Mother. I really doubt that I'll have any guests."

"I'm sure your sister will stay here quite often," Delores pointed out.

"Andrea?"

"No, dear. If Michelle is going to help you in the bakery, she may want to stay overnight with you on Fridays and ride to work with you on Saturday morning. That way she won't have to walk to The Cookie Jar. And don't forget that she'll be going off to college a year and a half from now. She may want to come back and visit you on her vacations."

"But . . . won't Michelle want to stay with you at your house?"

"I'm not sure what I'm going to do with the house, dear. I don't need three bedrooms, and . . ." Delores paused and began to look sad. "Your father and I bought that house together right before you were born. And every time I go around a corner, I expect to see him there."

Hannah was immediately contrite. "I'm sorry I brought it up, Mother. I never meant to make you sad. Of course the house has a lot of memories for you."

"It's true. And I'm not sure how I feel about that. Sometimes I feel a greater sense of loss when I don't see him sitting in the living room, or puttering around with his woodworking out in the garage. At other times, the memory of our life there makes me happy. I guess what I'm trying to say is that I have to find out if I can cope with staying there. If I can't, I'll move to another place. If I can, I'll stay. Does that make sense to you?"

"It makes perfect sense."

"Grandma Knudson told me that a lot of women want to move when their children are grown and their husbands die."

"But she didn't do that. She's still here in Lake Eden, living in the parsonage."

"That's right. And she described how she managed to cope when Reverend Knudson died. She said she was all prepared to move before the new minister arrived, but that was when her grandson, Reverend Bob, accepted the call to come here to Lake Eden to be our new minister. And since he was still single, he asked her to stay and keep house for him."

"So she stayed."

"Yes, but not before she repainted the whole inside of the house in different colors. She said it wasn't that big of a project because since she'd planned to move, most of her things were already packed and out of the way."

"I can understand why she wanted to make the parsonage look different."

"Yes, and she even bought some new furniture and rearranged the rest. The only room she didn't change was her sitting room, and that was because Reverend Knudson had regarded it as her room and he never used it."

"Did that work to make her less sad?"

"Yes, she said that the parsonage looked totally different inside and only good memories were left."

"Like the bird tree?"

"That was one of the memories she mentioned. She told me that it was her husband's idea in the first place. He loved birds and when she first met him, he took her bird-watching with him. Reverend Knudson was the one who began to recruit the local children to help decorate the bird tree and teach them about winter birds. After he died, she decided that she wanted to carry on the tradition. She said she continued doing the things that made her happy and changed the things that made her sad."

"Do you want to repaint *your* house, Mother?" Hannah asked the obvious question.

"I think so. I've always wanted a sunshine yellow bedroom, but your father didn't like the color. And I wish the kitchen were a cheerier color. The living room could certainly use new wallpaper, maybe something with stripes instead of the paisley that your father was so fond of. And the bathrooms are getting terribly shabby. I could paint the walls and buy new towels to match."

Delores was smiling now, and Hannah decided to keep her talking about redecorating the house. "How about the furniture? Would you buy new?"

"I don't really need to buy new, dear." Delores gave a little laugh. "Have you seen the inside of the old woodshed in the backyard lately?"

"No, I haven't been in there for years."

"Well, it's filled with the things I found at estate sales and auctions. Most of the furniture I stored out there is in very good shape. I may need to reupholster some of it, but that's not difficult. And some of the wooden pieces need refinishing, but that would be a good project for me."

"You're right, Mother," Hannah agreed. Delores was always happier when she was involved in a project.

"Let's go see the bedrooms, dear," Delores said, leading the way through the living room and down the long, carpeted hallway.

"Here's the guest bathroom," Hannah said, stopping at an open door and flicking on the lights. "Good! There's a shower."

"And a nice little vanity in front of the mirror with a stool under it," Delores pointed out. "I'm glad the guest bathroom isn't just a powder room. Al told me that the one-bedroom units have powder rooms right off the living rooms. He said they call the powder rooms guest bathrooms, but they're very small rooms with a sink and a commode. This one is really a second bathroom."

Hannah turned off the bathroom lights and they went across the hall to look at the guest bedroom. There was a large closet along one wall with mirrored doors. The room was good-sized and there was plenty of room for a double or perhaps even a queen-size bed.

"That window will have to be curtained," Delores said, walking over to look outside. "It's right next to the covered staircase outside. I probably have curtains we could use until you find what you want."

"You're right, Mother," Hannah said, walking over to look. "Anyone walking up the stairs can see right into this room."

What they'd just done suddenly struck Hannah. Delores was talking as if they'd already rented the condo unit and Hannah was thinking along the same lines. As they left the spare bedroom and walked down the hallway to the master bedroom, Hannah found herself hoping that she'd be able to afford the rent.

"It's huge!" Hannah gasped as they stepped inside the master bedroom. "There's room for a king-size bed, a dresser, and even an easy chair with a table."

Delores walked over to look out the window. "It has a nice view of the pine trees in the distance and the planter below. You can see the building on the other side of the planter, but it's not intrusive."

Hannah walked across the room to inspect the master bathroom. It was large with a vanity that ran along one wall and a mirror above it. There was a stool beneath the vanity that could be pulled out for anyone putting on makeup or styling hair.

"Come look at the shower," Delores said as she opened the glass door. "It's huge."

"You're right." Hannah began to smile. She wouldn't have to be careful about bumping her elbows when she washed her hair in the shower.

They exited the master bathroom and went back into the bedroom, where Delores opened the set of double closet doors that exposed the master closet that covered one entire wall. "Do you like this place, Hannah?"

"I love it. But how much is the monthly rent? I have to make sure that I can afford it."

"It's not as inexpensive as a two-bedroom at The Oaks." Delores named a new apartment complex in the opposite direction. "But you'll be getting a lot more. I know someone who lives in The Oaks and it's closer to town, but it's noisy because a lot of young singles live there. This complex is farther from town, but it's quiet and it's fairly secluded. And it has a lovely view of the pines and the surrounding countryside."

"You're right, Mother. The Oaks is right next to the highway, and this complex is further away. But the big question is, can I afford it? I don't even know how much money is left in my college fund. And what am I going to do if The Cookie Jar doesn't bring in enough money to take over the rent when my college money runs out?"

Delores smiled at her. "I'm going to tell you what your father would have told you. I've heard him give advice to other people who were starting a business. All you have to do to make The Cookie Jar a success is to sell good products and believe in them. It'll be slow at first and you mustn't fall into the trap of biting off more than you can chew. Open your coffee shop and sell cookies and coffee. That's all you have to do. Just concentrate on selling coffee and cookies, and make a profit that way. You can branch out later if you have time and the energy to do it."

"Dad always said not to spread yourself too thin."

"Yes, he did. And your father was a wise man."

"And you're wise, Mother," Hannah told her.

"Thank you, dear. Your father told me all this when I wanted to start an antique shop in town."

Hannah was puzzled. "But you didn't open an antique shop."

"No, I decided that I didn't have enough product and I had to buy more antiques before it would be worthwhile. And I was having so much fun collecting things, I never got around to actually opening any kind of business."

"Do you think you'll ever want to open a shop like that?"

"I don't know. It's a possibility. And your father told me exactly how to do it. I learned some important things from him over the years." Delores reached out to pat Hannah's shoulder and then she turned around. "Now, let's go talk to Al and find out exactly how much this place costs and when you can move in."

# Chapter Twelve

Hannah stood back to look at her partially stocked pantry. She'd bought only bare necessities at the Red Owl and she planned to order flour, sugar, eggs, and other products in bulk once she actually opened for business.

The next item on her to-do list was to learn how all the existing appliances operated and test them to make sure they were in good working order. She brought in a chair from the front room and pushed it over to the stainless-steel work island. Then she opened the instruction manual for the industrial oven and sat down.

The chair was a bit too low to be comfortable, and Hannah reminded herself to find stools that were the right height. She flipped the manual open and began to read. The instructions were written in English and she was thankful for that. She'd read operating instructions that appeared to have been translated from a foreign language and they had been so convoluted that they were completely undecipherable.

Once she'd familiarized herself with the instructions, Hannah went to the walk-in cooler to retrieve one of the extralarge metal mixing bowls that were on one of the shelves inside. Then she went to the pantry to find the ingredients she needed to bake Cashew Butter Blossom Cookies.

Hannah had decided to use a stackable series of small and large bowls that she'd found in the cupboard, and she'd washed them in the sink. There were at least two dozen of them and when Michelle and Lisa came to join her, she'd ask them to read the manual for the dishwasher, stock it with the metal mixing bowls she hadn't yet washed from the shelf in the walk-in cooler, and run a load of dishes and utensils.

All the ingredients she needed for the Cashew Butter Blossom Cookies were in a grocery bag she'd set on the counter. Hannah carried it to the workstation, along with the clean mixing bowls, and the set of measuring cups she'd also hand washed in preparation for mixing up a test batch of cookies. She had her favorite mixing tool too, a large wooden spoon that had belonged her to great-grandmother. When she baked cookies in volume for The Cookie Jar, she'd use the industrial mixer. But right now, when she planned to bake her first test batch, she didn't want to take the time to look for the attachments, wash them, and learn how to use the mixer.

Hannah added the sugar and the salted butter to the bottom of the metal mixing bowl. She'd left the butter out on the work island to soften and all she had to do was unwrap it. She added the cashew butter she'd purchased at the grocery store, placing it on top of the butter in the bowl. Then she used her great-grandmother's spoon to mix them together. Two teaspoons of vanilla extract came next, and she stopped to spray her measuring cup with nonstick cooking spray before she measured out the molasses. Once those were stirred into the butters in the bowl, she added the baking soda, baking powder, and salt.

Unfortunately, Florence hadn't carried chopped cashews at the store, so Hannah had bought them whole. She opened a can, got out a clean chopping board, and chopped them herself with one of her favorite knives.

Once the cashews had been added to the mixture in the bowl, Hannah used a whisk she'd purchased to beat the eggs. She added them to the mixing bowl, mixed them in thoroughly, and opened the sack of all-purpose flour.

She measured the flour, adding it in increments to her

bowl, adding it to her other ingredients. She'd learned from past mistakes that if she let all of the flour sit on top of the other ingredients before she attempted to mix it in, not only would the flour tend to fly out of the bowl when she stirred it, but it would be doubly difficult to achieve a smooth mixture.

When her dough was thoroughly mixed, Hannah smiled in triumph. Now all she had to do was preheat the oven, get out the chocolate star-shaped candies she'd found in Florence's candy aisle, shape the cookies on the cookie sheets that she would line with parchment paper, top them with one of the chocolate stars, and bake them.

Hannah covered her mixing bowl with plastic wrap and walked to the oven. She had placed the manual on a nearby counter, opened to the correct page, and she read the instructions a second time. Then she opened the oven, hung an oven thermometer on one of the revolving shelves so that she could make sure that the oven was calibrated correctly, and reclosed the oven door.

"Here goes nothing," Hannah said aloud as she turned the knob to the ON position to make the racks revolve. Then she pressed the red button to ignite the gas.

There was a whooshing sound from inside, and Hannah smiled in relief. It was the same sound her mother's gas fireplace made when it ignited. The oven was operating just as the manual had said it would. Now all she had to do was wait for the light in the center of the temperature indicator to go on and her oven would be preheated.

While Hannah waited for the oven to preheat, she began to shape the cookies. She had completed only two sheets of cookies before the oven beeped to show that it was at the proper temperature.

Hannah opened the oven door. One glance assured her that the oven had reached and was maintaining the proper temperature. The oven heated fast and that was a good thing. It meant that she could bake first thing in the morning if she mixed up the batches of cookie dough before she left for the day and kept them in the walk-in cooler overnight. She shut the oven door again and hurried back to the workstation to shape the rest of the cookies.

"So far, so good," she said, even though there was no one around to agree with her. She worked rapidly, forming round cookies and topping each with a chocolate star. As soon as she completed enough cookie sheets to fill the revolving shelves, she carried the cookie sheets to the bakers rack that Alex and Veronica had left. The bakers rack had multiple shelves and it was equipped with wheels so that it could be easily rolled to any location in the kitchen. It would be a real step saver and Hannah promised herself that the next time she made cookies, she'd wheel it over to the workstation to receive the filled cookie sheets and then wheel it to the oven.

It was time to bake and Hannah smiled as she placed the cookies on the revolving racks inside the oven. The cookies needed to bake for ten to twelves minutes, so she set the timer for ten minutes. When the bell on the timer rang, she'd look through the glass on the oven door to see if the cookies had browned enough. When they were golden brown, she'd take them from the oven, slip the cookie sheets onto shelves in the bakers rack, and wait for them to cool. That shouldn't take long since the shelves were similar to wire racks, and air would circulate around each cookie.

Hannah went back to the workstation to gather her baking utensils and mixing bowls. She carried them to the sink, intending to wash them by hand, but she realized that they didn't have to be cleaned immediately. She simply rinsed them out in the sink and placed them in the industrial dishwasher. Once Lisa and Michelle figured out how to work it, they could wash her baking utensils and mixing bowls. It was a perfect way to test the dishwasher to make certain that it operated well.

As she walked past the oven, Hannah glanced at the timer. She still had five minutes to go, so she went back to her chair at the workstation and opened the instruction manual for the industrial mixer. As she read the instructions, she felt a sense of relief. Although it was four times larger than her mother's stand mixer and could mix up enough cookie dough to fill all the racks in the industrial oven at once, it operated exactly the same.

The timer sounded and Hannah jumped up from her chair to see if her cookies were done. She looked through the door, saw that they were a nice golden brown, and removed all the cookie sheets to place them on separate shelves on the bakers rack. The cookies would need to cool for at least ten minutes before she could taste one to see how successful she'd been. She went back to her chair at the workstation and sat there, wishing that she had brought coffee to go with her cookies.

The solution to the coffee problem popped into her mind and she rushed to put on her coat. Hal and Rose's café was only a short distance away. She could hurry down there, get a to-go cup of coffee, and be back here by the time her cookies were cool enough to test.

A scant three minutes later, when she opened the door to the café, Hannah breathed in the scent of burgers grilling, onion rings browning in the deep fryer, and roast beef roasting in the oven. She was tempted to take one of Rose's excellent burgers back to the bakery with her, but she reminded herself that her mother was taking them out to the Corner Tavern to have Double-double hamburgers in less than three hours' time. Hannah ordered coffee from Luanne Hanks, one of Rose's best waitresses, and hurried back to the bakery with her take-out coffee.

Once she'd returned her parka to the rack of hooks by the back kitchen door, Hannah walked over to touch one of the cookies on the bakers rack. It was still slightly warm, and that was the perfect eating temperature for a freshly baked cookie. She chose two cookies and carried them over to the workstation to taste them.

The first taste was wonderful and Hannah gave a little sigh

of satisfaction. Her recipe had worked perfectly. She ate her cookie slowly, taking time to savor the flavors, and then she bit into the chocolate star on the top of the cookie. "Great combination," she said aloud.

"What's a great combination?" a familiar voice asked from the main room, followed by a second familiar voice that added, "And what smells so good?"

"Cashew Butter Blossoms," Hannah told Lisa and Michelle as they came into the kitchen. "They're the first batch of cookies I baked and I just tasted them. I bought two little cartons of milk at the Red Owl this morning and you can get them out of the walk-in cooler. I have straws, too."

"You got the walk-in cooler working?" Michelle asked her.

"Yes, and it was easy. All I had to do was turn it on. The oven's more complicated, but I followed the instructions in the manual and it works perfectly."

"And it's calibrated right?" Lisa asked.

"Perfectly," Hannah answered, impressed by Lisa's question. Lisa's mother was a very good baker and she'd taught her daughter well.

"I'll get the milk," Lisa said. "I want to take a look at the walk-in cooler. I've never seen one of those before."

"Okay," Michelle agreed. "And while you're doing that, I'll get us a couple of cookies and bring us two chairs from the coffee shop."

Hannah noticed that Michelle had already called the main room a coffee shop and she gave a little smile. It was obvious that Michelle had confidence that Hannah's new business would succeed.

"We'll have to look for stools that are tall enough to fit here," Michelle remarked as she carried in the first chair. "Mother told me that this was the workstation and it was taller than the tables in the coffee shop. We talked about bar stools, but I think they'd be too tall. We should probably ask Hank down at the Municipal Liquor Store if we could bring one of his bar stools here to try it out and see if it works."

"Good idea," Hannah told her. And then she marveled at how sisters, raised by the same parents, could have such different personalities. Andrea was an artistic perfectionist, two characteristics that usually didn't go together. Michelle was a realist who was practical and also creative. And she was . . . Hannah paused, thinking about it for a moment. She wasn't sure exactly *what* she was. She was certainly gullible when it came to love, since she had believed that Bradford Ramsey was going to marry her.

"The cooler's just wonderful, Hannah!" Lisa plunked the cartons of milk down on the stainless-steel surface of the workstation, effectively interrupting Hannah's thoughts. "You can mix up all the cookie dough you need for the next day's baking and let it chill in there overnight. Then all you have to do in the morning is take it out, let it warm up a little, and bake it."

"That's right," Hannah said with a nod. It was obvious that Lisa was also practical. "Here comes Michelle with the second chair and a plate of cookies. Let's taste them. I need to know what you think of them and please don't be afraid to tell me if you don't like them. I can always correct anything that doesn't work."

"They smell delicious, but I already told you that when I came in," Lisa said. "And they look great, too."

Michelle sat down in the chair she'd just brought and reached for a cookie. "Lisa and I skipped lunch because they were having grilled cheese and they always make them so far ahead of time, they're cold. Now I'm really hungry and I'm dragging. This cookie should fix me up just fine."

"Two at the most," Hannah warned her. "We're going out to the Corner Tavern with Mother tonight and we should save ourselves for their Double-doubles."

"And their French fries," Lisa added.

Michelle laughed. "And their onion rings," she said.

"Okay. Let's taste," Hannah told them, reaching for her cookie.

All three of them bit into their cookies at the same time. For a moment, there was silence and then Lisa exclaimed, "Oh, boy!"

"Oh, boy is right," Michelle agreed. "These are every bit as good as your Cocoa-Crunch Cookies."

"I love the taste of cashews with chocolate," Lisa commented.

"So does Mother," Hannah told her. "She even mixes her can of salted cashews with chocolate chips so she can eat them together."

"I'll have to try that!" Michelle said, taking another huge bite of her cookie. "Mother knows her snacks."

"Really?" Lisa looked surprised. "But she's so thin."

"She's usually a little heavier," Hannah explained, "but she's always watched her weight. And the way she's been eating lately, she'll get back to her ideal weight in record time."

"Especially if you keep on baking these," Michelle told Hannah, and then she turned to Lisa. "Mother's going to practically inhale these cookies while Hannah reads to us tonight. You'll see."

# CASHEW BUTTER BLOSSOM COOKIES

Preheat oven to 350 degrees F., rack in the middle position.

2 cups white *(granulated)* sugar
1 cup salted butter *(2 sticks)* softened
½ cup cashew butter
2 teaspoons vanilla extract
⅛ cup *(2 Tablespoons)* molasses *(I used Grandma's Molasses)*
½ teaspoon baking soda
1 teaspoon baking powder
½ teaspoon salt
½ cup finely chopped salted cashews
2 large eggs, beaten *(just whip them up in a glass with a fork)*
4 cups all-purpose flour *(pack it down in the cup when you measure it)*
13-ounce bag Hershey's Kisses *(or milk chocolate stars)*

Prepare your cookie sheets by spraying them with Pam or another nonstick cooking spray or lining them with parchment paper.

**Hannah's 1st Note: This recipe is easiest to make if you use an electric mixer to prepare this dough.**

Place the white sugar in the bowl of an electric mixer.

Add the softened butter and mix on LOW until it's well blended, then beat on MEDIUM speed until the mixture is light and fluffy.

Mix in the half-cup of cashew butter and beat on MEDIUM speed until it is well incorporated.

**Hannah's 2nd Note: Cashew butter is easier to measure if you spray the inside of the measuring cup with Pam or another nonstick cooking spray and also spray the blade of your rubber spatula. Pack the cashew butter down in the cup and level it off with the prepared spatula. The cooking spray makes it easier to get all the cashew butter out of your measuring cup. You can also use this pre-sprayed cup to measure the molasses.**

Mix in the vanilla extract and the molasses. Beat until they are well incorporated.

With the mixer running on LOW speed, sprinkle in the baking soda, baking powder, and salt. Mix well.

Add the finely chopped cashews to the bowl and mix them in on LOW.

Add the beaten eggs and mix those in thoroughly.

Mix in the all-purpose flour in half-cup increments, mixing after each addition.

**Hannah's 3rd Note: If you mix in your 4 cups of flour all at once, you may find it spews out of the bowl when you turn on your mixer and you end up with flour all over your kitchen floor!**

Mix until all your ingredients are thoroughly blended and then shut off your mixer and scrape down the bowl.

Take the bowl out of the mixer. Scrape down the sides of the bowl with your rubber spatula and give your Cashew Butter Blossom Cookie dough a final stir by hand.

Let the dough firm up for a few minutes on your kitchen counter as you sit down and enjoy a couple of the Hershey's Kisses or chocolate stars.

Form the dough into walnut-sized balls and arrange them on a greased cookie sheet, 12 to a standard-size sheet.

Press the Hershey's Kisses or chocolate stars, point up, into the middle of your cookie balls, flat side down. They'll look like flowers or blossoms after they're baked and that's why they're called Cashew Butter Blossom Cookies.

Bake at 350 degrees F. for 10 to 12 minutes, or until the edges are just beginning to turn golden. *(Don't worry—the chocolate won't melt in that length of time.)*

Cool your cookies on the cookie sheet for 2 minutes and then remove them to wire racks to finish cooling.

**Hannah's 4th Note: If you used parchment paper on your cookie sheets, just pull it off the cookie sheet, cookies and all, and onto a wire rack. The cookies can cool right on the paper.**

Yield: Makes approximately 8 dozen delicious cookies, depending on the size of the cookie dough balls. You can cut this recipe in half, but if you do, use ½ teaspoon of baking soda and ½ teaspoon of baking powder.

**Hannah's 5th Note: If you have any chocolate stars or Hershey's Kisses left over, the baker deserves another treat!**

# Chapter Thirteen

The words she had feared were there on the front page of the newspaper she'd bought at their last stop. Her cousin was in jail, along with several of the men he called his employees. They'd arrested him shortly after they'd received the package of double books she'd mailed in New York. And Lenny, his right-hand man, was there too, on a murder charge.

She turned the pages of the paper to find the rest of the story. One of her cousin's men had broken down during police interrogation and had exposed his whole illegal racket. The authorities had charged Lenny in several murders, and the paper called Lenny a "hit man" for the mob. The federal prosecutor had assured the reporter that Lenny would be behind bars for the rest of his life, that this time they had him dead to rights, burying a body in the backyard of his aunt's house in Brooklyn.

She gave a soft little cry as she read the name of Lenny's most recent victim, but there were no fellow passengers near enough to hear her. The train was still boarding and the club car would not open for them until all the baggage had been loaded and the conductor had walked through the cars to check everyone's ticket.

Tony was dead! Her husband was dead! She felt faint and the club car began to dim in front of her eyes. The couches, and tables, and chairs began to revolve around her until everything was spinning out of control and she could see bright, sparkling lights blinding and twirling at the edges of her vision. They twirled toward the center, creating a wave of dizzy heat in her mind, and then everything faded into oblivion.

She could see light behind her eyelids and she let them open slightly. She must have dozed off for a moment because everything seemed to be happening in a dream. There was a newspaper on the floor near her feet and she wondered about that for a moment. Was the newspaper hers? Had she dropped it when she'd fallen asleep? Or was the newspaper a part of the dream that she was still experiencing. She was struggling to find an answer to those questions when a man spoke to her.

"Excuse me, ma'am. Is this your newspaper?"

She startled awake and her eyelids flew open. "Oh! Yes, it's mine. I must have fallen asleep."

The man smiled and she realized that she liked his face. He was older, perhaps the age of her grandfather, and he looked both kind and concerned.

"Are you all right?" he asked her.

"Yes," she replied quickly, taking the newspaper he held out to her. "I couldn't seem to sleep last night and I must have dozed off."

He smiled at her and it made her feel as if he were actually interested in what she'd said. "It's not always easy to sleep on a train," he told her. "That's why I always book a compartment when I go to visit my sister. To tell you the truth," he said, leaning down a bit closer to her, "it doesn't always help. I was in here last night and I almost came over to talk to you then, to ask if I could order some cocoa or hot milk for you."

"I wasn't . . . talking in my sleep, was I?" she asked him, suddenly afraid she'd said something strange. She knew that she talked in her sleep. Her family had told her about that. What if she'd mentioned how desperate she was to escape what had happened in New York? And what if she'd mentioned how worried she was about her husband's safety?

"No, you didn't say a thing," he reassured her. "But you were restless and I was concerned for you."

"Thank you!" She felt like crying with relief, or perhaps it was simply because a perfect stranger had been kind enough to be so concerned.

"Would you like some cocoa now?" he asked her. "I'd be happy to ring for the porter."

"Thank you very much, but I'm fine. I had coffee with my breakfast."

"I noticed. I saw you in the dining car and I had to refrain myself from ordering something more nourishing for you, especially in your condition."

He knew! She felt her cheeks flame with embarrassment. Did everyone who'd come into the club car know that she was expecting a baby? She pulled her oversize raincoat a bit closer around her and wondered if she could pretend that she hadn't understood the meaning behind his words.

"How long will it be now?" he asked her.

"Ten to twelve weeks," she answered honestly. Since he knew, there was no reason not to tell him.

"Is that what your doctor told you?" he asked, sitting down in the chair across from her. "You don't mind if I sit here, do you?"

"I . . . no. I don't mind at all," she answered, feeling a small jolt of surprise because she truly wanted him to continue to talk to her. "Yes, that's what my doctor told me the last time I saw him."

"And how long ago was that?"

"Almost two months ago. I . . . I couldn't keep my last appointment with him."

"Because you were traveling?"

"Not exactly. It was because I was . . . preparing to travel, and I . . . just couldn't go to his office."

"I see." He smiled at her and again, it was a kind smile, a caring smile. "Your doctor was wrong," he said.

"How . . . do you know?"

"Because I'm a doctor and I've delivered hundreds of babies. You're only a week or so away from having your baby now."

"Are you . . . you're certain?"

"I'm wise enough to know that a doctor can never be certain. Babies arrive when they're ready and that may or may not be on our timetable. Still, I believe I'm right when I say it will happen within a week, but not much longer than that."

"But . . . that can't be right! I have to find a place to live. And I have to wait until . . ." She stopped speaking, as she remembered the words she'd read. Then tears filled her eyes and she wished that she'd stayed with Tony, that they'd been together even in death. But there was the baby, Tony's baby, to think of. She took a deep breath and attempted to quell her panic and look much calmer than she felt.

"I'd like to help you if you'll tell me what's wrong," he said.

He was clearly concerned for her. She could see it in his eyes. "It's just that I . . . I'm not . . . ready!" she told him.

"Babies don't wait for you to be ready." He reached across the space between them to take her hand. "Don't worry. I've delivered hundreds, perhaps even thousands, of babies. You'll be perfectly fine and so will your baby."

"That's very . . . comforting," she said, giving a sigh of relief. "And it's very kind of you to be concerned."

"Nonsense," he dismissed her tearful gratitude with a wave of his hand. "Is this your first baby?"

"Yes."

He reached up to ring for the porter. "You still have time to prepare. Did you eat anything besides toast for breakfast this morning?"

"Yes, I did," she told him, beginning to feel more comfortable at answering his questions.

"What did you eat?"

"I . . . I had strawberry jelly on my toast. And I had cream and sugar in my coffee."

He shook his head. "That won't do, my dear. You'll need . . ."

He stopped and gave a little wave as the porter appeared at the entrance to the club car. "Ah! Here's Alvin now." He turned to the porter. "My niece needs something good to eat, Alvin. What would you recommend that's light, but packed full of nourishing goodness?"

The porter looked surprised. "Doc! I didn't know that she was your niece!"

"Well, she is. Introduce yourself to Alvin, my dear."

She smiled and it was a genuine smile. "I'm Rose," she said, giving him the first name that popped into her head. "It's nice to meet you, Alvin."

Lisa gave an audible gasp. "Do you think Essie was writing about *our* Rose?"

"No." Delores answered quickly. "Rose McDermott has lived in Lake Eden all her life. She dated Hal in high school and married him right after they graduated. They worked for the former owners of the café, and when they retired, Rose and Hal bought it. I know for a fact that Rose has never been anywhere near New York."

Lisa looked a bit downcast. "I didn't know that. I'm sorry I thought that it could be her."

"That's all right," Hannah reassured her. "I was thinking the same thing."

Michelle turned to smile at her friend. "I was thinking the very same thing." Then she turned to Hannah. "Please read more, Hannah. This is getting really exciting."

"Nice to meet you too, Miss Rose," Alvin said with a smile. "My apologies. I didn't know you were the Doc's niece."

"You couldn't have treated me any better if you'd known," she told him.

"So what would you recommend, Alvin?" the doctor asked him.

"The best thing would be oatmeal, but it weighs heavy on

your insides. And it's warm in here, so I wouldn't say oatmeal. How about scrambled eggs with cheese?"

"What kind of cheese, Alvin?" the doctor asked him.

"Cream cheese. None of that artificial cheese that isn't cheese at all. And I might mix the cream cheese with a little sharp cheddar or shredded parmesan for flavor. And I'd serve those scrambled eggs with biscuits and plenty of butter."

She smiled at Alvin. "Just hearing you describe it is making me hungry."

Alvin looked pleased as he turned to the doctor. "How about it, Doc? Do you want me to go make it?"

"Yes. And while you're at it, make one plate for me, too. I didn't think I'd be hungry this soon, but my niece is right. I'd like to try those scrambled eggs of yours."

He waited until the porter had left and then he turned to her again. "Is Rose your real name?" he asked her.

There was no need to lie, so she shook her head. "No, it's not."

"Will you tell me your real name?"

"No, it would put you in danger."

He gave a slight nod. "So you're running away from something or someone?"

"Yes."

"Your husband?"

"No! Never!" She was horrified at the thought and it showed clearly on her face. "I love my . . ." She stopped speaking and tears filled her eyes. "I *loved* my husband."

He was silent for a moment, obviously thinking about what she'd told him.

"Your husband is dead?" he asked, drawing the obvious conclusion.

"Yes," she said . . . and then she glanced down at the newspaper he'd handed back to her. "They killed him!"

"Who killed him?"

"I can't tell you. That would put you in danger, too."

"And you're running away from the people who killed your husband."

It wasn't a question, but she nodded anyway. "Yes, I promised him that I'd keep our baby safe."

"The people who killed your husband would hurt you if they found you?"

"They'd kill me," she corrected him. "And they'd kill our baby, too. I promised my husband that I'd go somewhere I'd never gone before and hide until he came for me. But now he can't . . ." She stopped to swallow past the lump of sorrow in her throat and blinked back the tears that formed in her eyes. "He can't come for me now."

"Alvin told me that you were traveling to California."

"I bought a ticket to California."

He caught her meaning immediately. "But you're not going to California?"

"No, but it's where they'll expect me to go."

He smiled at her. "So you're throwing them off your trail. That's very clever."

"It was my husband's idea." She stopped to dab at her face with a tissue. "I think he knew all along that they would kill him. But . . . but he . . . he stayed behind to give me a chance to get away."

"I can see why you loved him," he said.

They were both silent for a long moment and then he extended his hand to her. "Shake hands with your uncle Jim. I'm the town doctor in Lakeview, Minnesota. I have a clinic in my house there, and I think that you should come home and stay with me."

She studied his face and saw that he was perfectly sincere. He was kind, he was caring, and he was the right age to be her grandfather. If he was right about when the baby would be born, it could be dangerous for her and for the baby to continue traveling. No one would find her in Minnesota, especially if he told everyone that she was his niece. Was this the right solution for her and for her baby?"

**"Uncle Jim," she took his hand and smiled. "Meet your new niece."**

There was complete silence as Hannah closed the notebook and set it down on the table by the side of her chair. Delores, Michelle, Lisa, and Hannah simply stared at each other.

"Oh, my!" Delores said at last. "I hope she's going to be all right."

"Do you think the doctor is right about when she'll have the baby?" Lisa asked.

Hannah shrugged. "I don't know. I haven't been reading ahead. I wanted to, but I didn't think it was fair to the rest of you."

"I don't know how you can keep from reading ahead now," Michelle told her. "It's just too exciting to put down."

"Hannah has always shown great restraint," Delores told them.

"I know," Michelle said, turning to look at Hannah. "If I was the one who had those notebooks, I would have locked myself in my room and read until the very end."

Hannah smiled. "Perhaps I'd do that, but Grandma Knudson said there isn't an end. Essie said she couldn't decide how to end her story and that's the reason she stopped writing."

"No ending?" Lisa asked, looking at Hannah in dismay.

Delores sighed. "Hannah's right. Essie told us that she never finished her story."

"Oh!" Lisa sounded as if she wanted to cry. "I can't believe there's no ending."

"I have an idea," Hannah said. "Perhaps if we read through everything Essie has written so far, we can think of the perfect ending for her book."

"You mean . . . we could finish it?" Michelle asked, staring at her older sister in awe.

"Yes. Or at least we could try. And if we tell Essie our

ideas for ending it, she might decide to choose one of our ideas and actually finish her story."

"That's a marvelous suggestion, dear!" Delores complimented her. "As a matter of fact, I think I already have an idea."

"I have one, too," Lisa said.

"You're right," Michelle nodded. "Essie may have pointed the way to the ending and all we have to do is recognize where she was going and why."

Hannah smiled at her youngest sister. "Let's exchange the ideas we have so far over coffee and something else that might unleash our creativity."

"What would that be?" Lisa asked her.

"Chocolate, of course. I made something else to test out the bakery's stovetop burners and the walk-in cooler. I brought home a box of them and put them in Mother's refrigerator." She turned to Delores. "Since Lisa and Michelle can't help with the champagne at the Christmas Ball, I thought we might have them pass plates of my creation around while you and Andrea serve the champagne. I think they'd go very well with champagne or white wine."

"That sounds lovely, dear," Delores commented.

"What did you make, Hannah?" Michelle asked her.

"Truffles . . . of a sort. They're not traditional, but they're really easy to make and the recipe sounded wonderful. A college friend gave it to me right after Nutella first came out."

"The chocolate hazelnut spread?" Lisa asked her.

"Yes, I'm calling them Chocolate Hazelnut Bon-Bons. They're a little like the Rum Balls that I always make for Christmas."

"I'd love to try one!" Delores volunteered.

Hannah, Michelle, and Lisa all turned to stare at the woman who'd eaten five cookies after polishing off a small dinner salad, a Double-double burger, a side of French tries, and half of Michelle's onion rings at the Corner Tavern.

"Maybe we should wait until tomorrow night," Michelle suggested, trying hard to keep the teasing expression off her face. "You can't possibly be hungry, can you, Mother?"

"I may not be hungry, but I know my responsibilities," Delores said quickly. "I'm obligated to taste one, or perhaps two, of Hannah's new creation." She stopped and gave a big sigh. "After all, this may be the last chance I get."

"What do you mean?" Hannah felt an immediate concern. Was her mother wearing herself out, planning the Christmas Ball? Was she genuinely ill? "Is there something wrong, Mother?"

"Yes, there *is* something wrong." Delores looked very serious. "You see, I tried on the outfit I planned to wear to the Christmas Ball when I came home this afternoon. It's my size, but it's a little too tight for me now. And that means I'm starting a diet at the end of the week. You girls have three more days to fatten me up before I can never eat anything good again!"

"Never?" Lisa sounded horrified.

"Well . . . perhaps *never* isn't precisely the right word. But I can't eat anything good again until I lose at least three pounds."

They were silent for a moment and then Lisa spoke up. "Maybe you don't have to go on a diet."

Delores looked surprised. "What do you mean, Lisa?"

"Is the outfit you were planning to wear to the ball your favorite outfit?"

"Not really. It's just that it's the dressiest outfit that I have and I wanted to wear something dressy."

"Then I have a solution for you," Lisa said. "You can eat all the truffles and bon-bons you want if you just go out and buy a new outfit."

# CHOCOLATE HAZELNUT BON-BONS

No need to preheat oven—this is a no-bake recipe.

½ cup Nutella
¼ cup salted butter *(½ stick, 2 ounces)* softened
¼ cup finely chopped hazelnuts *(measure AFTER chopping)*
½ teaspoon vanilla extract
2 cups powdered *(confectioners)* sugar *(do not sift)*
1 small box food picks or long toothpicks

2 cups *(12 ounces by weight package)* semi-sweet chocolate chips *(I used Nestlé)*
1 rounded Tablespoon salted butter, softened

**Hannah's 1ˢᵗ Note: If you can't find food picks in your grocery store, you can buy them in a party store or a restaurant supply store. They look like toothpicks, but they have a colored cellophane decorations on one end and you've probably seen them used on cheese platters or with platters of little appetizers.**

Prepare your pan by lining a cookie sheet with wax paper.

Use a wooden spoon or fork to mix the Nutella with the ¼ cup softened butter in a medium-size bowl.

336

Sprinkle the ¼ cup finely chopped hazelnuts on top and mix them in thoroughly.

Add the vanilla extract and mix that in.

Add the powdered sugar in half-cup increments, mixing well after each addition.

Cover the bowl with plastic wrap and place it in the refrigerator for at least one hour so that the mixture will firm up. *(Longer than one hour is fine, too.)*

Using impeccably clean hands, roll pop-in-your-mouth-size balls from the Nutella, butter, and hazelnut mixture.

Stick a food pick into each ball and place the completed balls on your prepared cookie sheet lined with wax paper.

**Hannah's 2<sup>nd</sup> Note: The food picks will make it easier for you to dip the balls in melted chocolate chips once they've firmed up.**

Place the cookie sheet with your Chocolate Hazelnut Bon-bons in the freezer for at least 1 hour. *(Overnight is even better.)*

When your chocolate hazelnut balls are frozen, prepare to melt your chocolate coating. *Leave your candy balls in the freezer until your chocolate coating has melted and you are ready to dip them.*

Place your 2 cups of chocolate chips in a microwave-safe bowl. Add the rounded Tablespoon of butter on top. *(I used a 1-quart Pyrex measuring cup to do this.)*

Heat the chocolate chips and butter on HIGH for 1 minute. Let them sit in the microwave for an additional minute and then stir to see if the chocolate chips are melted. If they're not, continue to heat in 30-second increments followed by 30 seconds of standing time until you can stir them smooth.

Take the cookie sheet with the candy balls out of the freezer and set it on the counter. Using the food picks as handles, dip the balls, one by one, in the melted chocolate and then return them to the cookie sheet. Work quickly so that the balls do not soften.

Place the cookie sheet with the Chocolate Hazelnut Bon-Bons in the refrigerator for at least 2 hours before serving.

When you're ready to serve, remove the balls from the refrigerator, arrange them on a pretty plate or platter, and leave the food picks in place so that your guests can use them as a handle when they eat them.

**Hannah's 3rd Note: If you plan to serve these at a party, you can either leave the food picks in place or pull them out and use cake decorator frosting with a star tip to cover**

the hole with a pretty frosting rosette. Then, if you like, you can place the candy, rosette up, in fluted paper candy cups.

Yield: Approximately 3 dozen Chocolate Hazelnut Bon-Bons depending on the size of the candy balls.

# Chapter Fourteen

"These are incredible, dear!" Delores declared, after tasting her first Chocolate Hazelnut Bon-Bon. "And they would be divine with champagne."

Hannah smiled. Her mother's approval meant a lot to her. "Do you think we should put them on trays and pass them?"

"Yes! That would be perfect, dear. What are you planning to wear to the event?"

"I'm . . . not sure."

"Do you have a cocktail dress or a ball gown?"

Hannah shook her head. "No, I've never attended anything like the Christmas Ball before."

"Well, that settles it then!" Delores smiled at all three of them. "I'm buying a gown for Andrea and I'll buy something dressy for all three of you. What's your favorite color, Lisa?"

"My favorite color?" Lisa asked, looking surprised.

"Yes, dear. If your closet looks anything like Michelle's, you'll need something to wear to a dressy event."

"But . . ." Lisa began to look distressed. "Really, Mrs. Swensen, you don't have to . . ."

"Nonsense! All three of you girls have pitched in to help me with this project. The least I can do is find something nice for you to wear. We'll meet at The Cookie Jar after school tomorrow and walk over to Claire's dress shop. I'm sure she'll have something appropriate for all three of you."

"How about you, Mother?" Hannah asked. "Are you going to buy something for yourself?"

"Perhaps." Delores looked down at the plate of bon-bons and sighed. "I may have to look for something new if you keep on feeding me delicious treats like this."

Hannah reached for the last dress that Claire had chosen for her. It was a beautiful shade of blue and she'd saved the best for last. If it fit, she'd tell her mother that it was fine. She absolutely hated to try on clothing, probably because it forced her to examine her image in the mirror and chide herself for eating that last French fry or piece of cake.

"Please fit," she whispered as she slipped the dress over her head and reached back to pull up the zipper. And . . . miracles of miracle . . . the dress *did* fit! It fell, whispering down over her hips like gossamer silk, minimizing her slightly too wide hips and slightly too large derrière. The bodice was snug, but not too snug, the sleeves were exactly the right length, and even more important than all those plusses, her image in the mirror made her feel beautiful.

"This is it!" she said to herself, since no one else was there. "A perfect dress for a perfect Christmas Ball."

"Do you like it?" Claire's voice floated through the crack in the dressing room door.

"Oh, yes!" Hannah answered immediately. "I love it, Claire. If Mother agrees, I really want this dress."

"And if she doesn't agree, you'll buy it yourself on lay-away?"

Hannah laughed. "Yes, Claire. I will."

They were all waiting when she emerged from the dressing room, Lisa in her lovely pink gown, Michelle in a sunshine yellow that made her hair shine, and Delores in a slinky black dress with brocade beading on the bodice.

"Perfect!" Delores declared, smiling at Hannah in approval. "That dress is just perfect on you, dear."

"It's beautiful, Hannah," Lisa added her vote.

"Stunning," Michelle smiled at her oldest sister. "I really like it, Hannah. You just have to choose this one."

"Then I will," Hannah agreed, smiling at all of them as she turned to Claire. "I'll take this one, Claire."

Once Claire had measured them for final alterations, Delores led the way back to her car. "Get in, girls. We're meeting Andrea at the hotel in ten minutes. I want to show you what we've accomplished before you go back to work baking."

Hannah could scarcely believe her eyes as she stood next to her mother and Andrea. "It's a miracle, Mother."

"I couldn't have done it without Andrea's talent for decorating," Delores told her, glancing at her middle daughter proudly. "The drapes and the valences are completely her idea."

"They look exactly the way they did in that photo that Rod gave you," Michelle said.

"But that was a black and white print," Lisa pointed out. "How did you decide on the colors?"

"I used my imagination," Andrea told them. "Gold seemed to complement the rest of the ballroom, once the floor was polished and resurfaced. And I thought the dark green was very Christmassy, especially since Mother told me that there would be decorated Christmas trees around the edges of the ballroom."

"How about the poinsettias on the tables?" Hannah asked her.

"I wanted red and green and that's why I had the borders of the sashes made in red velvet. Trudi agreed with me completely."

"Trudi Schumann?"

"Yes, she made the curtains and didn't charge us a cent. She said that it was the least she could do for Essie."

Hannah knew she must have looked puzzled, because Andrea continued. "Trudi told me that Essie took Cliff under her wing when his parents died. She told me that Essie was like a second mother to him and he used to do his homework with her at the hotel until Trudi picked him up after work. She told me that sewing the tablecloths and drapes was her way of repaying Essie for helping with Cliff."

"That was a horrible accident." Hannah gave a little sigh, remembering how shocked she'd been about one of her classmates losing both parents in such an awful way. She'd had nightmares for several nights after imagining how terrible it would be if something like that happened to her own parents.

"You might not know this, Hannah," Delores said, "but right after you went off to college, Cliff enrolled in community college and got his B.A. in business management."

Hannah was surprised. "I had no idea he'd gone on to college. I knew he was working for Dad, of course."

"Your father gave him time off from work so that he could attend class."

"That was nice of Dad," Hannah said, remembering how Cliff had gotten the job at her dad's store and still feeling vaguely uncomfortable about how Lars had offered Cliff a summer job if he'd invite Hannah to her senior prom. It had been bribery, pure and simple, but she hadn't known at the time and she'd had a marvelous time at the prom.

"And now Cliff's going to manage your father's hardware store," Delores added. "He can't buy it right away, but he's arranged to finance it with timed payments." Delores looked a bit concerned. "It's what your father would have wanted. When I went to Howie Levine's office to get my copy of the will he drew up for us, Howie said that Lars mentioned Cliff to him once and he'd said that he wanted to promote Cliff to manager and take a little time off for himself." Delores looked sad for a moment and then she smiled. "Your father was always a great judge of character, so when I told Howie that I didn't want to manage the store, he said he thought that Cliff would be a logical choice for the job."

Hannah nodded. "Dad was right. The store looks good. I was in there just the other day, buying my reading lamp."

"I hope that selling the hardware store doesn't bother you, Hannah." Delores looked a bit apologetic. "Perhaps I should have consulted you."

"It doesn't bother me at all," Hannah reassured her. "I think Cliff is a perfect choice. I know Dad liked him and he was a big help in the store."

"What do you think of the job the Otis Elevator people did with the old elevator?" Delores asked them.

"It runs just fine," Michelle said. "And it looks good, too."

Lisa nodded. "I just love the mirrors. Did they put them up?"

"Yes, but they coordinated with Cliff. He donated the mirrored panels for the sides and the back."

"And that means Essie can ride up in her wheelchair," Andrea said. "A couple of men from town said they'd carry her up, right in her chair, but Mother thought the elevator would be much easier."

"How did you get Otis to fix it?" Hannah asked Delores.

"I told them about Essie and how she'd lived here all of her adult life. And I told them that this was her fondest wish."

"And then we went out to talk to the owner of KCOW-TV," Andrea added. "That was Mother's idea."

"And the program director agreed to run a free ad for Otis Elevator during the special they're going to run tomorrow," Delores said with a smile.

"KCOW's doing a special?" Hannah asked, turning to her mother in surprise. "How did you ever work that? They never do anything for free."

"I have my ways. We're hoping it'll promote the ball and help to sell more advance tickets. The money will go to help Essie get the help she needs."

"Does Essie know about this?" Hannah asked.

"No, we decided not to tell her. Both Grandma Knudson

and Annie think Essie is too proud to take what she would regard as charity. I'm telling you girls, but please don't say anything to anyone else. We're going to let everyone think that the ticket sales are for the cost of the champagne and the dessert buffet."

"Then we should buy our tickets," Lisa said. "We want to help Essie, too."

Delores shook her head. "No, girls. You're already doing enough to help Essie. Just keep on baking so she can see the Christmas Cake Parade again. She talks about how beautiful it was almost every time we visit her."

"Is she . . . ?" Lisa stopped speaking and swallowed with difficulty. Then she cleared her throat and Hannah knew that Lisa was thinking about her own mother. "Is Essie getting worse?"

"Doc Knight says no. Grandma Knudson asked him. But Essie told Annie that she doesn't think she'll live much longer. Annie said she asked Essie why, but Essie wouldn't tell her."

"That's so sad!" Lisa said.

"I know. The Christmas Ball is very important to her, girls. And every day she asks me to thank you for baking all the cakes for the Christmas Cake Parade. She told us that the first cake piece was the most beautiful sight in the world."

"Did she say how many cakes there were?" Hannah asked. "We couldn't really tell from the photograph. All we saw were the candles and the cakes themselves weren't visible."

"I'll ask her tomorrow," Delores promised. "I'm sure she knows. She said she dreams about that beautiful sight almost every night because it's such a happy memory."

"Did Essie ever mention the kinds of cakes that were in the parade?" Hannah asked.

"Not specifically. She just told us that the cakes were all sizes and shapes. And, as I told you before, Hannah, there was a large cake that was shaped like a Christmas tree that led the parade."

"Was it a fruitcake?" Michelle asked, giving a little shudder at the thought.

Delores laughed. "No, dear. That *is* one of the things that Essie told us. There were no fruitcakes in the cake parade. And right after she said it, she laughed."

"Essie doesn't like fruitcake either?" Lisa guessed.

"Grandma Knudson and Annie and I certainly got that impression. There are quite a few people who don't like fruitcake."

"It's probably because of the citron," Hannah told them. "Many people think that the flavor of citron is too strong."

"That's exactly what I don't like about it," Michelle agreed.

"I must admit that I'm not fond of it either," Delores concurred. "Your father used to say that he thought there were only a limited number of fruitcakes in existence. He speculated that the people who got them for Christmas saved them in their refrigerator all year. And then they gave them to someone else on the following Christmas."

"That's funny!" Lisa began to laugh and so did everyone else.

"Perhaps you should experiment with making another kind of fruitcake," Delores suggested to Hannah. "You could make one with chocolate and fresh fruit instead of citron."

"I'll do that, Mother," Hannah promised, "but not before the Christmas Ball. We have only three days to get everything ready."

"Yes, dear. I know," Delores said, giving a little sigh. "I'm well aware that we're short on time. I just hope that we can get everything done before the big night."

"We will," Andrea promised. "The decorating is almost complete."

"And we're right on schedule with the baking," Hannah

told her. "The Christmas Cake Parade and the dessert buffet really won't be a problem."

"Oh, good!" Delores looked slightly relieved. "We're almost done with the repairs here and the electrician managed to hook us up with lights in the kitchen and ballroom. With all of us working hard, we can give Essie another Christmas Ball memory that she'll treasure for the rest of her life."

# Chapter Fifteen

"I love your beef stew, dear!" Delores complimented Hannah on the bowl of Hunter's Beef Stew that she'd just eaten. "I wish I could have more, but Claire took my measurements this afternoon."

"And if you have a second bowl, you might not fit into your new dress?" Michelle asked.

"That's it, exactly. But perhaps that depends."

"Depends on what, Mrs. Swensen?" Lisa asked her.

"On what we're having for dessert. If it's something I'm not particularly fond of, I might decide to have more stew instead."

"Other than fruitcake, is there any dessert that you don't particularly like?" Hannah asked her mother.

"I'm sure there is. I just can't think of what it is. There's got to be something, don't you think?"

She faced a trio of grins as her eyes traveled from face to face. "Well . . . perhaps there doesn't have to be any other dessert that I don't like." She turned to Hannah. "What did you bake, dear?"

"Ultimate Butterscotch Bundt Cake with Cool Whip Butterscotch Frosting. And we picked up some vanilla and some chocolate ice cream on our way here."

"Ooooooh!" Delores got up from her chair and took her

bowl to the sink to rinse it out. "There's no way I want to miss that!"

"I thought of a dessert that you might not like, Mrs. Swensen," Lisa said when Delores returned to the table.

"What is it, dear?"

"Chocolate sauce drizzled over dill pickles with a dish of chocolate ice cream."

Delores considered that for a moment and then she smiled. "Actually, that sounds rather interesting. Do you use dill pickle slices or whole dill pickles when you make it?"

Lisa's eyes opened wide in surprise. "I . . . I don't know. I've never tried it. I just thought it sounded like an awful combination."

"Actually . . . it might just be good. Dill pickle slices over strawberry ice cream is a good combination."

All three girls stared at Delores in disbelief and she laughed. "Don't worry, girls. I won't ask for that anytime soon. The only time I ever tried it was when I was pregnant with Hannah."

"Mom says that pregnant ladies get cravings for all sorts of weird things," Lisa said. "How about Andrea? Do you think she'd like strawberry ice cream with dill pickled slices?"

Delores shrugged. "I don't know, but I wouldn't be surprised. I know that she's always loved strawberry ice cream. And she likes dill pickles, too. We'll have to ask her the next time we see her."

With all of them working, it didn't take long before they were sitting at the kitchen table with coffee for Hannah and Delores, and tall glasses of milk for Michelle and Lisa. Hannah had cut generous slices of Ultimate Butterscotch Bundt Cake for all of them, and the ice cream cartons, complete with scoops, were sitting on the kitchen table.

"Let's taste it without ice cream first and then you can tell me how you think we should serve it at the Christmas Ball," Hannah suggested.

"Why don't we cut it, put the slices on little plates, and let everyone decide for themselves," Michelle suggested.

"Good idea!" Delores praised her youngest daughter. "It would certainly be less work if you didn't serve it with ice cream."

"Not necessarily," Hannah said. "We could put a tub of ice on a side table, open the ice cream cartons, and let everyone scoop their own if they wanted it."

"Then they'd have it for the other Bundt cakes, too," Lisa pointed out. "And we wouldn't have to scoop it for them."

"You'd need coffee ice cream for that wonderful chocolate Bundt cake of yours," Delores said. "We should taste all the cakes first and decide which ice cream flavors complement them. Then we can ask Florence to set those aside for us."

"We should taste all the cakes?" Hannah asked her. "I thought you were going on a diet, Mother."

"I am, but I know my duty. I've already tasted the Ultimate Lemon Bundt Cake and I think I'd choose vanilla ice cream with that. And I think either vanilla or coffee ice cream would go with the chocolate cake."

"Or chocolate," Michelle said. "Some people are real chocoholics, Mother."

Delores nodded. "You're right, of course."

Hannah took a sip of her coffee and picked up her fork. "Here goes nothing," she said as she cut off a bite, popped it into her mouth, and chewed.

Except for little sighs of pleasure and the sound of forks clinking against the dessert plates, there was silence for long moments. They were all intent on analyzing the complex flavors of Hannah's cake.

"Wonderful!" Delores said with a smile as she set her fork on her empty dessert plate.

"Which ice cream flavor did you think was best with the cake?" Hannah asked her.

"Oh, dear!" Delores said, looking surprised. "I forgot to try any of the ice cream. I imagine some people will want it à la mode, but I preferred it plain."

"I had a little vanilla ice cream and it was good," Lisa told them.

"And I had a little chocolate," Michelle added her opinion. "That was good, too."

"I'm with Mother on this one," Hannah admitted. "I forgot all about the ice cream and just ate the cake."

"Then I have a suggestion," Delores said with a smile.

"What's that, Mother?" Michelle asked her.

"I think we all owe it to Hannah to test her cake both ways." Delores picked up her dessert plate, pushed back her chair, and got to her feet. "Come on, girls. Duty calls."

# ULTIMATE BUTTERSCOTCH BUNDT CAKE

Preheat oven to 350 degrees F., rack in the middle position.

4 large eggs
½ cup vegetable oil
½ cup cold whole milk
8-ounce *(by weight)* tub of sour cream *(I used Knudsen)*
1 box of white cake mix with or without pudding in the mix, the kind that makes a 9-inch by 13-inch cake or a 2-layer cake *(I used Duncan Hines)*
5.1-ounce package of instant butterscotch pudding mix *(I used Jell-O, the kind that makes 6 half-cup servings.)*
12-ounce *(by weight)* bag of butterscotch chips *(11-ounce package will do, too—I used Nestlé.)*

Prepare your cake pan. You'll need a Bundt pan that has been sprayed with Pam or another nonstick cooking spray and then floured. To flour a pan, put some flour in the bottom, hold it over your kitchen wastebasket, and tap the pan to move the flour all over the inside of the pan. Continue this until all the inside surfaces of the pan, including the sides of the crater in the center of the pan, have been covered with a light coating of flour. Be sure to shake out the excess flour.

Crack the eggs into the bowl of an electric mixer. Mix them up on LOW speed until they're a uniform color.

Pour in the half-cup of vegetable oil and mix it in with the eggs on LOW speed.

Add the half-cup of cold milk and mix it in on LOW speed.

Scoop out the container of sour cream, and add the sour cream to your bowl. Mix that in on LOW speed.

When everything is well combined, open the box of dry cake mix and sprinkle it on top of the liquid ingredients in the bowl of the mixer. Mix that in on LOW speed.

Add the package of instant butterscotch pudding and mix that in, again on LOW speed.

Finally, chop up the butterscotch chips in a food processor or blender and then sprinkle them into the mixer. Mix in the chips on LOW speed.

Shut off the mixer, scrape down the sides of the bowl, and give your batter a final stir by hand.

Use a rubber spatula to transfer the cake batter to the prepared Bundt pan.

Smooth the top of your cake with the rubber spatula and place it in the oven.

Bake your Ultimate Butterscotch Bundt Cake at 350 degrees F. for 55 minutes.

Before you take your cake out of the oven, test it for doneness by inserting a cake tester, thin wooden skewer, or long toothpick midway between the sides of the circular ring. *(You can't insert it in the center of the cake because that's where the crater is!)*

If the tester comes out clean, your cake is done. If there is still unbaked batter clinging to the tester, shut the oven door and bake your cake in 5-minute increments until it tests done.

Once your cake is done, take it out of the oven and set it on a cold stovetop burner or a wire rack.

Let your cake cool for 20 minutes in the pan, but no longer than that.

Use your impeccably clean fingers to pull the sides of the cake away from the pan. Don't forget to do the same for the crater in the middle.

Tip the Bundt pan upside down on a platter and drop it gently on a towel on the kitchen counter. Do this until the cake falls out of the pan and rests on the platter.

Cover your Ultimate Butterscotch Bundt Cake loosely with foil and refrigerate it for at least one hour. Overnight is even better.

Frost your cake with Cool Whip Butterscotch Frosting. *(Recipe and instructions follow.)*

Yield: At least 10 pieces of decadent butterscotch cake. Serve with tall glasses of ice-cold milk or cups of strong coffee.

# COOL WHIP BUTTERSCOTCH FROSTING

This recipe is made in the microwave.

6-ounce *(by weight)* bag of butterscotch chips *(or measure one cup of chips, which is roughly half of an 11-ounce by weight bag)*
8-ounce *(by weight)* tub of FROZEN Cool Whip *(Do not thaw!)*

**Hannah's 1st Note: Make sure you use the original Cool Whip, not the sugar free or the real whipped cream type of Cool Whip.**

Place the cup of butterscotch chips in your food processor or blender. Chop them into smaller pieces so that they will melt faster.

Place the Cool Whip in a microwave-safe bowl.

Add the chopped butterscotch chips to the bowl.

Microwave the bowl on HIGH for 1 minute and then let it sit in the microwave for an additional minute.

Take the bowl out of the microwave and stir to see if the butterscotch chips have melted. If they haven't, heat in 30-second intervals with 1-minute standing times until you succeed in melting the chips.

Take the bowl out of the microwave and let it sit on the

countertop or on a cold stovetop burner for 15 minutes. This standing time will thicken the icing.

When the time is up, give the bowl a stir and remove your cake from the refrigerator. Frost your Ultimate Butterscotch Bundt Cake with the frosting and don't forget the crater in the middle. You don't need to frost all the way inside the crater. That's almost impossible. Just frost an inch or so down the cavity.

Return your cake to the refrigerator for at least 30 minutes before cutting it and serving it to your guests.

**Hannah's 2nd Note: You can also use this icing on cookies. It would be wonderful on any cookie with a vanilla, chocolate, or butterscotch taste. I especially like it on Old Fashioned Sugar Cookies and Cocoa-Crunch Cookies. Just make sure that the cookies are cool when you frost them.**

Yield: This frosting will frost a batch of cookies, a 9-inch by 13-inch flat cake, a Bundt cake, or a round two-tier layer cake.

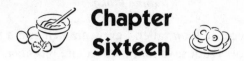

# Chapter Sixteen

As she rode up in the elevator, Hannah did something very unusual. She actually looked at her reflection in the mirrored walls. Her mother, Claire, Michelle, and Lisa had been one hundred percent right. The color of her dress was perfect with her hair. And, wonder of wonders, Bertie at the Cut 'n Curl beauty parlor had actually managed to tame her curly red hair into some semblance of normalcy.

The elevator stopped, the doors opened, and Hannah began to smile as she spotted Andrea and Mayor Bascomb moving through the crowd with trays of champagne. Michelle and Lisa were following them with trays containing the truffles that they'd made. She waited for a moment, watching as the huge crowd of guests reached out, one by one, for the truffles. Delores had been right about how well the confections would complement the champagne.

As she entered the beautifully decorated ballroom, a tall, well-dressed man left the crowd and hurried to intercept her.

"Hannah!" he greeted her with a smile as he gave her a little hug. "You look great!"

"Thank you!" Hannah smiled back, but it took her a second or two to place him. "Cliff! I didn't recognize you at first. For some reason, you look even taller than you did in high school."

"That's because I *am* taller. I grew an inch and a half after we left school. Trudi says that I was a late bloomer."

"How's Trudi? I haven't seen her since I've been back."

"She's fine. I just came out to ask you to save me a dance." This time Hannah's smile was much more than polite. "Really?"

"Yes. We had so much fun at the senior prom and I wanted to dance with you again. And . . . well . . . there's someone I'd like you to meet."

"Who?"

"Someone I'm . . . interested in, but I'm not sure. You're the smartest person I know, Hannah, and if you like someone, I know they're a really good person."

"Is this someone you're thinking about hiring, Cliff?" Hannah asked the obvious question.

Cliff began to smile. "Not exactly. But it *is* someone I might ask to marry me. I just don't know if I'm making a mistake. And I really don't want to do that. I'd value your opinion, Hannah."

Hannah gave a little sigh as she thought back to her failed romance with the assistant professor she'd planned to marry. "I'd like to meet her, but I'm not sure you should value my opinion about something like that. I've made some bad mistakes in the romance department myself."

"So have I. And that's why I'm asking you. I think it's important to get an outside opinion from someone you trust."

"Okay, it's a deal. But you have to do something for me, too."

"What's that?"

"You have to help me carry out the big platter with the Christmas cake I baked. We're going to turn off the lights and hold a Christmas Cake Parade just like the one Essie remembers at the first Christmas Ball. It's a really big cake and I need a strong guy to help me carry it, especially because the only lights will be the candles on the cakes."

"I'll be glad to help you, Hannah."

"Thanks, Cliff. There's one other thing I'd like you to do for me."

"What is it?"

"I want you to love the hardware store as much as Dad did."

Cliff smiled and gave her a little hug. "That's easy, Hannah. I already do."

The first person Hannah saw as she entered the ballroom itself was Essie. She was sitting in a wheelchair that someone had decorated with green and gold garlands that perfectly complemented Essie's deep red velvet ball gown. Instead of wearing her hair in a bun, the style she'd worn for years, her silver hair was now cut shorter and it curled beautifully around her face. Her makeup was perfectly applied, and Hannah made a mental note to ask Delores if she'd helped Essie get ready for the ball. In her wheelchair throne with a sparkling tiara on her head, it was obvious to everyone there that Essie was the queen of the Christmas Ball.

"You look lovely, Essie," Hannah greeted her.

"Thank you, dear. And so do you. That dress you're wearing is the perfect color for you. Have you seen your mother yet? She's here with Annie and Grandma Knudson."

"I haven't greeted Mother yet. Tonight, we're like ships that pass in the night. I got here early to help set up for the buffet, and then I dashed home to get ready. When I got to her house, Mother was already gone and so were Michelle and Lisa."

"Well, they're here now and your mother's been telling everyone what marvelous bakers you girls are. She told me that you were going to hold a Christmas Cake Parade! Is that true, dear?"

"Yes, it is. Michelle and Lisa got all of their friends to help us carry in the cakes. And Cliff Schuman promised to help me lead the parade with the largest one."

"Wonderful!" Essie smiled, but she seemed distracted by a man who'd just come into the ballroom. Hannah studied his face and came to the conclusion that he was a stranger. She turned back to Essie and asked, "Do you recognize the man who just came in?"

"I'm not sure. There are quite a few people here that I don't know."

"That's probably because of the television interview you did for KCOW. Mother told me that it was picked up by some major networks and it was shown as a human interest story all over the country."

"That's true and some people may have come just out of curiosity. That man looks familiar, like someone I used to know years ago. When are you holding the Christmas Cake Parade?"

"As soon as Mayor Bascomb greets everyone and officially tells your guests about the first Christmas Ball. When he gets up to speak, I'll go back to the kitchen to light the candles on the cakes."

"Is the orchestra going to play for the parade?"

"Yes, but they recorded the music because there won't be enough light for them to play. They gave Mother a recording. And after the parade, the lights will go back on and they'll play music for dancing."

"Perfect! This is all so wonderful, Hannah! Thank you for organizing all that baking. Tonight will be a full circle for me, Hannah. Now I won't have to wait and worry much longer."

Hannah tried not to show how puzzled she was by Essie's comment as she hurried back to the kitchen. What an odd thing for Essie to say! An unwelcome thought flashed through her mind on her way down the hallway that led to the kitchen. Did Essie's words about completing a full circle mean that she thought she would die tonight? Or was Hannah simply reading too much into what Essie had said?

# ULTIMATE CHRISTMAS BUNDT CAKE

Preheat oven to 350 degrees F., rack in the middle position.

1 cup shredded coconut *(pack it down when you measure it)*

¼ cup *(4 Tablespoons)* all-purpose flour *(You will be dividing this into Tablespoons.)*

8 ounces *(by weight)* candied pineapple wedges

8 ounces *(by weight)* candied red cherries

8 ounces *(by weight)* candied green cherries

12-ounce *(by weight)* bag of white chocolate chips or vanilla baking chips *(11-ounce package will do, too—I used Nestlé)*

4 large eggs

½ cup vegetable oil

½ cup cold whole milk

1 teaspoon coconut or vanilla extract

8-ounce *(by weight)* tub of sour cream *(I used Knudsen)*

1 box of white cake mix with or without pudding in the mix, the kind that makes a 9-inch by 13-inch cake or a 2-layer cake *(I used Duncan Hines)*

5.1-ounce package of instant vanilla pudding mix *(I used Jell-O, the kind that makes 6 half-cup servings)*

Prepare your cake pan. You'll need a Bundt pan that has been sprayed with Pam or another nonstick cooking spray and then floured. To flour a pan, put some flour in the bottom, hold it over your kitchen wastebasket, and tap the pan to move the flour all over the inside of the pan. Continue this until all the inside surface of the pan, including the sides of the crater in the center of the pan, have been covered with a light coating of flour.

Put the coconut in the bowl of a food processor and chop it up into much smaller pieces by using the steel blade in an on-and-off motion.

Place the finely chopped coconut in a bowl on the counter.

Sprinkle 1 Tablespoon of flour *(from the 4 Tablespoons you measured)* in the bottom of the food processor bowl. Place the candied pineapple wedges on top of the flour.

Sprinkle another Tablespoon of flour on top of the pineapple wedges. Place the red candied cherries on top of that flour.

Sprinkle another Tablespoon of flour on top of the red candied cherries. Place the green candied cherries on top of that flour.

Sprinkle a final Tablespoon of flour on top of the candied green cherries.

Process the flour and candied fruit in an on-and-off motion with the steel blade until everything is chopped into small pieces.

Add the candied fruit and flour mixture to the bowl with the finely chopped coconut.

Put the white chocolate or vanilla baking chips in the bottom of the food processor bowl. In an on-and-off motion with the steel blade, chop the chips into small pieces.

Place the chopped chips in another bowl on the counter. Now it's time to start mixing up your cake.

Crack the eggs into the bowl of an electric mixer. Mix them up on LOW speed until they're a uniform color.

Pour in the half-cup of vegetable oil and mix it in with the eggs on LOW speed.

Add the half-cup of cold milk and the teaspoon of coconut or vanilla extract. Mix them in on LOW speed.

Scoop out the container of sour cream and add it to your bowl. Mix that in on LOW speed.

When everything is well combined, open the box of dry cake mix and sprinkle it on top of the liquid ingredients in the bowl of the mixer. Mix it in on LOW speed.

Add the package of dry instant vanilla pudding mix. Beat it in, again on LOW speed.

Finally, sprinkle in the candied fruit and coconut. Mix them in thoroughly on LOW speed.

Shut off the mixer, scrape down the sides of the bowl, and give your batter a final stir by hand.

Use a rubber spatula to mix in the chopped white chocolate chips by hand. *(The reason you've chopped them into little pieces is so the pieces are lighter and won't sink down into the bottom of the Bundt pan.)*

Use the same rubber spatula to transfer the cake batter to the prepared Bundt pan.

Smooth the top of your cake with the spatula and put it into the oven.

Bake your Ultimate Christmas Cake at 350 degrees F. for 55 minutes.

Before you take your cake out of the oven, test it for doneness by inserting a cake tester, thin wooden skewer, or long toothpick midway between the sides of the circular ring. *(You can't insert it in the center of the cake because that's where the crater is!)*

If the tester comes out clean, your cake is done. If there is still unbaked batter clinging to the tester, shut the oven door and bake your cake in 5-minute increments, testing after each increment, until it tests done.

Once your cake has finished baking, take it out of the oven and set it on a cold stovetop burner or a wire rack. Let it cool in the pan for 20 minutes.

After the 20-minute cooling time is up, put your impeccably clean fingers on top of the pan and pull the sides of the cake away from the pan. Don't forget to do the same for the crater in the middle. This will make certain the cake isn't sticking to the sides and center of the Bundt pan.

Tip the Bundt pan upside down on a platter and drop it gently on a towel on the kitchen counter. Do this until the cake falls out of the pan and rests on the platter.

Cover your Ultimate Christmas Bundt Cake loosely with foil and refrigerate it for at least one hour. Overnight is even better.

Frost your cake with Cool Whip White Chocolate Frosting. *(Recipe and instructions follow.)*

Yield: At least 10 pieces of incredibly good and very rich cake. This cake is wonderful with vanilla ice cream on top. Serve with tall glasses of ice-cold milk or cups of strong coffee.

# COOL WHIP WHITE
# CHOCOLATE FROSTING

This recipe is made in the microwave.

8-ounce *(by weight)* tub of FROZEN Cool Whip
   *(Do not thaw yet!)*
6-ounce *(by weight)* bag of white chocolate or
   vanilla chips *(I used Nestlé white baking chips –
   half of an 11-ounce bag will do just fine)*
1 teaspoon coconut or vanilla extract

**Hannah's 1ˢᵗ Note: Make sure you use the original Cool Whip, not the sugar free or the real whipped cream.**

Place the Cool Whip in a microwave-safe bowl.

Add the chocolate chips to the bowl.

Microwave the bowl on HIGH for 1 minute and then let it sit in the microwave for an additional minute.

Take the bowl out of the microwave, then stir to see if the white chocolate chips are melted. If they're not, heat them in 30-second intervals with 30-second standing times in the microwave until you succeed in melting the chips.

Stir in the vanilla or coconut extract and let the bowl sit on the countertop or on a cold burner for 15 minutes to thicken the frosting.

When the time is up, give the bowl a stir and remove your cake from the refrigerator.

Frost your Ultimate Christmas Bundt Cake with the frosting and don't forget the crater in the middle. You don't need to frost all the way down. That's almost impossible. Just frost an inch or so down the crater.

**Hannah's 2nd Note: While your frosting is still soft and sticky, you can decorate your cake with more candied pineapple and red and green candied cherries if you wish. The top looks great if you make a circle of the red cherries on the outside of the top, a circle of candied pineapple just inside the red candied cherries, and then a circle of green candied cherries inside the candied pineapple.**

Return your cake to the refrigerator for at least 30 minutes before cutting it and serving it to your guests.

**Hannah's 3rd Note: You can also use this frosting on cookies. Simply frost and let your cookies sit on wax paper on the kitchen counter until the frosting has set and is dry to the touch.**

Yield: This frosting will frost a batch of cookies, a 9-inch by 13-inch cake, a Bundt cake, or a round two-tier layer cake.

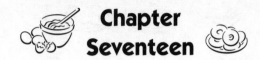

# Chapter Seventeen

Hannah smiled as she came into the hotel kitchen with Cliff. Michelle and Lisa were staging the cake parade in a line that wound, snake-like, around the edges of the huge counters and appliances that filled the room.

"Oh, look!" Hannah said to Cliff. "Lisa and Michelle have already lined everyone up with the cakes they're going to carry."

Cliff looked amazed as he surveyed the long line of cakes. "And you actually baked all these cakes?"

"Yes, but I had help. Michelle and Lisa walked to The Cookie Jar every day after school to bake with me."

"This one is amazing." Cliff pointed to the massive cake, shaped like a Christmas tree, that sat on the kitchen counter closest to the door. "Is this the Christmas Cake that you were telling me about?"

"Yes. It's the lead cake in the parade."

"It's beautiful," Cliff said admiringly. "Does it pull apart?"

"Yes, we baked miniature Bundt cakes and arranged them in an ascending tower to form the tree. We started with an almost full platter on the bottom, and each tier of the tree has a smaller number of miniature Bundt cakes."

"Did you frost them separately?"

"Yes. And then we stacked them up and used the drizzle icicle frosting to tie them together."

"Very clever! And it's beautiful!"

"Make sure you tell Lisa that. The design was her idea."

"The red and green cherries look like Christmas ornaments."

"That was Lisa's idea, too. The cake is really heavy though. Are you sure you can handle it if I help you carry it?"

"Let's see." Cliff picked up the platter with surprisingly little effort and held it aloft. "It's not a problem, Hannah," he assured her. "I can carry the cake by myself. The bags of concrete mix that I stack in the hardware store are a lot heavier than this. You just walk next to me and look pretty."

"Well . . . if you're sure . . ."

"Don't worry. I won't drop it. Besides, you'll be busy lighting the candles when Mayor Bascomb finishes his speech."

"*If* he ever does," Hannah retorted, and she was rewarded by a laugh from Cliff.

"I know what you mean, Hannah. I don't think the people in Lake Eden realized how long-winded he could be when they elected him. But I think he's beginning to wind up now."

They were silent, listening to what they hoped was the end of Mayor Bascomb's welcome speech. His amplified voice reached the kitchen and Hannah picked up the fireplace lighter she'd brought to light the candles they'd placed on top of all the cakes and began to light them.

"Thank you all for attending this wonderful event tonight. And thank you to our guest of honor, Essie Granger, for her years of service to the Lake Eden community. Please remain seated at the tables around the perimeter of the ballroom for the Christmas Cake Parade. And a big thank-you from all of us to Hannah Swensen, who, with the help of Michelle Swensen and Lisa Herman, baked all of the cakes for the parade."

There was applause from the guests in the ballroom and Hannah felt her cheeks turn warm at the unexpected praise.

"We will dim the lights so that you can see the parade in

all its lighted glory. Please stay in your seats and do not move around the ballroom during the ceremony."

"Smart move," Cliff said in a low voice. "I was wondering how they'd do that."

"And now, ladies and gentlemen, I urge you all to enjoy the Christmas Cake Parade!"

As Andrea dimmed the lights, very slowly so that Hannah would have time to light all the candles on the assorted cakes, the orchestra leader turned on the Christmas medley that they'd recorded. Hannah spotted Rod Metcalf with his camera, standing in a good vantage point against the ballroom wall, and she knew that there would be photos of the parade in the next issue of the *Lake Eden Journal*.

She lit the candles on the huge Christmas tree cake last and as Cliff picked up the cake, she turned to the Jordan High students in line.

"Are we all ready?" she asked them. "And do you all know where your cakes will be placed?"

There were nods all around and Hannah drew a deep breath as the medley of Christmas carols played. "The last two out are Lisa and Michelle, and they'll turn off the kitchen lights. Let's go!"

The light in the huge chandelier overlooking the ballroom had dimmed all the way as they emerged from the kitchen door. Hannah and Cliff led the parade to Essie's wheelchair, and Hannah leaned down to give Essie a kiss on the cheek. Then they continued past the wheelchair in a giant loop around the edges of the dance floor. The applause from the spectators built up to a crescendo and Hannah smiled as she walked with Cliff.

Hannah heard a man's voice over the familiar strains of "Silent Night." "I found you, Sharon," the man said.

A moment later, there was a sound Hannah had never expected to hear at the Christmas Ball. A shot rang out and there was a muffled scream as a bullet hit its mark.

By the time a second round was fired, Hannah had pinpointed the location of the shooter by the flash from the muzzle of the gun. Luckily, she was only a few feet away. She plucked a miniature Bundt cake from the top of the Christmas cake and threw it toward the origin of the gunfire as hard as she could. She heard a gasp as the cake hit its mark and she threw a second cake, and a third and a fourth as the lights began to come on.

There he was! The man she'd noticed as she'd greeted Essie, the stranger both Essie and Hannah had spotted. He was down on the floor, rubbing at his face, when Sheriff Grant and Andrea's husband, Bill, pulled his hands behind his back and cuffed him.

"It's the stranger Essie kept staring at earlier," Hannah told Cliff. And then she shouted, "Who did he hit?"

"Essie," Doc Knight answered. "Clear the way for us! Hurry! We have to take Essie back to the hospital right now!"

Since Bill had left with Sheriff Grant and the cuffed shooter, Hannah, Michelle, and Lisa went to sit at Andrea's table to hear Mayor Bascomb, who was speaking at the microphone. For once, their mayor was struggling for words as he urged everyone to stay calm and to please return to their seats. Then he asked everyone to stay to honor Essie and said that if she were here, she would want everyone to stay until the end of the evening. He mentioned that Essie had told him she wanted the Christmas Ball to be her thank-you to the Lake Eden community for enriching her life and giving her a home she loved.

A few people left after the mayor's speech, but most of the guests stayed. The orchestra began to play again, the cakes were sliced and served, and conversations began to start once again. Some couples began to dance to the music that the orchestra was playing, and gradually, more people filled the dance floor. It wasn't an entirely normal revelry, the way more large parties in Lake Eden were, but it was no longer hushed and somber.

Andrea sat with her cell phone out on the table. Delores, Annie, and Grandma Knudson had followed Essie to the hospital. Hannah knew that all three of them would be sitting in the small lobby outside the operating rooms, waiting for word about Essie's condition. Delores had promised to call Andrea the minute there was any news. She had already called once to say that Essie was still in surgery and so far things were going well.

"Drink your champagne," Andrea insisted, gesturing toward the glass that Mayor Bascomb, himself, had carried to Hannah. "One glass won't hurt you and maybe you'll stop shaking."

Hannah took a sip even though she didn't feel at all like celebrating anything. Champagne was for special occasions like weddings, engagement parties, milestone birthdays, and New Year's Eve. It was not for nights when someone you respected and had come to love had been almost killed by a bullet from a stranger's gun.

Andrea's cell phone rang and she answered it immediately. Everyone close to her was watching and they all looked hopeful as Andrea ended the call and walked toward the microphone.

"That was Mother," Andrea reported. "Essie is out of surgery and her prognosis is good. She's still unconscious, but Doc Knight told me that was to be expected because the second bullet grazed her head. Essie's vital signs are good and they're waiting for her to regain consciousness in the recovery room at the hospital."

It was good news and spontaneous applause broke out as Andrea walked back to her table. People began to smile, but Hannah wasn't quite ready to smile yet. She'd seen Doc's worried expression as they'd taken Essie down to ground level in her wheelchair, and she suspected that he had been putting the very best spin on things for Andrea and the Christmas Ball guests.

Cliff approached the table and Hannah managed to smile

at him. Once he'd realized what was happening, Cliff had set the Christmas tree cake on a vacant table and rushed to see if Sheriff Grant or Bill had needed his assistance.

"Julia and I are going to leave now," Cliff told her. "Will you have lunch with me at Hal and Rose's café sometime next week?"

"Sure. That would be nice."

"Great. If it's okay with you, I'll invite Julia to join us so that you can get a chance to talk to her."

"That's fine with me," Hannah said quickly.

"Good. One other thing, Hannah. Julia said that your Ultimate Lemon Bundt Cake was the best she'd ever tasted."

"What did you think of it?"

"I liked it a lot, but personally, I loved your Ultimate Christmas Bundt Cake even more."

"Thanks, Cliff. And thanks for being here to help me tonight."

"No problem. I'll call you when I set a time for lunch."

Cliff walked off and Andrea gave Hannah an assessing look. "Do you think you might be . . . interested in Cliff?"

Hannah thought about that for a moment. "Cliff's a friend. I think that's it, Andrea. And he already has someone he's dating. I know you like Cliff and I hope you're not too disappointed."

"I'm not. You have to find somebody that's right for you."

"Like you did?" Michelle asked her.

Andrea smiled. "Yes, exactly like I did."

"You met Bill when you were a junior in high school. Do you think I should start looking?" Michelle asked.

"Not yet," Andrea answered quickly. "You have to go to college. If the time is right, you'll meet someone there."

"But you didn't go to college," Lisa pointed out.

"That's true, but I didn't want to go to college. And the moment I met Bill, I knew that he was the one."

"How about you, Hannah?" Lisa turned to her. "Did you

meet someone in high school that you thought might be the one for you?"

"Not me," Hannah answered quite truthfully.

As the conversation between Andrea, Lisa, and Michelle went on, Hannah realized that she'd told the truth. She wanted a man in her life . . . eventually. But right now she was content with her new business, her new condo, and her family in Lake Eden. The future might bring other choices for her, but for right now, she was content.

# Chapter Eighteen

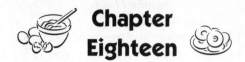

Hannah felt a sense of foreboding as she drove to Lake Eden Memorial Hospital. Essie was still in a coma and Doc Knight wanted to see Hannah. Hannah parked in one of the spots marked for visitors, and opened the outer door to the lobby with hands that were shaking slightly. The trembling in her hands was not from the cold, although it was less than ten degrees above zero. She had no idea why Doc Knight had specifically asked for her.

She opened the inner door and stepped into the lobby, heading straight for the desk and the volunteer who was sitting there. "Doc Knight called and said that he wanted to see me this morning."

"Could I have your name, please?"

"Hannah Swensen."

The volunteer gave Hannah a big smile. "Of course. I saw you at the Christmas Ball and your mother told me that you were going to open a bakery and coffee shop on Main Street."

"That's right." Hannah was puzzled. It was clear that the volunteer knew Hannah's mother, but Hannah didn't recognize her. She looked familiar, but Hannah couldn't quite place her.

"I'm Diane Jamison. I went to school with you, but I moved away when we were in the third grade.

"Diane!" Hannah began to smile, remembering that she'd liked Diane in grade school. "And now you're back in Lake Eden?"

"Yes, I married one of Cyril Murphy's mechanics last year. It's good to see you again, Hannah."

Hannah felt a bit embarrassed. "I'm sorry that I didn't recognize you, Diane."

"That's okay. I didn't recognize you either. Hold on a second and I'll page Doc Knight for you."

Hannah and Diane chatted for a few minutes while they waited for Doc Knight. Diane said she'd just signed a contract with the Little Falls School District to teach second grade and Hannah invited her to the opening of The Cookie Jar. They had almost run out of conversation when they spotted Doc Knight coming down the hall.

"I'm glad you're back in Lake Eden, Diane," Hannah told her.

"Come with me, Hannah," Doc Knight said, reaching out to take her arm. "I'll take you to my office, where we can talk."

"Essie's okay, isn't she?" Hannah asked the moment they entered Doc's office.

"She's still in a coma, but her vitals are good. I have every hope that she'll come out of this."

"Is she still in the recovery room?"

"No, she's stable and we moved her to I.C.U. I want to monitor her very closely."

"Is there any way that I can see her?"

"Yes. Normally, we'd only allow family, but since Essie doesn't have any relatives, I'm allowing certain friends to see her for a limited time. You're one of them. I'll take you there in a bit, but I need to talk to you first."

Hannah took a relieved breath and nodded. "What is it, Doc?"

"Essie left a note for you."

"But . . . how could she do that? Mother told us that Essie

was unconscious when you took her to the hospital. And when she called Andrea, she said that Essie went straight into surgery."

"That's completely correct. Essie left the note in a drawer of her bedside table right before we left for the Christmas Ball. The nurses didn't find it until this morning."

Hannah gave a little gasp. "She wrote it *before* she went to the ball?" she asked.

"That's the logical deduction."

"Then she must have known that something awful might happen to her."

"Either she knew or she suspected," Doc Knight corrected her. "And yes, Hannah. I came to the same conclusion."

"Essie did say something rather odd when I got to the ball-room and went over to greet her. First she complimented me on all the baking we did. And then she said, *Tonight will be a full circle for me, Hannah. Now I won't have to wait and worry much longer.* That scared me, Doc. What do you think Essie meant?"

Doc Knight looked every bit as puzzled as Hannah had been by Essie's words. "I don't know, Hannah."

"Do you think she knew that someone was going to try to . . . to kill her?"

"Some people do seem to know when death is approaching, but that's usually when they have a terminal disease. One of my patients, an elderly man with lung cancer, told one of my nurses not to change his bed, that he wouldn't be needing it that night. And he drew his last breath no more than five minutes later."

"But Essie wasn't terminal. Isn't that right?"

"That's right. When she first came to the hospital, I told her that she was malnourished, anemic, and dehydrated. We were taking care of all those problems, including the injuries from her fall. She knew she was healing and that she was feeling much better. I really don't believe that Essie believed she was dying."

"So it must have been the Christmas Ball? Essie believed that she'd die at the Christmas Ball?"

Doc Knight shrugged. "Perhaps she knew something that we don't know, some danger she was risking by going to the ball. As I said before, Hannah, I just don't know what was going through Essie's mind when she wrote that note. Open it and read it to me. Maybe then we'll have a better idea of her mental state."

Hannah opened the note and pulled it out of the envelope. She was almost afraid to read what was written there in Essie's fine, spidery hand, but her curiosity prompted her to read it.

"Dear Hannah," she read aloud. "Thank you for being my friend and making the Christmas Ball happen again. And please thank your mother and Annie and Grandma Knudson for me. I believe that this is the end of this long journey for me. Please find the beaded purse that I carried to the Christmas Ball. One of my nurses took me on a tour of the kitchen and while she was talking to your sister and Lisa, I hid it in an empty drawer. Please go there to get it and give it to Annie at the Children's Home. She can use it to help the children. Now is my chance to get rid of the evil that took my baby from me. Once he kills me, he'll stop looking for my baby. That's all I ever wanted. Please remember me with kindness, Hannah. And help me to thank the people of Lake Eden for giving me a safe place to live out my life."

Tears came to her eyes and Hannah brushed them away. "I don't understand, Doc. What was she talking about? Essie didn't have a baby, did she?"

Doc Knight shook his head. "Not that I know of. I do know that she didn't have any children with Alton. I started as an intern in Lake Eden right before she married him."

"Then it must have been before that. Or . . . in another place." Hannah thought back to the notebooks that Essie had written and the story about the young pregnant woman

on the train. "Did Dr. Kalick keep any records of his patients?"

"He kept meticulous records. They're all in the basement
of the hospital. Would you like to go through them?"

"Yes, I have to figure this out, Doc. I need to know what
Essie meant. All this is a puzzle and I have to solve it for her."

Hannah climbed the steps to the second floor ballroom.
She'd borrowed the key from Rose at the café, claiming that
she'd forgotten several platters in the hotel kitchen. She
could have gotten the key from Delores, but her mother had
gone out to the mall and Hannah hadn't wanted to wait until
Delores came back home.

The wind was blowing as she unlocked the door to the
hotel. Hannah locked it behind her and began to climb up
the stairs. The staircase was drafty and the wind howled, rat-
tling the doors on the second floor. It was a bit eerie, being in
this huge, empty hotel all by herself.

Hannah passed the two doors that led into Essie's make-
shift apartment. She stopped at the main door and said a little prayer that Essie would regain consciousness and recover
from her injuries. She thought of the lovely hibiscus picture
that Essie had hung on the doorframe to decorate her bedroom and gave a little sigh. Essie had done her utmost to make
her surroundings cheerful and homey. She hadn't been able
to afford many extras, but she'd always had a smile and a
fond greeting for any Lake Eden resident she'd met on the
street. Essie was an inspiration to everyone in town.

The kitchen was at the rear of the ballroom and Hannah
felt a pang of regret as she entered the empty ballroom. The
decorations were still up, waiting for removal later today.
Delores had assembled a work crew to take everything
down, including the drapes, to be stored away just in case
they held another Christmas Ball in the future.

Hannah flicked on the kitchen lights and walked through

the spotless kitchen. The students that Michelle and Lisa had asked to help with the cleanup after the ball had done a wonderful job. She'd have to remember to bake something special for them during the upcoming holidays.

As she began to pull out drawers, looking for Essie's beaded purse, she found herself hoping that no one had found it and given it to Andrea or Mayor Bascomb at the end of the evening. She worked her way around the perimeter of the kitchen, pulling out drawers, looking inside, and shutting them again. There were so many drawers, it reminded her of one of her great-grandmother's favorite analogies, *Like looking for a needle in a haystack.*

Hannah was down to the last three drawers when she found it, the pretty beaded purse that she'd found in Essie's rooms and taken to Essie in the hospital. Hannah put it inside her own saddlebag-size purse and turned to leave the kitchen.

As she walked across the ballroom floor, Hannah heard the windows begin to rattle. The wind was blowing even more forcibly and it was making what Hannah imagined was a keening sound. Had something happened to Essie at the hospital? Was the wind keening for her?

"Nonsense!" Hannah said aloud, hurrying to descend the staircase to the ground floor. Her imagination was running away with her, rushing past her sense of reality and making fanciful and rather frightening conclusions. But the wind kept howling in a high-pitched wail and Hannah felt the hair on the back of her neck bristle with an emotion very close to dread.

Hannah rushed down the remaining steps and pulled out the key Rose had given her. She unlocked the door and attempted to pull it open. But the door wouldn't budge. The wind was too strong. She struggled for long moments and then the wind abated slightly and the door opened, almost blowing her off her feet as she stepped outside. It was a bad storm and there was no way she could walk home in gale winds like this.

Icy needles of snow stung her face as she rushed to the café. She struggled with that door, fighting against the gusts of wind, until she could rush into the warm haven of the interior and shut the door behind her.

"I was just coming to help you with the door," Rose said. "Did you find what you needed, Hannah?"

"Yes, thanks, Rose." Hannah handed the hotel key to Rose. "I'd better get back to The Cookie Jar."

"You're walking?"

Hannah nodded. "It seemed silly to drive when it's only a couple of blocks."

"I'll give you a cup of hot coffee to go before you leave. It's really blowing out there and you're going to get cold on the way. They call it *wind chill* for a reason, you know."

Rose was right and Hannah clutched the cup of coffee in her gloved hand all the way to The Cookie Jar. Even though the coffee was still warm, she was shivering as she unlocked the door and entered the warmth inside. Thank goodness the gas and the electricity were on! She didn't even want to think about how cold it would be if the furnace wasn't running.

She walked over to the industrial oven even before she'd taken off her parka and set the temperature dial to preheat it. She wanted to bake a batch of cookies before she went back to her mother's house. She'd been thinking about a new cookie, a cookie that would be appropriate for Christmas, one that would be pretty and reflect the holiday season.

As Hannah mixed up her favorite sugar cookie dough, she began to smile. When Essie came out of her coma, they would celebrate by having some of these cookies with her. Annie had mentioned that Essie had served hot chocolate with candy cane sticks for stirrers when they'd arrived at the hotel after school to do their homework. Essie had told them that it was one of her favorite winter drinks, and the cookies that

Hannah planned to bake would be perfect with hot chocolate and peppermint sticks.

Once she'd mixed up the dough, using peppermint extract
instead of the vanilla extract she usually used, Hannah chilled
the dough and rolled cookie balls with it. Instead of rolling
them in white granulated sugar, she mixed green decorator's
sugar with white sugar and used it to roll half of the cookies.
She used red decorator's sugar for coloring in the second half
of the batch so that some cookies would be red and white on
top and others would be green and white. A Hershey's Kiss
would top every cookie and duplicate the flavor of the hot
chocolate and peppermint that Essie loved.

The Suburban, which she now called her "cookie truck,"
was toasty warm by the time Hannah reached her mother's
house. She'd started the engine and turned on the heater before she'd loaded up the cookies to take with her, and warm
air was blowing out of the heater vents.

Hannah used the garage door opener that Delores had
given her to open the garage door and pulled her cookie truck
into the double garage. Her mother's car was there in its spot.
Delores was home and Hannah was glad that she'd put dinner up in the slow cooker before she'd left this morning.

"Oh, good! You're home!" Delores greeted her as Hannah
came in the door. "I just made coffee if you want some."

"Thanks, Mother. I do," Hannah told her, hanging up her
parka and going to the cupboard to get a coffee mug. She
poured herself a cup, carried it to the kitchen table, where
her mother was sitting, and dashed back out to her cookie
truck to retrieve the cookies she'd brought home with her.

"What do you have, Hannah?" Delores asked, as Hannah
came in with the large, foil-lined box.

"Peppermint cookies with chocolate on top. I'm going to
call them Minty Dream Cookies."

"Oooh! Peppermint and chocolate are two of my favorite
flavors. We can have one now, can't we, dear?"

"Of course." Hannah lifted off the foil and handed her mother a cookie. "Have two, a red one and a green one."

"Thank you," Delores took a bite of the red cookie and began to smile. "The red one is excellent!" she pronounced. "Now I'll try the green one."

"They're the same, Mother. The only difference is that I used red sugar on one and green sugar on the other."

"Perhaps, but I'd like to test it out for myself," Delores said with a laugh, taking another bite.

Mother and daughter sipped coffee and crunched cookies for several minutes and then the kitchen phone rang.

"I'll get it," Hannah said, reaching up to grab the receiver of the wall phone next to her chair. "Hello?"

"Hannah!" Hannah recognized Andrea's voice. "Is Mother there? I need to talk to her right away."

"She's right here," Hannah said, handing the phone to her mother. "It's Andrea."

"Hello, dear," Delores greeted her. Then there was silence for several minutes while Delores listened. "Oh, dear!" she said at last. "Is Bill very upset?"

There was another silence and then Delores spoke again. "All right, dear. I'll tell Hannah. She'll want to know."

"You'll tell me what?" Hannah asked the moment her mother had hung up the phone.

"The man they arrested is refusing to talk," Delores said. "They don't know who he is. He refuses to give them any information and he doesn't have any identification on him."

"Did they take his fingerprints?"

"Yes, but it'll take a while to get that information back from the federal authorities. And that means they still don't know if Essie was his intended target or if he was shooting at someone else."

"I heard him say something about Sharon."

Delores nodded. "So did Leroy Schmidt. He was standing right next to the man when he fired."

"When will Sheriff Grant have news about the finger-prints?"

"Bill told Andrea that it'll be at least a week or two before they hear anything and it could be even longer."

"Another mystery," Hannah said with a sigh.

"Another?" Delores asked, and it was clear she was intrigued. "What do you mean, dear?"

"Let me stir the chili in the crockpot and I'll get you another cup of coffee. Then I'll tell you all about it."

# MINTY DREAM COOKIES

DO NOT preheat oven—dough must chill before baking.

1 cup melted butter *(2 sticks, 8 ounces, ½ pound)*
1 cup powdered sugar *(don't sift unless it's got big lumps and then you shouldn't use it anyway)*
½ cup white *(granulated)* sugar
1 large egg
1 teaspoon peppermint extract
½ teaspoon baking soda
½ teaspoon cream of tartar *(critical!)*
½ teaspoon salt
2 cups plus 2 Tablespoons all-purpose flour *(don't sift—pack it down in the cup when you measure it)*

¼ cup white sugar in a small bowl *(for coating dough balls)*
¼ cup white sugar in another small bowl
approximately 3 Tablespoons red decorator's sugar
approximately 3 Tablespoons green decorator's sugar
approximately 5 dozen Hershey's Kisses

Melt the butter in a microwave-safe bowl or in a saucepan on the stovetop. Add the cup of powdered sugar and the half cup of granulated sugar and mix thoroughly. Let the mixture cool to room temperature.

Mix in the egg and the peppermint extract.

Add the baking soda, cream of tartar, and salt. Mix until everything is well combined.

Add the flour in one-cup increments, mixing after each addition. *(You can add the 2 Tablespoons of flour to the last full cup.)*

Cover your bowl with plastic wrap and chill the dough for at least one hour. *(Overnight is fine, too.)*

When you're ready to bake, preheat oven to 325 degrees F. with the rack in the middle position.

While your oven is preheating, either spray your cookie sheet(s) with Pam or another nonstick cooking spray or line them with parchment paper.

Add the red decorator's sugar to one bowl of white sugar and mix it in with a fork from your silverware drawer.

Add the green decorator's sugar to the other bowl of white sugar and mix it in.

Use your impeccably clean hands to roll the dough into walnut-size balls.

Roll half of the dough balls in the bowl of red and white sugar.

Roll the second half of the dough balls in the bowl of green and white sugar.

Place the sugar-coated dough balls on a cookie sheet, 12 to a standard-size sheet.

Unwrap the Hershey's Kisses and place one, point up, on top of each sugared dough ball. Press it down so that it will stay in place.

Bake your Minty Dream Cookies at 325 degrees F. for 10 to 15 minutes. *(The cookies should have a tinge of gold on the top.)* Cool the cookies on the cookie sheet for 2 minutes, then remove them to a wire rack to finish cooling.

**Hannah's Note: If you used parchment paper to line your cookie sheet, just pull the paper, cookies and all, over to a wire rack.**

Yield: Approximately 5 dozen crunchy, buttery, sugary peppermint and chocolate cookies.

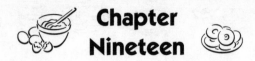

Lisa, Michelle, Hannah, and Delores were sitting in the living room munching on Minty Dream Cookies, Hannah's new peppermint and chocolate Christmas cookie. They'd eaten the chili that Hannah had made, along with slices of homemade garlic bread and a crispy salad that Lisa had made out of shredded cabbage, shredded carrots, and pineapple chunks in a sweet vinaigrette dressing.

Once she'd finished her cookie, Hannah switched on the reading light she'd purchased and prepared to read from Essie's last notebook.

"I can't believe that this is the last notebook," Lisa said, settling back in her seat.

"Me neither," Michelle echoed her sentiments. "How about you, Mother?"

"I feel the same way," Delores replied with a sigh. "If Essie would only wake up, we could ask her if she liked any of the ways we thought of to end her story."

Hannah heard the concern in their voices. Lisa, Michelle, and Delores were every bit as worried about Essie as she was. She made an instant decision and pulled out the note that Doc Knight had given her.

"Essie left me a note," she told them. "I read it to Doc Knight, but I didn't know if I should let anyone else read it. I think you need to know what was going through Essie's mind as she was getting ready to go to the Christmas Ball."

Hannah unfolded the note and read it aloud. After she finished, there was shocked silence for a long moment and then Delores spoke. "But Essie didn't have any children, did she?"

"I don't know and neither did Doc Knight, but he let me go through all of Dr. Kalick's records. There's nothing in there about Essie giving birth to a baby."

Lisa looked thoughtful. "Could it have been before she moved to Lake Eden?"

"Of course. But somehow, I don't think so."

"Then the story that Essie wrote in the notebooks was partially true?" Michelle asked.

"Maybe, but maybe not. All I know is, I have to find out."

"How can we help?" Delores asked immediately.

"I don't know. Let's read what's in Essie's last notebook and maybe it'll give us some clues."

"And maybe it won't," Michelle pointed out.

"That's true, too." Hannah had to agree with her youngest sister. "But I think we all owe it to Essie to read it and find out."

**She looked out the window and realized that snow was falling. The man she now called her uncle Jim had given her his guest room and helped her to change into his wife's nightgown. He'd told her that after his wife died, he'd kept all her clothes because he couldn't bear to throw them out or give them away. He said the clothes were old now, and she was welcome to use anything that might fit her. Then he'd urged her to rest and left the room.**

**"Broth?" He reappeared in the doorway with a mug of what smelled like chicken soup.**

**"Oh! Yes, please," she replied, welcoming the warmth as he handed the mug to her. "Thank you. You're very kind."**

"Not at all," he said. "You need to keep up your strength. Since this is your first baby, it could be a while before you can hold your baby in your arms."

"No!" she said, shaking her head. "If I hold my baby, I won't be able to do the right thing. And I have to do the right thing."

"And you've decided on that?"

"Yes, I have to give up my baby. I don't want to, but I promised my husband I'd keep our baby safe. And that's the only way. No one can know where I am or that I had the baby."

His eyes were sad as he looked into her face. "All right, my dear. If you're sure about this."

"I am," she said firmly. "I've been thinking about this ever since I found out that my husband was killed. They may find me, and they may kill me. But if I give up our baby, the baby will have a chance to live."

He closed his eyes for moment and then he sighed and gave a little nod. "All right then. Try to get some rest. And call me if the contractions wake you. Please don't worry, my dear. I promise you that I'll keep your baby safe."

"How awful!" Delores breathed. "What a horrible decision she had to make."

Michelle looked as if she wanted to cry. "Please tell us that this isn't the end of Essie's book, Hannah."

"It's not. There's a little more."

"Read it," Lisa begged her. "This is just too sad for words!"

When he'd left her alone, she got out of bed and went to the small desk that sat under the window. She pulled out a drawer and found the stationery and envelopes he'd placed there. She wiped the tears from her cheeks with the handkerchief he'd given her, picked up the pen that was on the desk, and began to write.

She had to stop several times to dry her tears, but at last the notes she'd written were in separate envelopes. They were the same, except for the names. Right after the baby was born, she'd give him the envelopes—one if her baby was a girl and the other if her baby was a boy.

They had discussed names right after she'd gone to the doctor and learned that she was pregnant. She wanted to choose those names, but what if Tony had told someone about it? It would be easier for them to find the baby if they knew the baby's first name. It was why she hadn't chosen either of those names. Instead, she'd chosen two new names. She had to take precautions to safeguard their baby.

Despite her efforts, there were tears on the envelopes. She thought about opening them and putting the notes in fresh envelopes, even pulling out the drawer to do that. But before she could reach out to get the envelopes, the first contraction began.

She gasped and cried out. She wasn't ready! But then he appeared in the doorway to help her back to bed.

"It's all right. I'm here," he told her.

"The notes," she gasped. "One for a boy and . . . one for . . ."

The contractions were coming so hard and fast, she couldn't finish what she'd started to tell him.

"I see them. I'll take the right one. It won't be long now, my dear. Your baby will be born very soon."

Hannah looked up and saw the shocked expression on their faces as she closed the last notebook.

"That's . . . all?" Delores asked her.

"Yes," Hannah answered. "That's all that Essie wrote."

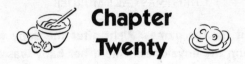

# Chapter Twenty

Hannah's sleep was uneasy, filled with dreams of crying babies and tear-stained notes. She opened her eyes at six in the morning, feeling tired and out of sorts. One glance out the window at the peaceful landscape below told her that the wind had abated sometime during the night and the snow stretched out like a pristine white blanket, covering her mother's shrubs and garden statues. The sun had not yet risen, but the moon was still visible, casting a cold blue light on the tops of snowdrifts that the wind had fashioned during the course of the winter storm.

Her shower was accomplished quickly and Hannah arrived downstairs in the kitchen in record time. She put on the coffee, sneaked out a cup before the machine was through brewing, and sat down at the kitchen table to enjoy her aromatic eye-opener. Today would be a busy day. They'd decided, the previous evening, to go in a group to visit Essie at the hospital in the early afternoon. Hannah planned to bake in the morning, freezing some cookies for future trips to see Essie, and make some calls from the landline phone that the phone company had installed. Then, if there was enough time, she would run out to the condo complex and take measurements for the new refrigerator she would order with Delores, make a list of the other furniture that would be necessary for her to buy before moving in, and drive back to pick up Lisa, Michelle, and her mother. Annie would meet them at the hospital, and Hannah planned to show her the note and give her the lovely purse that Essie had made.

Five minutes later, Hannah had just finished putting Oven French Toast in her mother's oven. She'd heard the shower start upstairs and she knew that either Michelle, her mother, or Lisa was using it. Lisa had stayed overnight and the girls were going to help her bake at The Cookie Jar this morning.

The phone rang and Hannah reached out to answer it. "Hello," she greeted the caller. "This is Hannah."

"Hello, Hannah," a familiar voice said. "This is Doc Knight, calling from the hospital. I'd like you all to come out around noon. Essie had a restless night and I think she's almost ready to regain consciousness."

"We could come now if you need us," Hannah offered.

"Noon will be time enough. It'll take Essie a while to prepare herself to open her eyes. She's still unconscious, but I've seen this phenomenon many times. And even if she's groggy when she first regains consciousness, she'll know that you're there."

"Do you want me to call Annie Winters?" Hannah asked.

"No, I'll call her. She can meet you in the waiting room and I'll call all of you in when it's time."

"All of us?" Hannah was surprised. They'd only been permitted to go in one by one before.

"Yes. When Essie is awake enough to talk, I know she'll want to see all of you."

Hannah was smiling broadly as she said her goodbyes and hung up the phone. She could hardly wait to give the girls and Delores the wonderful news. Essie was coming out of her coma and this morning their breakfast would be a real celebration!

Annie was sitting in the waiting room when they got there, and Hannah, Delores, Michelle, and Lisa greeted her warmly.

"I can hardly wait to see Essie again," Annie told them. "I

know Doc told us that Essie might be able to hear us even though she was unconscious, but it's hard to talk to someone who doesn't respond. I just hope she really does wake up and know who we are."

"She will," Hannah said. "Essie's going to come out of it. We . . . all of us . . . have to believe that."

Annie nodded. "You're right, Hannah. Essie always said that positive energy could work miracles. We have to keep a positive attitude and believe that Essie will be with us again very soon."

"You love Essie, don't you?" Lisa said, turning to Annie.

"Yes, I do! Essie was like a mother to me. Once, a long time ago, I forgot and called her *Mom.*"

"What did she do?" Delores asked.

"She gave me a hug and . . ." Annie stopped to blink back tears, ". . . she said that she couldn't love me more, even if she were my real mother."

There was a tinkling sound and Hannah recognized her mother's arpeggio ringtone. "Your phone, Mother," she said, gesturing toward her mother's purse, which was sitting on the chair next to her.

"I swear I'll never get used to this cell phone," Delores said, opening her purse and pulling out her phone. "Hello?" She listened for a moment and then a puzzled expression crossed her face. "It's Andrea," she told them. "She says Bill called her with news about the man who shot Essie."

They all waited silently while Delores took the call, but they didn't learn much from Delores's end of the conversation. *I see,* and *Oh, my,* and *I'm glad you told me,* didn't reveal the subject or the nature of the call.

Delores said goodbye and put her cell phone back in her purse before she turned to them. "Bill called Andrea from work," she told them. "He said that Sheriff Grant took the shooter into the interview room again and Bill and another deputy were there as observers. Sheriff Grant asked him his name and the man still refused to give it. He's been refusing to identify himself ever since they took him into custody. Of course they took his fingerprints, but the federal authorities haven't gotten back to them yet."

"So they still don't know who he is?" Annie asked the question that was in everybody's mind.

"No. If he's ever committed a crime, his name will be in the register. But if he hasn't . . ." Delores stopped speaking and sighed. "There's more," she said, beginning to frown, "and it's not good news."

Hannah leaned forward in the uncomfortable plastic waiting room chair. "Tell us, Mother. Please."

"Sheriff Grant continued to question the man. Bill told Andrea that the sheriff is a real expert at getting people to talk, but the shooter wouldn't budge. He just kept saying things like, *I won't tell you that*, and *No comment*. Bill said that Sheriff Grant used every interrogative tactic in the book, but none of them worked."

"So they still don't know his name or why he shot Essie?" Hannah asked.

"That's right, dear. And it's even worse than that. Sheriff Grant tried to break the man down by telling him that he'd better pray that Essie wouldn't die because the sentence for attempted murder would be a lot less than actual murder. And that was the first time the man spoke."

"What did he say?" Lisa asked, clearly interested in Delores's account of the interrogation.

"He said, *She didn't die?* in this shocked voice. And Sheriff Grant said, *That's right. She's in intensive care at the hospital. They removed the bullets and she's recovering.*"

"What did the man say to that?" Annie asked quickly.

"He just yelled *No!* in this really loud voice. Bill told Andrea that the man sounded outraged that he hadn't killed Essie. And then he grabbed his chest and fell forward, face-first, on the table. Sheriff Grant told Bill to call for the paramedics while they tried to resuscitate the man. When the paramedics came, they rushed the man to the hospital, but he died on the way."

"So they still don't know why he did it, or even if Essie was the intended target," Hannah said.

"That's right, dear."

"And we still don't know why he yelled, *I found you, Sharon!* right before he pulled the trigger."

Delores nodded. "There were three women named Sharon at the Christmas Ball. Sheriff Grant brought them in for interviews, but none of them could shed any light on the shooter's identity or why he shot Essie."

"It's a mystery," Hannah commented, hating the idea that they might never know who the shooter was. "Essie might know. I asked her who he was earlier that night and she said he looked a little like someone she used to know years ago."

"Then Essie is the only one who might be able to solve this mystery," Annie said with a sigh.

Hannah was quiet for a moment and then she shook her head. "Not necessarily. A mystery is like a puzzle. You need all the pieces to complete it." And then she drew the small beaded handbag out of her purse and handed it to Annie. "Essie left this for you. She hid it in a drawer in the hotel kitchen and I retrieved it before the storm hit us yesterday. Essie left instructions to me in a note she wrote before she left the hospital for the Christmas Ball."

Annie looked surprised. "Do you mean . . . Essie *knew* something might happen to her at the ball?"

"It seems that way to me. Look at the handbag and then read the note. And see if you can put any of the puzzle pieces together for us."

"It's beautiful," Annie said, and then she opened the purse and looked inside. "There's nothing inside except a handkerchief, a comb, and a lipstick." She closed the purse again and smiled as she turned it in her hands. "Essie put her favorite flower on the outside." She held it up so that they could all see it. "The rhinestones in the center of the rose sparkle so much, they look almost like diamonds in the light."

"Let me see, Annie," Delores said, beginning to look excited as Annie handed her the purse and she examined it. "I didn't notice this when I saw the handbag before, but there are some rhinestones that are larger than the rest. And . . . I don't think they're rhinestones!"

"Could they be diamonds?" Hannah guessed.

"I'm not a jeweler and I'm not completely sure, but they *are* larger. And they sparkle more brilliantly."

"You don't suppose . . ." Annie stopped speaking and gave a little gasp. "Someone left two diamonds in the charity box at the Children's Home. And there was a note on the envelope saying that they were to be used for my college tuition! But . . . that's not possible. Essie didn't have the money to spend on diamonds."

"Wait a minute," Hannah said, her mind spinning fast as she remembered what Annie had said about the design of the flower. "Why did you say that the flower on the outside of the handbag was a rose? It looked like a hibiscus to us."

"It *is* a hibiscus. But the hibiscus is called *Rose of Sharon*."

"Oh!" Hannah gasped. "Essie's real name was Sharon!"

"Essie's story!" Michelle's expression mirrored the same expression of shock that was on Delores's, Lisa's, and Hannah's faces. "Essie's story is true!"

"And she ended it with the notes that the mother wrote before she gave birth to her baby." She turned to Annie. "You said that you came to the orphanage as a baby. Did they give you your name?"

"No, it was in a note from my mother. She said that she had to give me up to keep me safe, that my father had died in the line of duty, and I should never forget that I was named after him."

"But your name is Annie," Hannah said, beginning to frown.

"Actually, no. Annie isn't my full name. They shortened it

at the Children's Home because there was an older boy named Anthony."

"Your full name is Anthony?" Lisa asked.

"No," Annie smiled. "It's the female version of *Anthony*. It's *Antonia*."

"Tony!" Delores, Lisa, Michelle, and Hannah all exclaimed, almost simultaneously.

"They would have called me *Toni*, but there was already a boy named Tony at the Children's Home." Annie stopped and began to frown. "Why do all of you look so shocked?"

"Because Essie is your real mother," Hannah told her. "She had to give you up for adoption to keep you safe from the man who shot her. He must have been her cousin, the one she worked for in New York. Her first husband, Tony, died to protect her and expose her cousin's illegal business. We'll give you the notebooks and you can read them for yourself. It's all there, Annie."

"Essie is *really* my mother?"

"Yes."

The most beautiful expression that Hannah had ever seen spread across Annie's face. It was pure joy and Hannah blinked back tears at the love she saw in Annie's eyes.

"Ladies?" Doc Knight called out as he entered the waiting room. "Essie's awake and she's stable. You can go in now."

"One at a time?" Delores asked him.

Doc Knight shook his head. "You can all go in at once. Essie's in good spirits and eager to see all of you."

"You first," Hannah said, waiting until Annie had gotten to her feet. "You may need a little time alone with her."

Annie shook her head. "She'll want to see all of us."

"All right, but you go in first," Delores backed up Hannah's decision. "We'll be right behind you, but we'll give you a few moments of privacy."

Annie looked slightly nervous as she entered the intensive care unit, but she led the way to Essie's room and went in to stand next to Essie's bed. "We're here, Essie," she said, leaning down to give Essie a kiss on the cheek. "I . . . I'm so glad you're all right! We all are! And I just want to tell you that I know what you've been through, and I understand that you had to protect me."

"You know?" Essie looked surprised. "How?"

"Hannah figured it out. You don't have to worry about your cousin any longer. He had a heart attack and died. You protected me from him all these years, but we're together now. There's only one thing I don't know."

"What is it?"

"I . . . I'm not sure what I should call you. I called you Essie for years, but I know that your real name is Sharon and my father called you Rose. What would you like me to call you?"

Essie began to smile. "How about *Mom*," she suggested. "And come here and give me a hug. I love you, Annie."

Annie bent down to hug her. "And I love you, Mom."

Hannah brushed away a tear. Then she turned to see Delores dabbing at her eyes with a tissue. Both Lisa and Michelle were wiping away tears, and all four of them were smiling. Hannah wasn't sure if they were tears of joy at Annie and Essie's happy reunion, or tears of gratitude that Delores had recovered from her depression and was back in their life again. The only thing she knew for certain was that she was happy to be home in Lake Eden again, glad to be back with family and friends, and delighted that Essie and Annie's Christmas miracle had come true.

# Christmas Cake Murder
## Recipe Index

# Baking Conversion Chart

These conversions are approximate, but they'll work just fine for Hannah Swensen's recipes.

## VOLUME:

| U.S. | Metric |
|------|--------|
| ½ teaspoon | 2 milliliters |
| 1 teaspoon | 5 milliliters |
| 1 Tablespoon | 15 milliliters |
| ¼ cup | 50 milliliters |
| ⅓ cup | 75 milliliters |
| ½ cup | 125 milliliters |
| ¾ cup | 175 milliliters |
| 1 cup | ¼ liter |

## WEIGHT:

| U.S. | Metric |
|------|--------|
| 1 ounce | 28 grams |
| 1 pound | 454 grams |

## OVEN TEMPERATURE:

| Degrees Fahrenheit | Degrees Centigrade | British (Regulo) Gas Mark |
|--------------------|--------------------|---------------------------|
| 325 degrees F. | 165 degrees C. | 3 |
| 350 degrees F. | 175 degrees C. | 4 |
| 375 degrees F. | 190 degrees C. | 5 |

Note: Hannah's rectangular sheet cake pan, 9 inches by 13 inches, is approximately 23 centimeters by 32.5 centimeters.

*Spring has sprung in Lake Eden, Minnesota, but Hannah Swensen doesn't have time to stop and smell the roses— not with hot cross buns to make, treats to bake, and a sister to exonerate!*

Hannah's up to her ears with Easter orders rushing in at The Cookie Jar, plus a festive meal to prepare for a dinner party at her mother's penthouse. But everything comes crashing to a halt when Hannah receives a panicked call from her sister Andrea—Mayor Richard Bascomb has been murdered . . . and Andrea is the prime suspect.

Even with his reputation for being a bully, Mayor Bascomb— or "Ricky Ticky," as Hannah's mother likes to call him—had been unusually testy in the days leading up to his death, leaving Hannah to wonder if he knew he was in danger. Meanwhile, folks with a motive for mayoral murder are popping up in Lake Eden. Was it a beleaguered colleague? A political rival? A jealous wife? Or a scorned mistress?

As orders pile up at The Cookie Jar—and children line up for Easter egg hunts—Hannah must spring into investigation mode and identify the real killer . . . before another murder happens!

**Please turn the page for an exciting sneak peek of Joanne Fluke's newest Hannah Swensen mystery TRIPLE CHOCOLATE CHEESECAKE MURDER now on sale wherever print and e-books are sold!**

# Chapter One

The chairs in Mayor Bascomb's outer office were uncomfortable and Hannah Swensen shifted her position. She'd brought the mayor's secretary, Terry Neilson, some sample cookies from The Cookie Jar, Hannah's bakery and coffee shop, and Terry was reaching for her third Vanilla Crunch cookie.

"These are great cookies, Hannah!" Terry told her, biting into the crunchy confection. "I'd better stop soon or Mayor Bascomb won't get any of these."

"Forget it, Andrea!" Mayor Bascomb's voice was so loud, they could hear it in the outer office. "Nothing you can say will change my mind. And if you keep it up, you're going to make me even madder! You and I both know that Bill was wrong to make that arrest!"

"Uh-oh!" Terry reacted to the angry words that they could hear, even though the mayor's office door was closed. "He's been in a horrid mood all week, and now he's on a real rant. I really hope your sister's got enough sense to leave before he says something really nasty."

Hannah sighed and shook her head. "Andrea won't leave. She's never walked away from a fight in her life. She's even more stubborn than Mayor Bascomb, especially when somebody insults her husband. And from what she told me, Bill was caught between a rock and a hard place. He had to arrest the mayor's nephew. The state trooper was standing right there, and Bill couldn't just let Bruce go the way he did the last two times."

Terry looked very apologetic. "I know. Bruce is a real menace on the road when he gets a snootful. I told the mayor that, but he never listens to reason when it comes to his brother's kid. He still thinks that Bill should have figured out a way to let Bruce go."

"But didn't the state trooper test Bruce for alcohol?"

"Yes, and Bruce's blood alcohol was twice as high as it should have been."

"I don't want to hear it, Andrea!" The mayor's angry voice interrupted their conversation. "My mind's made up, and your husband is history. He won't even get a job as a dog-catcher as long as I'm the mayor of Lake Eden!"

Both Hannah and Terry listened, but they couldn't hear Andrea's response. This made Hannah proud of her younger sister. So far, Andrea hadn't yelled back. The fact that they couldn't hear her meant that Andrea was still using a perfectly reasonable tone of voice, but Hannah knew that couldn't last forever. Eventually, Andrea would lose control and she'd give the mayor a piece of her mind!

"I'm impressed," Terry said admiringly. "Andrea's really keeping her cool."

"Yes, she is . . . so far. But she's always been very protective of her family. If Mayor Bascomb keeps this up, she'll snap."

"I almost wish she would. Nobody else has the nerve to tell him when he's being a you-know-what. Did Andrea tell you that Bill came in to talk to the mayor yesterday?"

Hannah nodded. "Yes, and she said the mayor refused to see Bill. That's one of the reasons Andrea came over here today. She promised me she'd be calm and reasonable, but she also said that she'd kick down his office door if he refused to see her."

"Do you think she actually would have done it?"

Hannah laughed. "Oh, yes. Maybe she wouldn't have succeeded. It looks like a pretty heavy door to me. But I know that Andrea would have given it her best shot. She's in mother-lion-protecting-her-cub mode."

"Enough!" Mayor Bascomb's voice was even louder than it had been before. "I've listened to your pathetic whining and sniveling for long enough. You're every bit as stupid as your husband!"

"Just one more thing, Mayor Bascomb. . ." Andrea's voice was louder and Hannah picked up her purse and Andrea's parka. "I think that'll do it."

"You mean Andrea's going to . . ."

"You bet," Hannah interrupted. "I know my sister and she can't take much more."

"You're the one who's pathetic!" Andrea's voice was almost as loud as Mayor Bascomb's had been. "You're nothing but a bully, and it's long past time that somebody stood up to you!"

"And you think that *you* can stand up to me, little lady?"

"I *know* I can! Bill's too much of a gentleman to take you on, but not me! Somebody's got to give you exactly what you deserve, you . . . you pig!"

Hannah jumped up from the chair. "Grab your coat, Terry! When Andrea charges in here, it's time for us all to get out of Dodge!"

"Right!" Terry grabbed her coat and purse and was pulling on her boots when they heard a sharp, stinging sound that was followed by a loud crash. "She slapped him?"

"That's what it sounded like to me. I think she slapped him right out of his chair!" Hannah hurried across the room and opened the door to the hallway. "Go out first, Terry. And stand out of the way. Andrea's so mad, she's going to explode out the door!"

Terry grabbed the plate of cookies that Hannah had brought and ran to the door. She had just stepped out, into the hallway, when Andrea came storming out of Mayor Bascomb's office. "Whoa!" Terry gasped, sheltering against the wall as Andrea raced past her. "Wait for us, Andrea!"

But Andrea didn't wait. She practically flew down the staircase and out into the street. By the time Hannah and Terry had managed to catch up with her, she was leaning against the old-fashioned, designer lamppost in front of the building, gasping for breath.

"Here, Andrea," Hannah, who had been holding her sister's parka, draped it around Andrea's shoulders. "Deep, calming breaths. It's okay. You're out of there now."

"I . . . I . . . I . . ."

"We heard," Hannah told her.

"I . . . slapped . . ."

"We know," Terry said.

"I . . . knocked . . . him . . ."

"You knocked him over in his chair," Hannah finished the sentence for her. "Put your arms in your sleeves, Andrea. It's cold out here and you're overheated."

"Nasty . . . bully," Andrea managed to say. "I . . . I should have killed him!"

"A lot of people feel that way," Terry said.

"But . . . all I did was. . . was slap him!"

"Nobody else has ever done that before," Terry told her. "They might have felt like it, but they never had the courage to actually do it."

Once Andrea had calmed down enough to zip up her parka, they walked to their respective cars. "That was a really loud crash," Terry said, as she unlocked her car door and slid into the driver's seat. "I wonder if you broke his chair."

"Maybe," Andrea gave a weak little smile. "I hope I did, but after the things he said about Bill, I should have broken his *neck*!"

# Connect with

## U s

Visit us online at
**KensingtonBooks.com**
to read more from your favorite authors, see books
by series, view reading group guides, and more.

for sneak peeks, chances to win books and prize packs,
and to share your thoughts with other readers.

facebook.com/kensingtonpublishing
twitter.com/kensingtonbooks

## Tell us what you think!

To share your thoughts, submit a review,
or sign up for our eNewsletters, please visit:
**KensingtonBooks.com/TellUs.**